First published by Gary Kinsley 2020

gkinsley@rishk.net

ISBN 978-1-83853-868-2

ISBN 978-1-83853-868-2

9 781838 538682

Printed in Hong Kong
by Regal Printing Ltd.
www.regalprintingltd.com.hk

ATTACK VECTOR

Gary Kinsley

To Dawn, Oliver, Thomas, and Amelia.

During the telling of this story I've done my best to stick as close as possible to accurate and real scenarios. The computer hacks explained here are real although I've tried to avoid being too nerdy and not to start looking like a cybersecurity training manual. More technical detail would bore the pants off anyone other than the most ardent technical engineers. So, if it's too technical or not technical enough – my apologies. The concept of hackers, black hats, white hats, code kiddies, actors, researchers – whatever you want to call them - and the seven-step kill chain is all real, as is the logic hackers follow when preparing and executing a hack. The Dark Web is also real and refers to a virtual underworld of cybercriminals where much illegal business is transacted. The Dark Web is of great interest to crime prevention authorities and the security agencies who themselves inhabit this murky virtual world and try to catch the real criminals. TOR (an acronym of The Onion Ring) is one in a number of real encrypted browser-like software used for anonymised communications in the Dark Web.

All the places mentioned are (or were at the time of writing) real, and for authenticity sake I've either lived in or visited these places many times, apart from North Korea. San Francisco, Palo Alto, Tel Aviv, Bermuda (book 2), Seoul, and Hong Kong are all truly fantastic places. The little tunnel Guy and Wendy run through during the chase in Hong Kong is very close to the former Excelsior Hotel, with its iconic bar in the basement, which I originally featured in the story. Sadly, the hotel was closed down while writing this book, so I had to go back and rewrite the references.

To add depth, history, and a context to the story, the historical references I've used are as accurate as possible. Stanislav Petrov really did apparently prevent a nuclear war between Russia and American in September 1983 by realising that satellite processed images were not the flashes from the rockets of intercontinental ballistic missiles as first thought, but were in fact caused by sunlight reflecting off shiny factory roofs close to real missile silos in North Dakota. A truly terrifying thought when considered, illustrating that however technologically smart we think we are; human common sense often prevails over computer generated conclusions. Let's hope in the brave new world of AI it remains so. Mr Petrov died a few years ago, hardly the household name he deserves to be.

The Soshi-kaimai policy, which forced all Koreans to take Japanese names during the Japanese occupation of Korea, was also real. Real too is the execution of Chang Song-thaek although I must confess to artistic interpretation here given there were several horrific (but conflicting) accounts of his death. It is hard to know the true circumstances, but the location and method of his execution, being obliterated by an antiaircraft gun, seems to be the consensus.

Unit 8200 in Israel is real, as is the Kirya building although this is not the main office housing Unit 8200. I linked them because of geographic convenience to the Sarona district, a very quaint and historic area of Tel Aviv. Likewise, the technical descriptions of the Rodong-1 and the functioning of the Yongbyon Nuclear Scientific Research Center are as technically correct as I'm able to make them.

The method I've used here to deliver the malware to the computer systems at the Yongbyon Nuclear Scientific Research Center may seem rather farfetched – actually nothing could be further from the truth. Using external USB devices to infect isolated systems is feasible and is believed to have been the method used to deliver the Stuxnet virus into the uranium processing centrifuges used in Iran, which when they exploded caused massive damage to the Iranian nuclear programme setting it back years. This is a fascinating story in its own right and was, in-part, the inspiration for this book.

Finally, this is the first book in a trilogy involving the exploits of

Wendy and Guy. At the end of this book I've included the Prologue of the second book for those interested in following the story. This features the infamous hack on the American National Security Agency (NSA). While the story of the hackers is speculative and fictional, the hack itself was real.

During the process of writing this book I drew upon the kind and generous help of colleagues, friends and family. On the technical side, I'd like to express sincere thanks to Clement Lee, Kev Hau, and John Goh (whose example code is featured in Chapter 5) for their excellent advice on cybersecurity and helping me apply what I know in theory to a true-to-life story. On cultural subtleties, I owe a big thank you to Israeli Eitan Fischgrund and Koreans Kriss Lee and Claire Mun for their insights into Israelis and Koreans, respectively. My undying gratitude to my super-smart friends and former colleagues Carris Chen and Sharron Drinnan, and my darling wife Dawn, for their brilliant assistance in proofing and correcting my appalling grammar, spelling, punctuation and generally everything I've written. Any mistakes remaining are entirely my fault. Finally, many thanks to John Jarrold whose pragmatic advice regarding the literary industry was both helpful and, more importantly, inspiring.

Gary Kinsley has worked in the cybersecurity industry for many years all over the world and takes a keen interest in the technology but also the actors who play in this space – both the good guys and the bad guys. Cybersecurity is a hugely complicated business both technically, legally, and philosophically, and he believes as the world becomes increasingly reliant on technology, including Artificial Intelligence, this will only become more so.

He has lived in Bermuda, Singapore and Hong Kong, but now resides in rural England with his wife and family. He can be reached at gkinsley@rishk.net

Books by this author include:

If you want Loyalty – Buy a Dog (non-fiction – business focused on the IT industry)

Attack Vector (1st book in the Guy and Wendy series. Fiction)

Deadly Protocol (2nd book in the Guy and Wendy series. Fiction)

Seven Pipers – working title (3rd book in the Guy and Wendy series. Fiction)

CONTENTS

Wonsan (On the eastern coast of what is now The Democratic People's Republic of Korea - North Korea). 4th December. 1941.

The young couple huddled tightly for warmth under their worn old woollen rugs in their small one room house. It was sunset, and what little heat the winter sun had offered during the day was lost. The freezing easterly wind, whipping straight off the Sea of Japan, forced everyone in the town to seek out any warmth as best they could. The couple's wooden house, in reality no more than a fisherman's hut, was very simple. Four large wooden posts were sunk into the ground at each corner. The raised wooden floor was pinned with wooden pegs to the four posts, and further pinned wooden planks made up the walls and roof.

In the summer they planned to paint or tar the house if they had any spare money. When the snowy wind was blowing, as it was now, it would find ways to whistle into the house between cracks in the planks. Their room had no light, unlike before, before the war. The paraffin lamp, which swung impotently from a peg in the ceiling was the only source but there was no paraffin for sale at the market now. All fuel supplies were limited on account of the war. So, the couple would simply cuddle, love each other, and love their tiny baby who was snuggled in the warmth of the muddle of blankets between them.

He was proud. They had been husband and wife for less than a year and their son was so young he could only suckle. They were so cold now it was winter but Park Min-ho was happy. He loved his wife so much. She was beautiful. She, and now their baby son was his whole world. She had given him her body and with it she had gifted him a healthy boy. He was honoured she had chosen him; he, a simple fisherman, as her husband above all others. She could have chosen any man in the town, any man in his whole country Korea, even in all of Japan if she so wished. But then they hated the Japanese.

His Korean Empire had been at war with Japan for over thirty years although he and his wife were not yet twenty. The Japanese had invaded his country in 1910 and now the news was that Europe was also at war. He had heard about Germans although Park Min-ho had never met one. Sometimes he wondered what they looked like. If they were anything like their Japanese occupiers, they were brutal.

Seoul was their capital city however Park Min-ho was mostly content to be a fisherman in Wonsan, his hometown. He'd never been to Seoul, it was a very long way away. At nights, in the darkness, together with his wife he talked of joining the Korean Volunteer Army. He bragged to his wife how he'd kill these despised Japanese soldiers who occupied their Korea with his fish-gutting knife. She listened to her husband talk, and she was proud that he was so brave, but she was happier that he was a fisherman, it meant he returned home to her every night. She had friends in the market whose brothers, boyfriends and husbands had gone to fight but they never returned. Besides, she reasoned, if her husband didn't fish how would they eat?!

During daylight he would take his nets from their house, walk down the wooden plank to the quayside and fish from his small boat in the bay off the coast of Wonsan. She would sell the fish he caught in the town market where she shared a stall with her sister. Their mother and father had been killed years before, so they were as close as twins and her sister loved her baby as if it were her own.

That night she had told her husband of a new Japanese warship that she had seen arrive and anchor in the bay. It had been damaged and needed repairs and supplies. The ship's sailors had come to the market and bought, but mostly requisitioned all the food that was available. They had taken all her fish today. She cried into the chest of her man, Min-ho, she'd made no money, so she'd failed her husband and their son. He stroked her hair and told her it was okay. 'I'll catch more tomorrow,' he reassured her.

The Japanese occupiers hassled her continuously. They called her 'Kinuyo' after a beautiful Japanese movie star she apparently resembled. Neither Park Min-ho nor his wife had ever seen a movie, only heard about them. To see a movie, they would need to travel to either the larger town of Pyongyang, which was many miles away to the west, or to the capital Seoul, which might as well have been the moon. Besides, his pretty wife didn't want to go.

'It scares me!' She'd said. Park Min-ho would never willingly scare his wife.

Today at the market the Japanese sailors wanted to know her Japanese name. In 1939, two years previous, the Japanese over-lords introduced the Soshi-kaimai policy, forcing all Koreans to take Japanese names. She didn't understand the law and didn't know what name to take, so they called her 'Kinuyo'. The sailors were rough, uncouth, smelt bad, and spoke a language she didn't understand. They were all rude, arrogant and angry. She had heard that further south, a few weeks ago on the 10th of December, a provincial government calling itself the Republic of Korea had declared war on the Japanese under their leader Kim Gu. She prayed they would beat the Japanese and do so without the help of her husband Park Min-ho. Then she wouldn't need a Japanese name. She was thinking this when she heard a faint noise outside the house.

With a sudden crash and a blast of freezing air, the short wooden door of their house suddenly blew in. At first, they thought it was the wind, but then came the sound of boots followed by loud

Japanese voices shouting words they didn't understand. They had an electric torch which shone light around the room and into their eyes. Park Min-ho instinctively jumped up. His wife instinctively pulled her baby to her breast and covered his head with her hand.

The head punch floored Park Min-ho before he had even got to his feet properly. Vicious kicks followed, fast and vigorous. Their hatred was bilious. His wife wriggled away into the corner of the room screaming as her husband lay helpless from the kicks and punches flailing down upon him. She wailed through abject fear for her husband.

'Kinuyo' was the only word she recognised. They used it like a taunt, laughing amongst themselves. One sailor grabbed Park Min-ho by the hair and hauled him to sit upright propped against the wall, with no regard for the pain it inflicted. Blood poured from his broken nose and shattered mouth. One eye was already swollen to closure. He gasped, struggling to breathe with broken ribs. Both arms limp beside him. They wanted him to watch. One sailor delivered a final brutal kick to his stomach rupturing his spleen. He would die slowly now, while helplessly watching them defile his wife.

Two sailors pounced on the young woman. She wore her hair down at night and one pawed at it, dribbling 'Kinuyo!' Another, the ringleader, fumbled with his trousers with one hand while he waved a knife in front of her face with the other. Its sharp tip was too close for her eyes to focus on clearly, but she saw the polished blade and her eyes blinked wide with terror. The fourth sailor ripped at her woollen shirt, but the baby was being held too tight, so he tore the tiny baby away, yanking it from her clasp. The baby was tossed like a dirty rag, screaming, without regard into a corner. Abandoned.

'No!' her sobs pleaded 'No!' She scrambled for her baby, but the sailors grabbed her, tore at her clothes and pinned her down regardless of her hysteria. They were all too heavy for her. Her clothes were ripped off in a frenzy as she struggled. With every passing second more of her was being exposed until she was naked. All four sailors used her body, scratching and lapping at her lactating breasts, laughing in front of each other, and grunting in front of her face through their rotten teeth. Their bodies and their rank breath stank.

She stopped fighting and instinctively screwed her eyes tightly shut from the horror. The pain numbed her as she tried to block out all sense of feeling. There were no feelings in her heart beyond hatred for her abusers and for the love for her husband whose life was now ebbing away. She couldn't look at him. She didn't want to see him watch her being shamed. She prayed, for his sake, that he was already dead so to avoid seeing her savage humiliation.

When the sailors were finished, her soiled and sweating body lay quivering on the wooden floor of the little room. Cold and fear convulsed her. Her mind was empty. She bled. The life had drained from her man, Park Min-ho. She saw he still had one eye open, but it was unfocused, lifeless. His son, lay motionless, abandoned and forgotten in the hut's corner. The sailor's leader removed his knife again from his pocket and stood over the wretched, bruised body of the once beautiful Korean woman they called Kinuyo. He grabbed a handful of her hair and pulled her up and head back. She no longer cared. The sharp steel knife slid easily into the side of her delicate throat and he quickly ripped sideward with his full strength, the muscles on his scrawny forearm flexing as he did so.

The last thing she heard was their laughter, then, 'Sayonara Kinuyo!'

Chapter 1. Wendy's Idea

Hong Kong. Saturday.

Wendy privately enjoyed the attention. She was, after all, confident in herself. She knew her own mind, knew her own body, and knew she was fit and attractive. Her frame was tiny. She barely stood 5'4" in her stockinged feet. She was painfully slim but elegant, lean and toned, her muscles enhanced by her newly discovered hobby, rock climbing; or more specifically in Singapore, wall climbing. She stood on the crowded platform of Hong Kong's Central MTR subway station and waited for the train. Now, ignoring the unsolicited attention she was getting, she considered her situation. She still wasn't entirely sure she was doing the right thing going to see Guy.

Guy had only agreed to meet her for breakfast twenty minutes ago and she'd sprung that on him. He was, after all, only a work colleague. On reflection she wondered if her choice of dress was appropriate. Her black high-heeled shoes accentuated her already long legs. Her indigo jeans were so tight they looked sprayed on. The white loose-fitting linen shirt hid her pinched waist; and her only concession to jewellery was an enormous man's watch on her small, feminine left wrist.

Her weakness was watches. They were usually heavy oversized men's watches, and Wendy was proud of her extensive collection. Today she'd chosen the black-faced Breitling Emergency, a gift to herself upon being offered her current job, a private reward she felt she deserved. Even when time didn't matter, she still delighted in looking at the functional watch face. It was hot. August on the Hong Kong MTR despite the air conditioning was always hot and humid.

The attention currently directed at Wendy was coming from a

rowdy gaggle of young lads; good-looking Chinese professionals speculating with each other if she was approachable. She was probably a little older than them she thought but she ignored them. She was approachable although she didn't want them to know that because today she had other things on her mind. On another occasion perhaps, if she had more time, she might have smiled across at the lads daring the bravest one of them to approach her. The spoils might go to the winner if he had the nerve and could maintain her interest for long enough. She would seduce him easily enough if he held her interest, but not today. Today was different.

Today she had an idea and her mind was preoccupied with forming that idea into a plan. Wendy knew more about cybercrime and cyberwarfare than she let on given her current job, and her keen brain was astute enough to see an opportunity when one arose. She was relying on Guy to help her form these ideas.

A whisper of a warm breeze stirred her still damp shoulder-length black hair giving her advanced warning the MTR train was approaching. Only twenty minutes earlier she had stepped out of her morning shower. She had awoken in her hotel bed with the idea taking shape; she guessed she had been dreaming, something to do with alpha waves or some such she'd once read. She showered quickly, squirted a spray of the Armani aftershave she had commandeered from a previous boyfriend (preferring the masculine smell to some flowery feminine perfume), and dressed quickly. The young lads she'd been attracting earlier were now forgotten and she boarded the train and stood while being jostled by little old Chinese ladies on a shopping mission. The automated voice announced in English, Cantonese, and Mandarin that the next stop was Wan Chai.

Wendy spoke all three languages being native Singaporean so navigating Hong Kong was easy for her. She liked Hong Kong although the smells of stale sweat and mothballs in the Hong Kong subway train were in stark contrast to the new plastic smell of the MRT subway in her native Singapore.

Her plan was simple enough, but she knew she needed an ally, as not all the parts of the plan were clear to her yet. She needed to talk to someone to help the plan to fully form. Guy would either help her or talk her out of such an ill-conceived and potentially dangerous idea.

Guy Anderson kept an apartment in Wan Chai. He was her older colleague with a smart brain, fast wit, and with his penchant for devilment she knew her plan would appeal to him if it was going to appeal to anyone. He would see it as a puzzle to be solved. As his Human Resources partner, she'd psychologically profiled him a couple of years ago and liked his balance.

She also liked Guy as a person. He wasn't classically handsome with his close-shaved head, large nose, glasses, and fondness for grandfather-like waistcoats, but nevertheless he was engaging and still attractive to her. She hoped he would like the element of risk, not to mention the possibility of a financial reward from her half-baked idea. Perhaps a well-placed pout and a flirt would inspire him to help her. More than likely he would simply be flattered she asked him.

It was a sunny Hong Kong August Saturday morning and Wendy had woken with her brain buzzing. Something she had seen in that meeting in Seoul the previous day had suddenly fallen into place during the night's sleep and she realized its implications as she sprawled in luxuriant nudity across her Four Seasons hotel bed. She jumped up with excitement and went to shower.

The idea had hit her, but she fast realized that alone she could do nothing. She let the warm soapy water wash over her soft skin as

17

she contemplated a potential partner. Guy! Perfect! Two minutes later, wrapped in a lush and extravagant towel and patting her wet hair, she was picking up her phone to call him and invite him to breakfast.

Wendy Chen worked for one of the largest cybersecurity consultancies in the world: Cyber Security Systems Ltd or CSSL for short. She was head of their Human Resources department in Asia or, as they preferred to call it now - Talent Calibration. It was an exciting job that challenged her intellect regularly and her patience daily.

The company was very progressive, with cybersecurity and data protection now being such a critical issue for businesses and governments alike. The company was growing very quickly and very profitably. Wendy had a good team of people working for her; to whom she delegated the boring and administrative tasks, giving her time to focus on the psychology of the prima donnas the company employed.

Being at the forefront of the battle against cybercrime, CSSL employed the very smartest 'researchers' the universities could churn out. 'Researchers' was the acceptable term for hackers. Many of them bordered on genius and this came with the high price of any thoroughbred, namely frail egos, mental instability, social awkwardness, chemical dependencies, and plain old eccentricity. This psychological melting pot made for an interesting professional environment and keeping the talent on the rails was Wendy's main job and one she relished. She saw them as her boys and girls and intellectual mothering was part of her job.

CSSL's main professional services included penetration testing, digital forensics, incident response and risk compliance consulting. Guy Anderson was one of their Senior Client Executives in Asia looking after their larger customers including the banks, insurance companies, and government departments. He was a good salesman and inspired the trust of CSSL's client base. Relative to the Researchers, the Senior Client Executives were low maintenance for Wendy however their massive egos created a different set of problems during her working day. Guy was one of the more rational people to deal with and, besides, she liked his sense humour and suspected she could trust him. He always seemed to her like an honest and reliable man. Squinting at her iPhone she speed dialled Guy's number.

'Guy. It's Wendy Chen. Did I wake you?' Wendy giggled.

'Nah, just back from the gym,' Guy lied. Truth was he had enjoyed a few beers with colleagues after work the evening before and was still feeling a little rusty. 'You still in Hong Kong Wendy?'

'Yeah, planning to have the week here on the way back to Singapore from Seoul last week. Hope I'm not disturbing anything?' she asked probingly. It quickly occurred to her that Guy might have had other plans and quite possibly someone in bed beside him. Wendy knew he wasn't married or, to the best of her knowledge, attached, but that didn't mean he slept alone.

She liked Guy; they worked well together, she respected him as a professional, and she enjoyed bantering with him socially. He had never mentioned another woman, or man for that matter, and it suddenly occurred to her then how little she knew about his personal life.

'It's always a pleasure to hear you so chirpy first thing in the morning,' he responded doing his best to stifle the scepticism from his voice. He knew from previous early morning meetings with her in the office that she was rarely chirpy first thing in the morning and she was best left well alone until after her second coffee at the earliest. Sometimes they had early morning management meetings and Wendy was prickly at best.

'What's up? Couldn't you sleep or just fancy coming to do a few weights in the gym with me?' he teased. Although they worked for the same company, they had never socialized together outside of work without a group of other colleagues present.

'I have an idea I'd like to share with you. Not over the phone though. Let's meet. I'll buy you breakfast if you're free,' said Wendy. In her heart she desperately wanted to hear him agree, however the pause on the line gave her cause to brace for a polite but definitive excuse. Her shoulders slumped. She was poised and waited for the rejection.

Then she heard, 'sure, I'd love to. It's a beautiful morning and what better way to enjoy breakfast than with a beautiful woman.' She knew he was a shameless flirt yet still her heart skipped. It surprised her how happy she was to realize she would be seeing him shortly.

'Great! I'll pull some clothes on and head over to Wan Chai,' where she knew he kept his apartment. She bit her lip with the realization she had shared her state of undress with him over the phone. That really was more forward than she had intended!

'Oh I shouldn't worry. Pop right over as you are,' came the predicable retort. 'I'll ping you the address and there's a great coffee shop downstairs.'

As Wendy dressed she contemplated the sense of what she was doing. Was she really considering something as serious as a cybercrime when the closest she had ever got to a crime in Singapore was chewing gum? Were that not enough, she found herself deliberately not bothering to put on a bra, just pulling on and buttoning up a loose-fitting white linen shirt, which lent a provocative silhouette to her curves and a delicious sense of permanent naughtiness. Hair still damp, jeans wriggled into, and a dab of subtle lipstick and she felt ready to face Guy. She caught her reflection in the hotel room mirror as she closed the door to head to the MTR station and grinned to herself.

She jumped off the MTR in Wan Chai and her heart was racing as she walked the 200 yards to the pinned address showing on her iPhone that Guy had sent her. She started to question the implications of all she was considering. Was the apprehension because she was provocatively dressed to meet a colleague for breakfast with whom an affair would be totally inappropriate and unprofessional? Was she excited to discuss something as serious as committing a cybercrime with a cybersecurity professional? Or was she actually really excited to meet Guy in a social context and had never admitted this to herself before? More to the point she wondered, why had he so readily agreed to meet her?

'No going back now!' She stoically confided to herself as she reached the apartment block near Queens Road East per the instructions on her iPhone. She decided to avoid buzzing the apartment number fearing Guy would come straight down. Instead she asked the aged security guard sat in the black marbled lobby to let her up to the 27th floor. Despite policy, he readily agreed as he scrutinized her body through the tight jeans and flouncy shirt, then failed miserably to suppress a leer as he swiped his security card over the lift sensor and hit the button for the 27th floor.

'Have a good day ma'am,' he grinned as the elevator doors closed.

A minute later in the well-lit corridor she rang the doorbell of the apartment number on her iPhone and anxiously arranged her hair, trying to suppress the butterflies in her empty stomach. As the heavy wooden door opened, she was treated to Guy's smiling face, fresh from the shower and smelling of soap, clean clothes, and aftershave. She stepped over the threshold, forcefully pushing him back into the apartment against the wall and, thrusting the full weight of her small body up against his, she kissed him squarely and passionately on the lips.

Seoul. The Previous Friday.

Kim Sung-han looked out the window of his dark and expensively furnished office across the Seoul skyline and stretched his arms above his head. It was getting late and the Seoul skyline looked beautiful as the sun silhouetted the high-rise tower blocks and Seoul's nightlife was beginning to wake up. Millions of people would be leaving their offices and heading to the thousands upon thousands of little restaurants tucked down the side streets off Seoul's main multi-lane roads. Their offerings of beer, soju and kimchi (the Korean staple of cabbage pickled in the brine of rotting fish guts, garlic, and chilli) served to complement the Korean national dish of barbequed meat.

Mr Kim watched the fading sunlight kaleidoscope across the Han River. The twilight driving multi-coloured oily patterns in the wake's of the few remaining boats puttering to their final berths for the night. Kim Sung-han's office was on the 69th floor of Han Electronics Tower. The penthouse office was one of the privileges of being the President and CEO of one of Korea's most progressive electronics companies.

This was how success felt he thought. In his early forties, he was still one of the youngest CEO's of a large Korean corporation. His busy mind had been nibbling at the edge of chaos theory to explain the scattering light patterns the river boats were making on the water's surface. This was a thought he would dwell on later; it might help with the development of the next-generation cameras deployed in the smartphones his company was famous for manufacturing. He grabbed his smartphone and tapped out a note to remind himself later. Striving for ever more sophisticated camera technology was a constant battle in the smartphone market.

He drifted back to his thoughts of success, his luxurious office, and the panorama of the city, indeed the country, he had influence in. Politicians would queue to meet him, and businessmen would fight to get on his calendar. He had power, real power, in the form of both money and resources to shape South Korea for the twenty-first-century. His ancestors would be proud: from their steel trading four generations ago before the Second World War to a world leading high-tech conglomerate today.

Seoul's formal business day was over although much business would still now be conducted in its bars and restaurants. He preferred to work late rather than suffer another formal dinner and excessive drinking, as was the Korean business culture. By nature he knew he was an introvert and a technologist. He was most happy solving logical problems - mathematics, computer code, and engineering issues. It was his father's wish that he would eventually takeover control of the business his four generations had built before him. In preparation he was sent to the best schools in Korea and the USA to study. A Masters in Electrical Engineering with a supplementary Computer Science Degree stood him in good stead.

He was a natural, he loved his subject and knew he was good. Even his own engineers, hired from Seoul National University and the Korea Advanced Institute of Science and Technology, the best universities in Korea, could still not blindside him with technology. He had an instinct for good engineering, and this is exactly what he was studying on the 32" monitor of his private computer on his desk right now.

The code was good, very good. His team had done a great job taking the framework of a programme developed by a consultant in the USA known to him only as Wolf and adapting and improving it yet further. Not so good as to look like it came from a government agency. That was always a dead giveaway. The American hackers employed by the NSA, CIA and FBI were too clean; code so precise it could only have come from one of these Agencies, a State sponsored activity.

'Those idiots,' he thought. He'd discussed it with his own Chief of Security, Mr S.C. Lee who had told him 'some of the malware even had expiry dates! What hacker in their right mind would bother to code in an expiry date on a computer virus?' But Kim Sung-han thought he knew, presumably one instructed by a lawyer considering the legal implications of State sponsored cyberterrorism on the Presidential term of office, he guessed. Sung-han smiled to himself. 'Fools!' he muttered.

The Russians and Chinese on the other hand were too sloppy, clumsy coding, errors everywhere, and inelegant. It was remarkable it even worked half the time. Not that it mattered or that they would care as they would simply recode more shoddy malware until something kind of worked. Most of these black hats just played anyway, 'code kiddies' they were disrespectfully called, and if they could make a bit of money from a ransomware so much the better for them. Mr Kim Sung-han hated sloppy coding but what he was staring at now was very tidy: economical coding and precise although not so exact as to betray the origins of the source. The one giveaway was the word 'wolf' hidden at the end of a line of script. Only those in the know would spot and understand that signature.

The malware could also be well hidden, embedded in pictures on spoof websites, hidden in .DOC files or .PDF files and such like. It could have come from anywhere. Russia would blame the USA, the USA would look to China or Israel, and China would have no idea if it were theirs or some other rogue actor in Europe, Africa, or Russia. 'Whatever,' Kim thought, 'The world would wake-up and take notice.' This code will trigger the biggest impact on geo-politics in decades and for the betterment of the economic underweight

South Korea had become he believed.

Kim was still thinking about the ramifications this code would have on the North's nuclear ambitions when he found himself absent-mindedly tapping the business card that was left lying on his desk. He looked at it: Wendy Chen, Vice President of Talent, Cyber Security Systems Ltd. He recalled the lady he had interviewed earlier that afternoon as a possible new head of Human Resources for Han Electronics International, Kim Sung-han's company.

Ms Chen was a Chinese Singaporean and presumably thought 'Talent' was a more fitting term than 'Human Resources' or even worse 'Personnel'. She went to great lengths to stress her focus was '…developing the psychology of the company and to groom the best staff for excellence.' He liked her. She was strong, sincere, and intelligent. She believed in herself and believed in what she told him. She was also an attractive woman. Not that this mattered to Sung-han as he was only interested in her professional capabilities and, besides, he was totally besotted by his lovely Korean girlfriend Lee Hyo-joo.

He had met Hyo-joo while he was giving a lecture to students at the Korea Advanced Institute of Science and Technology (KAIST). She was a postgraduate and had been in the USA studying computer science. Being studious, she seemed to attach herself to him with the pretence of discussing engineering and computer programming. From the moment he first saw her she had bewitched him. Seeming to show total interest in him one minute and then almost completely ignoring him the next, he wasn't sure if she deliberately liked to taunt him or if this was her indifferent style towards all men. Sometimes she was attentive and other times quite distant. However, it worked. The more time he spent with her, the more time he yearned to spend with her.

26

Lee Hyo-joo was fourteen years his junior, slim, beautiful, enigmatic, with long black hair that fell all the way down her back. She had approached him after the lecture and bombarded him with a dozen questions. They fell in step along the corridor as he headed to meet the Dean for lunch. He heard himself inviting her for lunch the following day and was amazed when she accepted. The subsequent stuffy lunch with the Dean passed in a bored daze of reflections on Hyo-joo as he counted down the hours to his lunch date the following day.

His wealth and status tended to attract many suitors although he had little time for girlfriends. Women had never really interested him. To him they were a flowery and disappointing distraction for the most part. He preferred the cold logic of computer code than the irrational and needy whims of women. He had a business empire to run, a job to do. Of course, he had dabbled with girlfriends, but he always found them unfulfilling, a waste of time mostly, only interested in their own vain looks and material possessions. Hyo-joo was different. She intrigued him. She taunted him. She was smart, close to his intellectual peer, and with an edginess that bordered danger; a youth and vitality that excited him both mentally and physically. He wanted to possess her like a good little Korean wife however she was frustratingly always just beyond his grasp. She made him work for the crumbs of attention she threw to him. He was still tapping Wendy Chen's business card as he contemplated seeing Hyo-joo soon.

#

In another part of the Han Electronics Tower, on a much lower floor than the heady heights of President Kim's 69th floor office, J.J. Oh sat at his desk in the Security Operations Centre. The SOC was windowless and over air-conditioned and it was his domain. He liked his job. Recruited straight out of university, Han Electronics had trained him well and promoted him on a regular basis. He worked hard, wore the company pin in the lapel of his casual jacket, and felt his career was progressing very well. His professional status in Korea was beyond his age and that of his peer group. His parents were very proud of him. Soon he planned to marry a pretty girl from the same church he attended every Sunday and his prospects at Han Electronics Inc. were very good. J.J. Oh was in the Security Department and while this typically meant network security, in charge of the firewall, access control, and intrusion detection software, his department also looked after the physical aspects of security in the building.

J.J. Oh randomly scanned the management consoles in the Security Operations Centre. Like most SOC's, there was a massive array of consoles and monitors showing the status of the network and building security. He was replaying some of the records from the numerous security cameras discretely positioned around the building. He was a huge admirer of the 'big boss' President Kim to whom he indirectly owed his career. He routinely viewed the feed from the security camera in Mr Kim's private office feeling that this somehow made him closer to the big man himself, when in fact he was five management layers removed. He had never personally met President Kim one-on-one and only ever saw him at the annual all-hands company dinner. Regardless, he had viewed the video feeds from his office so often he felt quite intimate with Mr Kim and had even learnt some of his mannerisms.

J.J. Oh was routinely watching a video stream from earlier in the day when Mr Kim was meeting with a rather attractive Chinese-looking lady with good legs. He probably lingered a little longer on the legs than he should have done, but then he was suddenly dumbstruck by her actions. President Kim had stood up and left the office for a moment. The lady with the legs uncrossed them, stood up from her chair, then went behind President Kim's desk, and started to read what was on his computer terminals.

If this weren't bad enough, she then appeared to remove a USB device from her handbag and plugged it into a USB slot on his personal computer which was so private it wasn't even network connected. Typing a few commands on the keyboard, she appeared to download something then she unplugged the USB device, placed it back in her bag, and sat down again, gracefully re-crossing those long legs in front of her. President Kim returned a short while afterwards and the meeting continued as normal. Shaking with the implications of what he had just seen, J.J. Oh replayed the video to make sure his eyes were not playing tricks on him and, perspiring heavily under his armpits, he grabbed for the phone and dialled his direct manager as fast as he could.

Kim Sung-han planned to see Hyo-joo this evening and he was looking forward to it. They would have a Korean dinner in a private room in one of their favourite restaurants in Gangnam. She would look immaculate as always. She didn't specifically dress to impress him, it happened to always be that way. His chauffeur would have picked her up in his black Hyundai Equus already and Sung-han would meet the car in the private parking bay beneath his office. She would smile and look radiant. They would usually drive in silence and after dinner the driver would take them back to Kim's apartment at one of the most exclusive residences in Seoul. She would stay the night without invitation. She would be classy, demure, and quiet in public but in the bedroom, she would take control.

Kim Sung-han was the boss in the office and everyone was fearful of the 'big boss'. In the privacy of the bedroom it was different; this was Hyo-joo's domain where she was very much the boss. She would shower and emerge from the marbled bathroom wearing a red silk gown then insist he shower. At first she would tease, feigning disinterest in lovemaking and in him. She let her silk gown slither snake-like over her frictionless skin whenever she moved. Occasional gaps in the red silk would reveal the perfect curves of a breast or a well-defined muscular thigh. He would try to engage her with alternating empathy and authority, all were wasted effort. She would be indifferent, cat like, until she was ready. And when Lee Hyo-joo was ready it was he who became passive.

He wasn't a confident lover so when Lee Hyo-joo took control he was happy to let her. Forcefully laying him on the bed, Hyo-joo would straddle him, letting the silk gown falling open around her exposing pert chest and a flat muscular stomach. Her powerful thighs would grip his waist as she slid onto him, while her long hair would fall over him, the perfumed red silk gown and long black hair enveloping him in a heady cocoon of erotic delight. Hyo-joo would slowly pick up rhythm, moaning and crying out as she bought herself to a climax, stopping only when she wanted. Sung-han, if he made a sound or said anything was ignored.

Afterwards she would be coy again, lying in his arms asking him about his day, their stock price, and the progress his company was making with any given technology. He would be honest with her, sharing his successes and frustrations. She would listen with interest, head on the pillow, offering opinions and advise where she could. He valued her thoughts and opinions, actively seeking her input. Tonight, however, he wanted to update her about this code. He would name it 'Stinger', a malware that would change the political balance on the Korean peninsula. A malware that would redefine a new, reunified Korea as a credible world power. A malware that would launch a nuclear device from the Korea peninsular.

Lee Hyo-joo was well aware of Stinger, in fact, the very observant would have noticed over the preceding months that it had largely been her idea or, more accurately, her chain of ideas. Lee Hyo-joo had not blatantly communicated the idea, that would be crass and most likely met with rejection, but instead she sowed the seeds, pulling the strings, slowly and discreetly manipulating the players, as would a puppeteer skilfully make her puppets dance. Stinger was a compilation of ideas carefully orchestrated by her and woven into a credible plan. That the plan would work depended on multiple variables, but it was a plan, and seemingly a very good one at that.

As they lay in bed, Kim Sung-han reclined on the huge pile of fresh linen covered pillows with Hyo-joo lying to his left, her head nestled on his chest, her right leg wrapped over his, and her hair splayed out in all directions. Sung-han gave her the update on Stinger. The code, originally developed by a hacker known to them only as Wolf, had been tested by his own engineers in Han Electronics and was found to work, in emulation at least. It was well coded and anonymous apart from the Wolf signature, a vice they would concede to the arrogant Wolf. Kim considered this project his baby, his idea.

His ancestors would be pleased he had not inherited their foundation and used it merely to create a larger company. To simply create more wealth would be a waste. Much rather, that would be instrumental in the reunification of Korea, and establish it as a world power. To reunite this frivolity of a country, divided along some arbitrary 38th parallel, and leave the legacy of a country, rightly, an economic equal too, or better than, either China or Japan. The Korean people deserved this, or so he unerringly believed.

Hyo-joo, with her head lying on his chest, ran her hand over his soft skin, her hair concealing her face from Kim Sung-han as she smiled to herself. Her plan was taking shape. The reconnaissance done and the weaponization completed, the third step in the cyber kill chain was now the malware's deployment.

As he lay there, his hand absentmindedly stroking her flawless skin and sharing this update with the woman he loved, Kim's private smartphone buzzed where it lay next to him on the bedside table. In moments of intimacy he would usually ignore it although this time he reached out, grabbing the vibrating phone, something instinctively making him glance at the text message. The message was from S.C. Lee, his Chief Information Security Officer, and it was marked 'CRITICAL!' Kim Sung-han suddenly sat up and heard the panicked voice of his CISO.

Kim Sung-han sensed the worry. 'Hello, what is it?' he asked.

Pyongyang, North Korea. Saturday Morning.

Three large portraits hung in pride of place on the light green wall behind General Park's huge and clear desk. The first picture, in the left, was of Kim Il-sung, the Eternal President of the Democratic People's Republic of Korea (DPRK). On the right, his son Kim Jong-Il. In the centre and the largest of the three, his grandson Kim Jong-un, the current leader of what the rest of the world calls North Korea. General Park smartly strode into his office in his usual dark green full-dress uniform then formally and precisely saluted the three pictures.

No one was watching but this was a routine he had followed his entire army career. Regardless of whether anyone was watching or not, he assumed the room was bugged with microphones and spy cameras and that everything he did and said was being eavesdropped upon, always. In the current climate of paranoia, it was best to tow the Workers' Party of Korea's (WPK) political line to the letter and be seen to be respectful to the leadership at any and every opportunity.

The rain lashed against his office window as he looked down at a battalion practicing their carefully synchronized marching. The hot dry spell had broken and today was going to be hot and wet, a respite from the weeks of brutal sun and humid summer heat. It didn't matter to General Park as the troop's pointless training would continue regardless, rain or shine or snow. The 60,000 men and women from twenty-two brigades in the Korean People's Army (KPA) under his command needed to be battle-ready. To the Party Leader this primarily meant impeccable marching skill exhibited at huge, irrelevant, military displays through the streets of Pyongyang. Most real North Korean military muscle came simply from the threat of their nuclear capability and their delivery vehicles; the crown being the medium-range Rodong-1 ballistic missiles so feared by North Korea's neighbours.

The huge conventional army was always an impressive show as well, but mainly put on for the benefit of their own repressed people who were being repeatedly told they were a world power. As the rain outside pummelled his office window, General Park considered how useful the flawless marching would be if, heaven forbid, they ever actually needed to march into real armed combat. Perhaps the enemy would simply surrender at the intimidation of such precision marching. He privately smiled at his own humour as his thought's turned to the matters of the day.

General Park slid behind his desk and settled starchily upright in his chair. His secretary came in and, following formal salutes, handed a buff folder with sheaves of papers containing the month's, the week's, and the day's itinerary along with routine intelligence reports. Reporting directly to the Chief of the General Staff, General Park's responsibilities included briefing the Chief on intelligence matters. Most of these consisted of Chinese PLA supplied reports of USA and South Korean troop and naval movements.

This morning the news was light as no specific joint allied force activities were in process near the Korean peninsula. General Park's own surveillance feeds were more helpful. These included feeds from 'fishing trawlers' across the South China Sea and the Sea of Japan, the two oceans on either side of the Korean peninsula. Also, from his spies in various countries including the USA, China, Australia, Hong Kong, England, Japan, and of course South Korea. Plus, lastly, his growing team of 900 computer hackers. These hackers were Chinese and Russian trained talented young software programmers who endeavoured to eavesdrop on everything and anything they could. The chaff would be separated from the wheat later.

Given the Chinese and sometimes Russian provided intelligence would be heavily edited, General Park placed much more reliance on his own sources. His hackers had the brief to create mischief and could be thanked for may of the worlds more toxic malwares. Working under names like Kimsuky and Lazarus his hackers formed into groups and created prolific malware and spyware. Much of it was primitive and clumsy. But they were improving and occasionally a virus, trojan, RAT, or ransomware would hit its mark.

Park was a career soldier, adopted by the army as an orphan in 1951 when he was only 10 years old. This was just after Kim Il-sung helped form the National Revolutionary Army, which latterly became the Korean People's Army, and had declared war on what became South Korea. He knew no other life than the army and relished every day, doing his best to exceed in every order he was given. Kim Il-sung, the Eternal President, spotted his talent as a young soldier and admired his dedication. He was brave, hardworking, and personified the communist Korea Kim Il-sung wanted to build. With the Eternal President's patronage, the young Park progressively moved up the army's ranks.

General Park now flipped through the routine intelligence report's and noticed the USS *Ronald Reagan* was again resupplying in Hong Kong. This irked the General as China, and of course Hong Kong was now part of China, was supposed to be North Korea's closest military ally. Every now and again there would be a diplomatic spat and Chinese Hong Kong would not allow a US ship to resupply in Hong Kong, but clearly not this week.

There was a sharp knock on the door and his secretary again entered, this time with a sealed report labelled 'For Your Eyes Only' and 'Highly Confidential'. Good! His bushy eyebrows rose as he looked up at the secretary. From one of his own agents thought General

Park. He dismissed the upright secretary and smiled to himself. This looked like it might be from Talon, code name for one of the undercover operatives the North had currently placed in Seoul, the capital of South Korea.

The General picked-up his elaborate silver letter opener from his desk and slid it beneath the security seal thus breaking it and allowing him to pull out the one crisp page. Indeed it was from Talon and, retrieving his English language copy of Chairman Mao's Little Red Book from his desk draw, he began decoding the ciphered text in the letter. Book cyphers were common and difficult to crack. Two people used an identical book and used a numeric sequence to express the desired letter, starting with page, line, word, and lastly letter, although careful to minimize vowel use as this aided codebreakers.

He enjoyed the irony of using the Chinese Communist Party leader's aphorisms as it lent humour to the dialog with Talon, thinking that she too would be fingering the exact same pages of her copy of the little book while thinking of him. All this while, contemplating the wisdom of China's great leader using the identical book to be the key to their private cipher.

Talon had been personally trained by him while he was Commandant of the training base at Pyongyang AAA Command. AAA Command was responsible for, amongst other things, Special Purposes Force Command covering special operations, SEAL, intelligence, assassination, and espionage including sending subversive agents into South Korea and other countries considered hostile to the DPRK. He had taken a keen interest in the career and development of Talon, in fact he had taken a special interest in Talon ever since she had been born.

As a committed member of the Korean People's Army his life was his work and his loyalty was to the Party. For this reason, he had never married. He had one affair as a young Major, however, with his military career on a fast trajectory, he refused to marry Lena. She was a simple village woman whom he loved but who he saw as unsuitable as the wife of a budding General in the KPA; instead, leaving her to the shame of bearing his illegitimate child alone. Although, emotion prevented him from completely separating himself from his biological daughter and, through a combination of direct orders, subtle influences, and money, he saw to it that she received a good education and at the age of fourteen she joined the 907th Army Unit. Again, with his remote influence, he oversaw her progression into the Special Purposes Force Command. By eighteen she had developed into a beautiful, fit, and bright young woman, responding well to the harsh intense physical training while diligently developing her foreign language skills and, of course, ingesting the political guidance of the Workers' Party of Korea.

Talon, her code name, was told her father had died shortly after her birth in 1993 while on a covert mission for the Democratic People's Republic of Korea and that she should be very proud but ask no more questions. She was happy to leave it at that. Although her schooling and the army had taken her away from her mother, she adapted by embracing her learning. By nineteen Talon had language skills and had mastered mountaineering, scuba diving, martial arts, demolition and firing multiple weapons including AK-47's, M-16's, RPG-7 and her favourite, the Russian made anti-tank missile the AT-3 Sagger. Aside the weapons, she had studied many military tactics including asymmetric war, guerrilla war, insurgency and counter insurgency. Finally, Talon was ready for the last stage of her training.

Talon was a model soldier and at twenty-one she was proud to serve her country, smuggled in Los Angeles, California, to perfect her integration with the imperialist West. There she specifically worked hard to acquire her American accent and understand the ways of a capitalist society. At twenty-three, AAA Command ordered her move to South Korea and there she was given her intelligence brief from the DPRK Reconnaissance Bureau.

Now, armed with her American Green Card under her false South Korean identity, she leveraged her good looks and sharp intelligence, and eased somewhat by a very healthy bank account facilitated for her by her KPA employer in North Korea, she was instructed to ingratiate herself into the upper echelons of South Korean society. From there she was instructed to move in political circles and feed back any information she could to her controller in the North.

She had done a good job. She had worked very hard to remove any vestiges of her North Korean accent and maintained her carefully crafted cover. Her insights and ability to assess snippets of information, coupled with rumour, enabled her to interpret and share the ebb and flow of the South Korean government whims and industrial thinking. General Park was rightly proud of his daughter, however what he read now on the sheet of crisp paper, having decrypted the message, sent a shiver through his body. A large electronics company south of the demarcation line had developed computer software aimed at attacking his nuclear missile facilities.

General Park sat back in his large office chair and stared, unfocused, through the window at the black clouds scurrying across the grey sky as if they too were motivated to move faster by this news. He pondered the significance of the news. He well knew their nuclear technology and missile launch systems were not state-of-the-art. They were mostly supplied with dated technology from Russia, Iran and Pakistan, with an assortment of aged gear smuggled in from China or through African rogue states. The Korean People's Army's nuclear capability was vintage at best. That said, as a deterrent and as leverage for aid negotiations, typically needed every three to four years when the Democratic People's Republic of Korea needed external food aid, banging the nuclear war drum worked perfectly. China would sit back while three generations of Kim leaders rattled their sabres, beat their chests, threatened war, and generally made a nuisance of themselves on the world stage.

Everyone knew eventually, South Korea, China and the US would throw a few million tons of food aid at North Korea, who would temporarily cease their sabre rattling and chest thumping until the next time the crops failed, and they needed help again. CNN and BBC viewers would soon lose interest and CNN would find another story to entertain their viewers and so General Park knew the world would keep turning.

The General mused the folly that was their muddle-headed agricultural, industrial, and economic model, and while not well travelled himself, he was worldly, veraciously reading everything he could about the West. Sadly, he saw no end to this depressing cycle. It had, after all, lasted three generations of Kim's. North Korea was too big an economic parasite to integrate into South Korea without killing its host (numerous studies on East Germany's integration into West Germany has shown that) and China didn't want North Korea either as they had more than enough of their own uneducated cheap labour, which was the only readily available commodity the Democratic People's Republic of Korea truly had to offer.

Sooner or later the West, and even China, would tire of the juvenile Kim dynasty's repeated failures and allow millions to die of famine in the hope of catalysing a civil uprising to overthrow the moribund leadership. Regrettably, General Park knew that he too would be counted amongst that cliquey band of incompetents; living proof that communism, while an interesting social experiment, was inherently and irreparably flawed like a cracked vinyl record. The worn wheels of diplomacy knew North Korea had no assets. There were no billions of cubic meters of oil underground or rich seams of iron ore or valuable precious metals easily accessible. Not even an educated workforce. The harsh point was North Korea was an economic irrelevance, only given humanitarian aid to prevent social and economic collapse and so avoid the burden of millions of starving to people spilling over South Korea and China, its two border-sharing neighbours. He sighed inwardly; they had failed.

General Park was maudlin, and the weather didn't help. Heavy water droplets still helter-skeltered down his windows. His thoughts turned to his very much missed old friend and comrade Kim Jong-un's uncle, Chang Song-thaek. As young men they had believed such wonderful communistic ideals. Then as middle-aged men they shared such a vision for their beautiful country, but as old men… well, they had been cheated of growing old together. He mused on this as he watched the rainwater droplets tumble drunkard-like down his window pain. Now he'd grown old and lonely and mocking.

The scurrying storm clouds outside seem to mimic the winds of change he felt stir in his own gut. He might not live to see the changes, but he hoped his daughter would. If the changes resulted in his own death so be it; he would simply look forward to drinking soju in heaven with his old friend Chang Song-thaek. He reached for his copy of Chairman Mao's Little Red Book. He owed Talon a response. 'Execute plan' were simply the two words he translated and ciphered into XCT PLN before calling for his secretary to send the encrypted message.

Palo Alto, California. June.

Palo Alto was stiflingly hot. Heat shimmers were coming off Route 101, the main artery running north-south through Silicon Valley. It was very heavy with traffic although at least today it was still moving. The aircraft coming into San Francisco's international airport were tightly stacked as usual on their final approach coming in over the bay. Had the curtains been drawn open, Craig might just see them from his east-facing aspect however the curtains were black hole opaque and never opened nor for that matter were the wire mesh that hung down behind them. The air conditioning in Craig's apartment laboured under the strain of trying to cool the naturally hot outside air coupled with the heat output from Craig's impressive array of computers, gaming consoles, monitors, servers, routers, firewalls, and other miscellaneous IT hardware equipment. All were carefully stacked and neatly racked in what Craig called 'Mission Control'.

Craig's mum would otherwise refer to Mission Control as 'Craig's Bedroom', a room she rarely ventured into. Craig was a slob in all sense should be plural of the word. Discarded pizza boxes and junk food wrappers intermingled with empty soda and energy drink cans cluttering every surface and obscured much of the drab carpet. For Craig's mum to venture into Mission Control would be met with howls of abuse and hysterical screaming from the code kiddie for hire – her son, and only child.

Jenny Sanchez, Craig's mum, actually had no idea quite what he did in his room. He would stay inside for days on end, venturing out only to use the bathroom and collect food. He had once told her he was a day trader, and this seemed to satisfy her. As it was, he would give her a wad of cash every month or so and this more than covered the bills so the arrangement, while not exactly loving, suited her okay.

Craig's own appearance changed little from day to day. A crusty, stained, black tee shirt stretched over an obese flabby white stomach which flopped over the top of a pair of equally stained and crusty faded cargo shorts betrayed the tidiness of his mind and his programming abilities. Contrasting the untidy, shabby and perpetually messy room, were the racks of neatly stacked and lovingly maintained computer appliances which hummed reassuringly in the dim light. While looking like a bowl of spaghetti to the uninitiated, all the multi-coloured fibre cabling connecting the latest gear in the computer racks were meticulously labelled and impeccably laid out. Craig's server farm coupled with flash storage array's, and the latest firewalls interconnected with the fastest fibre networking infrastructure made Craig's Mission Control as formidable as any datacentre offered by a bank, telco, or cloud service provider.

Truth was that Craig knew he had progressed a long way since his code kiddie days. Originally computer coding had been his passion adapted from his hobby in school. He was passionate about computer programming and found he had an aptitude for it, a feeling for him almost a sixth sense. Good coders were intuitive. Artists. Craig's computer programming started with simple applications, but he soon found it more challenging and intellectually rewarding to try and reverse-engineer other people's programmes rather than to develop his own. Had he been a little slimmer, a little cooler, a little better looking, and a little more sociable, he would probably have turned his talents to sports, graffiti, or skateboarding like the other kids of school age.

Craig had been none of these. Fat, nerdy, pimply, awkward, and with little attention paid to his bodily hygiene, he had been ostracized at school and latterly at university, which he subsequently dropped out of. Being friendless and girlfriendless didn't bother Craig as his mind was always on his computers anyway and he knew he could always pay for sexual gratification online without even needing to be polite.

Craig had been readily accepted into University California, Santa Cruz (UCSC); forty miles down the road, past San Jose, and over the hill on the Pacific Coast. At first he had enjoyed the complete change of pace with Santa Cruz being something of a throwback from the 1960's and 1970's. After a while though he tired of his classes and found his self-taught hacking skills taking precedence over his lectures. His lecturers bored him. They didn't share his passion for breaking things.

With the advent of crypto currencies, Craig had found he could now monetize his talents and apply his coding skill to building malware others were prepared to pay for, specifically ransomware. The beauty of ransomware was receiving the untraceable extortion payments, which had become easy via blockchain based crypto currencies. His first attempts at ransomware were inelegant but they did the job well enough.

The encryption code could be propagated to target companies who would invariably pay his 'consulting fees' to have the now locked and useless data files decrypted and so usable again. Initially he targeted organisations in healthcare: doctor's surgeries, hospitals and such like. Craig knew these were regulated industries entrusted with lots of patient health records and typically these organisations had very sloppy IT security rendering them easy targets for black hat hackers like himself.

These organisations would discreetly pay the crypto currency ransoms rather than deal with the public humiliation, not to mention the costly litigation and probable fines, by confessing to having been hit with a data theft or ransomware attack. They would then hope the extortionists were honourable enough to send the decryption codes. They rarely were. Craig thought it laughable how amateurish these companies were, and how they'd be so desperate to pay his ransom demands.

Craig found he could make a credible living honing his hacking skills by acting as a white hat hacker also. These 'honest' hackers are employed by penetration testing (pen-testing) organisations trying to develop their own secure environments. They would invite and willing pay a reward for anyone who could penetrate their secure environments, hence exposing any overlooked vulnerabilities.

'It is rather like paying a burglar to try and break into your home and giving him a reward if he does,' Craig explained to anyone who'd listen. Of course, many white hats by day may become black hats by night. So, as Craig got better at winning hackathons and hacking competitions and preforming his penetration testing duties, he was also busy building viruses, botnets, ransomware, and anonymizers for his own illicit darker activities.

As sponges mop up water so Craig mopped up malware and hacking tools. His own datacentre held a carefully indexed database of malware equal to that of any antivirus software company or government security agency. The library of malware tools stored on his computer servers was only surpassed by his extensive library of pornography.

\#

Craig's mum, Jenny, despaired when Craig dropped out of university and simply remained in his room, gaming, or so she thought. Increasingly he spent days on end in his room and she was frustrated to think she would have to support him financially on her meagre salary as a waitress in a local diner. Twenty-three years ago, Jenny had been pretty and blond, the classic B-52's *'Love Shack'* Californian babe. She grew up in the valley and loved the Californian lifestyle, never really considering any alternatives. While not ambitious, life was good. She was gregarious, naturally shapely, had long blond hair and a pretty smile. She had avoided the artificial enhancements so favoured by other girls of the same generation and this gave her an unconscious and natural confidence in her own beauty.

Throughout her teenage year's Silicon Valley was getting rich on all the IT companies. Hewlett-Packard had really kicked things off in the 1960's and now Apple, Cisco, Oracle, Google, Facebook, Amazon and a myriad of smaller companies seemed to be making every other guy a multi-millionaire through their Initial Public Offerings. Jenny was desirable, she was part of the party circuit, and she assumed one day she would marry well, while not being in any particular hurry. Jenny wore tight, white, cropped tee shirts to show off her midriff and worked as a waitress in the neon lit bars on Palo Alto's strip. Most nights, like all the other girls in her coterie, she was occupied with juggling the many party invitations she would receive to kick on later after the bars had closed.

One Sunday morning Jenny had awoken with a hangover, a little worse than usual, on an unfamiliar sofa in a classy apartment in Mountain View with the groggy realization she had gotten rather too high on cocaine and tequila the previous evening. Her missing knickers and stippled, sticky thighs also told her she'd had unprotected sex, a rule she promised herself she'd never break. The young and fiercely good-looking owner of the house looked vague about who she was and even vaguer when she asked him the name of the guy who she may have slept with the previous evening.

'It was quite a party! You and your girlfriends seemed to be having a lot of fun!' he had rather glumly said while squinting at Jenny through puffy red eyes. Then he dipped his head to snort his first line of cocaine of the morning, gesturing her towards the coffee machine as he did so, with the hand not holding the powdery, tightly rolled $100 bill.

Jenny Sanchez had the impression that strange, half naked women waking up in his apartment was not at all unusual. Jenny declined the offer of coffee, found her bag, gave up trying to find her underwear and made a swift exit. She was desperate for the seclusion of a private taxi and a shower back in her own apartment. These were all IT guys, young professionals with Porsches, huge amounts of disposable cash from vested stock options, and a determination to live life to the full. Like a good groupie, she didn't begrudge it at all; she actually loved it. But four months later the tummy bulge was beginning to show, and nine months later baby Craig was born, largely closing that chapter on Jenny's days as a Californian party chick. Now she was single mother with a fatherless child and a social circle that had evaporated faster than San Francisco's morning mist.

Twenty-three years later, confirming her original misgivings, her son was a programming recluse who rarely spoke to her. He seemed to be financially self-sufficient though as he had no problem giving her four or five thousand dollars every month to keep the apartment supplied with electricity and him supplied with unhealthy junk food and energy claiming soda drinks.

#

Craig cracked his knuckles, stretched, and yawned exaggeratedly then continued flipping through the financial news blogs of the day. Spending so much time in the darkened room, he frequently lost all track of time and indeed whether it was even day or night.

He slept when tired, coded when motivated, and researched when bored of both. The small green, red, yellow, and blue coloured lights on the computer racks flickered hypnotically as the cooling fans hummed and the management consoles told Craig they were all as they should be. Like all good hacker's first move, he needed to do his reconnaissance, and today he'd just found himself researching a new target.

He had previously read a press release from a particular computer manufacturer boasting of a sizable deal with a large American credit rating agency, Union Credit Inc. Many computer manufacturers liked to publicise big customer wins, flaunting their customers like trophies. No computer equipment was 100 per cent hack-proof and Craig was familiar with many of the vulnerabilities of this particular manufacturer's servers and software. A quick check of LinkedIn and he was looking at a score of programmers who had either previously worked for, or were still working for Union Credit Inc. Seeing their Photoshopped pictures and self-professed technical skills and experience on the LinkedIn pages enabled him to form a profile of the hardware and software the credit agency used. Depending on how they had designed and configured their network would determine how easy this would be to hack, or not. At least he knew what to expect.

Following his debut with viruses and ransomware, Craig went on to cut his hacking teeth by building botnet malware. The name 'botnet' was created by combining the words 'robots' and 'networks' then abbreviating them into the term 'botnet'. Botnets are the protocols Craig used to exploit multiple other computers across the Internet which, are in turn, controlled by the botnet's originator known as the 'Botnet Herder'. Craig had achieved a fair degree of notoriety in the dark, swirling mists of anonymous hacking circles and was looking for a signature, a way to make a name for himself, to brand himself.

Black hat hackers congregated in the Dark Web, the online virtual underworld of pimps, arms dealers, paedophiles, drug dealers, fences, killers and hackers. Craig knew the Dark Web is a marketplace for every conceivable criminal activity so far invented by mankind. Everyone on the Dark Web used an alias and Craig felt he needed one too. The name of the creator of a botnet malware is known as the botnet herder or botnet shepherd, and it's the bot herder who control their botnets remotely. The only part of Craig that is larger than his ample lily-white belly is his ego, and, like many celebrity hackers, he craves notoriety and recognition for his work from his peers. Just as an artist will sign their work, so hackers like to leave some small signature so those in the know will admire the coding and the audacity of a well-executed hack.

Craig knew the trick with botnets is maintaining a low profile so as to exploit zombie machines that are used without the owner's detection. Craig's signature was to code 'wolf' into his command and control code. Originally he liked the idea of the name 'The Shepherd', a pun on herder, but it sounded too meek, too biblical, too benign. Mulling on the term shepherd, it struck Craig that the logical ornery of a shepherd was a wolf. 'Now that's a code name worthy of a top black hat on the world stage,' thought Craig.

Wolf was gaining celebrity status. He had a following, a fan club of other hackers who loved his work. He was a rock star in the underworld of cybercrime. He would get commissions. His opinions were sought, and his advice was asked. If his university classmates could see him now – the virtual equivalent to the handsome quarterback all the girls wanted to date. Well, in the opaque world of the Dark Web you could be anything you wanted to be, and Wolf wanted to be a God to whom all others grovelled.

Wolf, along with other black hats, are aware hacking follows seven logical steps known prosaically as The Cyberattack Kill Chain. The first act is Reconnaissance: researching likely targets and building an understanding of the target and the computer systems they use. Then would follow Weaponization: deciding what software tools to use, the actual vulnerability which would be exploited that would be used to execute the hack. The third step is Delivery: physically loading a malware into the targets network, the virtual equivalent of a house break in. Then follows Exploitation: activating the payload of malware for the task it was designed for on the network, much like how a burglar would rummage through draws looking for hidden valuables. This is followed by the fifth step, Installation of the malware into the target destinations, be they hardware or software: the virtual equivalent to safe cracking.

The hack now complete, the penultimate task is to take 'Command and Control' giving the hacker access to the target's computers and software then issuing specific instructions such as download all your data files. Lastly, Act on Objective's, the ultimate goal of the hack: this could include encrypting files as in ransomware, shutting down a computer, steal these datafiles, or issue instructions such as 'send my bank account $1m now', or even deliver instruction codes for missiles launches, and so on.

Wolf found this power physically arousing. Done properly, Exploitation and Installation would take seconds, minutes at most, however the lead up to this could take weeks or months if planned properly. Good Reconnaissance was key. Craig loved the research as much as he loved sidestepping the network security demonstrating he was smarter than the average security professional. Above all this, he loved coding his beautiful weapons, handcrafting his own tools - the cyberweapons he would deploy for his own financial gain.

In addition to his own hacks, he was happy to undertake commissions. It paid well and he knew the hack's could never be traced back to him. The only clue would be the Wolf signature somewhere in the code string and this would only ever be found by someone who knew what they were looking for, true aficionados of good malware coding.

Craig had recently undertaken a very interesting commission. He had been approached via the Dark Web by someone simply known as Talon. Talon had given some very specific instructions on the launch management systems of a Russian-made missile defence system. Simply put, they wanted to override this system and have the ability to trigger the launch process. The system was old, so old in fact Wolf needed to brush up on some older programming languages. This made the job easier in some respects as the code was not designed for security although harder in other respects because he had to learn the commands. The general public assume modern weapons are sophisticated but it is remarkable how many are actually run on very antiquated technology. Regardless, Wolf accepted the commission and built his baby he christened 'Stinger', the malware which took command and control of a missile launch system that could irreversibly trigger a missile launch. He idly wondered if he would ever see the results of his handiwork on the news. At US$250,000 for the job he didn't really care. It was still a nice thought.

#

Union Credit Inc. seemed to Wolf to be much like any other standard financial services company. Not having to actually deal with money, they assumed they were less vulnerable to hackers than banks. After all, there was no money to steal. Their offices were magnificent; a red marble, glass and hardwood temple to capitalism. Based in downtown San Francisco, their self-important senior executives had views spanning east over the Golden Gate Bridge then, following clockwise, the panorama across Alcatraz, Treasure Island, and South San Francisco down to Hunters Point. The staff's cubicles were functional in contrast to the boardroom and executive offices where no expense in opulence had been spared. The datacentre, stylishly designed and displayed behind thick glass, had the very latest in biometric physical security. Retinal scans were needed to even gain access to the room. Designed to impress their clients with their diligent attention to apparent security, Union Credit Inc. loved to host visitors in their office to see how a twenty-first century, world-class data collection and credit rating agency worked.

Wolf, the reflection of his chubby face looking back at him from his huge production monitor on his main desk in Mission Control, carefully studied the website of Union Credit Inc. He was looking at pictures of the datacentre to see the equipment used. He already had the LinkedIn profiles of many of their staff. He had even sent a few malwares via embedded code in fictitious CV's to their trendy Human Resources job board, purely to test the sophistication of their firewalls and sandboxes. These malwares were all blocked. Predictably, he was pleased to see. Nothing like throwing a few dummy punches to test your opponent's reflexes.

While Union Credit Inc.'s prime location offices in downtown San Francisco were state-of-the-art in their IT and security infrastructure, less glamorous was the off-site backup facility Union Credit Inc. rented further south along Route 101 in Sunnyvale. Moffett Field, an old military airbase, was a sprawling mass of old buildings on land once use to hangar blimps deployed to patrol the Pacific coast during the wars. Many of the old buildings were sturdy enough still and were rented out to the IT companies that had sprouted like mushrooms along the length of the 101.

One such building was used by Union Credit Inc. as their backup and disaster recovery facility. Logically, a close replica of their datacentre in the San Francisco headquarters, this facility was used for close to real-time backup and duplication of every computer task that happened in the headquarters datacentre. Encased in concrete and enmeshed in a steel Faraday cage, the same brand of computer servers, routers, and firewalls were setup in racks in this failover facility. This way Union Credit Inc.'s data was protected from power failures, computer viruses, and even earthquakes that could interrupt the business in their more plush head office seventy miles away.

However, one possible tiny oversight caught the interest of Wolf. While the backup datacentre itself was literally rock solid given the concrete and steel making access virtually impossible for all except the authorized personnel, the local area network seemed to extend to a couple of computers in the adjacent administration office. Outside of the Faraday cage, in the administration office, sat two rarely used, dusty old computers that dealt with the physical aspects of access to the building, including swiping staff security badges and performing retinal scans to employees needing physical access. These were still networked to the datacentre itself. However, also connected to this same network was an old legacy printer for the occasional need to print off worksheets and the like for the contract maintenance staff. That was precisely the chink in the armour a good black hat like Wolf would be looking for.

Craig clapped his hands, scratched his fat tummy and smiled. As his thoughts drifted off towards his porn collection, he had that tingle that told him Union Credit Inc. was about to become the next unwitting victim of the Wolf.

Hong Kong. Saturday Morning.

He wasn't quite sure what shocked him more. The fact that she had so forcefully pushed him up against the wall with such strength and agility for a small woman; the fact that she was kissing him so passionately, a pleasure he had hesitantly pictured although never guessed would ever actually happen; or that look of sheer determination in her dark eyes as she did both. Quickly getting over the surprise, Guy reciprocated the kiss. Her lips were soft but the kiss was firm, aggressive, pushing hard against him with her lithe little body. She had put her arm around the back of his neck to pull his head down to meet hers. Loving, no. This was pure, unbridled passion. She wanted to be held and kissed hard. He intuitively knew this was no game to her.

Rapidly overcoming the fact that he hadn't actually been consulted about the kiss she was so rudely stealing, he decided to make the best of it. He slid his arms around her waist, sliding his hands up beneath the baggy shirt and feeling the frictionless softness of the skin on her lower back. He kissed her hard in return, his stubbly chin rasping against her soft cheeks. She bent into his embrace as his manly hands supported her smooth back, sliding ever higher. He was further surprised when his fingers failed to trip over a bra strap where he had expected to find one. He discovered there simply was no bra.

Guy straightened himself, coming to his full six-foot height, while still holding Wendy tight. The effect was to lift her clean off her feet, the black stiletto heels dangling six inches above the floor. This enabled him to break the kiss and gently lower her back down while placing a few inches of space between them without fully letting go. He studied her face, looking deep into her innocent eyes. The braless torso was a giveaway. She wanted sex. While the thought of her nakedness beneath the shirt caused an immediate and potentially embarrassing arousal, he didn't want to be seen as such a pathetic pushover. If she was going to simply use him for sex it would be on his terms. Not that the idea of sex right there and then didn't appeal to him, far from it. He simply wanted to play a part in the choreography. Wendy gave him her most impish grin. Guy studied her face silently as he contemplated his next move and his sheer good fortune on this sultry Saturday morning.

'Well I didn't see that coming!' Guy said. 'Can I assume it was an uneventful Friday night for you?' he quizzed, assuming her partying the previous evening in Lan Kwai Fong with the other girls they worked with had been a complete washout.

Wendy blushed and sidestepped the last question. 'Would you believe me if I said I didn't see that coming either?' Her face was burning up with embarrassment. She didn't quite believe her own forwardness and now she was feeling rather self-conscious. After all, they were colleagues, and her behaviour was entirely unprofessional.

Guy smiled, well aware of the awkwardness. He needed to take control of the situation. There were three potential courses of action. Firstly, he could kiss her passionately again while pulling her into his apartment, unbuttoning that shirt which he so urgently wanted to do, and have quick carnal sex with this beautiful little woman. Or secondly, he could act nonchalant and invite her into the apartment on the pretence of coffee; although this too would likely degenerate quickly into sex he suspected, his firm erection now pushing against the inside of his jeans was reminding him how he desperately wanted to have sex with her. Lastly, he could suggest they have leisurely breakfast per their original plan, giving them both an opportunity to pause and consider what they both wanted at a more languid pace. They could always come back to his apartment afterwards if their conclusions were consistent with the first two options.

He was wracked with the decision. He utterly wanted to pleasure this passionate little woman right now but somehow he sensed this relationship was probably worth more than quick sex and intuitively he wanted to take a little time to nurture it. Up to now he'd always admired Wendy from afar, her beauty, her confident stance, and sharp intellect. But, unable to resist a little more exhilaration though, there on the doorstep Guy reached forwards with his right hand and with the back of his fingers gently brushed the shirt where he could see her breast stood proud against the fine linen shirt. She didn't flinch or step back. She simply watched his eyes, he was tender, and she was happy and willing to let him touch her. After all, she'd instigated it. She was sensitive there and liked the intimacy of his gentle stroke. He was admiring her face and scanning her in detail now, searching for her thoughts. Guy liked the high heels, tight jeans, and stark white shirt. She liked this feeling and watched his serious face as he processed the image of this lovely woman.

Looking up at him, she noticed for the first time his casual Saturday morning dress. Shaved head, old jeans, worn and faded blue business shirt slightly frayed at the collar with the cuffs rolled-up, and unshaven but smelling of soap and freshly applied aftershave. She had not often seen him in casual wear. The look suited him.

After a moment he grinned and said, 'come on, let's grab a coffee!' He stepped backwards to retrieve a set of keys off a side table in the hallway then took her hand and stepped out of the apartment closing the door behind him. She gave him a practiced pout but nodded readily in agreement.

'You look nice!' he said, while they rode the elevator down to the lobby. He was compelled to say something to distract from the irritating muzak playing in the background of the elevator, a particularly grating electronic monotone version of *"Hotel California"*. He had thrust his left hand into his jeans pocket so as to hide the erection. She had slyly noticed anyway and was pleased with the effect she had on him. He desperately hoped this would subside before they reached the lobby and met the security guard.

Wan Chai traffic was the usual sensory overload. It was a loud smelly chaos with a cacophony of horns tooting and buses belching exhaust smoke on Johnston Road adding to the claustrophobic heat. They comfortably held hands while dodging traffic and walked to the nearby café. She spotted their reflection in the café window as they entered and privately thought how they made a handsome couple. He had not mentioned the kiss, however holding hands felt perfectly natural and said more than words ever could. They crammed into the café, ordered two lattes and croissants at the glass fronted counter and found a high-top table to sit at. Café hubbub enveloped them.

'That was a rather delightful way to start the day,' he smiled. The heady smell of fresh roast coffee intermingled with the sweet smell of the pastries and easy-going conversations. Then cutting straight to the point Guy said, 'now what's this idea you wanted to share with me, or was that merely a lame excuse to steal a kiss off a poor, lonely, vulnerable old man first thing on a Saturday morning?'

Wendy mocked shock and said, 'you're hardly vulnerable, or an old man and the kiss didn't take much stealing I noticed!' a wry smile on her lips as she blew at the foam on her latte.

Guy gave a deep and sceptical 'Hmm'. Uncharacteristically he was lost for a quick retort.

Wendy pondered her croissant then munched a large bite from it, her dark eyes looking up and to the right as she collected her thoughts while pushing a rogue crumb into her mouth with her forefinger. Then, trying not to spray croissant crumbs everywhere she started.

'Well, I had a meeting in Korea last week with Mr Kim Sung-han, the President of Han Electronics. It was really an interview as he's looking for a worldwide Vice President of Talent Management. The headhunter connected us and a couple of days ago we had a very constructive conversation. I'm quite inspired by the company and the job Mr Kim wants done.'

'Go on,' said Guy, 'So you're really here asking me for career advice?'

She threw her head back and laughed out loud. 'No, it's way more exciting than that. You see it all started when he stepped out of the meeting. I guess he needed to pee or something, as he made a quick exit and asked me to excuse him for a couple of minutes.'

'And you did what exactly?' Guy noticed the impish grin again and having no idea where this was going knew he'd need to tease the story from her.

'Weeell.., I noticed Mr Kim had two computers on his huge desk and, assuming he had the recruiter's notes about me up on the monitor, I couldn't help but take a quick peep at what was on the screen to see what the headhunter had said about me. This is where it gets interesting! On the first monitor he did indeed have emailed notes about me but on the second monitor he was looking at a stream of programming code. Normally I'd not be interested in the code although I did sneak a look and the quick glance blew me away. I saw the word "wolf" and knew from CSSL meetings this is the signature of an infamous hacker.'

The Wan Chai café was loud and busy on Saturday mornings and other customers were bustling past the couple. Guy was oblivious to them. Leaning in towards Wendy he said, 'so go on!'

'I wasn't sure exactly what I was seeing at first. Being an inquisitive sort of girl, I pulled my keyring out of my handbag and found the thumb drive attached to it. I always carry it for my important files. I inserted it into the USB slot and downloaded a quick copy of the code so I could review it later.'

'You did what!?' Guy exclaimed, sitting back aghast, then realizing he had said this much too loudly as other people in the café paused their conversations to look at him.

Wendy hunched forwards conspiratorially. 'Well I didn't really mean to copy the file. It struck me as intriguing and, before I really considered the morality of what I was doing, the file was copied over to my thumb drive, the keyring was back in my handbag, and I was sat nonchalantly back in my chair when Mr Kim walked back into his office. I don't think he suspected a thing.'

'I'm horrified you'd blatantly steal software off the President of a potential employer's computer. I'd never have taken you for a common thief!'

Wendy bit into the last of her croissant and wiped the flakes of pastry from the corners of her mouth. 'I didn't take myself for a common thief either,' she sighed, 'however I think I've rather hit the jackpot with this one.' She reached into her handbag and pulled out a neatly folded piece of A4 paper. She unfolded it and laid it on the table in front of him. It was a printed page of part of the programming code.

......

```
if [ "$syscheck" == "rodong_lcct" ]; then ($syscheck = a system
check to see if it's inside the rodong launch control centre terminal)

tpi_bypass_kit (bypass Two-person integrity check TPI - two-men
rule or four-eyes principle)

wait_order

else (if it's not inside the launch control centre terminal)

search_krnetlink (kr missile launch network)

fi (fire rodong-1 love Wolf)
```

......

Guy studied this; his eye's widening as he did so. The black commands
were code, whereas the bracket was a layman's explanation of what
the commands did. At one point, realizing the seriousness and
implications of what he was reading, he looked around scanning
the other customers in the café fearing that someone else might be
reading this over his shoulder. No one was. His brain was racing
considering first the implications of what he was holding and then
secondly quite what to do with this information. 'Where's the USB
now?' he asked Wendy.

'Here in my handbag,' she replied knowing he was hooked. 'I
printed the last page of the programme for you to make it easier
to read.'

He stared at Wendy for a long time, trying to second-guess her thoughts. 'You know what the Rodong is? Do you think this is some kind of a hoax, a joke? What do you plan to do with this Wendy?' A rush of questions suddenly coming to his mind all at once.

'Yes, the Rodong is a large missile, and both good questions,' she replied. 'Firstly, we need to find a way to test if this software is actually real and not a hoax, although the fact that I found this on Mr. Kim's private computer would suggest whatever it is, it's serious. He runs a multi-billion-dollar empire that includes one of the largest IT companies in the world. I can't imagine he would have time for much frivolity. As to what to do with it, I guess that depends on the answer to the first question.'

Guy studied the bubbles on his coffee as excitement at the potential implications of what she had just involved him in coursed through his veins faster than the caffeine in the coffee. 'I believe I can help us there. I'm no techie but one of my good mates is excellent and is on contract to a client of CSSL. He owes me a favour.' Guy picked up his mobile phone, thumbed the icon for his address book and found John Choo's number.

'Hey John, it's Guy. Hope I'm not catching you at an inconvenient time. I've a favour to ask.'

'No problem Guy. I'm taking the kids to Little League football. What's up?'

'I'm looking at a page of code script. It looks like it's a malware designed to take command and control of the launch sequence for a missile system, although it could be a hoax. Any way to test it to see if it's for real?'

'Are you for real Guy - launch system for missiles? Where did you get that? Is this normal for CSSL?' asked John, the surprise unconcealed in his tone.

'Ah, I'd rather not say how I got it.' Guy was scowling across the table at Wendy nonchalantly sipping her coffee, the picture of innocence. 'And I'd prefer if we could keep this separate from CSSL for the time being,' he said to John.

Despite being Hong Kongese by birth, John grew-up and was educated in Sydney, Australia, and spoke English with a very exaggerated Aussie accent. He replied, 'no worries mate. Bring it over to my place in Discovery Bay in an hour and I'll take a look. We'll be back from the footy by then.'

An hour later, on the sunny mid-summer Saturday morning, Wendy and Guy disembarked from the ferry and arrived in Discovery Bay. They had taken the thirty-minute fast ferry ride and then the short walk to John's apartment. Guy knew it well, Discovery Bay is a residential area on the Island of Lantau, close to Hong Kong's airport, but it was Wendy's first time to visit. The easiest way to reach "DB" is via a regular ferry running from Pier Three in Central Hong Kong. Their arrival at the address coincided with John and his boys. His two young boys were excitedly discussing the football game, reliving their goals, their dives, their tackles, and their kicks, as a plump, friendly-faced Filipina domestic helper was trying patiently to cajole them towards the bathroom to clean up.

John greeted Guy with a warm handshake, a pat on the back, and a raised eyebrow gesturing subtly towards the attractive woman accompanying him. 'Let me introduce my colleague, Wendy Chen,' said Guy with strong emphasis on the word colleague.

John gave a wide smile and shook Wendy's hand. 'G'day Wendy.

Come on in you guys. My wife, Chew Ying, is out shopping this morning.' Wendy warmed to John immediately and, slipping off her high heels, stepped over the threshold into the apartment. The marble floor tiles were cool on her bare feet. As a Human Resources professional, she prided herself on her intuition regarding people, and John, with his honest smile and strong handshake inspired an easy trust. In another room she could hear running water and splashes from the excitable children followed by a squeal from the domestic helper who had presumably just taken a soaking.

'You fella's go easy on May!' shouted John through the apartment, presumably referring to the soaked domestic helper. Laughter, squeals, and yet more splashing water was the only reply.

John led them into his spacious lounge where three large computer monitors were arranged to give 120 degrees surround vision, with every conceivable gaming attachment sat mutely on a low gaming table in front of the monitors. Several sets of headsets, consoles, joysticks, and sound speakers were carefully positioned, suggesting that both John and his lads were serious gamers when not at work, school, or football lessons. An intimidatingly large black computer sat on the floor under the table with an array of formidably blinking red, green and blue LED's, as if to say, 'I'm watching you!'

John flipped on the monitors and ran up a session with only a black screen and a command line. Like most techies he preferred the command line to some fancy graphical window to input commands.

'So, what've you gotta show me?' asked John. Wendy reached into her handbag and cautiously passed the USB device, still on the key ring, to John. John took the USB device reverently, sensing Wendy's concern about what was on it. Whilst the USB device was, of course, quite inert, the potential sensitivity of the software on it lent a gravitas to Wendy's movements. John was about to plug the

USB device into a slot on the computer but then hesitated.

He bent down to the computer and unplugged a cable. He then turned off the Wi-Fi router and asked Guy and Wendy to turn off their mobile phones completely. He stood up and found the kid's mobile phones turning these off too. Lastly, he found May drying her wet hair with a towel in the kitchen and asked her to kill her mobile phone also. Surprised by the request she obliged anyway and turned her phone off and then said, 'shall I make coffee sir?'

The kids now dry and dressed came into the lounge to see what the adults were all doing, gaming they had assumed. They had hoped for some new challengers they could thrash with their dexterous little fingers. They were disappointed to be met with a scrolling black screen sequencing through a software install script; nothing exciting there, at least not to two nine-year-old twin boys. May, her hair damp and baggy tee shirt still wet down the front, came into the living room carrying a tray of coffees and some biscuits neatly laid out on a plate. The kids, unimpressed, went off to play in their bedroom and the three adults stood in silence expectantly watching the script load.

John was looking at the huge screen shaking his head in wonder. 'It's too elaborate to be a prank. It's very good. I ran it in a sandbox that emulates a real environment and it executes for real.' Guy well knew sandboxes were the concept of running virtual computer sessions that were used for testing software in safe environments before going into real production systems. For this reason, sandboxes were a useful tool for testing new software. They were also effectively used as a cyber defence tool by executing files in a safe or 'sandbox' virtual machine so that in the event of any malware being present in a file, the file could be quarantined before the malware could infect and do any damage. John thoughtfully unplugged the USB device, ran some quick commands to backup the software to his own remote drive, and then erased any trace of the programme on the computer. He then reconnected the cable and the Wi-Fi and turned the mobile phones back on. His natural smile had gone.

John passed the USB back to Wendy then looked seriously at Guy and Wendy in turn. 'I've no idea what you've got there guys or what you've managed to get yourselves into, but that programme is no prank. It's real code and it executes. I'll put it this way, if I had missile silos connected to that computer,' John said gesturing to the intimidating looking large black box with randomly flashing LED's under the gaming table, 'the missiles would be flying to their target destinations by now.'

'Any clues who it belongs to or who's the target in the coding?' asked Guy.

John looked thoughtful and nibbled on one of the biscuits May had bought in. 'My guess,' said John, 'is that this is some hack attempt on an unsophisticated missile defence system. I say unsophisticated as it's using an old version of Linux, an open source version of Unix. Because it's open source it's easily accessible to countries not strictly governed by USA export regulations so that would be countries like Pakistan, assorted African failed states, North Korea, some Eastern European countries, Afghanistan, and some Middle Eastern countries.'

Guy and Wendy shot a look at each other. John went on, 'I'm not so up-to-date with defence systems however Western countries using modern systems will have moved on from this old version of Linux many years ago. It was robust, although primitive. The malware is good though; it's well coded by a very good hacker. It's elegant, fast, and unstoppable once installed and triggered to execute. It's also going to be hard to detect by typical antivirus software. My guess is the target devices won't even know they've been penetrated until it's too late.'

'So, this malware could actually trigger a missile launch if successfully deployed on a target computer attached to a missile defence system?' asked Wendy.

'Absolutely right!' said John. 'One more thing, watching the script run, I noticed the word "wolf" at the end of a command line. It was odd because the command was executed before the word appeared, meaning the word was superfluous and useless. The rest of the coding was tidy so that makes me think this was deliberate, a signature perhaps, as it was intentional but has no other function. I'll dig around a bit and see what I can find out about Wolf, but if its who I think it is…' he left the statement unfinished.

The kids were getting rowdy in their bedroom so Wendy and Guy took that as their cue to leave. John saw them to the door while the still damp May scurried behind tidying up the coffee cups and biscuit remains.

'Thanks for the favour John. I owe you,' said Guy shaking hands again.

'Look,' said John in all earnest when they reached his front door, 'you saw me turn the Wi-Fi and all mobile phones off. I did that because computers, and particularly mobile phones, are very easy to hack and terribly vulnerable to spyware. Without you knowing it they can take photos, betray your location, record your conversations, and see all the app's you've ever used. I thought I was being melodramatic for a minute, to heighten the tension so to speak, better safe than sorry I thought, but now I'm bloody glad I did. What you've got there is very dangerous in the wrong hands and my advice mate is you throw that bloody USB device into the Hong Kong harbour and pretend you've never seen it.'

Wendy waved back at John as they walked away, the two boys waving from behind him, then a thought suddenly struck John and he shouted to them, 'Hey Guy, a quick afterthought, if the owner of that knows you've got it, they're going to be really pissed and really keen to get it back!' Guy paused, then turned and gravely nodded his thanks, that was his fear too.

Chapter 6. Semtex

California and Tel Aviv. July.

His breathing became laboured. Being massively overweight, any kind of exertion would have him panting like a dog. Today was treat day. He had to regulate his vice, knowing full well he had an unhealthy perversion that would consume all of his time if he let it. It was another hot day in the valley and the air conditioning in Mission Control was working flat out to keep the temperature at the constant desired 21 degrees. Despite this, Craig was sweating profusely. He had already enjoyed a couple of hours surfing regular porn. Now he was in a live chat room using the Dark Web where an Asian-looking girl with poor English was performing for him. He was paying with bitcoins, a commonly used cryptocurrency, and she was readily doing whatever he asked. She looked very young and hastily applied make-up failed to conceal a few purple bruises. It was hard to tell exactly how young she was, but Wolf didn't care.

All he did care about was the position of the camera and the creativity of the increasingly degrading and lewd acts he demanded her to perform for him. Regardless, she enjoyed doing this, didn't she? The money was certainly good. The payments were high although how much of that the girl actually saw was another matter. Craig's bitcoins would be sprinkled liberally, virtually, over her barely pubescent naked body so long as there were no hesitations at his progressively bizarre requests. He could also hear an older female voice, the owner of which was off-camera, speaking commands in the girl's local language, Chinese maybe, Indonesian possibly. He didn't care. Occasionally the voice would speak to Craig in broken English to clarify if she had really heard him correctly. 'Yeah, you heard right lady,' Craig would demand in his loud Californian drawl. His order would be hastily relayed in the local language.

The girl had an array of toys of increasingly perplexing colours, shapes, and sizes. Craig's enthusiasm to see them deployed seemed to show no sign of waning. Still the bitcoins flowed. The girl on the monitor was now openly crying, shaking with pain, humiliation, and a fear of repercussions if the customer wasn't satisfied. Craig didn't care which so long as his goals were met, the girl's humiliation adding to his pleasure. At last, following a succession of gasps and grunts Craig slumped back in his chair wiping his hand with a small towel and lastly on his cargo pants. Having transferred the last bitcoin payment a few moments before, the session on his main screen went blank.

After a bathroom break to clean-up, mop his lank hair, and cool down, Craig went back to Mission Control and launched his browser for the Dark Web again. Now, with the Asian-looking girl long forgotten, he had other matters to deal with. Some Dark Web users were still using Tor, the defacto browser for the uninitiated, although many black hats were now developing and promoting their own polymorphic code that promised even greater anonymity for the nefarious activities being performed over the dark web. Today Craig wanted to go shopping.

#

Tal Bar-Lev enjoyed his job. Fresh out of university in Tel Aviv, he had been recruited by Unit 8200 as a Researcher. He had scored top marks in his Computer Science degree at the Technion Israel Institute of Technology and specialized in communication protocols, something very useful to the Signal Intelligence (SIGINT) capabilities of the Israeli Intelligence Corporation who operated Unit 8200. Unit 8200 was widely regarded as one of the most advanced cyber-intelligence agencies in the world. Technically in a permanent state of war, the Israeli's were given very wide latitude in their intelligence gathering activities. Unlike many western countries, Unit 8200 was largely unencumbered by personal privacy laws and trivial bureaucratic matters which questioned eavesdropping techniques and personal data collection. In short, Unit 8200 did pretty much anything it wanted wherever it wanted. From his perspective, Tal didn't care so long as his bosses gave him recognition for his brilliance.

Today was routine for Tal. He was sitting under the florescent lights in his blue walled cubicle in the highly secure offices of Unit 8200 situated in The Kirya, Israel's military high command building in the middle of Tel Aviv. After work he had planned to head over to the Sarona area across the street to meet Dorit, the current focus of his affections. Dorit was also serving her obligatory military duty. She was in Special Forces. She was super fit and was trained in multiple weapons, explosives, and unarmed combat. She confided in Tal once that she had killed a man during a skirmish in the Gaza Strip and was totally unphased by it. Tal, by contrast, was a total nerd but between them there was spark, compatibility, a mutual respect, and surprisingly, a physical attraction.

Tal was scratching his stubbly beard and monitoring traffic on the Dark Web. The usual rogues were dealing in drugs, weapons, blood diamonds, personal identities, stolen credit card numbers, and human trafficking around the world. Network traffic over the Dark Web was all encrypted with offshore VPN's, anonymizers, and onions (the security layers on the browsers), preventing the real computer servers' IP addresses and therefore the individuals behind them from ever being identified. However, there were often patterns of behaviours and, while the individuals could rarely be identified or even less likely caught, spotting common threads and narrowing the actors down to a geographic area was possible with a bit of training and some beautiful software programming. Tal considered his work 'beautiful' and the ever-changing security landscape kept it interesting for him.

Tal had recently been involved in a project where a black hat had attempted to take down the entire telephone infrastructure of a Western European country. The various tools being used coupled with the style of coding suggested a very specific team of black hats and looked to be coming from perhaps one person in one physical location. Known as a Distributed Denial of Service or DDoS attack, the idea of the malware was to create multiple botnets and have them all send a massive volume of email traffic at the exact same moment so totally overloading the target telecoms network. These DDoS attacks were very effective, and very hard to prevent. The target network would simply overload, the routers and servers would stall, and the countries telecoms networks would be taken down for hours, days, and even weeks in extreme cases. It was vandalism at best, an act of war at worst.

In this case, Tal and his colleagues had first been able to trace the source of the attacks to one province in China. They then further narrowed this down to one district on the edge of Beijing and finally to one building. The building was interesting. While in a typical industrial area, the nondescript building had no markings, company logos, or any other apparent method of identification. More curious still, the building had few windows, an elaborate array of satellite dishes and antenna on the roof, and seriously hostile perimeter security. The perimeter was a mix of thick mesh steel fencing topped by razor wire and one double gated entry point operated by biometric security.

'Got yah!' said Tal out loud. To Tal it clearly looked like a People's Liberation Army operation. Tal and his colleagues, feeling mischievous, effortlessly hacked some of the nearby traffic cameras that overlooked the building's one entrance gate and over the course of two months captured images of the few staff that seemed to come and go. Surveillance complete, Tal and his team sent their intel up the chain of command to their bosses in The Kirya.

This in turn found its way to Mossad, the national intelligence agency of Israel, who alerted the grateful Western European country of the potential impending DDoS attack on their telecom's infrastructure as a gesture of goodwill. Of course, the gesture would be 'banked', to be bought out in future political discussions when needed.

Presumably, the diplomatic backchannels leapt into action because, not six hours later, the hacked traffic cameras in Beijing showed all the staff from the facility being led out of the drab building by fully uniformed and armed PLA guards. The dull brown unmarked brick building was left seemingly abandoned. Tal wondered if the grainy faces of the staff being led out of the building belonged to the infamous APT3 group. A team of hackers rumoured to be attributed to China's Ministry of State Security. Tal privately admired their skills, they were good, although he knew that he, and others in Unit 8200 were better.

Today something new piqued Tal's interest on an otherwise dull shift. Some slimeball on the West Coast of the USA had come off a particularly perverted live paedophile porn site and was now trying to buy explosives. Odd behaviour and didn't meet the usual profile of criminals using the Dark Web. They usually stuck to their unique areas of specialization, being drugs, arms dealing, data theft, etc. To jump from child pornography to buying Semtex was something altogether uncharacteristic. Tal stretched, rubbed his eyes under his wire-rimmed glasses, glanced at the picture of Dorit wedged into the seam of his large desktop monitor, and then let his thin nimble fingers fly across the keyboard. The amounts of Semtex required seemed to be very small; hardly enough to start a war, perhaps enough to blow a safe he wondered. He would check with Dorit later, she would know. *'This merits a little further investigation,'* thought Tal. Had this Dark Web user cum paedophile turned bank robber or even domestic terrorist perhaps? This was a bit out of his scope however interesting nonetheless on an otherwise routine day.

#

Wolf had become anxious in recent months. He was totally confident in his own ability to remain anonymous on the Dark Web and his hacking exploits, while notorious, were mostly very discreet except to the few who recognised his precise coding and the word 'wolf' imbedded somewhere in the deployed malware. However, recently he had started to worry what he would do were his Mission Control to be breached.

As smart as Wolf was, and like most involved in criminal activities, he always carried that niggling concern that he may have missed some small detail which would expose him. Wolf didn't think he would fair very well in a state penitentiary. Mission Control, his cluttered bedroom in his mum's apartment off Middlefield Road in Palo Alto, was vulnerable to two groups. Firstly, there was the NSA. In the unlikely event the FBI, NSA, CIA or other law enforcement agencies were able to track him down, or at least trace the IP addresses of his computers to his physical address, they could get warrants and raid his mum's apartment. Seizing the servers would be catastrophic as there were terabytes of incriminating data. A jury might be lenient towards cybercrime but less so towards the child pornography. Irrationally though, his bigger fear was that he himself became the target of a hack. Being a first division hacker did leave oneself open to being the target of hacks, both by law enforcement and other black hats who would love the kudos of taking out a fellow actor as a matter of professional gamesmanship.

In the event that he was caught, Wolf wanted to ensure he could take down Mission Control in a heartbeat, quite literally. His smartwatch was programmed to digital trigger, a software programme that would immediately destroy the hard drives and backup storage in

Mission Control. All he needed to do was to dial one specific phone number, a command he could issue from his smartwatch. Wolf's natural paranoia went so far as to ensure this same mobile number would be dialled in the event of his pulse stopping. Of course, his smartwatch monitored his pulse. Craig wasn't myopic to his tremendous girth and unhealthy diet. While young, he hated the thought that if he did have health issues his beloved software would be available to them who could decrypt it. And while decryption was difficult, it wasn't impossible.

The process to disable Mission Control was simple. He could manually dial a specific mobile phone from his smartwatch or in the event of his pulse stopping the number would be dialled automatically. This in turn powered two huge electromagnets placed next to the server racks in Mission Control. The magnets, so energized, were powerful enough to scramble and turn all the data in those computers into binary mush, the IT equivalent of a bullet to the brain. Craig was careful, and the smartwatch was always well charged and rarely removed, upon which the software could be deactivated temporarily.

In the four years since Wolf had rigged the super powerful electromagnets to erase everything on the computers in Mission Control he had never even come close to a mistake. But were the magnets enough? Magnets do scramble the computer memories for sure, however, forensic experts can sometimes still recover some data and there's always the risk of a power cut preventing the magnets from charging, although he did have backup batteries they too might fail. Moreover, were he to be raided by a SWAT team they would likely kill the power to the building first, rendering the electromagnets impotent aside the single-point-of-failure backups. As Wolf became more prolific he feared this was not enough. He needed an even more definitive solution. Prompted in part by Hollywood, Mel Gibson gave him the idea. What he really needed was for the whole room to vaporize.

His Dark Web browser spun into life and in no time at all Wolf soon found several suppliers of explosives. A little research convinced him Semtex charges were probably the best suited for the job. Semtex was stable and inert until detonated, able to be operated within a wide temperature range, precise, and mouldable for maximum precision. Curiously, Wolf found it hard to buy small quantities. If he had wanted truck loads that seemed easy, presumably ripped off from army bases or demolition companies. But, for a couple of kilogrammes, nobody seemed interested. With a little perseverance though Wolf found a willing supplier and was invited to meet at a remote truck stop a few miles east of San Jose.

Route 130, Mount Hamilton Road, ran up over the mountains east of Silicon Valley and eventually linked up with Interstate 5. It was picturesque on a normal day as the road ran through Joseph D. Grant National Park, however today Craig's mind wasn't on the views. He had received the directions by WhatsApp and found the truck stop diner on the roadside as per the instructions.

#

Tal and Dorit sat on the seats outside the bar in the balmy Tel Aviv afternoon air and ordered a beer from the waitress. Sarona was made up of old building and full of trendy bars and restaurants. It was a bit pricey but convenient, being close to the railway station and closer still to the offices of Unit 8200 where Tal worked. Tal's shift had finished and Dorit had been training, the sweat was still encrusted on her tanned skin, and now she too had finished for the day. It was late afternoon and the Tel Aviv sun had lost its strength. The day had been hot and Mediterranean dry. Dorit was conscious of badly needing a shower however cold beers with Tal took precedence. Besides, he wouldn't mind if she was still sweaty, he liked her musk. After a beer she would invite him back to her small flat and make love to him. She had not had sex all week and was looking forward to seeing Tal as much as she hoped he was looking forwards to seeing her. They could shower later. After the small talk about their respective days, Tal got to the point that was on his mind.

'What do you know about Semtex?' asked Tal.

Dorit raised an eyebrow. 'What do you want to know?' she asked somewhat taken aback. Occasionally he would ask her cryptic questions which she presumed were work related. She knew better than to ask directly as he would not be able to discuss his work. She respected that.

Tal studied her for a moment over his wire-rimmed glasses. Her strong features matched her personality. She was a strong woman, heavily built, and muscular. The deep brown eyes, full lips, and long black hair, now worn down, gave her the femininity he admired. 'Well, I'm curious why someone would want to buy small amounts,' he said. 'Usually if needed for demolition or even combat presumably you'd want a lot of it.'

Dorit took a slug of beer from the cold glass. 'Semtex has a lot of applications,' she said, 'Yes, demolition usually requires multiple bricks as does underwater work, depending on the size of the job. Even terrorists will buy as much as they can get their hands on.' She studied her beer, the way the condensation had formed on the glass, pondering the scenarios. Tal let her consider without interruption. At last she looked up and said, 'Semtex has a long shelf life, stores easily, and has a wide operating temperature range. Someone buying a small amount probably has one small job in mind and isn't interested in offloading a larger purchase. It suggests someone who's not a regular user but needs to make a one-time explosion. Assuming it's not legitimate, I'd guess blowing-up a safe, a car, or perhaps a small hole in a building. Plastic explosive is ideal for these kinds of jobs.'

Tal smiled at her. 'You're a star! I'd come to the same conclusion,' he said.

They finished their beers and, before any moment of awkwardness or Tal suggesting a second beer, Dorit took the initiative and said, 'Any plans this evening?' She rested her hand on his across the table.

'No,' said Tal smiling at Dorit.

'Come on,' she said, 'my place.' She grabbed his hand and with her well-defined arm pulled him to his feet without protest.

#

Wolf sat in the diner on Route 130 east of San Jose as instructed. The diner was typical of any other off-freeway diner anywhere in the USA. Neon signs advertised Coca-Cola and beers; the menu was predictable and appealed to truckers, bikers, and tourists. Outrageously large servings of everything fried were delivered with free-flowing coffee or soda. He felt a little awkward amongst the truckers and bikers, however given his size and unkempt appearance no one paid much attention to him. They assumed him to be just another super-sized trucker chowing down on a full all-day breakfast of eggs, bacon, and pancakes.

Two guys in well-worn combat jackets and dusty jeans slid into the same booth and faced Craig as he chewed on a mouth full of eggs and bacon, a gob of grease trickling down his chin. Craig looked awkward and intimidated, as if cornered by the schoolyard bullies. He felt very much out manned. He didn't see the dusty old pickup truck they had arrived in although he could picture the look right down to the gun rack in the back.

'They say Grey Wolves are an endangered species around these parts,' said one to the other, pointedly looking at Craig as he said it. The other brother said nothing. 'Good hunting though,' replied the first as if to reinforce the point. Their similar features apparently betraying they were brothers.

Craig spluttered and gulped, still trying to swallow the mouthful of food. His mouth has suddenly gone dry. He tried to smile lamely. 'I'm Wolf,' he said. 'You guys must be the Marx Brothers?' This is the name they had given him following their contact on the Dark Web.

The lad's eyed Craig with scepticism. He was awkward, overweight, sweating heavily, and clearly as uncomfortable as a rattle snake on hot tarmac. They considered if he was law enforcement but he looked so far removed from anything remotely official he had to be for real. 'You planning a firework party?' asked the talkative brother.

'Something like that,' replied Craig, his appetite now waning, so he pushed the plate away and drew the back of his hand across his greasy chin. 'You can help me?'

'Sure, can't we Bill?' replied the brother. Bill looked younger, he was bearded, with a tatty, well-worn, frayed army cap hiding greasy shoulder length hair tied in a ponytail. Bill nodded slowly; his unblinking eyes fixed on Wolf trying to make out exactly what he was.

'Bill don't say much!' said the older brother to Craig. Craig nodded. 'He sees a lot and gotta nose for the cops. Bill don't much like cops. Good judge of character though is Bill!' The older brother was presumably the brains of the two. Craig didn't know his name and didn't want to either. These were hard men and harder to age. Both looked in their early forties but had worn badly. They were probably ex-military, of low rank, fit, disciplined, considered, and now seemingly worked in construction or such like. They didn't suffer fools.

The waitress, an older lady wearing a rather dated and faded pink uniform, arrived with two mugs and poured the brothers' coffee without asking or saying anything. The trio sat in silence and waited for her to leave. 'I'll be back to get your order in a minute,' she said unsmiling, sensing their unease. Still the three said nothing.

Craig was reluctant to say anything either. He didn't want to offer any information about himself and certainly didn't want to ask any questions of these two fearing they would be suspicious. Suddenly the foolishness of his predicament dawned. These guys secreted danger. The smell was even stronger than their body odour mixed with cordite, lingering like an aura around them.

'Come with us,' the older brother said abruptly. They all rose and Craig was left to throw a handful of green bills on the table, unmeaningly tipping generously. The breakfast remained half eaten and the coffees untouched. They walked out through the 'In' door and across the huge parking lot outside the diner. Space was plentiful as trucks were able to turn and park, some even staying overnight. The Marx brothers battered old pickup was parked at the far edge of the lot, well away from the diner and well out of earshot of anyone with nothing else to do parked close by. Anyone snooping would be easy to spot a mile away. They walked towards the pickup and around to the far side, the vehicle now obscuring them from the road and the diner itself. Waste ground surrounded them. The three were alone and no one was watching.

What happened next caught Craig completely off guard. The older brother rapped Craig hard on the back of his knees and Bill, the younger brother, suddenly pulled a battered revolver out from the back of his pants. 'Kneel!' he commanded in a tone higher pitched than his appearance would suggest. Craig instinctively raised his hands but the 'kneel' command was compelling. Craig sank to his knees as instructed, awkwardly, and as quickly as his bulk would allow, one knee resting in the dust at a time. 'You government or a cop?' squeaked Bill. 'Military?'

'No, neither,' said Craig shaking his head vigorously.

'Anyone put you up to this?' retorted Bill again in his effeminate tone, this time pushing the barrel of the steel grey revolver into Craig's mouth.

Craig shook his head, or more accurately wobbled his jowls, in denial. His mouth had suddenly become as arid as the dusty carpark and he was unable to talk and reluctant to shake his head too vigorously through fear the gun might accidentally discharge.

The Marx brothers looked at the forlorn slob of a guy kneeling in front of them. It lasted seconds although it felt to Craig like hours, the pause excruciating. 'Got the cash?' the older brother asked eventually. Craig sensed they were indifferent to letting him live or blowing his fat head all over the parking lot.

Craig moved his head up and down and slowly reached into his back pocket, assuming he had foolishly been rolled. The cold gun barrel still rested deep in his mouth, the bitter taste of gun oil on his tongue. Craig pulled the pre-agreed $500 from his pocket and slowly passed it over to the brothers, no thought given to fingerprints or DNA. The older brother took the cash and flipped through to confirm the value. He nodded to Bill. Bill withdrew the gun from Wolf's mouth and opened the passenger door to the pickup. He jumped in as his older brother walked around to the driver's door and jumped in also, starting the engine in a plume of oily black exhaust smoke.

Craig was still on his knees looking crumpled in the dust then, just as the pickup pulled away, the rear tyres churning up two great plumes of dirt-yellow dust, Bill threw a heavy parcel on the ground in front of Craig and shouted, 'We added a couple detonators too. Call it goodwill,' then the pickup squealed away to the sound of the Marx Brothers fading laughter.

Wolf had his Semtex.

Chapter 7. Strategic Rocket Forces Command

Pyongyang. Saturday.

2013 had been a bad year for the Democratic People's Republic of Korea, General Park reflected. Diplomatic efforts had seemingly been progressing well since the young leader Kim Jong-un's succeeding to power from his stolidly traditional father. In the corridors of western governments, it was widely thought the fresh-faced new leader would want to nudge his country towards a more progressive economic model, given he was educated in Switzerland and so living and seeing how a civilized western democratic country really worked.

While proud Swiss shopkeepers would collectively wash their doorsteps and pavements clean outside their shopfronts every morning, the Chinese Communist Party leaders were alarmed that their doorstep was about to cosy up to the imperialist West. The North Korean border was only a few hundred miles from Beijing. For centuries China had successfully managed to keep most of her borders vague, with disputes in the west with India, and in the east in the South China Sea, with pretty much all of their East Asian neighbours. The Chinese's infamous Nine-Dash line map of the South China Sea clearly documented their acquisitive territorial ambitions. The People's Republic of China desperately wanted to avoid North Korea becoming allied with the West, however, neither did they want to break their status quo with this failed state.

As his black military limousine swept under escort through the grey featureless streets of Pyongyang, General Park mused that 2013 was the year his then boss's boss, Kim Jong-un, had shown his true colours. Any notions the people had about the boy revolutionizing the country or straying from his father's tactics were finally, publicly, and irrefutably quashed. Taking control of North Korea upon his father's death in 2011, the new Party Leader Kim had played his hand close to his chest. 2013 saw all this change. Within a matter of weeks he had issued several aggressive edicts. Firstly, he had ordered the restart of all nuclear processing facilities at the main Yongbyon nuclear complex. Then he attempted to buy further nuclear and chemical weapons from China. Then the DPRK successfully bought two MIG-21 fighter jets, albeit they were caught en route and impounded in Panama. Lastly, he scuppered the fledgling joint venture with the South Korean funded Kaesong Joint Industrial Park, halting operations at 123 South Korean factories and recalling more than 50,000 North Korean workers.

Moreover, and more personally painful for General Park, the young Kim had a purge on his own leadership, persecuting and removing any liberals he didn't wholly trust or believe were totally committed to him and the Korean Workers' Party. Perhaps all that saluting at pictures had paid off and General Park was thankfully untouched. The removals though were epic. Not happy to simply strip his staff of their positions or even publicly shame them, he staged elaborate and public executions for the world to see.

General Park now sat proudly in the leather seat in the back of the limousine and vividly recalled those memories from years ago; the utter horror and humiliation as he was expected to smile through and then vigorously applaud the death of his good friend Chang Song-thaek.

Chang Song-thaek was Kim Jong-un's uncle and was always part of his father's inner guard in Kim Jong-il's regime. A lifetime soldier and member of the Workers' Party of Korea, many in the Party considered he was number two to Kim Jong-il. In 2012, Chang was arrested, charged, and found guilty of attempting to overthrow the younger Kim, although how he could have possibly been discovered still wracked Park's brain. The charges were quite accurate however, the mystery was how they had been discovered given such extreme attention being paid to their secrecy. Following what North Korea passed for a court martial which, General Park reflected was a simple reading of the charges, a verdict of guilty was then given and the death penalty decreed. Chang was held for the remainder of the year in a tiny military prison cell while preparations were made.

It had been a bitterly cold day. All senior members of the military and government were assembled at Gang Gun Military Academy in a suburb of Pyongyang on that freezing, windy December day in 2013. Ice heavy grey clouds and snow flurries filled the air. Without their overcoats and in full military dress they were formally marched onto the bleak parade square and made to stand, shivering with cold and fear. They stood in-line thirty feet from a wooden post securely driven into the ground.

At 12 noon Kim Jong-un arrived and stood on his slightly raised platform to belie his stature. He was predictably met by sharp salutes from his staff. He gave the order and Chang Song-thaek was brought from his cell and strapped to the wooden post. On this freezing day he wore only a thin prison issue dark blue jumpsuit with no hat, no uniform, no medals, and no opportunity to salute the Party Leader. He wore no blindfold and briefly glanced at some of his comrades, though careful not to linger on anyone specifically. Pulling himself upright as best he could, he stared square at his nephew. His dull eyes were sad; the intelligent shine had gone out forever. Kim Jong-un held the stare with his familiar fat smile sat upon his moon face, his latest hairstyle being hidden by a thick fur hat.

Five uniformed corporals grabbed the oiled green tarpaulin and hurriedly pulled it away from an imposingly large shape revealing the steel machine which also stood on the frozen parade ground. The machine was a Russian ZPU-4s. The weapon had four barrels, each firing 14.5mm rounds. The assembled crowd looked wide-eyed in horror. A small yet audible gasp emitting from many of them, 'Surely not!' The nephew, always enjoying the limelight, raised his arm as the five corporals scurried onto their position's beside and behind the weapon. Allowing a pause for effect, Kim held up his arm for what seemed like an eternity. Would he capitulate now, his point proven? Was he even considering a change of heart, sharing a joke to scare the crap out of everybody; so to demonstrate to them without a shadow of a doubt how powerful their young esteemed leader really was? The uncle and nephew held each other's gaze, no remorse showing on either.

Then the arm dropped, Caesar-like, to the deafening clatter of 600 rounds per minute anti-aircraft thunder.

General Park recalled the moment with a shudder. The 14.5 calibre rounds didn't just hit Chang Song-thaek, they ripped him apart. The initial shots sent a puff of vaporized blood into the freezing air around him as clods of flesh and gore splatted the mass of assembled onlookers. This was why they were stood so close. They weren't meant to simply observe the punishment, they were meant to taste it! The spray of arterial blood coated the Generals. Those with spectacles witnessed the death of their colleague through a film of crimson. Their uniforms were pelted with lumps of unidentifiable meat which had once made-up the person, their colleague, Chang Song-thaek. Most gagged and some lost composure and were retching. A few, to their extreme humiliation, had involuntary bowel movements while they remained standing to attention.

After twelve seconds of fire, which seemed an eternity, the frozen ground was turned into a funnel shaped bloody smear of red with a few pale lumps of unrecognizable skin, muscle, and white bone. In the freezing air the final wisps of warm condensation were dispelled from the bodily remains along with the panting breath of onlookers, and a lazy waft of smoke from the gun barrels.

Chang wasn't simply shot, he was publicly vaporized. Not even the wooden post remained! Kim Jong-un, the grandson of the State's founder, continued applauding. The sound had been previously inaudible over the noise of the Gatling gun. All others present realized the cue and promptly, if reluctantly, started applauding too. This went on for minutes. The smiling Party Leader surveying his splattered and bloodied staff and the now scarlet sprayed, frozen parade ground. After a few minutes of vigorous applauding, to ensure all his staff 'got' the message, he stepped off his small platform and walked back to the warmth of the building, leaving his stunned staff to reflect on their positions, the freezing wind forgotten.

#

General Park remembered that day and the death of his friend like it was yesterday. The hatred he felt at that moment towards his leader still stuck to him like the flesh, blood, and shards of bone had stuck to him on that cold December day years ago. Despite the warm yet wet summer weather, General Park shivered involuntarily at the memory. He was heading to give his superiors an update on the week's military and intelligence matters. This was a formal process where he would state their military preparedness and convince the Pyongyang AAA Command they were 100 per cent ready for war if ordered or provoked. The Party Leader would often attend in person and be told nothing other than good news regarding their status, with any bad news carefully delivered later in private.

Intelligence reports were seized upon like food rations by the nations underfed troops. In the plain windowless meeting room, hidden in the labyrinth of underground Government offices in Pyongyang, the reports from the Reconnaissance Bureau were picked over like a carcase by vultures, and discussed. The game being to second-guess the malicious intentions of the imperialist West. General Park would play along and make much of his intelligence provided by his network of fishing trawler surveillance boats and his spy network in other countries.

Today he planned to give graphic descriptions of the USS *Ronald Reagan* and her support flotilla. He would embellish the fighter aircraft elements and produce maps of her route and manoeuvres. She had departed Hong Kong and was now heading north into the East China Sea. The convoy had passed the US naval base at Okinawa and was likely to conduct manoeuvres with South Korean naval vessels. He always spoke with a matter-of-fact authority. Other's opinions and comments would be politely entertained but he knew, as the provider of the data, his opinions were the only ones that mattered. That was until the Party Leader himself joined the meetings. Then whatever muddle-headed, hare-brained idea the young President came up with would be marvelled at for its foresight and wisdom.

#

As part of his portfolio, General Park also oversaw the Missile Guidance Bureau which was established in 1999. That year several disparate missile units under the Korean People's Army Ground Force Artillery Command were reorganized into a single missile force, which has since been renamed the Strategic Rocket Forces, one of the Party Leaders great ideas. 'Strategic Rocket' sounded so much cooler than 'Missile Guidance' they all agreed. The Strategic Rocket Forces is mainly armed with surface-to-surface missiles designed and built by the talented young designers trained by the KPA, although they also still supported older Soviet and Chinese missiles. Much to General Park's ire, he rarely had a chance to test his missiles these days although the Rodong-1's, also known as

Hwasong-7's were well tested and stable. These were the delivery platform for the nuclear warheads should they ever be needed.

Some of his nuclear arsenal was housed at Yongbyon in a purpose build silo close to the nuclear processing facility. It was standard practice not to keep the warheads close to the missiles themselves, minimizing damage in the event of an accident. That said, he didn't want the warheads and the missiles too far removed in the event of an attack either. He was expected to promise the Party Leader that the Strategic Rocket Forces would be able to launch on both Seoul and Tokyo within ten minutes of an attack, a drill they practiced almost weekly.

General Park's limousine sped down the grey sided ramp that lead to the access tunnel for the underground complex that served as the government offices; extensive, well concealed and almost impossible to target in the event of a pre-emptive attack. The labyrinth ran for over five miles and today's meeting was in one of the newer sections of the continually expanding system. The car and motorcycle escorts turned their lights on and drove for a further ten minutes underground before eventually finding the new subterranean car park and coming to a halt.

The General grabbed his briefcase of notes as a soldier in uniform opened his door and smartly saluted. Park eased out of the car, feigning a slow dignity to hide his age-induced stiffness from the subordinate soldiers. The Strategic Rocket Forces directly reports to the Supreme Commander who, judging by the number of vehicles already parked and very heavy security presence, would join today. Kim Jong-un's attendance would have everyone jittery, however, General Park was well prepared as usual and could handle any rational questions. The irrational ones though could floor him occasionally. He found it was usually better to try and second-guess the Supreme Commander as best one could.

The meeting room was little more than a sparsely furnished bunker. It was artificially lit, eerily quiet, and still smelling of damp concrete, the acidic lime offensive. The Government of North Korea was almost entirely housed in this underground city now so to avoid their enemy being able to take out the countries leadership in the event of war or, more importantly, an attempt to bomb Kim Jong-un out of existence. The twenty Generals sat around a large oval shaped table, all with one aide stood smartly behind them. The Supreme Commander sat as usual at the head. The briefings followed their normal format with most of the twenty Generals' updates being met with bored indifference from the Supreme Commander. Their infantile attempts to ingratiate themselves were tiresome.

For General Park there were multiple questions, some designed to trip him up. Was one of the other Generals making a play for his own position he wondered? Probably. Regardless, he followed his usual routine and answered the loaded questions with acute diplomacy using supporting data from his own Reconnaissance Bureau. If the Americans were only half as aggressive in attacking North Korea as their own Generals were at slyly and stealthily attacking each other politically, there would be no Democratic People's Republic of Korea he mused privately.

General Park was happy to brief the Supreme Commander that missile drills continued to confirm the Strategic Rocket Forces were fully ready with constantly alert soldiers and missiles which could be armed and fuelled within a matter of minutes. This was a slight exaggeration as the volatile rocket fuel had to be carefully processed and loaded with extreme care into the rockets themselves. In the event of usage in anger, a few minutes would likely make little difference.

For some reason, the Supreme Commander of the KPA Kim Jong-un was interested in the vulnerability of the KPA's missile sites from cyberwarfare attacks. It seems the leader was somewhat familiar with some of the work General Park's 900 black hats had been doing. A recent gem had been to release an antivirus software called SiliVaxine. It had been liberally distributed in South Korea and Japan. Amusingly the core code was actually based on a very old version of Trend Micro's software (a legitimate antivirus software made by a credible Japanese antivirus software maker), however, in this case with the specific malware signatures deliberately removed. This rendered the users of the so-called antivirus specifically vulnerable to particular viruses which would be intentionally overlooked by the user's computer. This was both ingenious and amusing although perhaps not so for the target recipients in South Korea and Japan's government, schools and the media.

General Park, perspiring slightly under his arms in the inadequate ventilation of the room, sensed his leader's whimsical interest in this subject and so supported and encouraged the free-flowing ideas of possible attack vectors against the hermit state's enemies. He also reassured President Kim that their own missile systems were completely safe from an outside cyber-attack by virtue of the fact that their networks were totally isolated. Nothing was connected to any outside computers, thus rendering them safe from a cyber-attack. In order for hackers to attack their systems, the computers would need to be physically attached to a wide area network providing physical access whereupon a brute force attack would be possible.

General Park continued and was careful to explain to his Supreme Commander that if he recalled it was due to his own foresight and wisdom that their computers would be in no way externally connected, and instead would simply be on their own unique, self-contained, standalone networks. This last ingratiating toadyism was completely untrue although it had the desired effect as the Supreme Commander did indeed remember it perfectly well and smiled as he nodded around the table to the other Generals present, gloating at his own genius. They all sagely agreed and vigorously nodded back.

On this note the briefing was considered over. The Supreme Commander of the KPA looked at his escorts who then led him from the viper pit of the bunker and back to his heavily armoured vehicle. Back in the meeting room the Generals took the opportunity to coagulate into little clusters of common interest groups, all sensing General Park was still very much in favour with the boss. Park surveyed the room and wondered where the next internal volley might be fired from. He was getting old, he was tired, and it would only be a matter of time before he was replaced but he wasn't quite ready yet, no not quite yet.

#

The black Russian-made limousine swept out of the underground city into the late afternoon daylight. The Army motorbike escort cleared the traffic on the roads ahead, although much of the traffic was bicycles. General Park settled back into the leather seats and considered the meeting and his performance. He was never relaxed after such meetings and replayed them though his mind; the looks, the words, the body language. He poured himself a soju, the Korean spirit of choice, from the bottle placed in the centre console. He preferred Scottish Whisky however he only kept that in his private collection. That would be for later.

He considered the logistics of his medium-range missiles. The Strategic Rocket Forces Command's main site was in the mountains near Yongbyon north of Pyongyang. This was North Korea's main nuclear facility and processed the spent fuel from North Korea's Russian-designed nuclear power stations. This was the source of plutonium for Strategic Rocket Forces Command's nuclear weapons programme and the location for the KPA's nuclear command and control centre. It was policy that the actual nuclear warheads would not be stored with the Rodong-1 delivery missiles, or as the South liked to call them the Hwasong-7's. It was also policy that none of the other silo-based launch sites, including Punggye-ri and the base in the Paektu Mountains, would be physically connected via communications networks. Instead, there would be multiple discrete and redundant networks that could relay communications. This was effective and safe, hack-proof.

General Park reflected and he was happy with the day's performance and poured himself another soju. The Strategic Rocket Forces Command also had fifty mobile launchers for the Rodong-1 and these were in a constant state of mobility via both rail and roads. Only the Supreme Commander Kim Jong-un could order the warheads to be mounted on the missiles; however, there were six semi-permanently mounted and stored underground at the Yongbyon plant. These were referred to as the 'first strike' missiles and could be very hastily fuelled, prepared, and launched with minutes of notice. In the event North Korea was attacked, these were to be the immediate retaliatory response. Some observers in the West doubted the Korean People's Army had perfected the technology far enough to create a nuclear warhead small enough to be mounted on a Rodong-1 missile. But they had. And it was this deterrent which had kept North Korea safe in recent years and it was this deterrent that was used to blackmail the West for aid every time the harvests failed.

The limousine slowed to turn into his barracks. The triple depth razor wire fencing and double gated security checks told him he was home. He was surprised to see more than half the bottle of soju had been drunk during his lonely journey. As his car stopped at the second security gate, his secretary was stood waiting for him with a message from Talon. It had been a decade since Kim Jong-un's uncle, Chang Song-thaek, his closest friend and mentor, had been found guilty of attempting to overthrow the state and was summarily executed. That had been the biggest purge and political shake-up since the death of Kim Jong-il in 2011. General Park thought it was about time to shake it up again.

Back in his office, following his usual routine he gave smart salutes to the three pictures on the wall, if a little unsteady, and then he sat at his desk, opened his draw, and reached for the little red book.

Seoul. Saturday.

He'd had a terrible night's sleep. As he shaved in the mirror of his tastefully styled marble bathroom, the face looking back at him was tired and drawn, with uncharacteristic dark shadows under his red eyes. He was still wrestling with the same problem which had bothered him all night. On one hand he was kicking himself for being so lax about security. He had left his personal computer turned on while he stepped out of his office leaving basically an unknown person alone in there. On the other hand, he was incensed that this woman, who he had instinctively trusted when she first sat down, would be so rude as to snoop on his computers in the first place. Beyond all this, he was gravely worried that his plan could now seriously backfire and destroy both him and ultimately his company were his scheme to be made public. With social media being what it was, public disclosure of the plot would be ridiculously easy. His only comforting thought was the police hadn't knocked on his door already and he hadn't yet received any contact suggesting blackmail.

'So, what is her plan?' he asked his reflection in the mirror. He had to believe she knew what she was stealing otherwise why bother. He wondered if she was even who she claimed to be. Maybe she was some foreign intelligence agency's attempt to infiltrate his company either for the purposes of industrial espionage or, more worryingly, they had somehow connected his company, Han Electronics, with Stinger, this computer malware which he believed could change the world.

The surveillance video quite clearly showed Wendy Chen inserting a thumb-drive USB device into the USB slot on his computer and then seemingly copying a file, presumably the one on the screen at the time. 'Surely she couldn't know what she was looking at simply from a stream of code, could she? Was this just an opportunistic time and place petty theft and she really had no idea what the file contained?' He hoped that was the case although he privately doubted it. That idea didn't sit well in Kim Sung-han's sharp brain.

#

Casting his mind back nine months, he wasn't really sure whose idea the plot had been in the first place. He recalled the seed of an idea being discussed at a dinner party hosted by the Korean Minister for Trade. The residence of the Korean Trade Minister was an opulent house in private grounds located in the Gangnam area of Seoul. This was an official senior government staff enclave used by politicians and some senior diplomats. It had been a cool autumn evening with cocktails and canapés served on the huge veranda overlooking the architecturally lit and manicured gardens before the formal dinner.

He was proud Hyo-joo had accompanied him and she looked utterly breath-taking in a long burgundy coloured evening gown finished with ruby and diamond jewellery adorning her elegant neck and hands. The jewellery was her own. Kim had wanted to buy her jewellery once, early on in their relationship, and suggested they went shopping to one of the more exclusive diamond dealers. He had even made an appointment for a private viewing. She had not-so diplomatically shrugged off the idea making it quite apparent she had her own money and wanted for nothing material. She had omitted to add 'from you or any other man', but her message to him was implied and clear. She wasn't his whore. This lack of materialistic desire made her all the more attractive to Mr Kim. Independently wealthy, Hyo-joo had made it very clear she wasn't going to be financially indebted to any man.

That evening she was looking radiant with her long crow-black hair cascading down the back of her low-cut dress. She was fit, very fit, and the toned muscles of her back revealed just enough to leave no doubt that the rest of her body was equally well defined. Complemented by the subtlest of eyeliner and a dark shade of lipstick, Lee Hyo-joo was simply, stunningly beautiful. The attention she garnered from the other male dinner guests was bordering on annoyance, but she managed it all with impeccable grace and humour.

He recalled it was an unusual dinner. The Minister had invited an eclectic mix of guests. In addition to the standard grey faced senior executives rolled out from the Korean chaebols, the large Korean trading houses that controlled all aspects of the South Korean economy, there were quite a few intellectuals from various NGOs and other international think tanks. The dining room was cool and exquisitely presented with traditional Korean art, furniture, and subtle décor. The exposed roof beams were decorated in traditional green, blue, and red paints that were still handmade and applied by one of Korea's "national treasures". These were the artisans whose skills were passed down from generation to generation and who could still make and apply the traditional paints; such was the seriousness with which Korea took this centuries old art form.

The typical politically weighted conversation had largely bored Mr Kim, but it turned interesting though when hypothetical unification with North Korea was discussed and the collective diners started to consider non-diplomatic ways to urge unification with the North. It seemed to start all well-meaning and good-humouredly, however, as the wine and soju flowed so more imaginative ideas started to be kicked around. He noticed Hyo-joo quietly and carefully prompt one of the diners to expand on his idea of spoofing a weapon's launch from the North to really test the mettle of the South Korean alliance and prompt a retaliatory defensive attack. The table of diners smiled benignly over their waiter-served kimchi and barbequed beef as the speaker embellished his ideas around what would happen should the North accidently suffer an unintended missile launch.

'Oh yes!' he went on. 'Something similar nearly happened with Russia on the 26th September 1983,' he had explained. 'Basically, a glitch in the software of Russia's early warning defence system triggered an alert to warn Russia it was under a pre-emptive nuclear missile attack from the USA. It was only the sharp wits of Mr Stanislav Petrov, the guy on duty whose job it was to monitor the early warning system that evening, that prevented a full nuclear retaliatory attack from Russia.' The table of diners fell silent, they were spellbound.

'Seriously? So what happened?' asked one diner unable to restrain his enthusiasm.

The orator knew his subject well and warmed to the audience realising he had their full attention. Some had even stopped chewing, gawping open-mouthed. 'Well, the Russian satellites accidently triggered an alert to say they were tracking at first one and then scores of missiles being launched from the USA. Specifically, this was from a known nuclear missile silo in North Dakota, and all aimed towards Russia. Russia had literally ten minutes to decide whether to retaliate before the missiles started hitting Russian cities. Russia went into full alert and was about to retaliate. Fortunately, the cool-headed engineer on duty, Stanislav Petrov, suspected the alert was a software glitch and took the gamble to declare it a false alarm.'

It was Lee Hyo-joo who then asked, 'you said "software glitch". Do you know what caused it?'

'Yes. Apparently sunlight was reflecting with such intensity off the metal roofs of some industrial buildings near the missile silos. The Russian satellites software mistook this for the flash of an Intercontinental Ballistic rocket's jet engine at launch,' smiled the orator, happy to have been noticed by Miss Lee.

He went on. 'I guess if you think about it, we wouldn't be sat here now if Mr Petrov hadn't declared it a false alarm.' The table, still shocked, pondered this thought for a while. The storyteller enjoyed the pause, sipping his soju, holding his audience as a skilled conductor holds his orchestra. He continued. 'If the North really did launch an attack, accidental or otherwise, the South would need to retaliate even if the attack was abruptly halted after a short time. The effect would be to catalyse a break in the status quo. Either both sides would go to war or, as in the 1950's with the beginning of the Korean War, one side would rapidly back down, presumably the North, again. So, while both China and Russia love to stir up rhetoric in the North, if it really came to an all-out confrontation with the Americans, I suspect they would both drop North Korea like a hot potato.'

As they were largely a group of industrialists, the diners couldn't help but get into the weed of the technology needed. Kim Sung-han had remained silent up to this point then found himself thinking aloud how such an attack might be prompted, dwelling on the hackability of the North's missile systems and what it would take to hypothetically break-in. He had really been talking to himself, but thinking out loud, so was surprised when he realised the rest of the table was graveyard silent and hanging on his every word.

His heart further skipped a beat when he realized Lee Hyo-joo was intently staring at him with a look of such admiration it completely caught him off guard. Her usual coy gaze under her long lashes and double eyelids had been replaced with a foundry like fire he had never seen in her before. After they left the party later that evening and returned to his apartment her passion was so intense during sex it bordered aggression and, although he had never admitted it, she had actually hurt him.

The next morning following the dinner, once the maid had served their coffee and left the balcony where they had enjoyed breakfast in the cool Seoul autumn air, she had asked if he had meant what he had said the previous evening, and did he really think it was possible? He didn't need to ask what she was referring to as he knew all too well and had expected her question.

'Yes, it's possible,' Mr Kim told her. Truth was he had spent half the night pondering this very question and had even scratched out a plan in his mind. The real question was did he have the balls to attempt such an audacious plan; he feared not. While an interesting intellectual problem, he had never thought of himself as a man capable of such bold geo-political actions, particularly not one which could potentially provoke a nuclear war.

That night he had lain between his linen sheets staring up into the rooms blackness. Hyo-joo was sleeping deeply and contentedly next to him. Her breathing usually relaxed and reassured him, although not that night. He loved to smell her sex intermingled with her faint perfume. They had not showered after the passionate lovemaking. Hyo-joo had climaxed loudly, crumpled down onto him, and was soon curled-up, purring like a kitten. The problem was complicated.

While South Korea would love to reunite with North Korea, economically it would be crippling for the South. The USA, Japan, and other first world countries had verbally offered support, however, the economic overhead would be tremendous, so much so, such reunification would take two generations to even attempt to rebuild back to the current developed state the South enjoyed today. Multiple studies on Germany's reunification in the 1980's had proved that, and the Germans reunification issues were tiny in comparison to Korea's. China and Russia on the other hand had no desire to see the two Korea's reunite. The current tragic economic mismanagement of the North simply meant the routine nuclear blackmail was unlikely to ever stop. But then the real cost burden to the rest of the world was negligible.

There were really three scenarios. Firstly, the North Korean leadership would unilaterally see sense and slowly start to relax tensions. Indeed, this was the current prevailing winds of negotiation with the USA and South Korea. Joint Korean Olympic teams would be formed, trade deals would be struck, foreign direct investment would flow. Eventually the muddle-headed state would emerge in the way other Communist states in Asia such as Vietnam, Cambodia and Myanmar had successfully evolved; progressive albeit slowly.

The secondly scenario suggested sooner or later there would be a military coup or a civil uprising in the North. This would be messy and leave the North vulnerable to outside intervention. It might work with a strong, benign leadership, however, interference from their neighbours would likely see this fail and the most likely outcome would be to evolve another strongman under even deeper influence from the Chinese.

Lastly, North Korea might push the West too far. Some small skirmish with fishing boats or a missile accident could provoke the impatient West, notably the Americans under a brash President, to at last take decisive action against the nuclear armed Democratic People's Republic of Korea once and for all. China and Russia, while angrily hopping up and down rattling their sabres, would threaten retaliation to support their North Korea ally, but this would ultimately stop short of direct intervention. Neither China nor Russia needed nor wanted a trivial no-winner war, after all, the Middle East had the monopoly on that role, and they kept the arms manufacturers in business. North Korea might prove to be an ugly war zone for a year or two but then this would blow over and the South would offer an economic lifeline, something the South believed the populous of the North really wanted anyway: to reunite with their rich cousins south of the DMZ.

Over breakfast on the balcony of his luxury penthouse apartment all those months ago Kim Sung-han shared his idea with Lee Hyo-joo. His idea was how the third scenario could be catalysed.

Later that morning, while Kim was at his office dealing with his usual business matters, a North Korean asset code named Talon, in the employ of the Democratic People's Republic of Korea's Special Purposes Force Command, dug out her copy of Chairman Mao's Little Red Book. Using their usual prepared cypher to encrypt a message, the message was passed to a courier who in turn transmitted it to a further encrypted receiver north of the 150-mile-long DMZ. One hour later, it was being decoded by General Park. It simply read 'PLN. NED US HCKR'. General Park picked up the phone to his Chief of Cyber Intelligence and explained he needed to find a US-based hacker for a project that could not be traced back to them in North Korea. The Chief smartly saluted to his superior and ran to his office to consult the Dark Web. Within thirty minutes he had made contact with someone using the pseudonym 'Wolf'.

Some months later, once the plan had been clearly thought through, Talon recovered the contact for Wolf and passed along her instructions with details of the software used in the missile launch systems. There were no niceties or personal information shared. A brief dialog of the coding instructions and an even briefer price discussion was had before the deal was struck, with the first instalment of the payment being made in a cryptocurrency. Wolf confirmed the payment had been received and commenced his reconnaissance, the first step in a good hack.

#

Kim Sung-han patted his freshly shaven face dry with a soft towel.

He wondered what the news today would bring. Would he get a knock on the door of his apartment and see the police standing there? Would the South Korean security forces storm his office building and humiliatingly lead him away in handcuffs for the world's press to televise? Would Wendy Chen or her associates make contact asking for a ransom or some other set of preconditions? He was racked with nerves, so much so he couldn't ever remember being this stressed in his professional career and as the CEO, he had been in some hairy situations.

Unbeknown to the CEO of Han Electronics, his own mobile phone had been corrupted by a hacker. SimJacker had been loaded via an SMS, which exploited a vulnerability in the phones own SIM card. The spyware on his personal smartphone had captured the message the previous evening from S.C. Lee, the Chief Information Security Officer at Han Electronics. The messages had been read and the salient part of the video reviewed. The wheels had already been put in motion for seven hours now to deal with Wendy Chen.

Kim Sung-han, the CEO of Han Electronics, threw his summer robe on and emerged from the bathroom. It was still very early, not even 6:00 a.m. yet and Lee Hyo-joo was also up. He saw her robed silhouette through the drapes preparing coffee for them both on the balcony. It was still too early to ask the maid to prepare breakfast. The sun had risen, but it was still low on the horizon and, although it promised to be another hot day, the morning was cool and fresh. Hyo-joo had retrieved a small suitcase and put it on the unmade bed. This was a sign she was planning to travel somewhere today. The case was as yet empty aside a small red book in the bottom. Sung-han had not paid much attention to the little book but then, seeing the front cover, realized she had packed a copy of Chairman Mao's Little Red Book.

It struck him as odd given he had believed her to be such an ardent capitalist. It occurred to him then that, regardless of how close they were, he at least had fallen deeply in love with her, he actually knew very little about her real opinions and influences. He decided when the time was right, he would gently probe her on her personal politics and her interest in the little red book he had seen. But now wasn't the right time.

As he stepped through the large glass floor to ceiling sliding doors onto the same balcony, Lee Hyo-joo smiled warmly and walked around the table towards him, encouraging the robe to fall open revealing her perfectly fit and completely naked body beneath. She threw her arms around his neck and kissed him affectionately on the lips, pushing her body into his. She was wide awake and fully charged despite the earliness of the hour. He thought perhaps she was feeling sexy and wanted to make love to him again given it was early and they were in no particular hurry at this hour. She then stepped back, retied the robe, stretched an exaggerated yawn, and pulled her hair free of the robe with both hands behind her head, her long black hair tumbling down her back as she did so. She gestured him towards the table where she had prepared fresh juice, fruit, and coffee. She sat opposite him and asked what he had planned for the day. Kim mumbled something about meetings then asked her how her day looked. He knew better than to confront Hyo-joo about her plans directly as she would only tell him what she wanted him to know, when she wanted.

'I'm going to be away for a couple of days,' she announced without specifying where she was going. 'I'm on the board of a company actually and, while I have minimal involvement, I am expected to attend the occasional meeting and sign various papers. I'll only be away for one, maybe two, nights,' she said, leaving it at that as she clearly felt enough information had been imparted. Sung-han knew better than to push for more. He nodded his acknowledgement.

He steeled himself. 'Darling,' he started, 'we need to discuss Stinger!'

Looking at him, pokerfaced over the rim of her coffee cup, a taste she had developed during her time in America, she said 'you want to deploy now? Are we ready?'

'We're not quite ready, no. The point is we have a problem. The malware has been stolen! A lady I met yesterday downloaded a copy of Stinger from my computer in the office.'

'It was only a copy? You still have the original code?' Hyo-joo enquired pragmatically holding a steady tone of voice, careful not displaying any emotion.

'Yes, the original code is fine. I've had it retested and all's good. She did no damage; merely helped herself to a copy of it. I'm not even sure if she knows quite what she's stolen.' Kim Sung-han paused. He half expected some recrimination, a look of disappointment or even a flash of anger, from Hyo-joo, however, she simply maintained her passive gaze, giving nothing away. It was almost as if she already knew.

Hyo-joo looked thoughtful, her porcelain features barely creased. 'We knew there would be issues we could not foresee, and I don't think you should be overly worried. No one apart from a very few of us know the true capability of Stinger or what it's designed to do. Only you and I truly know the full implications of what we desire. Maybe your thief doesn't know what she's stolen. Has she been in touch with you looking to blackmail or to extort a ransom?'

'No, none of that. Not a word yet. I still think we need to bring the delivery date forwards. Let's deliver the 'gift' as soon as we can and not wait for the Korean Worker's Party Foundation Day anniversary parade on October 10th.'

She nodded agreement. 'You're wise,' she said, not in her coy and patronizing way but with sincerity, as she didn't want him losing his nerve now. 'Let's bring the plan forwards. It's Saturday morning and I'm back in two days, three at most. Do you think you'll be ready? Can you be ready by then? I want to be with you, here! I want to spend every minute of this ride with you as we see history being made together.'

He looked grave, shivered in the fresh morning cool air, and forced a nervous smile at her. She stood up and walked around the balcony's breakfast table, cupped his freshly shaven face in both her hands, and kissed him with passion on the lips. The robe fell open again. This time she left it open and fed his hands inside.

California. Saturday Morning.

Craig's mum shouted, 'See you later hon. I'm off to work,' as she closed the front door of their apartment and set off down the steps to her car parked in the parking lot below. Jenny now worked in a diner across the 101 in San Carlos. It was stress free and suited her friendly, outgoing personality, although the base salary was poor. Whilst her hips had spread a bit for sure, she was still an attractive woman for her age. She kept her blond hair long and the few grey hairs when they appeared, were promptly treated. The growing lines around her eyes she could downplay with a little more make-up. She hadn't married, not because she hadn't wanted to, simply that as a single mum she'd not had time to meet and date. *Perhaps, one day I still will, when I met the right guy*, she thought.

Jenny Sanchez found her upbeat attitude and ready smile meant the tips from her regular customers could support her modest needs perfectly well. Random guys using the diner would hit on her from time to time too. Secretly she desired to play along, however, the face looking back at her in the mirror every morning as she applied her make-up returned a sardonic smile and shook its head. She wasn't unattractive, only aging. Dreams of marrying a rich IT professional making millions from the latest IPO had evaporated when she fell pregnant with Craig. She wasn't bitter. She was pragmatic and got on with life as best she could. Privately she wasn't unhappy and saw no desire to change much. Craig never needed money and his work, whatever that was exactly, seemed to pay him well enough to give her money every month. He bought anything he needed, mostly computer gear, and always gave her enough cash for bills and supplies. In this regard, he was a good son.

She doubted her son, ensconced in Mission Control, had heard her leave but it made her feel better to wish him well every time she came and went from the apartment. Besides, it was close to the full extent of their dialog these days. As a child, she had loved him wholeheartedly and he doted on her. As he hit his teenage years, so the reality of who he was struck home. He was the bastard result of a drug addled party between a nerd software programmer and a pretty, cheap, and naive party girl. He became bitter and, despite her desperate pleas, he distanced himself from her. He stopped considering her wishes and now, like an old married couple, they just lived in the same apartment more out of routine and indifference to change than any emotions a mother-son love could elicit.

Craig had heard her leave and grunted a quiet response under his breath, 'Baa bitch'. He was busy, in the zone, as he liked to think when he was coding or gaming and he hated interruptions. His eyes did flick momentarily to one of the many monitors above his main screen, the one tracking the tiny hidden camera that oversaw the front door and parking lot. Sure enough, there went his mother. The day was already getting hot and he watched her climb into the tired old silver Ford, wind the windows down to dispel the hot and fusty car air, then reverse out of the parking space. He relaxed, lapsing even deeper back into his zone.

#

The American credit rating agency, Union Credit Inc., had unwittingly left an unsecured Wi-Fi enabled printer attached to a network segment, which also rather clumsily happened to be attached to the rest of the network in the backup datacentre in Sunnyvale. Parking close to their disaster recovery facility in Sunnyvale one night a few days previously, in his mother's borrowed silver Ford, his 'borrowed' mobile phone was easily able to connect to the printer's Wi-Fi. The printer was functional. However, it was old and used a simple version of the Linux Operating System, which was designed to be light, quick, and reliable. However, and regrettably for Union Credit Inc., it wasn't particularly secure. This made it the ideal attack vector, the perfect launching platform for Wolf's malware payload. For Wolf, step three in the kill-chain, deploying his malware on the printer had been easy. He had been reconnoitring this company for months looking for a vulnerability, and now he smiled to himself.

His malware was simple and small. A little C++ coding enabled him to brute force access the printer, then take command and control of the printer which, in turn, would enable him to use the IP address of one of the network attached personal computers. From here Wolf would assume the identity of an authorized user. With some further malware and a few commands, which he'd make later when he was back in his chair in Mission Control, he'd established himself with full network administrator rights then he'd be able to go pretty much wherever he pleased within this company's data networks.

Union Credit Inc. had diligent access controls in their production datacentre in San Francisco, but not so in the back-up centre. This ultimately allowed Wolf access to all the credit records of the individuals and companies stored on the credit rating agency's backup databases. As the backups were synchronized to be real-time with the San Francisco headquarters, the data was current. Such detailed records being current commanded a good price on the Dark Web, the meeting place for cybercriminals in the IT world. Many black hat actors would be keen to buy and exploit this data, which could be resold many times.

Many legitimate companies would also be keen to come by the data too and not ask too many questions about its source. With cybercrime, it was always the fault of the hacked company's sloppy security policies, and not the recipients of the stolen 'goods' who got the bad press, and usually fined under privacy laws. Craig had clapped his hands in glee and squirmed in the seat of the old silver Ford as his Remote Access Trojan was downloaded to the printer. He knew such records being so current could be worth as much as $1 to $5 each on the first day of their theft, and Wolf suspected he would be able to download around 10 million records. Not bad for a night's work!

Over the quiet hum of the air conditioners back in Mission Control, Craig rolled his huge bulk onto his left buttock and squeezed out a rich and noisy fart from his flabby arse, grimacing to himself at the smell. 'Get a load of that baby!' he said out aloud followed by 'Phew!' as he exaggeratedly waved his hand in front of his nose. He was in a good mood. Wolf was sweating profusely as the adrenaline of the hack coupled with his third caffeine-loaded energy drink in quick succession was kicking in. He was excitedly bouncing up and down in his chair as his fat fingers quickly flowed over the keyboard like mercury.

His RAT, the Remote Access Trojan he'd deployed on the printer attached PC previously had fulfilled its task, he was now enacting the fifth step in the chain and had installed another piece of code he'd designed giving him command and control of the back-up servers. At last Wolf affected the algorithms to act on his objective - the download of millions of personal credit records to his servers.

Wolf was proficient. He had opted for a chunk download as opposed to a covert channel download. The covert channel download was sneaky, slower, and broke the data into multiple small files and then downloaded one every few seconds. Stenography, the term for hiding the files in plain sight, was classy although he knew it might trigger a security management alert and data loss prevention software might spot unusual behaviour and enact a shutdown of the servers and network.

The chunk download was more practical albeit slightly less elegant. This method used Wolf's ciphers, custom software that Wolf specialized in coding. These ciphers would encrypt the data and save it all into one very large file, and then download all in one data dump. Inevitably, the forensic investigation would find this in no time, however, by then the hack would be complete, the data exfiltrated, and that was that. The records would already have been copied, downloaded to Wolfs servers, and then put up for sale on the Dark Web within an hour.

The credit rating agency would be left with an expensive and publicly embarrassing mess to clear up. Following the inevitable C-suite resignations, a collapsed share price; then the subsequent criminal investigations, fines, shareholders class action lawsuits, legal costs, etcetera, Union Credit Inc., would likely never recover. The only clue the forensic investigators would find would be the word "wolf", Craig's calling card that his ego would not allow him to forego, written somewhere in the string of the weaponized malware code, deployment of which had been facilitated by his RAT on the original attack vector – the old printer network. Pretty girls at UCSC might not appreciate Craig, but hackers in the shadowy underworld of cybercrime would learn Wolf had struck again and collectively smile and nod appreciatively.

Wolf's own servers physically sat in the computer racks in Mission Control. He couldn't bring himself to trust public cloud providers or any other servers not within his immediate control. His old school approach to his servers had worked well for him and, besides, they were untraceable to the authorities or other hackers for that matter. Anonymizers were software that utilized multiple zombie computers around the world and used the IP addresses of those computers to have multiple logical hops; the files hopping from one anonymous server to another before reaching Wolfs destination servers.

The zombie computers Craig exploited were simply other people's computers, hacked solely to use their IP addresses making tracking his own computers nigh on impossible. This was Wolf's botnet. His sophisticated form of malware which hijacked other people's computers randomly, purely for the purposes of giving his communications multiple hops and so obfuscating the originating or destination computers, namely, the servers in Wolf's own Mission Control.

Wolf wanted to protect his intellectual property. In addition to the large electromagnets installed to wipe the data in a hurry, he had now gone one-step further. The Semtex he had sourced from the Marx Brothers was now carefully moulded around the computer racks. Wolf didn't believe he would ever need it, but his line of work was unpredictable. Wolf's confidence in his own brilliance in covering his tracks was absolute, but he wasn't entirely naive either and occasionally doubts would creep into his mind.

The contract he'd fulfilled a few weeks ago he had called 'Stinger', and while it was stimulating, it was clearly at the extreme end of industrial espionage, if not blatant cyberwarfare. This end of his business attracted some very talented and brutal people, not to mention the world's smartest hackers employed by infinitely well-resourced law enforcement agencies around the world. He had no doubt "Wolf" was a pin-up on many a virtual situation board in FBI, NSA, CIA, GCHQ, PLA, and Mossad offices around the world; and the guy who could take down the Wolf would become a legend.

Jenny was having a busy morning in the diner, smiling her friendly smile and hurrying around pouring more coffees. There was a large computer fair happening nearby and many of the delegates had descended on the diner for lunch. 'Tips should be good today,' she thought. She overheard their technical conversations and recognized many of the terms although they meant little to her. She thought about her son's bedroom and all his computer gear. She thought to note down some of the terms she was overhearing and ask Craig what they meant later. She considered she should take an interest in his work perhaps and try to bond with him through the joys of TCP/IP. Unfortunately, as she would later come to reflect, that wasn't going to happen.

#

The sunny Palo Alto streets were tree-lined, pleasant, and not too busy during the day. The residents were largely young professionals and so all at work during the week, and either exercising, socialising, or sleeping-in at weekends. Most worked in the numerous IT companies that followed Route 101 from San Francisco to San Jose. Palo Alto, being the location of Stanford University, was the epicentre of the Silicon Valley boom and most of the older residents had sold up years before to cash out of their simple wooden houses to make way for the massive influx of nouveau riche.

Talon parked her rental car under the shade of a tree in a side street off Middlefield Road, on the edge of downtown Palo Alto. She sat in the driver's seat and carefully screwed the silencer onto the threaded barrel of the Glock 19 9mm, her preferred sidearm. Despite the hot day, she wore latex gloves. She hated the smelly gun oil on her manicured beringed fingers and, pragmatically, she needed to avoid gunshot residue. She had picked up the Hermes handbag containing the weapon from the concierge at the hotel. She had checked into the hotel, situated a little to the south of San Francisco earlier that day after disembarking the comfortable Korean Airlines flight. Immigrations queue's at SFO had been light and she felt comfortable and refreshed, ready to go to work.

Her thoughts flicked briefly to her boyfriend who she had loved and left in Seoul that previous morning. Now she sat in the driver's seat of the hire car she had picked up at San Francisco International Airport earlier using a false driver's license and ID. She had driven down Route 101 to the address provided in Palo Alto and parked in the quiet, tree-lined side street off Middlefield Road. A quick scan of the street and adjacent houses told her there were no cameras overlooking the car. No one to watch her movements. The car's GPS might give her away later, however, she would be long gone by the time the police connected those dots.

The street was simple enough with small, discrete houses, each worth many millions given the Silicon Valley location. Her orders had been quite clear. She had received them in three separate WhatsApp messages. WhatsApp messages were encrypted at an elementary level and these messages were themselves coded. Disguised to look like sexually suggestive texts of affection, with many aubergine and banana icons, they appeared to be sent by an acquaintance she had met in a bar in Seoul; simply the usual messages between two new lovers. Nothing the deep packet inspection software so favoured by security agencies would flag. If only they knew!

Her shapely black stockinged leg extended from the car, and she exited, ready for work. She stood, buttoned the jacket on the dark designer suit, arranged her long dark hair around her face, then grabbed the black attaché case off the back seat, and locked the car doors. Tall and slim, she blended into the middle-class street perfectly and, apart from her apparent beauty, no one would look twice or think she looked out of place. She would burn her clothes later given the gunshot residue.

Talon walked around the block to the address given on her WhatsApp message's. She had memorized the address and then dumped the phone it was received on in a trash bin at the airport, careful to wipe it with a hand-sanitising alcohol swab first. She walked up the steps and rang the doorbell at the given address, careful no one else was watching. She held the black attaché case. It looked professional, such like a realtor or lawyer might carry as flipping property in this area was commonplace. She looked slick and not a bit out of place, given the rest of her ensemble.

Wolf heard the bell ring. Canvassers were usual in this area and would typically be ignored. Craig took a habitual glance at the monitor displaying the camera on the sunny aspect of the front door and parking lot. Irritation at being interrupted was quickly replaced by intrigue as he regarded the form of the beautiful Asian lady with the designer suit and black attaché case ringing his doorbell a second time. Pizza delivery was usual but apart from that the doorbell was untouched. Asian with a black attaché case probably meant a payment thought Craig. Cryptocurrencies were usually Wolf's method of payment although cash was always handy too.

Cryptocurrencies were all well and good, but he still liked the liquidity of good old hard currency in his hands from time to time and so occasionally he asked his smaller regular clients to pay in cash. He didn't recognize this lady and his payments were always transacted at a busy public location. It occurred to him no one should ever know his address. Regardless, his greed and her beauty motivated him to find out more. Even if she was only a realtor or canvasser, where was the harm in having a chat? Craig heaved his obese form out of his chair and padded towards the front door. He didn't recognize this courier, if that's what she was, but she was so pretty.

Talon was the consummate professional. Regulating her breathing, she merely stood nonchalantly waiting for the door to be answered. Her right hand was on the silenced Glock tucked in her Hermes handbag looped over her left arm. The attaché case now stood on the floor beside her. She heard the shuffling of someone heavy approaching the door and, once opened a crack, she gave her best engaging smile so as to disarm the apprehension of the apartment owner, after all, they may be armed too.

Craig's first instinct was to check the body of the woman at his front door. He pulled his leering gaze up from her expensive Christian Louboutin shoes, shapely legs, to her bust provocatively hidden behind a lacy bra and cream silk blouse, then finally up to her face to reciprocate her smile. Hopefully she would reference someone he knew well and hand over the attaché case resting on the ground. If it was his lucky day she might even be part of the payment from a satisfied customer. He would invite her in. Such bonuses had been known, albeit in a bar usually followed by a pre-booked motel room close by. But who cares when she was stunning? And here she was, standing in the sun on Wolf's doorstep.

Two quick silenced bursts hit Wolf square in the chest. She was so fast, his smile hadn't even had time to turn to shock. Once Talon recognized his face from the picture, which wasn't hard, she withdrew the Glock from her bag. Her training taught her to fire in bursts of two quick shots then re-aim. On this occasion she knew two rounds would do the job. She saw with instant satisfaction both were near heart shots, the bullets tearing through flesh, bone, and lung. If he wasn't dead before he hit the floor he would bleed-out within a minute. She reviewed her handywork, then re-aimed and quickly fired two more for good measure, retaining the other rounds in the event of a problem while escaping the scene.

She watched him stagger back into the apartment, falling backwards against the wall, knocking over a small side table as he fumbled for purchase. The Glock 19 was a powerful weapon. With sound suppression though it was not so powerful as to knock a near 400-pound man clear off his feet. Craig had staggered, shock having more impact than the bullets that slammed into his chest and ripped through his ribcage into his heart and lungs. He looked uncomprehendingly at her, mouth moving but no words forming. Talon stepped carefully forwards, grabbed the front door handle, and pulled it closed. Usually she would put two more shots into the head to ensure a definitive kill, but she saw there was no need today. Turning around, she placed the hot weapon back into her handbag, picked up the attaché case, and walked away, surreptitiously checking if anyone had seen the event. No one had.

Wolf's pulse became weaker as he bled-out. He had slumped backwards and was half propped against the wall inside the front door. He blinked in shock at the method of his death, unable to comprehend why he had been shot and worse how he could possibly have been tracked down. He even spared a moment's thought to consider if he had fumbled an anonymizer. Laying in the entrance hall of his mum's apartment, his lungs and heart being punctured by the four shots, he was unable to speak. Orange foaming blood bubbled and gurgled with the movements of his lips, the air unable to form the words in his blood-clogged vocal cords.

The smartwatch on his wrist tracked his wildly fluctuating pulse, racing at first, then exponentially slowing. Wolf's eyes slowly closed. His brain functions slowed and then finally stopped as the life left his quivering body. Lastly, his weakening pulse finally ceased altogether. As programmed, the smartwatch sent an alert to the iPhone it was synchronized with and in turn, a small piece of software triggered an electric current to charge the enormous magnets placed next to the computer racks. The magnets quietly hummed into life, scrambling the magnetized memory of the server's hard drives, then after a few seconds a second electrical circuit connected the detonators on the carefully positioned Semtex. The ensuing explosion ripped through Mission Control, Jenny's apartment, and the two apartments either side.

Talon had just turned the corner from the apartment when Mission Control exploded. The blast was strong enough to knock her to her knees, shattering windows around her, tearing leaves from trees, and sending a shock wave down the street. Talon hadn't expected that and her ears were ringing, although now the explosion had bought an eerie silence to an otherwise peaceful neighbourhood on a hot California day. At first, she was confused as smoke billowed from somewhere behind her, leaves swirled around, and debris was now raining down around her.

Quickly the assassin regained her senses. Her knees and palms were scratched and sore, but she stood, regained composure, checked she had not left any smears of her own blood on the pavement, and briskly, not hurriedly, covered the distance to her hire car. Talon opened the driver's door and slid in. Her stockings had torn, and her knees were chaffed and bleeding. Her palms were red and bruised from the fall having ripped the gloves she had worn for the actual shooting. She started the engine and, while maintaining the urban speed limits, she carefully put as much space between herself and Palo Alto as possible while heading back northwards towards San Francisco airport. It was an hour before her ears stopped ringing.

A little later that Saturday afternoon, on a derelict bit of waste ground south of San Francisco, a long-haired Asian-looking lady could be seen dumping designer clothes and a black attaché case into an old waste bin, dousing them in barbeque lighter fluid, and throwing a match on the lot. The gun had been wiped down with surgical alcohol along with the Hermes bag to be passed back to the concierge when she arrived back at the hotel later. The Korean lady then returned to her hotel, wiped down her exposed skin and hair with surgical alcohol, showered for a very long time and put on a comfortable jumpsuit.

She checked out of the hotel, returned the hire car after wiping down the interior with yet more surgical alcohol, and caught her Korean Airlines evening flight back to Seoul, business class. As the aircraft taxied, she settled into the large comfortable seat, sipped a glass of champagne, and read *The Economist*. No one would be any the wiser. As far as US immigration was concerned, Lee Hyo-Joo was a typical Korean business woman, representing her typical Korean IT company employer, having typical meetings in Silicon Valley. Nothing unusual there.

Hong Kong. Saturday Afternoon.

Spray splashed the huge windows as the fast ferry sliced through the wake of the container ships as she sped back from Discovery Bay. The route crossed the commercial shipping lanes which crisscrossed Hong Kong harbour. All sizes of boats competed for a space on the congested Victoria Harbour, from the smallest sail boats competing in "round the can's" regattas, to Macau turbo-jet hydrofoils, the world's largest containerships, and the goliath of warships – the American navy aircraft carriers.

Wendy and Guy sat, subdued, side by side cocooned in the ferry from Discovery Bay back to Central, both were quiet with their own thoughts. The large twin hull ferry flew across Hong Kong harbour, the journey taking less than thirty minutes. The ferry seated hundreds of people on the two decks and they were fully enclosed, barely noticing the waves which gently rocked the highspeed boat. The Discovery Bay ferries were practical in contrast to the romantic Star Ferries that chugged in relay, daily, between Hong Kong and Kowloon to the north of Hong Kong Island. Fans of Hong Kong loved these quaint, iconic little green iron ferries, named after stars, that were open to the elements, a legacy of the British past. The Discovery Bay ferries were, by contrast, simply large practical white commuters.

Looking out through the large salt encrusted windows, they barely spoke, still coming to terms with what John had showed them and with his parting warning still resonating. Clearly both were thinking the same thing at the same time when Wendy suddenly said, 'I'm sure I wasn't seen lifting the software from Mr Kim's computer.'

'Did you notice if the room had cameras Wendy?' Guy pragmatically asked, trying to keep any trace of scepticism from his tone. She was clearly anxious.

'Well, I can't say I really looked. I was more concerned about Mr Kim coming back in and catching me red-handed using his computer. That was my only thought at the time.'

It was true. So long as there were no cameras, Mr Kim would unlikely think to check his computer to see if it had been tampered with in his absence. Unless Wendy had been seen on a discreetly placed camera, she might have gotten away with this rude and risky indiscretion. Guy shared these thoughts with Wendy to placate her.

'But if I was caught on camera John's going to be right, I'm in deep trouble.'

'Yes,' agreed Guy, welcoming of the opportunity to be level headed. 'We need a contingency plan. John's suggestion of dumping the USB drive is a bad one if we need to prove to the authorities what we've found or potentially even as leverage with Mr Kim.' The ferry banging over the waves helped create background noise and their conversation didn't need to be too muted.

'Perhaps we can go to the British High Commission or the Singaporean Embassy and ask for protection once we've told them what we have,' suggested Wendy.

'Possible,' shrugged Guy. 'I'm sure the British spooks would be very interested in this, but I can't second-guess the Singaporean Government, although they too rely on implied American defence support so they would likely be helpful. How much they'll care for our personal safety though I've no idea. We could even try the US

Embassy, however, neither of us are US citizens so simply getting in would be a pain in the arse, let alone talking to someone in a position of authority.' They both grunted in unison at that suggestion and looked, unfocusing, through the sea spray etched window at the container ships in Hong Kong harbour. Looking through the port side windows, Guy pointed to a massive grey shape in the distance to the left. 'That's the USS *Ronald Reagan*,' he said. 'One of the largest aircraft carriers the US fleet, and a state-of-the-art warship apparently. It's based out of Japan and stops in Hong Kong from time to time when on Pacific Ocean patrol. You can't get within a mile of it when it's here.'

Wendy seemed unimpressed at this and murmured 'boys' toys,' as she nodded absently.

The Discovery Bay ferry docked in Central, as it always did, at Pier 3. From there the two meandered down the gangplank and up the wide concrete steps towards the covered walkway connecting the Pier with the IFC building. The IFC is one of the largest skyscrapers in Hong Kong, housing expensive offices, an up-market shopping mall, and the classy Four Seasons Hotel. The IFC or International Financial Centre, prides itself on being one of the newest, tallest, shiniest, and most desirable locations on Hong Kong Island for shops and offices alike. Any typical day would see both expensively clad office workers hurrying through while picking up coffees, as well as wealthy tourists browsing the latest designer labels.

Intuitively Guy knew Wendy didn't want to be left alone yet, so without asking, or being invited, he wandered along beside her as they entered the shopping mall and drifted on towards the hotel. Today though the overpriced designer clothes held no appeal for Wendy who, under more normal circumstances, would at least check a few window displays and probably pop into a couple of shops when she had a spare moment... But not today.

The hotel lobby, accessible through the mall, was huge and airy. High ceilings and architectural lighting lent an air of friendly professionalism. There was some seating in the lobby, but without too many comfortable seats as that might encourage loafers. People were expected to check in, check out, meet friends and clients, however, hanging around with no purpose was discouraged and the aura of opulence simply made people who couldn't afford to stay there feel awkward. Perhaps it was because of this, that as Wendy and Guy wandered through the lobby, he happened to spot two characters who looked somewhat out of place. They were Asian for sure, although he suspected probably not Hong Kong Chinese, the dark jackets looked too awkward on them for Hong Kong nationals. They wore smart dark suits that were somehow sharp but not in the way a businessman might like the cut to show the suit was well tailored.

Guy was quick witted enough to not look directly at them. In fact, since leaving John's apartment in Discovery Bay, he had been thinking, if the Koreans were already on to Wendy, how would they go about finding her, and in what form would an approach take. Guy feared by simply phoning all the quality business hotels and asking for 'Wendy Chen' would probably strike lucky within an hour or two. Wendy would have had no thought or reason to hide her identity.

Guy was discreetly scanning the lobby for anyone who might take more than a passing interest in Wendy. As a beautiful leggy Asian woman, she did rather stand out in a crowd and was used to being noticed. This didn't bother Guy as he was known to appreciate a beautiful woman himself. What he did notice though, when he saw the two dark suits, was the subtle nod between them. Being the archetypical gentleman, he had held the door open for Wendy when entering the hotel lobby then he had lingered back far enough to let her walk a few paces in front of him. Guy wanted to put a little space between himself and her. Not enough for her to notice so as to alarm Wendy, but enough to make it look like she was alone and that they weren't necessarily together.

Wendy was oblivious to this and oblivious to the two dark suits and therefore just assumed Guy, like any good dog, was walking to heel. As they approached the lift, Wendy rummaged in her bag for her room key and Guy, as nonchalantly as possible, pretended to fumble in his jean pockets for his fictitious room key also, again to give the appearance to any on-lookers they weren't together. He prayed Wendy wouldn't blow his rouse by suddenly turning and talking to him or even worse touching him.

As the lift doors opened, he gallantly and a little flamboyantly gestured for to her to go first. To an impartial observer it would simply look as if he were trying to make a good first impression on a pretty lady he might be able to strike up a conversation with while in the lift. Wendy gave a peculiar smile, stepped ahead of him, but thankfully said nothing. Guy stepped in behind her and, without causing alarm, quickly pressed the button to close the lift door in case the suits were close behind them. They weren't close enough to share the same lift although they had moved towards them. In the lift he waited to see if Wendy had noticed the suits as presumably she would say something immediately if she had. She was clearly clueless, making a comment about being glad to be back in the hotel and needing a shower.

'You might need to hold that thought for a bit babe,' said Guy, as they got out of the lift on her floor.

'Why!' she exclaimed, looking at Guy with genuine anxiety.

'I'm not sure yet. We'll find out in a moment.'

As they walked down the beautifully appointed corridor with

tastefully overlit pictures, Guy saw what he wanted - the emergency exit door. It was a fire door with an oblong shaped wire mesh impregnated glass window in the middle, leading to a stairwell and the service elevator. He pushed the emergency exit door open assuming he had triggered an alarm somewhere in the bowels of the hotel. Regardless, if his worst fears were confirmed, it wouldn't matter. He pulled Wendy through the door and let it close ajar. He ran the few steps to the service elevator and pressed the call button. Through the wire-reinforced glass they could see the door to Wendy's room a short distance up the corridor. He put a finger to his lips to gesture silence and they waited, peering through the glass back towards Wendy's room. Wendy had no idea what Guy was up to, but it spooked her and she was pale, her eyes grilling Guy for answers.

They didn't need to wait for long. Within two minutes Guy's stomach knotted as he saw the two dark suited men emerge from the elevator on their floor and, by checking the room numbers, started moving towards Wendy's room. This was too much of a coincidence. This was Guy's moment of realisation; they were in way over their heads. Wendy sensed the fear in Guy as her own realisation hit home hard. Guy took a few steps back and hit the call button on the service lift again, and this time heard the whine of the lift motor as it started up towards their floor. The two suits stopped outside Wendy's room and quickly scanned the corridor in both directions. They each drew from their shoulder holsters a small calibre sidearm previously concealed by their dark jackets. Whoever these men were, they were not the Hong Kong police.

One suit rang the doorbell and waited patiently for several seconds. Again, looking up and down the corridor to confirm they were still alone. There was no answer. One of the suits aimed his weapon at the door lock and fired two quick rounds. The door surround splintered in a shower of wood and the second suit kicked hard blowing the door inwards with a deafening bang. They nimbly stepped in, both hands gripping the weapons raised in front of them. They moved with precision looking every inch the professionally trained hitmen they were.

The service lift dinged and its doors clattered open. Guy grabbed Wendy around the waist and bundled them both into the lift without a second thought. He punched the button for the ground floor then repeatedly stabbed the button to close the doors. He assumed, rightly, the hitmen would see the room was empty and untouched, realize they had been spotted in the lobby, and that Wendy had given them the slip, probably through the emergency exit. He had also assumed they would be onto them within seconds.

'I'm sorry I've gotten you into this mess,' babbled Wendy, her eyes wide in terror. 'They were here to kill me weren't they!' she said, more a statement than a question. Guy hugged her and didn't answer; it was rhetorical. The elevator ride down to the ground floor took an eternity.

'We need to get out of here fast,' he said, assuming a control he didn't feel entirely sure he had. 'I saw those guys in the lobby although I'm not sure they paid any attention to me. You're the target.' Guy bit his lip and kicked himself for the stupidity of using the word 'target'. If she wasn't feeling scared enough already, it was like he had hung a huge shooting range target on her back with bright red and white concentric circles and a big red bullseye in the middle.

'Oh God, I'm sorry. I didn't mean target,' he fumbled.

'Yeah you did, and I realise that I am. I can't believe they're on to me so quickly,' she said. 'They must have me on camera downloading the file. I feel so foolish. They could have the file back but that wasn't what those guys were doing here, was it?' Guy didn't answer.

The lift reached the ground floor and hotel staff scattered as they rushed out of the opening doors and spun around to catch their bearings. They took off towards a pair of large double doors with a green exit sign above it. Steel plates covered the doors halfway up for trolley protection, and they burst through it into the late afternoon heat and a gaggle of hotel staff who were stood around smoking and loitering outside the door on their tea break. Guy and Wendy were outside the hotel but on the staff entrance side where all the trade deliveries to the hotel were made. Guy grabbed Wendy's hand and they turned right to run towards the shopping mall. The startled hotel staff were calling from behind them, but their calls were in vain. Wendy and Guy were running as fast as they were able.

Right at that moment Guy spotted another suit. He wasn't one of those from inside the hotel as they must still be making their way down from the room. This one was looking straight at them while talking into his shirt cuff. Clearly, he was in touch with the first two, and possibly more. Guy guessed these guys had come in force. He assumed he too was armed, why else would a man wear a jacket in the August heat. Guy frantically pulled Wendy along, and pushed through a pair of glass doors into the IFC shopping mall. They could easily be chased in the mall although the chance of them being murdered outright in the mall was unlikely. It was the weekend and there was the usual throng of Saturday afternoon shoppers and the mall was congested. Men and women were looking in shops while bored children ran around and played chase in the huge airconditioned space.

The air conditioning was pleasantly cool in the mall and the couple sped along as fast as they could without breaking into an outright run. Wendy had slipped off her high heels and now carried them in one hand. She was barefooted for both speed and comfort. The cold floor tiles were a relief to her feet. Trying not to bash into people and so leave a trail of annoyed people bringing attention to them, they zigzagged through the dithering shoppers who were blissfully unaware of the present danger so close to them. The one suit was still trying to follow Guy and Wendy and was constantly speaking into his shirt cuff. Thankfully, he had not pulled out a weapon but, all the same, he still had them in his sight as he too weaved through the throng and was gaining on them.

Guy guessed the other dark suits would soon join the chase and he steered Wendy towards the mall's main entrance. He recalled this was the fastest way to the MTR, Hong Kong's subway system. He gambled, wondering if they could shake off their pursuers there. Looking over his shoulder, he saw that one other suit had now joined the chase. This guy had a pox scared face and tightly shaved haircut. He wasn't one of the hotel pair either. Guy guessed this one must have been covering the front entrance of the hotel. There was now four angry, radio-connected, armed Asian men in suits chasing after them and two of them had Wendy and Guy in view. These guys looked like they meant business. Guy presumed they were Korean or Chinese Triads hired by Mr Kim or his security detail and they had been commissioned to do Wendy harm.

Wendy and Guy skipped through the mall slalom like, dodging Saturday shoppers. They realized finding the police would be futile. If these killers caught up with them, they assumed they would kill whoever they needed to kill in order to honour the contract to dispatch Wendy, the thief! Guy's brain was racing, and he could feel Wendy was flagging. He thought one option was if they could dive down into the MTR system in the hope that a train was in the station then jump on just in time to have the doors close and the train pull out ahead of the suits. But, and he realised it was a big 'but', that assumed there was a train in the station already. If there were no train at the platform, and there was a two-minute wait until the next train arrived, they would be cornered by the suits with no exit options. The suits were too close. They would be upon Wendy in a matter of seconds.

Guy cursed, that plan was no use. This was Central station and the actual train platforms were still a long walk away. The Airport Express train station was closer but again they only ran every seven minutes. They reached the main entrance to the mall and the huge four lane escalators servicing the first floor from the ground floor. Guy and Wendy flew down the long escalator and reached the bottom in time for Guy to look back up and see two of the suits had reached the top already, they were only a matter of seconds behind them. Guy pulled Wendy through the mall's huge glass doors as a red Hong Kong taxi was alighting an elderly lady shopper. The couple ploughed headlong into the back of the taxi, ignoring the queue of shoppers waiting for the next taxi, and screamed at the driver, 'Drive!' The driver looked shocked and took a second to assess the situation. Guy, expecting this, shoved his hand in his jeans pocket and threw two brown HK$500 notes over to the front seat and again forcefully said, 'Drive!'

The driver saw the pair of brown notes, put the column gearshift into drive and pulled away quickly, merging with the traffic. Guy and Wendy, catching their breath, turned and looked out of the rear window in time to see the two suits running from the mall and across the pavement onto the road, merely seconds behind them. The suits stood in the road and glared at the departing taxi, catching their breath. As they did so, a black Mercedes screeched to a stop in front of them, the rear doors opened, and they jumped into the back seat of the car.

Chapter 11. Forensics

California. Saturday Afternoon.

Detective Brendon Butterfield was a minority in the San Francisco Police Department. Yes, the SFPD had its diversity ratios to adhere to, although Butterfield didn't believe his position was merely to assist those ratios. He believed he was in his job because his was good at his job. He had earnt the respect of his colleagues and his superiors. He successfully bucked every stereotype of a Californian cop. He was dark-skinned, African-American, tall, lean, powerfully built, fashionably dressed on any occasion, and obsessive about a healthy lifestyle. He wouldn't be seen dead eating a doughnut, rarely drank alcohol, and used the gym and adjacent health-food bar most days. Despite his job women found him attractive.

His ancestral route to the US was interesting. Having Nigerian origins generations ago, his kin only made it as far west as Bermuda, their slave ship being fortuitously shipwrecked on the small cluster of islands in the early 1800s. His ancestors settled in Bermuda and prospered. Then in the 1950's his grandparents made the decision to move from Bermuda to San Francisco in search of the American dream. Eventually his family made it all the way to the America's, only 200 years later than planned.

Detective Butterfield still spoke with a Bermudian accent. This legacy from his parents and their parents was often the butt of his colleagues' humour. They would mimic giving street directions in his slow Bermudian drawl, 'You gooow dooown deee rooood, den dee turn right...' He would laugh along with them, albeit a little tiresome. It was true, he didn't have a typical Californian accent, but the girls didn't seem to mind. It was an easy icebreaker, 'I love your accent. Where are you from...?' The flat vowels and T pronounced as a D in the Bermudian vernacular sounded easy going, laid-back, and somehow inspired trust. This trust people found reassuring in a cop and they would open up to him, preferably about the crime he was investigating.

Today Detective Butterfield was wearing crime scene coveralls and was carefully probing his way through the wreckage of what had once been three, average, two-storey apartments near downtown Palo Alto. The coveralls were worn on the pretence of not contaminating the crime scene, however, Butterfield was meticulous about his clothing and shoes and didn't want the blackened remnants of the apartments dirtying his expensive attire. It was bad enough that the burnt smell of the still smouldering remains would cause his suit to smell of smoke for the rest of the day. Habitually pulling up the creases at the front of his trousers so as not to stretch the expensive cloth over his knees when he crouched down, he tried picturing the apartments. He was trying to understand what on earth had happened. He looked up at McKenzie, the forensic lead who he only knew as McKenzie; he didn't have another name as far as Butterfield knew.

'Hey McKenzie. Wassup?'

'Hey! Mind your nice shoes Butterfield! This charred wood will play havoc with those fine leather polished church shoes you're wearing.'

'Yeah, yeah, mind your plastic sneakers don't melt either!' retorted Butterfield. 'What we got?'

'We've got one body. It's a Caucasian male, currently a John Doe. He's a big guy and was blown clear across the parking lot by the blast. Body's over there,' McKenzie said, as he gestured vaguely to the right with his free arm. 'It looks like he was in front of the blast when it occurred. The body also has what looks like a minimum of three gunshot wounds, maybe four, to the chest, delivered perimortem I'd say, although I'll need to do a full autopsy to be sure. There's no gas in the house and no obvious causation of the explosion so, a blast of this size, looks like explosives. I can't quite see why someone would be shot and then blown-up; seems like overkill to me. Not a gang-banger kill either I'd say. Remnants of the house are interesting though. There seems like a ton of electronics gear had been at the centre of the blast judging by the amount of metal and shrapnel strewn around.'

Unlike some other more arrogant detectives, Butterfield always held the CSI guys in high esteem. Keen to let McKenzie do his thinking for him, Butterfield asked, 'You think he was making explosives?'

'Possibly a good old-fashioned home-grown terrorist with a cause,' replied McKenzie, always happy to share his opinions. He knew the implications of what he was saying. The word 'terrorist' meant automatic involvement of the FBI. 'But in this case I'm not really sure. Bomb makers who manage to blow themselves up are usually working on, or transiting the explosives when they go off. That doesn't appear to be the case here.' McKenzie stood, looking around, he was thoughtful.

'Likewise, assuming the holes in John Doe's chest are perimortem and not because of the explosion, I'd bet he was killed first and then an explosive device was badly deployed to hide the murder.' Butterfield rubbed his tightly cropped hair as McKenzie continued. 'It's an odd one for sure. And the explosion was huge, way more than needed to destroy one murdered body. Extensive damage has been done to the two adjoining apartments as you can see. Whoever triggered the blast wasn't familiar with the handling of explosives would be my guess.'

Butterfield grunted in appreciation. He went over to inspect the body. Sure enough, he was a huge man, massively obese. The back of his body was very badly damaged from the explosion. The skin and flesh which covered it had been mostly ripped off and charred by intense heat. The smell of burnt hair and meat permeated the detective's face mask. Shrapnel from what looked like electronic components and metal casings were embedded in the remaining flesh and bone. It took three of McKenzie's CSI team to help roll the body over to see the chest wounds. Indeed, they did look like gunshots fired from a weapon at close-range. Fire had done much damage to the front of his body too, although not nearly as much as to the back, and there was less embedded shrapnel suggesting the explosion came from behind the body, the force of the blast then launching it across the carpark.

Debris from the wrecked apartments had strewn rubbish all around the neighbourhood and the cleaning crews would be a long time clearing up the mess. There were now over twenty police units, all with lights flashing, closing the surrounding streets. Multiple fire crews from Palo Alto and adjacent stations, together with the CSI trucks, blocked the neighbouring roads. The Crime Scene Investigation teams were stooped over busy collecting debris, taking photos, and documenting measurements.

'They're in for a long night,' said a rueful McKenzie. It was now mid-afternoon, and some were already erecting tents as makeshift labs to protect the unprocessed parts of the crime scene. The other members of law enforcement mingled around and speculated, unable to enter the crime scene while CSI did their work.

Butterfield was using his iPad to dialogue with his office. Seems the apartment was owned by a Jennifer Sanchez and there was no mortgage on the apartment even though Jennifer's only employment was as a waitress in a local diner. She was unmarried and lived with her son, Craig. Craig was a university dropout from University of California, Santa Cruz where he had been studying Computer

Science before dropping out. He seemed to make negligible tax returns every year, albeit they were always credible and on time. Equity Trader was his stated profession. Butterfield guessed the large charred body in the parking lot had been Craig Sanchez, however, with no priors, not even parking tickets, he didn't seem to fit the profile as a terrorist, or for gang wars, the criminal underworld, or even a robbery gone wrong.

None of this made much sense to Butterfield. There were the remains of one body in the parking lot, clearly blown 60 feet by an explosive blast, and the wreckage of three apartments, presumably triggered by an artificially created explosion. Computer racks and equipment seemed to be at the centre of the blast, and he had noticed the charred remains of a smartwatch melted onto the roasted skin of Craig's left wrist. The size of the body didn't lend itself to someone who appeared deeply health conscious. So was the smartwatch purely a fashion accessory or was this person using it for health reasons? he wondered. Furthermore, the sternum and three ribs were seemingly punctured, probably by bullet wounds.

If that weren't enough of a quandary, Butterfield sighed when he saw things were about to get even more complicated. A large black Ford SUV drove up, announcing the FBI's arrival. This could only mean a possible connection to terrorism was now implicated in Detective Brendon Butterfield's crime scene. The four suits spilled from the SUV and viewed the scene, their dark sunglasses being flipped open and positioned in practiced unison.

As Butterfield mulled the scenarios, McKenzie came out from one of the makeshift tents and wandered over to where Butterfield stood. He held up a sheet of paper with what looked like hieroglyphics scattered over a page of spectrometer readings and waved it to show Butterfield. 'We've found Semtex, Detective,' announced McKenzie with a proud smile, 'This has just got a whole lot more interesting.'

'That it has,' thought Butterfield, *'That it has!'*

Detective Brendon Butterfield raised himself up to his full intimidating height, thrust his broad shoulders back, which he noticed were still aching slightly from the previous day's gym session, and walked calmly across to the black SUV. *'Might as well confront this head on,'* he thought, as he removed the protective coveralls and shoe covers.

'Good afternoon,' he said, with an easy smile to the assembled FBI squad. They had done him the courtesy of not crossing the taped police line yet. 'I'm Detective Brendon Butterfield, SFPD. I'm leading this investigation.'

The FBI squad flashed badges and the older tall grey-haired agent introduced himself as Senior Agent Mick Adamson then quickly introduced his three other colleagues, who nodded at the mention of their names but remained hidden behind their dark glasses. Adamson went on, 'We had reports of an explosion and a possible terrorist involvement.' As Adamson scanned the quiet residential street in sleepy Palo Alto, his raised eyebrows betrayed his scepticism that this was a hot bed of ISIS activity. He was also shrewd enough to not jump too quickly to preformed opinions.

'Glad you got here so quickly,' said Butterfield, feeling friendly, 'I was about to call you in. We may well have a terrorist angle here. My forensic team advised me this mess,' he gestured vaguely around, 'was as a result of Semtex. We have one body, presumed to be Craig Sanchez, a 23-year-old day trader who lived at this address with his single mother. He appears to have received several gunshot wounds to the chest prior to the explosion. Forensics are still processing the scene; however, it appears we have a lot of electronics, presumably computer equipment, that seems to have been close to the origins of the blast.'

'So, we have Mr Sanchez getting shot and the killer then rigs a bomb to the computers Mr Sanchez used for his day trading. Dubious trades or money laundering possibly?' offered Adamson. His underlings were tapping notes into their smartphones.

'Possibly,' agreed Butterfield nodding slowly. 'Mr Sanchez has no priors and no known affiliations to any radical or political organisations. In fact, we're struggling to get anything on him at all. For someone who lived on the web, we've remarkably little intel on him.'

'Mind if we look around?' asked Adamson.

'Sure, but stay out of the CSI guy's way. You can have a full copy of my report in a couple of days when the labs come back with their finals.' With this concluding statement, Butterfield walked back to his car and waved farewell to McKenzie, who looked heavenwards while gesturing at the FBI agents.

Butterfield planned to drive north on the Interstate 280, back to San Francisco. The 101 would be more direct, however, traffic would be snarled up with commuters this time of day. He was based out of the 3rd Street precinct in the city. It suited him, being close to downtown and his small tasteful apartment. As he drove the sun was getting lower now to his left and the harsh Californian air temperature was cooling down, promising a much more comfortable and balmy evening ahead. Regrettably, Butterfield foresaw he would have no chance to enjoy this evening, having to write up the case notes with what he had found out today. He couldn't see how this would playout yet and he was missing a motive for the murder.

Shooting a guy and then rigging the place with explosives didn't make a lot of sense. If the objective was to kill someone then presumably the killer had done that with the chest shots. A further headshot would have definitively concluded the job, quickly and easily. If the objective had been to destroy evidence, why not simply torch or bomb the place, keeping the occupant alive long enough to be killed in the fire. The death could then be made to look accidental, albeit suspicious. A professional would have done that. His phone rang and, by pressing the button on the steering wheel of his BMW, he answered the call, muting his music at the same time.

'McKenzie, hey, what's happening? Found something?'

'You might want to get back here, Butterfield. A woman claiming to be the owner of the apartment and presumably the mother of the vic' has just turned-up, she's rather hysterical.'

He glanced at the dashboard clock. 'Thanks McKenzie. Sit her down and I'll be there in ten.'

He swung the white BMW around and gave the M6's engine the good news. The car launched itself up the road as if sensing the urgency like a greyhound out of the traps. Butterfield loved this car. The engine growled, the assisted gear changes were instant, and the acceleration pushed him deep into the black leather seat. The best bit of his job was his ability to really use his car to its full potential on the city streets and, while not technically legal, his badge relieved him of any awkwardness. His widening white smile contrasted to the colour of his skin and his music was back on and loud.

Jennifer Sanchez was distraught. She had come home from her shift at the diner and was unable to pull up at her apartment due to the congestion of police cars and emergency vehicles blocking the road. She had run under the police tape and was close to tripping over the debris of what was left of her apartment when one of the CSI team caught her around the waist and steered her away from the remains of the building.

She had blurted out who she was and demanded to know where Craig, her son, was. At that moment she had spotted the ominous blanket covering a large bulbous shape 60 feet away in the parking lot. The investigators were still combing the area around it. She had run over to the human sized hump and, before anyone could stop her, had pulled back the plastic sheet covering the remains. She gagged and covered her mouth, unable to even scream. Jenny swayed, sank to her knees and wailed. 'My son!' was all she could say, repeatedly.

Butterfield parked the M6 as close as he could get. The acrid smell of hot tyre rubber and brake dust was immensely satisfying. He closed the door and walked briskly towards the sound of wailing. This was Jenny Sanchez he presumed, owner of the apartment and mother of the deceased. If enjoying his car was the best bit of the job, he knew what was about to happen was the worst! He flashed his badge to the distraught woman and introduced himself as the investigating officer. Jenny nodded in a state of shock. Butterfield used his gentlest Bermudian tones to illicit a calm confidence. His first step was to get her to relax and focus on him. Shock was a terrible emotion, the brain did the strangest things, and he needed to ask Jenny questions.

He walked Jenny towards the back of an ambulance which had its doors open for business but no customers as yet. He sat her on the rear step, shaking his head at the hovering paramedic. The clinical smell of antiseptic intermingled with the faint smell of burning, the remnants of the explosion and Jenny's apartment. There were no fires now; only the charred shards of two people's lives, which lay scattered randomly over the surrounding area. Jenny rested her elbows on her knees, put her palms over her eyes, and sobbed uncontrollably. Brendon Butterfield silently offered a clean white handkerchief from his pocket. He always carried one for such occasions. The act of giving a small considered gift to a distressed woman, no matter how tough she was, created a subtle bond. She was now subconsciously indebted to him for the tiny gesture. It made the predictable questions easier to answer when they came. Detective Butterfield waited a full five minutes for Ms Sanchez to regain a modicum of dignity before he sat on the step of the ambulance next to her and gently started asking the questions.

#

By early evening, his interviews had achieved as much as he felt they would. Brendon Butterfield was in his local gym benching 120lb with his Jewish Israeli friend, Eitan. They would often meet in the evening and, while having little in common professionally, they both enjoyed the same gym discipline, frequently spotting for each other when their routines coincided. Brendon had little idea about cybersecurity despite Eitan's enthusiastic attempts to explain what he did for a living. Eitan, who worked for one of the many cybersecurity start-ups in Silicon Valley, wouldn't tire of trying to educate Brendon. Brendon suspected Eitan's ramblings were more to do with him defining his own thinking than trying to educate the slow-learning Brendon. The fact that Brendon had sought out Eitan to work out with this evening wasn't entirely coincidental.

'So, explain to me again how hackers work?' asked Brendon nonchalantly, as Eitan grunted through his tenth repetition. Eitan didn't need inviting twice. He launched into his favourite subject. After a fifteen-minute monologue about code kiddies, white hats, grey hats, black hats, hacktivists, state actors, deep webs, dark webs, malwares, trojans, anonymizers, and his grandmother's use of social media, Brendon had at least a seminal idea of what hackers were and how they worked, although he felt the last point was somewhat off-topic.

'Then it's quite possible, a hacker who was a good coder could simply sit at home, write malware, and use it themselves or sell it to others to use for a considerable profit,' continued Brendon, 'and us guy's, I mean law enforcement, would be none the wiser?'

'Exactly right,' said Eitan, warming to his subject. 'Hackers use VPNs, sorry, Virtual Private Networks to try and hide their online movements and anonymizers to exploit other people's computers so that, even if the trail can be followed, it's hard to figure out whose trail it is.'

'It's almost impossible to capture these people then?'

'Depends how good they are,' smiled Eitan, his dark cropped beard breaking into a grin. 'Like any profession, some hackers are good and others less so. Good hackers love to play games with law enforcement, leaving breadcrumb trails to see if they can be followed. Law enforcement and cybersecurity companies, like ours, lay virtual honeypots to try to trap the hackers. For the most part, it's all done anonymously. The goal of the hacker is to not be caught and the goal of cybersecurity firms is to prevent the malware from working thus stopping the hack or the attack. Actually catching an individual hacker is much, much harder. This is where you guys come in and it depends how badly you want the hacker and how naughty he or she has been. What really makes it hard is international jurisdictions. Even if you could trace a hacker, to say Romania, North Korea, or China, what are the chances of you prosecuting a case there? Close to zero I'd guess.'

Brendon and Eitan were so deep into their discussion they had forgotten the weights and drifted towards the fruit bar to order high protein shakes, so thick you needed a spoon to 'drink' one.

'Let's say I'm a hacker and I get raided by the police, hypothetically of course,' stressed Brendon, 'How would I quickly remove evidence that I was a hacker?'

Eitan clapped his hands together, provoking a few glances from other patrons. 'I knew it!' roared Eitan embarrassingly loud. 'Palo Alto today. You're involved!' Eitan's huge smile betrayed the fact that, while Brendon had positioned this as an innocent conversation between two friends, Eitan had all along suspected there was more to this than idle curiosity or small talk on Brendon's part.

Brendon was momentarily irritated he had been so transparently caught out, but his big black Bermudian face creased into a laugh too. Play-punching Eitan on the arm, he said, 'I'm unable to comment on any ongoing Police investigations. You'll surely be the first to know when I can,' giving the standard stock answer the police always gave the press during an investigation.

'Look,' said Eitan, charged up again at the excitement of helping in a real-life police investigation, 'code is written on computers and stored on their local hard drives and probably local backups. Deleting files and records never truly removes the traces and experts can recover even deleted files. Hackers know this. To really remove all traces of software in a hurry, you need powerful magnets or a huge hot fire to completely trash the memory of a computer. Physically frying the computer's memory is the only effective way to remove all evidence. Do you think today's explosion in Palo Alto was a hacker waving goodbye?'

'You saw it on the news?'

'Online, yeah. Police are saying an explosion destroyed a residential street and the one death was that of a self-employed day trader. Failed day traders usually put a bullet through the roof of their mouths. Taking out the whole street is plain excessive. There must be more to it than this!'

'I'm beginning to think so,' confirmed Brendon quietly.

Eitan and Brendon parted on the steps of the gym. The evening was beautifully warm and breezy, cooling them after the workout. Brendon's parting request was to ask Eitan not to mention this conversation to anyone else. Then he sat on the steps and checked for new emails on his phone. McKenzie had sent through some further evidence although nothing shed any more light, only more detail.

Jenny had formally identified the obese body as her son, Craig. The Semtex belonged to a batch stolen from a demolition site six months ago in Orange Country. At best he could tell trying to reassemble the scene, the Semtex, along with large iron magnets, appeared to have been placed around an array of computer equipment in one of the bedrooms and this was the centre of the explosion. Lastly, Craig had died of four well positioned gunshot wounds to the chest, fired at close range shortly before the explosion.

Butterfield typed back a quick and genuine note of thanks, knowing how the CSI guys loved to be stroked for their genius. He stretched and jumped into his BMW M6 to head back to his police precinct on 3rd Street to start writing his report.

Meanwhile, Eitan headed home on his CycloCross bike, mulling on what he could piece together from what little Brendon had implied more than told him. This was exciting; he had to share it. Eitan had been in California for only three years. He liked San Francisco but missed his native Tel Aviv. In San Francisco, there was a large Jewish community, good kosher food he could eat, and lots of bars to enjoy, however, San Francisco didn't have the edge of Tel Aviv. He missed his close circle of Israeli friends with whom he had done his obligatory military training and then worked with for a couple of years in Unit 8200.

Once home, he hung the bike on the purpose built bike rack secured to the wall of his apartment, slumped on the sofa with his latest Apple computer on his knees, and set up a VPN to his old brother-in-arms, Tal Bar-Lev, in Tel Aviv. Despite Brendon's parting warning, Eitan thought Tal would enjoy this story.

Tel-Aviv. Early Sunday Morning.

He hated this shift. One of his colleagues, Ziv, had pleaded to swap shifts and Tal Bar-Lev begrudgingly agreed. He was a team player, but it had been a hard decision. When his colleague Ziv had called, Dorit, his girlfriend, was fast asleep in bed next to him, comfortable wearing her faded army green singlet and shorts. Now it was 2:00 a.m. and Tal was back in his claustrophobic cubicle in Unit 8200's facility in Tel Aviv and struggling to wake-up.

Predictably, after their one beer, Dorit had dragged him back to her apartment that night and promptly made demands on his body, demands he had only been too pleased to concede. He had only had two hours sleep before Ziv called him with some lame excuse and a promise to cover his arse at some unspecified point in the future when he needed it. Tal groaned agreement and slipped out of bed carefully, kissed a still sleeping Dorit on the forehead as he did so. He scribbled a note for Dorit and made his way back to the imposing multi-storey brick Kirya building that housed his division of Unit 8200. 'This shift is going to need a lot of coffee!' he groaned to himself, refilling the coffee maker in the communal canteen and rubbing his already sore eyes.

Tal was settling into the shift's routine of reading surveillance reports, watching satellite feeds, and monitoring the activities of several persons of interest when his screen pinged an incoming chat dialogue. 'Can you talk?' flashed in a chat room on the bottom right of Tal's monitor. It was Eitan, his friend in California. Tal glanced at the world clocks on the wall and discovered it was still early evening there. He was rather envious of Eitan if he admitted it. They had studied together at the Technion Israel Institute of Technology and then both found themselves with Unit 8200, the cyber-intelligence division of the Israeli army. Tal enjoyed the work and had opted to stick with his job in Unit 8200, possibly in part due to Dorit, whereas Eitan had left after the obligatory two years and got into the commercial side of cybersecurity, landing a plum job which took him off to San Francisco. Tal also suspected Eitan had connections with, and did occasional work for MOSSAD, the Israeli intelligence agency, however, this was never discussed.

Tal hit the connect button and positioned his headset back over his ears. They seemed to have developed the habit of speaking in Hebrew when chatting over the secure VPN. Tal would typically multitask and type away at other work while his friend talked. They started with the pleasant formalities of work, life, family, and, from Eitan of course, share-prices' and money. Eitan then asked if Tal had seen the news regarding an explosion in Palo Alto. Tal's nimble fingers instantly flipped to a browser and found the story. Quickly scanning the piece and sensing Eitan's change in tone, he asked Eitan the reason for the question.

'I'm friends with the cop investigating the explosion,' bragged Eitan. 'He thinks it's very suspicious. No obvious reason for the blast, no apparent motive, and in a street with no gas main.' He went on, 'looks like the guy was officially a day trader but he went to an awful lot of trouble to make sure his computers were totally destroyed today. He vaporized his own apartment and the two either side. Looks to me like the centre of the explosion were the computers themselves suggesting a deliberate explosive device.'

This piqued Tal's interest. Someone going to the extent of physically blowing up their computers suggested they had a lot of serious shit to hide. Tal recalled a few weeks before, when he was following a paedophile code-named Wolf who had been actively looking to source Semtex. He had even asked Dorit about Semtex, the malleable plastic explosive. 'What's the name of the cop, Eitan? I'll see what I can find out.'

'Detective Brendon Butterfield, SFPD,' obliged Eitan. 'Sounds like the FBI are also interested,' he added helpfully.

'Leave it with me Eitan,' Tal replied as he killed the VPN.

Forty-five minutes later, he was wide awake and intrigued by his new, self-appointed mission, his fresh coffee was cold and untouched. Tal was reading the email exchanges between the forensics CSI investigator, McKenzie, and Detective Brendon Butterfield.

Over the years, Israeli Intelligence had left multiple backdoors into countless telecom networks all over the world. If the traffic was encrypted this made reading emails difficult and required a different approach to surveillance. In these case's it required a breach of the physical devices at either end of the network so the mails could be read before encryption or after decryption. It was not an insurmountable problem although tiresome and time consuming. If the traffic were unencrypted all that was needed was a little deep packet inspection and the trillions of emails sent around the world daily could be scanned and read, with a bit of filtering and fiddling. Keyword searches like 'Butterfield', 'Palo Alto', 'explosion' and 'day trader' soon revealed a slew of dialogue. Some dialogue was encrypted, presumably the FBI, and some was unencrypted, in this case Detective Butterfield's dialogue with McKenzie the CSI lead.

Tal began to compile a dossier. It was clear that the casualty, one Craig Sanchez, was a self-employed Equity Trader, as far as the IRS was concerned, who lived with his mother in a quiet neighbourhood of Palo Alto, south of San Francisco. His body was found to have been blown through his front door and across the road by an explosion in their apartment that originated in a bedroom filled with sophisticated computer equipment. Mr Sanchez had died just before the explosion from four well-placed gunshot wounds to the chest. The accuracy of the shots suggested someone very familiar with small firearms and that it was quite possibly a professional kill. The forensic scientist, McKenzie, suspected a health monitoring device as a function of a smartwatch on the deceased's wrist actually triggered the explosion, which was itself caused by the plastic explosive Semtex. It's likely, large electromagnets were primed to first scramble the hard drives on the computers before the Semtex completely obliterated them. It seemed Mr Sanchez was very keen to cover his digital footprints.

This all rang a bell. It was the Semtex connection that did it for Tal, remembering the conversation with Dorit. He consulted his recent notes, a probable hacker of interested, mascaraing as a day trader, and now murdered. Furthermore, an explosion resulting from Semtex. 'Ah yes, here it is' he said to himself seeing the reference he'd made to the hacker who surfed extreme pornography on the Dark Web. Assuming he was ahead of the police and the FBI, Tal was able to add to his suspicions that Craig Sanchez was also the black hat hacker known as Wolf.

Wolf had successfully hacked multiple organizations for his own personal financial gain, was a hacker-for-hire, and a compulsive viewer of paedophile pornography. In addition, Wolf liked to sign his work so as to enjoy recognition and notoriety in the cliquey black hat forums. He concluded that Wolf was killed either because of a hack involving stealing money from some particularly unpleasant people or to silence him for malware he had developed where the customer needed complete anonymity and no audit trail. Tal would need to share this with his superiors. It was perhaps routine, but it was interesting and might have wider political ramifications.

As Tal, Eitan and every other Israeli understood, Israel was formally and very publicly at war with neighbouring Palestine. It's a messy and likely unsolvable situation of territorial control and religious ideology. Subtler than this were the time-worn enemies of the

Jewish faith across the world. These enemies included the Arab states and their various Muslim factions as well as individuals, usually prominent Christians in the West, who despised Jews for a plethora of reasons and would be happy to see harm come to them and, by default, to their homeland of Israel. Combined, all this meant Israel had few friends and even their friends needed to be carefully understood. The result was the birth of one of the most sophisticated and progressive intelligence agencies in the world. One that was in a constant state of alert. The cyberthreats Unit 8200 followed were sometimes state sponsored, often real, and happened in real time.

Curiously, as Tal turned his researcher brainpower to investigating Wolf, he tripped over some interesting dialogue in an old Dark Web forum that has been archived a few months previously. The dialogue was between a hacker he believed was the same Wolf, aka Craig Sanchez in Palo Alto, and what appeared to be a Korean Intelligence Services operative, identifiable only as Talon and based in Seoul, South Korea.

It seemed Talon had a particular interest in missile launch systems for the Hwasong-7, or the Rodong-1 as it was called in North Korea, and how the launch protocols might be hacked. Tal noted these missile systems were a North Korean adaption of an old Russian design, however, they still formed the basis of North Korea's mid-range missile defence systems and were believed to be the medium range delivery vehicle for North Korea's alleged nuclear warheads. It was true there was scepticism about North Korea's ability to actually deliver such a weapon; Israel's enemies had been lining up to buy them from the North Koreans for years with no success. However, Tal considered, someone keen to hack such a system was interesting and it presumed some inside knowledge of North Korea's missile capabilities.

'Was it possible that Talon was North Korean?' wondered Tal. Craig Sanchez's death had just gotten very interesting. Tal, being the diligent researcher, compiled his data, extrapolated and explained his conclusions, then marked his dossier "urgent" and sent this up to his superiors for their deliberation.

Chapter 13. Sheppy

Hong Kong. Saturday Afternoon.

The smelly roads in Hong Kong around Central, Wan Chai, and Causeway Bay are always heavily congested on Saturday afternoons. Wendy saw today was no exception. A heavy, humid mugginess added to the sticky heat and exhaust pollution. The city sleeps-in Saturday mornings but by late afternoon Hong Kong is alive. The streets and malls are busy as people go about their shopping chores or meet-up with friends. Eager students study together in coffee shops, heads down in huddles. Women drift like lost souls around over air-conditioned shopping malls checking the latest fashion's and sale prices. Young men meet their friends and play basketball in the public parks while older men enthusiastically watch on. A common theme to all of them is food.

Hong Kong has a multitude of restaurants packed with people eating or waiting to eat. The better dim sum and noodle shops will have lengthy queues outside, adding pavement congestion to the road congestion. Women waft their faces with fans in a useless attempt to cool themselves in the August heat and to disperse the unremitting smell of traffic fumes. Social eating underpins the fabric of society in Hong Kong and this is never more apparent than on Saturday afternoons and evenings. As the sun begins to set, taking the sky through all shades of orange, blue's and purple's, the Hong Kong cityscape becomes a Benetton of dancing neon colours overlaid with a rhythm of car horns and shop music spilling out over the busy pavements. Millions of people leave their cramped apartments and take to the streets to find somewhere to dine.

Under less stressful circumstances Guy would usually take time to enjoy this moment of the day. Sitting somewhere, perhaps with a cup of tea or a cold beer, purely to enjoy the beat of the city, the smells, the noise, the colours, and to watch people bustling about their business like busy ants. When viewed with detachment it's a beautiful, objective, and even an amusing view of humanity. Right now though, he was in a cold sweat and panicking. He had told the driver, after several changes of mind, to take them to Time Square in Causeway Bay, the heart of congestion. They had to shake off the black Mercedes. At least this taxi driver was quite young and appreciated there was a sense of urgency albeit he was not fully across all the facts yet, something that was about to be rudely corrected.

Guy told the driver it was an emergency. 'No, we don't need the hospital,' and repeated the driver could keep the HK$1,000 so long as he went as fast as his could. Given the fare would typically be about HK$50 this was probably the best tip he would get all month. Stepping up to the challenge the young driver was weaving his red taxi between lanes and running amber lights were possible. This incurred frustrated honks from other drivers, but these were duly ignored with the oblivion only learnt at a Taxi Driving Training School.

The Mercedes was struggling to keep up and a gap between the two cars was emerging. Having hastily picked up the other two suits outside the IFC building, the Mercedes had quickly sped after the taxi carrying Guy and Wendy. Until Wendy and Guy's taxi driver had fully understood the situation, assisted by the HK$1.000, the Mercedes had covered the distance between the two cars quickly, leaving only three or four other cars between them. But now the taxi driver was getting into his stride, the gap through the congested traffic was more like six or seven cars separating the hunter from his prey.

Multiple identical red taxis were joining the melee of traffic at one intersection as they sped eastward along the wide Lung Wo Road, and Guy hoped perhaps the Mercedes driver would get confused as to which one they were in. He and Wendy were keeping low on the backseat, peering out of the rear window trying to watch for their black pursuer. The daylight was fading now. Blurred shades of grey and neon reflections were taking over from the daytime sunlit definitions. The suit driving the Mercedes had the same thought and realised he needed a way to easily identify the taxi Guy and Wendy were in.

To his horror, Guy saw a suit standing up above the height of the cars about six cars back. His first thought was they were out of their Mercedes and were sprinting along the road trying to outrun the moving traffic. Then he realized the suit was in the middle of the lane and way higher than the other car roofs. The suit had opened the Mercedes sunroof and was standing up through it to get a better view of the cars ahead. Steadying himself and getting a purchase by wedging one foot against the lip of the sunroof he could raise himself to his maximum height. The suit suddenly pulled a firearm from his shoulder holster previously hidden by his dark jacket. He aimed and fired two quick shots over the roofs of the six cars separating them and into the rear window of the taxi.

Glass exploded into the taxi. Wendy and the driver simultaneously shrieked. Guy had seen this coming and had grabbed Wendy's head, pushing her hard down into the back seat and throwing himself over the top of her upper body. There was no sign of the bullets actually entering the taxi but the sound of the gunshot and the glass shattering was deafening. The terrified occupants of the taxi were showered with small crystal-like pieces of glass.

'Drive!' barked Guy.

It took a moment for the driver to react. The HK$1,000 tip was now the least of his concerns! He quickly pushed the driving column gearshift into a lower gear while gunning the accelerator.

The taxi's back wheels began spinning and grey smoke belched from them as they tried to get purchase on the tarmac. The taxi slewed from side to side, sliding sideways as it careered across the incoming lane of traffic. His adrenalin had kicked in now, as the taxi driver regained control and skilfully dodged the scattering cars while cutting across a six-lane intersection and briefly driving against the flow of oncoming traffic.

The Mercedes braked hard and attempted to follow, however, the rogue taxi had upset the traffic flow and the line of oncoming traffic was confused and had lost its natural equilibrium. Cars and vans began to swerve in all directions. A large double-decker bus, covered in the yellow livery of some cosmetic advertisement, its momentum carrying it way too fast to react in time, slammed hard into the side of the Mercedes bringing it to an abrupt halt. Broken glass, black plastic, and wing-mirrors sprayed across the road accompanied by a loud, deep crunch as the car was shunted along the road. The Mercedes' airbags instantly exploded enveloping the occupants, all except one, the suit, who had fired the gun. He was still stood half out of the sunroof trying to regain his balance.

With the force of the bus impact he was ripped clear of the car and thrown headlong against the side of the bus his arms flailing and his face set in horror as he realised his hopeless fate. As if in slow motion, his broken body concertinaed onto the wall of the bus, crumpling on impact with a sickening squelch, the body first cracking and then bursting like a balloon. It hung momentarily, a red smear against the yellow bus, then fell to the ground in a mangled, bloody heap to the horror of the involuntary onlookers.

The young taxi driver, now driving more by panic than thought, steered the snaking taxi back across the intersection and onto the lane heading in their original direction. All the traffic behind them had now stopped due to the bus accident. He was shrieking incoherently in Cantonese and continued driving east joining Gloucester Road. The traffic was heavy on Gloucester Road and the driver was forced to slow. He then pulled over to the side, shaking uncontrollably. His adrenalin was waning, and shock was setting in. Guy looked around to gather his bearings. They were close to Causeway Bay, good. He had the embryo of an idea.

The taxi driver was going to be of no help from here on, still babbling and banging his steering wheel with his clenched fists. Guy opened his passenger door, grabbed Wendy's shaking hand, and helped her from the car as fragments of broken glass fell from the creases of her clothing. She too was shocked but seemed unhurt. Guy could now hear sirens in the far distance. The traffic on Gloucester Road was slowly streaming passed them as normal and no one was paying them any attention. The remnants of the sunset still brightened the far western sky over Kowloon and the evening was turning fast into dusk.

Guy opened the taxi's front door, the acrid smell of tyre rubber still pungent. The two HK$500 bills were still beside the young driver on the front seat. A quick inspection confirmed the driver was unhurt, only shocked. The driver stared back at him, wide-eyed, his mouth still moving but now with no sound coming out. Guy reached into his pocket and pulled a further two HK$500 notes from his fold of cash. He removed his handkerchief from the other pocket and wiped them over quickly. Using the handkerchief to hold them, he passed the notes to the driver who instinctively accepted the two bills like a beggar receiving alms. Guy picked up the two on the seat that would still have his fingerprints on them and placed them back into his pocket. The HK$1,000 wouldn't nearly cover the cost of the rear window but it was a generous tip for such a short, albeit traumatic journey.

Wendy had put her shoes back on and was standing on the pavement, she was closer to Guy's height again. For such a manic afternoon she looked remarkably composed. She's a strong woman, he thought, lesser people would have gone to pieces before now. He looked at her, looking for signs of distress. She held his gaze in return, her dark eyes searching his as if for answers. Discretely he had wiped the door handles of the taxi with the handkerchief and thrust it back into his jeans pocket.

Hong Kong immigration used fingerprints for biometric security, therefore he assumed the police had access to everyone's fingerprints. He couldn't clearly recall all the things they had touched so he at least wiped down the obvious. Perhaps he was being paranoid because they hadn't actually done anything wrong, however, given they had unknown Asian hitmen chasing after them and shooting-up Wendy's hotel room doors and taxi windows, he assumed avoiding the police was probably wise until they had a clear plan.

Guy glanced back down the road and startled, 'Surely not!' Wendy, sniffing a problem followed his gaze. Quite clearly, 200 yards away two men in dark suits were running towards them.

Guy groaned loudly, 'what the…, shoes off again dear. We're not out of this quite yet!'

They ran across the three-lane carriageway dodging cars and trucks to get to the Causeway Bay side of the road, hoping the slow-moving traffic would delay their pursuers. Scrambling over the concrete reservation in the middle, they dodged cars on the even busier westbound carriageway bringing them down on the Causeway Bay side of the Gloucester Road. They looked back. Their pursuers were doing the same. Cars were sounding their horns and breaking to avoid the crazy men. Guy guessed the Mercedes was undrivable and perhaps two of the suits were injured and put out of action.

154

Regardless, these two had continued on foot and were now running, fast. They must tire soon he hoped.

Wendy and Guy joined the throng of pedestrians on the pavement, ducking and diving between them. The suits were still following although they were not catching up. If anything, they were falling back. They must be getting breathless Guy thought; however, they were fit, probably military trained, and very determined. Guy and Wendy ran between the building which had once been the famous Excelsior Hotel and the adjacent shopping mall. Guy suddenly grabbed Wendy's arm and dragged her into a dark stairwell. They were both panting. The dirty stairwell lead down into an underground carpark.

'We can't hide here,' she panted, 'they're not far behind!'

'We're not going to hide here. Follow me!'

Unbeknown to many people in Hong Kong there is a passageway that runs under the busy Gloucester Road adjacent to the old Excelsior Hotel to the harbour front. It's a small tunnel, only tall enough and wide enough for two people abreast. It carries water pipes, telecom lines, and rats, and it links one side of Gloucester Road to the other. The passageway emerges on the harbour front where the landmark Noon Day Gun is situated. A quaint historical tradition in Hong Kong is the firing of one round, every day at noon, from an old naval gun facing out across Hong Kong's famous Victoria Harbour.

Through the tunnel they carefully ran, Wendy prodded on by Guy. Guy was banking on the suits neither seeing them access the tunnel nor knowing of the tunnel's existence. Wendy and Guy stopped short of exiting the tunnel on the harbour side, waited, and listened. Hands on knees they bent double and gasped to catch their breath.

Minutes passed as they continued to listen. The tunnel was empty. Their breathing returning to normal. No one had followed them through the tunnel. It worked! They had given their pursuers the slip.

Guy was thoughtful, now they had time to figure out what to do next. Wendy was rubbing her sore and raw feet. Guy looked sympathetically at Wendy then asked for her mobile phone. Removing his own from his back pocket he added them together. He turned both phones off and looked about, feeling around behind some exposed thick iron water pipes running alongside the wall in the tunnel at head height. Guy found a concealed dry place behind a rusty bracket. He hid the phones as well as he could then turned and emerged from the tunnel.

Wendy looked around, at the tunnel behind them and across the black water of the harbour. The lights of Kowloon beautifully illuminated the Kowloon skyline and the reflections danced on the water. 'What now?' she asked.

'I have an idea,' said Guy. They turned left and walked along the harbour front towards the lights of the Royal Hong Kong Yacht Club. The evening air was still warm and the marina to their right was full of beautiful yachts becalmed on the inky black water of the storm shelter. They followed the harbour wall round as it snaked right into the yacht club itself.

'Just look like you belong,' suggested Guy. They wandered through the front door of the Yacht Club and up the green carpeted stairs through into the club's trophy decorated bar. They paused to look around then headed on outside to the bar's airy veranda. Wendy had her shoes back on and seeing her tousled reflection in a trophy cabinet instinctively toyed with her hair in a vain attempt at dignity.

On the veranda they looked around again like they were expecting to meet friends, so they aroused no suspicion. Guy spotted a table with a couple of half-finished drinks the waiter hadn't yet cleared. He grabbed them and pressed one into Wendy's hand. Below them, metal security gates separated the club buildings from the pontoons. The pontoons were used to reach the yachts fortunate enough to have a berth linked by a pontoon. These lucky skippers didn't need a club sampan to ferry them to and from their mooring.

Guy held Wendy's free hand and they meandered back down the stairs. An electronic keycard operated the lock on the gates. Guy was careful to time their approach with a skipper coming off the pontoon towards the clubhouse. Raising his glass to the skipper, Guy bid him a good evening then grabbed Wendy's waist as she wobbled convincingly on her high heels. She grinned at the skipper, wordlessly raising her lopsided glass too, with a naughty smile and the hint of a wink. The yacht owner scanned Wendy appreciatively, smiled back warmly, and held open the heavy metal gate for them, bidding the pair of them a good evening and assuming full well they would.

Guy led Wendy along the floating pontoon. Her shoes were back in her hands and the cool wood soothed her sore feet. They walked along the pontoon until Guy found *Sheppy*, a Prestige 500 belonging to his old mate Mike. The flybridge motor yacht was absolutely beautiful; fifty foot of pure white hedonistic luxury. Guy's familiarity with the Royal Hong Kong Yacht Club was largely thanks to Mike who moored *Sheppy* there. Mike loved his boat although rarely used it and even more rarely spent any money maintaining it. A couple of times a year Mike would rally a few mates and, in exchange for a few hours giving it a good clean-up, Mike would produce slabs of ice cold beers, an extensive cheese board, and fire-up the two outrageously powerful Volvo engines and take her for a spin around the harbour, weather permitting.

Having done this on a number of occasions Guy was very familiar with the boat. He knew the lock to the cabin was faulty and sat there more for decoration than function. Wobbling the lock a few times to ease it free, he slid open the hatch, and the lower door. Careful not to be observed, he helped Wendy down the steps and into the dark, spacious cabin below.

Guy fumbled for the switches in the darkness. He located the small emergency light that illuminated the master lighting panel thus allowing him to flip on all the lights. The inside of the yacht's cabin came alive. The scene was one of opulent comfort. The deep pile mushroom coloured carpets screamed out to be stroked, while the deep white leather sofas beckoned to be sprawled upon. Subtle up lighting accentuated the tastefully fitted white ash and teak fixture. Helping her down the last few steps Guy welcomed Wendy in and closed the hatch behind them. Wendy, in awe of the yacht, slumped onto a white sofa and massaged her sore feet. Guy opened the fridge door to find a bottle of chilled white wine. He poured two glasses.

'We're safe now,' sighed Guy, careful not to say 'you're safe.' She needed to know she was not alone and, despite the mess she was in, he had now made it as much his problem as it was hers.

Sat on the large comfortable sofa rubbing her chaffed feet, Wendy looked suddenly tired. Guy passed her a glass of the chilled Chardonnay he had found and they chinked glasses. She gave him a weak smile. It was only 8:00 p.m. but the day had been manic and they were both now quite exhausted. The last couple of hours had been a blur of fear and adrenalin.

Guy slumped next to Wendy and said, 'Well today has been a day full of surprises. I never predicted any of this when I woke up this morning.'

Wendy looked sheepish and was about to apologise again but knew it was pointless. She had nearly got them both killed and it was unfair to Guy. After all, despite a certain chemistry between them and a shared sense of humour, they were still only work colleagues.

They slowly relaxed, both enjoyed the wine in silence for a while, neither finding the words nor wanting to talk, both calming down from the exertion of the chase. All credit to Mike. He kept a well-stocked cellar, thought Guy whilst again admiring the fit out of *Sheppy*. The wine was both cool, delicious and very welcome. Guy would replace it he privately pledged. He was about to give Wendy's glass a top up when she asked, 'Is it possible to get freshened up on this boat?'

'Sure, let me show you how it all works,' Guy said, as he led her by the hand carefully down spiralling steps to the master suite. The huge room was filled with a large king size bed covered in fresh oyster coloured sheets. The rest of the room bore identically coloured fittings and décor to the cabin above. The stylish lighting though was more discrete and tastefully toned down giving the bedroom a seductive appeal. There were wave shaped portholes above the waterline at eye level presumably giving a great view when out of the berth, although now they simply looked onto the yacht's hulls moored on either side of *Sheppy*.

Guy showed her how to use the shower in the equally luxurious head. This was finished off with gold coloured taps and fittings. He was pleased to see Mike, more likely one of Mike's female guests, had been thoughtful enough to ensure the shower was well stocked with feminine body washes, shampoos, conditioners, and an assortment of other apothecarial potions only a woman would know what to do with. He also noticed the head was well stocked with plenty of fluffy clean towels. Guy left Wendy to her shower and returned to the plush lounge deck above to refill his wine glass.

Guy's eyelids were drooping when sometime later Wendy's voice yelled up the steps between the two levels inviting Guy to take a shower. He came back down with Wendy's recharged Chardonnay. She was wrapped in a plush full-sized white bath towel while drying her hair with another. She smiled her thanks back up at him as she took the glass and paused the drying to take a sip of the chilled wine.

Guy too was grateful to let the hot water wash away the day's sweat and fear. He had no clear plan as to how to get them out of this predicament, although right now, in the luxury of this environment, he didn't want to think about it. He was relieved to have lost the dark-suited goons and be in a safe place where they wouldn't be found while they figured this problem out.

Clean and scrubbed, Guy emerged from the head with his damp towel wrapped around his waist. Wendy was still sat on the edge of the bed where he had left her, her hair sufficiently dry now. She stood up and stepped towards him.

'Now, where was I,' she murmured, her arms enveloping his neck. She moved closer and reared up on tiptoes to kiss Guy full on the lips for the second time that day. The towel fell away revealing her perfectly naked body, pinched waist, and flawless soft skin. This time the kiss was loving, not the aggressive head-on collision of the morning. It was deep, timeless, and seductive. Their tongues discovering each other's while their hands instinctively ran over the others body. She liked the width of his shoulders and firmness of the muscles beneath. He loved the curve of her rounded, soft bottom and, when he stooped to kiss her breast, the gasp of delight as she threw her head back, arching her back and pushing her chest fully forwards. Her nipples were sensitive, and she loved having them kissed. Wendy pulled the towel from Guy's waist. Her hands stroking his waist, hips, and then wasting no time to dive lower. She held him tightly, appreciating his full state of arousal.

She dropped to her knees, letting her lips and tongue run over his body. He gasped and shuddered. His mind suddenly reciting the twenty-six times table and thinking of Chelsea's last game of the season, then forcing himself trying to recall who they were playing in their first match next season. He didn't want this to be over too soon and Wendy was an exponent. She was looking up at him, her dark eyes gauging the degree of his pleasure.

Just when her technique was about to get unbearable and Guy feared he was going to peak, he gently pulled her to her feet and lifted her up on to him, his hands supporting her perfectly peachy bum as he did so. She was surprisingly light. She wrapped her long legs around his waist, her arms around his neck, and kissed him deeply. He was careful not to penetrate yet. He stepped towards the bed laying her down as gently as possible. She lay back, stretching her arms up above her head, her legs sprawled wide open, hungry and welcoming.

Guy paused for a moment to appreciate her form, enjoying this image. It wasn't lost on him that this was the first time to see her in all her naked magnificence. Her hairless body carefully prepared earlier in the shower for this moment, for him. Guy kneeled on the bed and slowly lowered himself onto her. Her breath came quick and fast. She moaned and thrashed. His weight pushing down onto her breasts held her beneath him. Her body was rocking with his. She squirmed and wriggled as Guy gradually built rhythm. Wendy was helpless. Her ecstasy had taken over from her emotions. Her body heaved, quivering and spasming as she cried out.

She felt her climax building, her breathing becoming rapid, her stomach muscles knotting, and then she burst. She cried out and gasped, throwing her outstretched arms back above her head. Her aroused breasts held tightly in Guy's hands as he pushed into her harder and faster. God she loved this moment. Her head thrashed from side to side and her eyelids fluttered as she screamed in delight. She had no idea what words, if any, were formed, she just needed to scream out. They were on the sea so who was to hear her anyway. Wendy arched her back. She wanted him all. 'Come on baby,' she heard herself say to him as she pushed herself harder against him.

She forced her eyes to open. She wanted to watch Guy. He too was close. He had a good body, a flattish stomach, but not skinny. His eyes were closed. The toned, hairy arms and manly hands were pressing down onto her chest. His fingers squeezing her tight although it didn't hurt. She was electric. She squeezed him with her pelvic muscles. Guy opened his eyes and stared into hers, pupils wide, shining. 'Come on,' she mouthed, her lips slowly accentuating every letter, 'Come on. Come in me please!' Guy peaked, shuddering, stopped moving frantically and rocked as he felt himself pulsing inside her. He paused, still kneeling before her, upright, spellbound, and then Guy slowly lowered himself onto her. His breathing still laboured. Wendy wrapped her legs tightly around him. She wanted this feeling to remain for a while yet.

Guy and Wendy slowly cooled down. He kissed her neck as she lay smiling. They snuggled, their bodies entangled and in no time were deeply asleep, all cares forgotten, for now.

Chapter 14. Protocol

Tel-Aviv. Sunday Morning.

One thing that could be said for his seniors, sat in the Kirya building in the hierarchy of Unit 8200, was that they did move fast, Tal noodled. Some would argue too fast on some things, occasionally making impulsive shoot from the hip decisions. But they did turn things around quickly, there being little subtlety to anything the Israeli armed forces ever did. Having sent his dossier up to his superiors, he realised he still lacked sleep and his red eyes were sore. He took the opportunity to splash water on his face in the washrooms and then grab a large coffee, one he planned to drink this time.

Following his coffee break, Tal's orders came back less than twenty minutes later: to continue to investigate everything he could find relating to this case, Wolf, and hacking North Korean missile facilities. Tal wished he had gotten more sleep as his brain wasn't quite as sharp as usual. Regardless, he sat in his non-descript little cubicle and tried to focus his muggy brain, while surrounded by his fellow elite researchers monitoring intelligence traffic around the world. In front of his large monitors, Tal tried to compile what he knew or suspected he knew and then what he needed to investigate further. He was struggling. His brain was tired, the thought processes felt like treacle, and it was hard for him to concentrate. His eyes stung under the artificial light and his blue walled office cubicle felt airless and oppressive. Either he needed to sleep, or he needed to get some air and borrow another brain.

Staff in this section of Unit 8200 within the Kirya building were not allowed to bring their mobile phones into their work area for security reasons. However, they did have lockers on another floor and this is where Tal headed after logging off his computer.

He couldn't sit still and knew if he stayed in his cubicle his arms would simply fold onto the surface of the desk in front of him. He would rest his head on them and surrender to sleep in seconds. He mounted the stairs to the floor where the lockers were housed and retrieved his phone from his locker. Tal auto recalled Dorit's number and sent her a text: 'Are you up?'

'Yes. I need to be at the camp at nine,' she replied.

'Meet me for breakfast? I need ideas.'

'Sure. I've an hour before I need to leave. I'll see you in fifteen.' Dorit was in a good mood. Tal hoped he was in part responsible for that after last night.

Fifteen minutes later, Tal had bought fruit, yoghurt, bread, and coffee and they were sat at the café in the trendy Sarona market, close to his office building. Dorit was dressed for work in her Israeli Defence Forces olive green Madei Aleph uniform, the sword and olive branch badge denoting her as infantry. Dorit was a big woman and the uniform fitted her well. Tal was privately proud such a shapely woman had chosen him for her lover. It was a warm Tel Aviv early morning. The sun was just up and already heating the parched earth. It was going to be another hot day in Israel. Aware he was about to disclose too much confidential information to Dorit, he first asked her for complete confidentiality. She readily agreed and being military, she was bound by the same confidentially laws as him anyway. They were not supposed to share intelligence with each other, however, Tal judged this wasn't really intelligence affecting Israel anyway. Tal summarized to Dorit what he knew already.

'A murdered hacker in the USA wiped then blew up his computers to remove all traces of his work.'

'Ah, the Semtex question,' Dorit noted.

Tal grinned privately but ignored her and went on. 'I suspect a Korean operative had commissioned the hacker to build code that could override the launch sequence of medium-range missiles believed to be used by North Korea. It's unclear if the Korean was working for the South, the North, another flag or organisation altogether. These missiles are believed to be capable of carrying nuclear warheads.' He paused for a moment. 'My orders are to continue to investigate but where to start?' He looked pleadingly with his dark brown eyes at Dorit for inspiration.

Dorit was enjoying her fruit and yoghurt washed down with fresh coffee. She looked fresh from a good night's sleep, her hair was still damp from the shower, and she smells good, thought Tal.

'What do you know about this Korean operative?' asked Dorit, her pragmatic mind thinking what her next steps would be if she were him.

'Nothing really. Only some dialogue I found on the Dark Web. It has since been removed by the senders; however, we had archived copy's, so I was able to find it. The black hat in the USA I believe was using the pseudonym Wolf. The Korean contact was using the codename Talon.' Tal was keeping his voice very low through fear of being overheard discussing his work. He reached across and held hands with Dorit over the table to suggest they were talking romantically should anyone from Unit 8200 happen to see them. She accepted his hand and continued to eat breakfast with her spare hand.

'Who might want to hack North Korean missiles and why?' asked Dorit, the question was rhetorical although it did get Tal thinking.

'Umm, good question. Quite simply, missile launch systems themselves are depressingly simple. You're right though. To actually hack a missile system is pretty much impossible. For one thing, they're not connected to other networks. They are completely isolated autonomous systems so getting a virus into a missile launch system is pretty well impossible. Let's say then, for the sake of argument, someone did manage to install a malware onto a missile launch system, there's not a lot they could do. To corrupt the system to disable it would be harmful and could delay a launch briefly although that's easily rectified. The whole launch software could simply be deleted and reinstalled from a backup. It's hardly the pinnacle of state-sponsored cyberterrorism! More a mildly irritating form of vandalism a script-kiddie might try, corrected after a five-minute reinstall. A bit like a naughty nephew resetting your playlists on your phone's music account.'

Dorit considered this, 'Can control of the launch system allow the missiles to be stolen? Fly them to a country that wants to use them?'

Tal loved her simplicity. 'No, it doesn't work that way. They only fly once and it's a one-way trip as they are designed to explode on impact when they get to where they're going.'

'What about a false flag attack?' she asked her man. 'Many a war has been started by one country pretending to be someone else. Even today the world doesn't know if it was Russia or the Ukraine who shot down the Malaysian Airlines flight over the Ukraine a few years ago. That was a serious ground to air missile attack. Could that have been someone taking control of another's missiles?'

Tal pondered this. Dorit had made a good point. Disabling the missiles was pointless. Unless the missiles were fuelled and ready for launch, simply triggering a launch would have no effect, rather like trying to strike a spent match. If they were nuclear capable and the warheads were fitted, which was unlikely anyway, precipitating a launch would be impossible as too many manual functions would still be needed. So, what was the purpose? Redirect the missiles and launch a false flag attack seemed the only scenario to go to this much trouble over, but surely this was also doomed to failure. The hack was useless unless someone already knew when the missiles were primed to be tested and that would assume inside knowledge of the North Korean's missile testing schedule.

'Possible,' conceded Tal, 'however very unlikely as this would assume inside knowledge of when the missiles would be armed, such as knowing the detailed drill schedule.'

Tal jumped up. The sweet fresh fruit, coffee, and seeing Dorit had energized him again. He needed to get back to work now. His break was over. He boldly kissed Dorit on the forehead and said he knew what he needed to do now.

She had second-guessed him and smiled up at him. 'You need to know what else it's going to take to launch those missiles and, when you've done that, you need to find out who this Talon is.'

'Yup,' he winked at her.

'See you tonight and get some rest this afternoon! You'll need all your energy for later,' she shouted after him with a naughty grin. He turned and waved, enjoying the tease. He jogged back from Sarona market towards the Kirya building that housed the senior generals of one of the most advanced intelligence gathering agencies in the world, Unit 8200.

Sat back in his cubical and scrutinising his terminals, Tal started digging up as much as he could find about the Rodong-1 or the Hwasong-7. The Rodong-1's are the workhorse of North Korea's medium-range ballistic missile arsenal; well tested, predicable and reliable. They aren't as sexy as the Hwasong-10's although these were much more temperamental, requiring a delicate and highly volatile fuel mixture. They also aren't as ambitious as the Taepodong range, the multi-stage intercontinental missiles North Korea were keen to threaten the USA mainland with. The Rodong's were easier to fuel using the liquid UDMH/AK27. They were also easy to launch from either static silos or mobile transporters and they could, it was believed, carry small nuclear warheads.

Tal started to research and compile the names of any notable people who had spent an uncharacteristically long time researching these systems, both in the public domain and on the Dark Web in the last twelve months. Beyond students, freelance journalists, and other defence contractors, several interesting characters started to emerge. One that struck Tal as particularly interesting as he had popped up several times was Mr S.C. Lee.

Tal discovered, this gentleman as it turned out, was the Chief Information Security Officer for Han Electronics, a huge South Korean technology company. Mr Lee reported directly into the President and CEO, Mr Kim Sung-han. 'Now there's a man who would have close to infinite recourses for some corporate sponsored and possibly even state sponsored espionage,' thought Tal. 'Why would such a chap be interested in North Korea's Rodong-1 missile programme? Han Electronics are one of the largest electronics manufacturers in the world, leading technology development in both consumer and manufacturing hi-tech,' Tal wondered as he scratched his stubbly chin. He loved this aspect of his job. 'Follow the breadcrumbs,' he said to himself.

Sat in his cubicle, Tal began to squirm in his chair, his fatigue now long since forgotten. Why would Han Electronics take such a keen interest in their neighbour north of the 38th parallel? This had to be more than neighbourly curtain twitching. Kim Sung-han was an interesting guy too. Born into the Kim family and heir apparent to the business, he was himself an accomplished technician and inventor with many patents under his own name, not to mention the thousands owned by his company. Tal scrolled through the many pictures available in the press and social media of Mr Kim. He was still quite young given his seniority, early forties, good looking, and influential, although not appearing to harbour any particularly aggressive political ambitions himself.

And what a stunning looking girlfriend! Seems the social pages in the Seoul media couldn't get enough of the beautiful and enigmatic Miss Lee Hyo-joo. There was little available about her. 'Strange,' thought Tal. The girlfriend of one of South Korea's most predominant industrialists was bound to have warranted a very social and public dissection. Mistresses in Korea were accepted, expected, and given due respect and privacy, however, Lee Hyo-joo was no mistress. Mr Kim wasn't married. This made Miss Lee potential wife material to one of Korea's most eligible bachelors and so open season as far as the Korean press were concerned. Who was she? Where was she from? How did she make her money? Lee Hyo-joo had done her utmost to avoid being too public with Kim Sung-han but some photos and commentary on them both did exist.

On a hunch, Tal checked airline reservations and manifests to see if S.C. Lee or his boss, Mr Kim, had been in California at the time of the death and latterly the explosion killing Craig Sanchez. As he expected he had no joy there. Messrs Lee and Kim wouldn't be so clumsy as to be directly involved.

Tal had an idea forming. He looked up and checked the array of wall clocks displaying multiple time zones around the world. He was pleased to see it was still business hours in Israel; Sunday being a working day, the first day of the working week in Israel. In South

Korea it was Sunday afternoon and they would still be enjoying their weekend but calls on a Sunday from Israel would be nothing unusual. He found the telephone number he wanted and picked up the phone and called the Israeli Embassy in Jongno-gu, Seoul.

Asking for the head of the office of Political Affairs, he was soon put through to the section head. Tal explained the Israel Defence Forces was looking to procure ruggedised communications equipment for field use. He went on to advise this was politically too sensitive for the normal conduit of the Trade Department so he had been tasked with trying to coordinate a trade delegation to visit Seoul and wanted to meet with various hi-tech' manufacturers in Korea, specifically Han Electronics. Tal advised he was going to send over a quick email explanation with an attached file containing further information and could the office of Political Affairs have this translated into Korean and sent to the marketing department at Han Electronics. 'And yes, I am aware it is a Sunday in Seoul however this is rather urgent and requires hasty arrangement given the seniority of the generals.'

Tal was quite prescriptive. The file he was about to send would be written in both Hebrew and English. 'Could the section head commission and forward this file to an outside translation agency to add a Hangul translation making the file readable in all three languages.' This letter formally introduced the trade delegation and briefly explained their requirements. It was imperative the translation agency use the current file and did not recreate another document. The document should then be sent from the external translation agency directly to Han Electronics, to save time of course, being the end of a business day in Israel although he respected it was still the Sabbath in Korea.

Tal continued, 'I need to get the introduction letter to Han Electronics as soon as possible, preferably today, then they can act on it first thing Monday morning Korea time.' Tal was quite insistent on this point. The head of Political Affairs readily agreed and said he would do it immediately, keen to be seen to be as helpful as possible to the Israeli Defence Forces.

Two hours later and he was in. Sure enough, the head of Political Affairs was good to his word and, despite being a Sunday (the translation agency was probably used to their Israeli client working on Sundays), had performed a quick translation, and then forwarded the file to their contacts at Han Electronics. A diligent employee in the Han Electronics' marketing department who was also working on a Sunday had seen the email on their smartphone and opened the file to consider the request from this potentially important customer.

Unbeknown to the diligent employee, smartphones have next to no security and these devices are one of the easiest ways to breach corporate security. The little piece of software code Tal had embedded in the innocent looking letter of introduction file was carried via the email attachment on the smartphone into the Han Electronics corporate network. A trade delegation from Israel was looking to procure army-ready communications equipment: it was a very good sales lead for Han Electronics!

The alert that the file had been opened flashed up on Tal's console. This came through quicker than Tal could have possibly wished for. 'Damn efficient these Koreans!' he murmured to no one in particular. Without their knowledge, the sophisticated malware, a dropper, was the third stage of the kill-chain attack. This enabled Tal to access the PC, load further malware and ultimately gave Tal command and control access of the marketing employee's office computer. He was then able to assume the identity of the marketing person, who it transpired was a diligent young lady called Amy Park, and from there had pretty much free reign to access all the other networks this computer was connected to within the Han Electronics organisation. This included the company's travel approval system.

Because the malware worked by emulating their own employees, it didn't attract any suspicion or trigger alerts. The company's management software would simply capture that an employee was doing some work on a Sunday afternoon, neither strange nor unusual for busy staff. After hacking the Systems Manager's access controls and granting himself sysadmin rights, Tal was able to assume other identities and change user permissions to his heart's content. Within two hours there was nowhere Tal couldn't go.

Twenty-seven Han Electronics employees had been in California at the time of the murder. Most looked like technical or business staff working with Silicon Valley suppliers or customers and all of these looked legitimate. He scanned them all but none jumped out at him as of particular interest. He would deep dive these later if other avenues of research reached dead ends. Tal scratched his beard, he was frustrated. He needed another approach.

It was of course still quite possible, even probable, that Wolf's death had nothing to do with Han Electronics or any of their staff but, like a dog with a bone, Tal couldn't leave this thought alone. He simply had a feeling. He decided on a different tack and started to look into the email account of S.C. Lee. Tal was impressed. He was an industrious fellow and had heightened security on his personal and project files. This was not unusual. Tal knew this was to avoid intellectual property theft in the high-stakes game of consumer electronics. These files were encrypted and were not going to be easy and most likely impossible to break into.

Regardless, the emails in the inbox were easy to read and scanning the usual management rubbish didn't reveal much except the usual big company administration of a senior executive. The emails were mostly in Korean so Tal used translation software; it was not perfect but he got the gist. There were several references to internal development projects however these were not very forthcoming as Mr Lee was diligent to save these quickly to encrypted archives.

He noticed there was a reference to a UAV project, a drone to the uninitiated. This was logical for a high-tech developer and it didn't strike Tal as odd either. Drones were a fast growing market. Tal seemed to be getting nowhere and he needed a different approach. He thought for a while then ran a quick scan on patterns of behaviour for S.C. Lee. Most of the emails seemed to concentrate around the usual working hours although he noticed two evenings before there had been a lot of activity late that evening seemingly around a video recording. This was with his subordinate staff, J.J. Oh, and also referenced the boss, Kim Sung-han. 'Interesting,' murmured Tal unconsciously to himself.

Tal followed the thread and, after rummaging around in the security files undetected with his administrator access, was able to find the video file that was causing all the excitement. The video was a feed from a security camera in Mr Kim's, the CEO's, own opulent office. The tasteful furnishings, large desk, and impressive cityscape view was a stark contrast to Tal Bar-Lev's tiny florescent tube lit blue cubicle in the windowless offices of the Kirya building.

A Systems Security Engineer called J.J. Oh had found the video that showed the CEO having a meeting with an Asian looking lady and then leaving the room. Mr Kim stood and appeared to apologise. As soon as he had left the room, the lady stood and walked around to read whatever was on his computer screens. She then removed a USB drive from her small handbag, plugged this into one of the computers, punched a few keys, then removed the USB drive, placed it back into the handbag, and sat down again, crossing her long elegant legs back into her relaxed pose. Shortly afterwards Mr Kim returned and they carried on talking. Tal surmised that unbeknown to Mr Kim the lady had copied a file. No wonder this had panicked Mr J.J. Oh and caused such a stir for Mr S.C. Lee, the Chief Information Security Officer for Han Electronics.

Tal glanced again at the array of world clocks on the wall. There were multiple clocks all accurately reading the time in various cities around the world. He realised he had lost track of the time completely. He was both weary and hungry plus his shift was close to ending. Tal scratched the tee shirt he wore and stood to stretch his jean clad legs. Dress sense in Unit 8200 was very informal except for the senior officers. He picked up the phone, called his supervisor, and asked for an overtime extension of his shift. 'Yes,' came the confirmation after Tal gave a summary of his research and explained he still wanted to pursue another couple of angles, adding this could be time sensitive. This was all too interesting to stop now, besides, if he could drag out his research until Dorit had finished her shift then that would be perfect. A little overtime would pay for a nice dinner with her.

At a loss for exactly what his next steps should be, Tal took time to update his file with what he had learnt so far. As a matter of protocol, he would need to do this anyway and he thought it might help him consider what to do next. He was looking at the pictures of Mr Kim and his stunning escort Miss Lee Hyo-joo. She was young, clearly fit, and toned, and carried herself with a confidence which reminded him of someone. Upright, square shoulders…; suddenly the thought struck him. Dorit! Was this woman military trained?

Tal sat back and wondered. The seed of a thought occurred to him. He wondered if she was aware of the data theft her boyfriend had experienced. On a whim he ran facial recognition software to scan her beautiful face and head into memory from every picture of her he could find. The facial recognition software captured twenty-six data points on her face including length of nose, space between eyes, dimensions of head, width of mouth, etc. He then went into the database of airport surveillance camera footage from airports all over the world. This was intelligence readily shared on a reciprocal arrangement between many airports globally, ostensibly as a prevention of a terrorist attacks following 911. He focused on Seoul and San Francisco and ran the image for the previous five days.

'Bingo!' Tal leapt from his seat with his arms raised like a soccer player scoring the winning goal in the cup final. His bemused colleagues sitting close by frowned at him. Sure enough, there was Miss Lee departing Seoul's Incheon International Airport on a Korean Airlines flight arriving in San Francisco on the day of the murder. She then departed twelve hours later; enough time for some shopping or business meetings in California, or perhaps something far more sinister. In fact, she was probably still on her return flight, as it wouldn't have touched down back in Incheon yet. 'What could have been so urgent?' Tal wondered.

Tal, feeling extremely smug, suspected he had discovered the identity of Wolf's assassin and a possible reason for his killing. This would be added to his dossier for onward consideration by his management. Three questions now bothered him. Should he share this information with his friend in California, Eitan? Who was the lady in the video of Mr Kim's office? And what was it exactly that she had copied off Mr Kim's computer?

Tal had worked nearly fourteen hours straight, but he had enjoyed it and felt invigorated. This was the part of the job he loved. It was a productive day and, like a cop on television, he had cracked or at least partially cracked his case through some good ol' fashion sleuthing and, of course, his forte, a bit of good hacking. He realised he should be tired and was looking forwards to seeing Dorit that evening. He had sent his updated report to his superiors and logged out from his shift. He went home to get a quick sleep knowing he would be pulled in again if they needed him to work on this still further.

Tal was fast asleep when the shrill ring of the telephone call came through three hours later.

Hong Kong. Early Sunday Morning.

Plug privately hated being called Plug. He was 37-years-old now for heaven's sake! He had been fast-tracked by Her Majesty's Civil Service after recruitment into the United Kingdom's Secret Intelligence Service, straight from reading history and mathematics at Oxford University in England. His age, intellect, and seniority all demanded that he be given more respect. The nickname had somehow haunted him his entire life after first being used at infants' school thirty years previous. The problem was it suited him so well.

'Damn it!' shouted Plug at a Junior Administrator as he slid a buff file onto his desk with a yellow notelet stuck to the front hand-scrawled with 'Urgent Plug!' He had already received a text to warn him of the urgency of the incoming file. Plug sat at his desk and glared at the Admin' in the British Consulate-General office who had dropped the file with the helpful remark, 'It's marked urgent, boss!' It was a Sunday morning and, although not formally a workday, staff in the Secret Intelligence Service were assumed to come to the office and check any secure or urgent communications anytime. Despite being a Sunday, Plug wore a light-coloured tailored suit albeit he had left his tie back at his home in Mid-Levels.

Regrettably, the nickname Plug fitted Andrew Smith better than the light-coloured tailored suit. His tall lanky form, thinning fair hair, exaggeratedly long neck, wing-nut ears, long pointy nose, goofy teeth, and lack of a chin didn't help to convince anyone to not call him Plug regardless of how much as he hated it. His entire life most people simply knew him as Plug without needing an introduction. His posting to the British Consulate-General in Hong Kong had happened three years previously and Plug was the senior MI6 operative albeit under the auspices of Trade Attaché. If the general public's expectation of an MI6 operative was the roguishly good-looking face of James Bond, Plug was most certainly the antithesis of this. Despite his goofball looks and social awkwardness, he was very smart, multi-lingual, and a very competent intelligence operative. His keen wit enabled him to skilfully navigate the dangerous and haphazard world of international espionage.

Plug stopped what he was doing and picked up the buff file. He opened it to see pictures of a crashed black Mercedes, a taxi with a missing rear window, and several grainy pictures of a Caucasian male with a pretty, slim, Asian female. The male looked familiar. The police report talked of gunshots being fired on the highway in Wan Chai heading towards Causeway Bay and an earlier incidence of gunshots being fired in the Four Seasons Hotel in the IFC, in Central. The two incidences' the Hong Kong police believe were connected and seemed to revolve around these two people. The room at the Four Seasons was rented by a Singaporean woman named Wendy Chen, and while not named here Plug believed the man looked like Guy Anderson, a Brit' he knew from meeting at various seminars and social events themed around cybercrime and its prevention. It was still early on this Sunday morning and already, while only into his second cup of tea, Plug could see the day was going to be an interesting one.

Sheppy barely moved on her mooring in the Royal Hong Kong Yacht Club's marina. Guy had woken at dawn and, feeling the soft naked warmth of Wendy still curled against him, he chose to lay there and consider their options rather than disturb the sleeping beauty next to him. She would wake soon enough to the realization of the terror of the previous day so let her sleep he reasoned. Besides, being between soft linen sheets with a beautiful woman aboard a luxury yacht was a privilege he didn't want to dispense with quite yet. He looked across at the pretty, innocent face of the woman he had made love to the previous evening. She was peaceful. Her chest lightly rising and falling with her slow breathing, steady as she dreamed. He gently kissed her forehead still wondering what he'd gotten himself into.

Guy stared up at the pale leather covered ceiling and knew they needed help. Wendy had stolen something precious and others were prepared to kill her to recover it. The threat was unlikely to go away until the stolen software was recovered, and, he feared, they were both dead. He rationalized this was beyond the help of the local police and wasn't sure they would even know where to start. Contacting them was probably pointless and protection unlikely to be offered. If the suits were monitoring the local police stations, like the one close by in Wan Chai, they would be dead before they made it through the front gate anyway.

He needed Interpol or the help of the British Consulate-General, at least they'd appreciate the need for their personal safety. Wendy was Singaporean, could her Embassy help he wondered? Probably not, they would do nothing to rile the Chinese. But who did he know, if anyone, at the British Consulate-General? Then it struck him, of course, Plug!

Guy had met Plug on many occasions and while he would not go so far as to call him a close friend, he was a good lad, professional, with an impressive understanding of the murky world of cybercrime. In fact, so much so, Guy assumed that whatever this Trade Attaché did, it stretched the definition of 'trade'. Plug had called Guy on several occasions to ask advice on hackers and various spywares and malwares. Guy never knew why and was shrewd enough not to ask, however, he assumed, based on the technicality of the questions, it was Secret Intelligence Service related. Regardless, Guy liked this sharp-witted, goofy chap and instinctively suspected he could trust him. A plan formed in his mind and eventually he kissed Wendy awake to tell her.

Under normal circumstances on a Sunday morning he would carefully slide out from the bed, make tea or coffee, pop out to buy fresh bread and juice, and then wake his previous night's date with breakfast in bed. This predictably, would precede another sex romp before getting up for the day. On this particular Sunday morning though he didn't want to scare Wendy by leaving her in bed and risk her waking up alone with the fear he had abandoned her on a strange yacht, albeit a luxury yacht, particularly after the events of the previous day.

Wendy woke refreshed, yawned, stretched, and listened to Guy's idea with her knees up to her chest and the duvet pulled up to her chin keeping her warm and modest. Guy sketched out his idea while sat on the side of the bed, a towel around his waist. She struck him as remarkably composed for someone who'd been chased and shot at the previous day.

'You think you can trust this guy Plug?' asked Wendy, unsure if she could trust anyone while in this predicament.

'I can't think of another option at the moment' suggested Guy, scuffing his shaved head and stubbly chin with his fingernails. 'It's not too early to call him now. You grab a shower and I'll go and recover our phones from the tunnel and pick up some breakfast. We'll call Plug when I get back. Don't leave the boat please and answer only to me. I'll not be long.'

Unlike the comfortably air-conditioned environment on-board *Sheppy*, there was no air conditioning in the British Consulate-General on Sundays much to Plug's annoyance and that of the skeleton crew who had to come to the office to work on alternate Sundays. The office was hot and stuffy, and the windows could not be opened for security reasons, so the staff used fans to stir the hot air around. Plug had read the police report and it was clear they had no idea what the incident was all about. It seemed that one person was killed in the Mercedes accident although the nationality of that person or that of the car's owner was not yet known. If the fellow captured in the security camera pictures was Guy Anderson, he was a British national and Her Majesties Consulate would afford the due privileges.

Plug's social phone, resting on his desk alongside the encrypted MI6 issued secure phone, suddenly buzzed and vibrated around the table. Plug startled, grabbed it and looked at the number and caller's name before he gave a slow smile and pressed the green button.

In an exaggerated WWII British Airforce accent, Plug heard the voice on the phone: 'I say, we're in a spot of bother old chap and could use a bit of a hand!'

'Good morning, Guy! Funnily enough I've just been reading about your "spot of bother" and wondered if you would think to call me,' responded Plug, with his perfectly normal Home Counties Oxbridge tone. He was doodling cartoon stickmen on the yellow notelet pad on his desk as he spoke.

'We seem to have attracted the interest of some rather unpleasant individuals,' replied Guy, 'Would you be able to meet?'

'I was thinking the exact same thing. Sounds like you are indeed in trouble,' said Plug. 'Remember that hotel where we last met? That Beating Cyber Crime event? There's a café in the lobby. Can you meet there in an hour? And do you think you're still in danger?'

Guy had returned to the boat and looked at Wendy's hopeful face while keeping his own expression neutral said, 'Yes, I recall the hotel, and yes.'

'Understood, then without giving me your location over an open phone line then, if you think you can get to the hotel safely, I'll pick you up in my car there. Let's skip the café, too public,' responded Plug.

'Thanks…,' Guy stalled, trying to recall his real name. He was going to say 'Thanks Plug' but felt this might be rude under the circumstances.

Plug rolled his eyes heavenward and smiled, picking up on the hesitation, 'No problem Guy. Her Majesty's Government is here to help. Just get there safely. I'll see you in an hour. It's Andrew by the way.' And he clicked off.

Guy had bought coffee and sandwiches while collecting their phones and realising they had missed eating the previous evening, he for one was starving. He assumed Wendy would be too. He had been careful to look out for the suits or any people that looked out of place, however, the short trip to recover the hidden phones and buy breakfast was uneventful. Once back on *Sheppy* he used his phone to make the call to Plug, leaving Wendy's turned off in case the suits could use it to trace her whereabouts.

They showered and found some clean shirts for both men and women in Mike's closet. They tidied the yacht to the best of their ability and left *Sheppy*. Guy carefully closed the main hatch and positioned the broken lock to make it at least look functional. The day was already sunny and warm. They walked back along the floating pontoon and through the Royal Hong Kong Yacht Club again, nodding politely at all they met, arousing no suspicious looks. Outside they hailed a taxi that had recently dropped off three young lads dressed for a day's sailing on the iconic harbour. Guy looked about and judged the wind. *Nice day for sailing he thought.*

'Shangri-La Hotel in Admiralty please,' Guy shouted to the elderly taxi driver. Wendy was suddenly hesitant to get in, an impulsive nervousness unsettling her following her last taxi experience. Guy squeezed her hand and pulled her gently into the car saying 'It's all right' in as confident a voice as he could muster. Although it didn't stop him instinctively looking behind them many times during the short journey from the yacht club to the hotel.

It was a short ten-minute drive to the Shangri-La and the wordless driver grunted as they alighted. Given Wendy was staying at the Four Seasons, it occurred to Guy that if the suits were looking to keep watch on other 5-Star hotels in the area this would be an obvious one to target. Fortunately, the British Consulate-General was literally across the road from the hotel so, rather than enter the lobby of the hotel, they lingered in the shadows behind one of the patron's Rolls Royce's that was parked strategically outside along with a smattering of Ferrari's and McLaren's keeping it company.

Plug, feeling a tingle of excitement, wrote a brief formal email to his Junior Administrator apprising him that he knew the man in the picture and the man had already initiated contact asking for help from the British Consulate-General. He was going to meet Mr Anderson to understand the situation and offer appropriate assistance to the British subject if required. He wrote an even more formal and even briefer email to his contact in the Hong Kong Police Force, thanking him for the original file and advising him he believed he knew the male subject and the Hong Kong Police could rely on the full cooperation of the British Government once he had more information to offer.

Given there had been firearms used in the previous day's altercations, Plug went to the locked steel cabinet and withdrew his own sidearm and shoulder holster. He was trained and authorised to carry a weapon although he rarely wore the trusty Browning 9mm. Most of the Service had now been upgraded to the Glock 17 but due to budget constraints Hong Kong was well down the priority queue for a weapon's upgrade. Plug was so unused to handling the sidearm he struggled to get into the shoulder holster, getting into an embarrassing tangle at his first attempt. Luckily the lightly staffed office meant no one saw him making a complete hash of this. Eventually, satisfying himself he'd not twisted the holster straps and that he had the full 13 rounds in the clip, the weapon was comfortably loaded, he tucked the side-arm away in its holster and wore his suit jacket to conceal it.

Guy saw the white Range Rover pull into the front driveway of the hotel. He quickly stepped forward and tapped on the window. Plug had seen him approach the car and tapped the button to unlock the central door locking. Guy quickly scanned the people milling around outside the hotel, mostly families of Sunday brunchers, then beckoned Wendy towards him, holding the rear door open for her to climb in. Guy closed the door and jumped into the plush front seat as Plug swiftly drove away and merged with the light traffic on Justice Drive. Plug looked over the back and smiled at Wendy. 'Good morning. I'm Andrew Smith, at your service,' he shouted over his left shoulder, then sighing he sheepishly added, 'but you might as well call me Plug as everyone else does.'

Wendy leaned forwards and replied, 'Nice to meet you Andrew. I'm Wendy Chen from Singapore.' They briefly and awkwardly shook hands. 'We're very grateful for your help!' Wendy said, feeling safe behind the tinted windows and with Plug. With his tall, gangly frame he was clearly no cage fighter, however, he did exude an air of quiet competence.

'I'll drive us to somewhere quiet and you can tell me what kind of trouble you've gotten yourselves in to. First things first, do you have mobile phones with you, and are they turned on?' he asked. They found their phones and made sure they were turned off completely. They talked as he drove. He first joined Cotton Tree Drive and then drove onto May Road and lastly Peak Road, parking in a secluded spot near Wan Chai Gap Park, close to the old Police Museum. There was a little café open to serve the hikers enjoying the park, so Guy and Plug bought chilled waters and returned to Wendy who stayed in the Range Rover. Now all back in the car together, Wendy and Guy explained the whole story to Plug leaving out only their lovemaking and the name of the boat they stayed on. Plug listened patiently from the driver's seat.

'Missile launch control system,' said Plug, once they had completed the story. 'You don't do things by halves do you Guy?' he said with a smile and refrained from judging Wendy for the theft. Privately he wondered if she was some form of agency operative herself. If she was, she was a hopeless amateur. She looked small sat in the back seat while she fiddled nervously with her Breitling Emergency watch, and his instinct told him she was not a spy, simply an overly curious woman who had bitten off way more than she could chew. She was clearly terrified at the reaction she had provoked.

'Based on what you've told me, I can only assume you've uncovered a covert operation by a South Korean technology company to build and control or trigger a missile launch in North Korea. Why they would want to do this is quite beyond me. South Korea has US missiles aimed at the North and so they don't need the North's dated technology. And why they would want to trigger a launch in the North is also hard to fathom. But then stranger things have happened!'

Plug surmised. Wendy and Guy looked at each other and shrugged. Plug went on, thinking aloud, 'Of course it's possible this was some academic exercise, a programmer's project for example, although why on earth would they then come after you in this way? They're clearly very serious and very worried about the software you've got.' Plug was quiet for a minute as his mathematician's brain considered the variables. 'I suppose it's not possible the reason these guys are after you has nothing to do with this software; some other unconnected reason for you being in trouble, Wendy? Jealous lover, drug cartel, bank heist gone wrong, eh?'

Wendy shook her head. 'I can't possibly think of any other reason and certainly none of the above. It must be this damn software I downloaded.' Plug stared, considered Wendy, and judged her to be genuine.

'Then whatever this is, it's way bigger than any intelligence we've gathered on Korea, North and South, for months, years even. Now, our first objective is we need to get you guys safe.' Plug reached across from the driver's seat, opened the glove compartment by Guy's knees, and pulled out a spare mobile phone. In doing so, his jacket fell open revealing the shoulder holster and Browning 9mm. Guy and Wendy both saw this and Wendy involuntarily shivered. Whatever Plug was, or knew, he had come prepared for trouble.

Chapter 16. Five Wise Men

Tel-Aviv. Sunday Afternoon.

The five men didn't often meet. For the five men to even be present in the same room was undesirable and was illustrative of the severity of the situation. The two men in pristine uniforms represented the pinnacle of the Israeli Defence Force's chain of command. The third, an older gentleman with large flappy jowls in a dark suit, and white shirt with an open collar topped by a small black skullcap, was the representative of the Prime Minister's office. He had a direct line of access to the Israeli Prime Minister himself. The fourth, studious looking, tall, and stickman thin, with a grey complexion, darting eyes, and a nervous disposition was the head of Unit 8200 Cyber-Intelligence. The fifth and least senior was Tal's immediate boss.

The large room in the middle of the Kirya building was sandwiched between two concrete lined lift shafts with steel reinforced concrete walls, floor, and ceiling. Although it looked like any other bland windowless meeting room with a tatty boardroom table and chairs, it was designed to be bombproof with no outside walls or windows. It had its own independent power supply, recycled air, and an exclusive fresh water supply. It was stuffy and stiflingly hot due to the old and woefully inadequate air conditioner that wheezed asthmatically somewhere in the roof space.

They had been talking over each other for an hour already in the oppressive, airless meeting room about Unit 8200's findings. Like most meetings in Israel, there was a lot of loud shouting, contradicting, and position taking. The emergency meeting was catalysed by a report submitted by one of the young researchers into intelligence gained about North Korea's missiles, and a possible attempt to gain control of the launch system; in this case potentially by South Korea, although, to all present, this seemed odd.

However, other intelligence sources provided to MOSSAD by her allies pointed to the fact that another rumour was circulating whereby Syria had approached North Korea regarding the purchase of an arsenal of short- and mid-range missiles. If Syria or Palestine were able to lay their hands on such weaponry, this would escalate Middle East tensions to a whole new level. Worse still, if these weapons were nuclear capable and tipped with North Korean nuclear warheads, Israel and her five million Jews could be turned into a large sheet of glass in milliseconds.

That some of Israel's neighbours were looking to acquire the North Korean Strategic Rocket Forces' Rodong-1, Hwasong-5 and 6 SRBMs (Short-Range Ballistic Missiles) was no surprise. These rumours had been abound for years and only China's firm hand on North Korea's government was probably all that was stopping a sale. Launch capable malware and South Korea interfering without MOSSAD, CIA, or MI6 knowledge was a recent and dangerous turn of events. The Prime Minister had been briefed and, as was his style, he had made no decision and instead demanded further information. Slightly less than three hours later, a phone call had been made to one Tal Bar-Lev, the humble young researcher who was trying to catch-up on his sleep.

After hanging up from the call, once again Tal was forced out of bed, bleary eyed and his body aching for more sleep. He pulled on his jeans and tee shirt and after a quick freshen up jumped back on his electric propelled bike and threaded his way back to his office in Unit 8200's section of the Kirya building.

Sundays were the first day of the week in Israel and so most people had a Friday and Saturday weekend of socialising, relaxing, and going to and from the beach. On Sunday afternoon, while most of the western world was having a day off work, Tel Aviv was a buzz with commuters. He had told his boss he would notify him as soon as he arrived and upon doing so was invited straight into the windowless and stuffy meeting room where he sat across a large table from five of his seniors. The only one Tal recognised was his immediate manager and he looked subordinate to all the others. Two were in uniform and their credentials were not questioned. These were big guns from MOSSAD, Israel's intelligence agency. Obviously his report had rapidly been escalated through the military hierarchy to this building's high command. Tal wondered what the hell was going on and if he'd done something wrong.

Tal's boss cleared his dry throat and prodded the buff file in front of him, Tal's report. 'This is good work Tal,' his boss started, the other members of the panel merely studied him stony faced. This was high praise in a culture not given to easily lavishing praise. 'We've all read the report but can you give a quick summary of how this started and what you've discovered.'

'Sir,' began Tal, realising he was expected to be precise and concise. 'Through a friend of mine in California I was told of a police investigation into the death of a suspected hacker in Palo Alto. My friend thought this was more gossip than intelligence, however, the dead individual I believe used the alias Wolf. He was on our database as a person of interest. I believe he was a black hat for hire and was responsible for several sophisticated ransomwares, multiple polymorphic malwares, and a handful of successful thefts of data. He also had a particularly nasty habit of commissioning extreme child pornography.' Tal paused and looked at the other men, but his audience was expressionless.

'I also believe he purchased the Semtex that resulted in the explosion which destroyed all evidence of his work following his untimely death. His death I believe was caused by a female Korean assassin who happens to be the girlfriend of Mr Kim Sung-han, the President and CEO of Han Electronics in South Korea. Her name is Lee Hyo-joo and I think she also used the alias Talon for Dark

189

Web correspondence purposes.'

Tal paused for questions at this point, however, there were none, only the stony faces. Tal, still slightly unnerved if he had done something wrong, continued. 'Lastly I believe Wolf was commissioned by Talon to develop a malware capable of assuming command and control of the launch systems for North Korea's Rodong-1 medium range missiles.' He paused, then added as an afterthought, 'The ones capable of carrying nuclear warheads! I further believe another actor possibly stole a copy of this malware from Mr Kim. That's the video I've included in my report Sir.' Tal paused again, perspiring slightly now.

'Do we know who this other actor is?' asked one of the Generals across the table from him. Even when talking the stern stony face barely creased and his eyes were hard and cold.

'No Sir, I've not got to that yet. I thought it best to provide a status report first, Sir.' Tal quickly glanced towards his boss for a positive reaction but was disappointed.

The General continued, 'Every October, North Korea celebrates its founding of the Workers' Party of Korea. This includes the mass parade and traditional display of military strength through the streets of Pyongyang. It's usual for them to test fire a number of missiles leading up to this as an international display of strength to the global audience. Our intelligence suggest North Korea is again looking to sell the technology for Rodong-1, or as the South like to call them, the Hwasong-7 missiles. Buyers would likely include our enemies. We're not clear if these two scenarios are connected or the part Han Electronics might play and we need to find out. If South Korea are looking to breach the security of the Rodong-1 missiles to the point where they can launch them, we need to know their agenda.'

Tal Bar Lev's boss stepped in once more, 'Bar Lev, go and identify the woman you believe may have a copy of the launch software and let's find out who she is, who she works for, and her agenda with the malware.'

At this he sensed his dismissal. Tal stood, smartly saluted, acutely aware of the large sweat patches that had formed under the armpits of his tee shirt and dismissed himself. He had never met such senior people before although he was well aware he probably shared the Kirya building with them. Being primarily an academic he was unsure how to behave in the presence of such power. Regardless, he had been given his orders and the spotlight was on him now. What had his Californian friend Eitan got him into he wondered.

Dorit took the call and was rather cool when she learnt her plans for the evening had been scuppered by her boyfriend having to work late. Regardless, she was military herself so a haphazard dating scene was a fact of life. 'I might see you later then,' was how she had left it. She would see him of course, she knew she would, but she would make him work a little harder if he was going to share her bed tonight. 'Treat them mean, keep them keen,' she said to herself with a smile.

Back in his claustrophobic cubicle, Tal scanned as many images as he was able to capture of the leggy woman who had met with Mr Kim in his office in the video he had obtained. He set about applying this to the facial recognition software he had used earlier to identify Lee Hyo-joo. He then overlaid this with images obtained from Twitter, Facebook, and LinkedIn then ran the sequence to start a scan. Like DNA databases, intelligence agencies around the world had methodically been scraping social media sites to digitally image faces for years. All pictures were digitised, indexed, and stored in terabytes of data farms in the eventuality they might one day be useful. The facial recognition software was able to capture fifty-two data points on the woman's head and face. This was good and Tal was confident the social media searches would turn up something soon. While he was waiting, he went to the pantry on his floor to get a much-needed coffee.

The earlier thought about Eitan made him contemplate what he should do about reciprocating the information sharing. He was sure Eitan and his policeman friend would doubtless be very grateful for knowing what he now knew. Sharing the intel would be a serious breach of protocol though, a criminal offence, and likely have him imprisoned if caught without a good explanation. Perhaps, had he not been so tired, his brain would have rationalised this differently but it seemed the right thing to do to share some of what he knew with his friend who had helped him.

He had not shaved in several days and, while he had showered earlier, he felt scruffy. He returned to his desk daydreaming of a shave, shower, and twenty-four hours straight sleep, preferably with his voluptuous Dorit lying next to him. Sitting back down at his desk with his coffee and a bagel with cream cheese, his computer presented him with a picture of a smiling Wendy Chen, a Singaporean Human Resources professional seemingly employed by Cyber Security Systems Ltd, a cyber-security consultancy. That is, unless it was simply a front for a more covert agenda. She seemed legitimate though as there was a long history of professional and personal photos, tweets, and pictures with friends going back years and showing her aging. Of course, this could all be completely fictitious and artificially created. Tal knew his trade though and felt he could usually spot the false identities. He studied the pictures and believed Wendy Chen was the real deal. *So why would she steal the software, and what did she plan to do with it?*

The facial recognition software was still compiling various pictures and Wendy's blog history when he was suddenly startled to see a police advisory posted to Interpol in Hong Kong just a matter of hours earlier. It seemed a lady matching Wendy Chen's description was captured in photographs posted by Hong Kong's police to other regional police agencies in a connection with two shooting incidents and a fatal car accident. 'Well, well, Wendy Chen! You are an interesting lady. What are you doing exactly?' he muttered.

His mind was made up. Eitan and his police detective friend should be made aware of this. Tal felt if Israel's defence was at risk, this channel of intel sharing was defendable.

California Saturday Evening. Hong Kong Sunday Lunchtime.

Eitan didn't usually contact Detective Brendon Butterfield; hardly ever now he came to think of it. They would meet at the gym and would often spot for each other when using the heavier weights. Conversation was easy between them and, although their heritage, background, religion, and professions couldn't be more different, they enjoyed each other's company and there was mutual respect, even friendship.

Brendon Butterfield was at home in his small tidy kitchen. He stood over the gas hob, browning a pan full of diced Monkfish. Bob Marley played in the background and Butterfield sang along, *'no woman no cry...'* The smells emanating from the pot were heady and complex. The lady he had invited over for dinner had been promised a traditional Bermudian fish stew with rum and peppers. He sipped the liquor in the pan and smiled, it tasted good. A WhatsApp message appeared on his phone and simply said, 'must meet you - have information.' Brendon was beginning to regret the previous conversation he'd had with Eitan. He was concerned he had professionally breached police protocols and given too much away regarding the Palo Alto explosion. He had specifically told Eitan to keep this to himself so whatever information Eitan now had presumed he had ignored that instruction. Brendon was riled to think his friend had not followed his wishes. *Well let's see where this leads, the detective thought.*

He knew Eitan worked in the cybersecurity industry and perhaps he had turned up something that could help his investigation. Having written up his report earlier he realised that, apart from documenting the situation and drawing a few scant conclusions based on the forensic evidence, he had precisely no leads and exactly zilch to follow-up on. This was not going to make his close rate statistics look good, reflecting poorly on him and his department. He hoped Eitan might have something to help relieve his now constipated investigation. Brendon turned off the heat and quickly added the sautéed fish to the pan of liquor. The fish stew would improve for standing a while anyway and his guest wouldn't arrive for another hour. He opened his car door, neatly folded his suit jacket over the passenger seat, and murmured, 'let's see what you got then Eitan,' as he fired his adored BMW M6 into life and blipped the accelerator. The throaty roar from the exhaust's always made him grin.

Eitan had refused to talk over the phone and insisted they meet. Sat in the designated Starbucks, Brendon had only enough time to order his Soy Chai Latte before seeing the form of Eitan on his CycloCross bike screech to a halt outside. Eitan waved the offer of a drink, too excited to waste time ordering.

He sat and promptly started gabbling in his animated Israeli accent. Brendon looked on benignly for a few seconds then held up a hand for Eitan to stop. He felt rather like a traffic cop he had seen in an old sepia picture of Front Street in his grandparent's hometown of Hamilton in Bermuda. The policeman, complete with white gloves and blue bobby's helmet, was directing the traffic on the town's only busy intersection. Eitan looked shocked at first, then smiled and stopped.

'Let's start at the beginning shall we?' pleaded Butterfield who had understood none of what had just been said.

'Right,' began Eitan, with an exaggerated sigh and intake of breath, 'Here's the thing. I can't tell you how I know this or any of the sources of the intelligence. I demand you respect my complete anonymity and I'll never testify to any of what I'm going to tell you and will deny it if you try to subpoena me.' That he had use of the word 'intelligence' and not 'information' was not lost on the detective. It sounded professional and implied an official conduit.

'OK,' agreed Brendon, 'go on.'

'I've a friend in Tel…,' he stopped short. 'I've a friend, he does, err, research into cyberwarfare and such-like. Well, he and I were chatting, and it seems the guy killed in the explosion was a suspected black hat, a criminal form of a computer software programmer. A hacker. He had been under surveillance, err, I can't say who by, and he was suspected of being a criminal programmer for hire with the pseudonym Wolf. He's thought to… Hey, can I get a reward for this or some tax breaks or at least future parking tickets waived?'

'OK,' agreed Brendon, 'Go on.'

'Really?'

'No! Of course not "really"! Go on,' scowled Butterfield; on questions of favours, Detective Brendon Butterfield was uncompromisingly moral, not through fear of breaking any law but rather he merely considered himself fundamentally honest. One of the good cops.

'Huh! OK,' shrugged Eitan, he continued. 'He's believed to be behind multiple cybercrimes, hacking banks and insurance companies and stuff. More interestingly, he's thought to have developed a malware able to assume command and control of missile systems, specifically those owned by North Korea.' Brendon leaned forwards, grabbed his phone, and started punching the keys to take notes; he had long since stopped making notes with pencil and paper. 'It's thought the South Korean's have a copy of this code or specifically a South Korean technology company called Han Electronics.' Brendon had heard of Han Electronics, in fact he recalled he even owned one of their rice cookers, rarely used but sat proudly on a kitchen surface in his apartment. 'You might want to look into a lady called Lee Hyo-joo. She's the Korean girlfriend of Mr Kim Sung-han, the President and CEO of Han Electronics in South Korea. She's also possibly the assassin who killed your man in Palo Alto.'

Brendon was intrigued. Eitan didn't only have information, he seemed to have somehow wrapped up the whole case for him! *If* any of this could be believed and validated of course. It wasn't lost on him that Eitan had used words like 'intelligence', 'surveillance', 'pseudonym Wolf' and he presumed 'Tel...' was short for Tel Aviv suggesting the Israeli Intelligence Service, possibly MOSSAD, was his likely source. Did Eitan really have links to, or perhaps even work for MOSSAD himself he wondered?

'There's one more thing you need to know Brendon,' Eitan leaned forwards conspiratorially. 'A Singaporean woman is believed to have stolen a copy of the malware from Han Electronics and is maybe in danger. She's now on the run in Hong Kong. How she came to know about it and steal it I'm not sure. Check out Wendy Chen. She works for a cybersecurity consulting company in Singapore.' Brendon could only raise an eyebrow and study the face of his Israeli friend. The bright lights of Starbucks did little conceal his smug expression, but Butterfield was impressed and looked upon his friend with renewed respect.

'I need to go to work' said Butterfield standing up. 'Send me those outstanding parking violations.'

As Butterfield swept out of the coffeeshop he heard Eitan saying behind him 'but I haven't even got a car yet...'

Detective Brendon Butterfield went back to his office and ingested all the information Eitan had given him. After checking airline manifests, a female called Lee Hyo-joo had been in California at the time of the killing of Craig Sanchez so that much of the story at least checked out. 'How did he learn all this!?' he wondered again. The rest though was all well above his pay grade and he pondered what to do with the knowledge. It was clearly of significance and might be important to the US intelligence services, although he had sworn to Eitan he would protect his identity. Still, he felt the information needed to be passed on. He opened the draw of his desk and found the disregarded business card of FBI agent Adamson he had clumsily thrown into the draw earlier, recalling he had offered to update the agent if anything of interest emerged. He guessed it just had. He looked at his watch and was glad the evening dinner for two was already prepared. One quick phone call and he'd still be home before his date arrived. Hopefully she'd be politely late.

'Senior Agent Mick Adamson,' came the gruff voice over the phone. Did Butterfield detect traces of an Irish or some British accent in there he wondered.

'Agent Adamson, this is Detective Brendon Butterfield SFPD. We met in Palo Alto earlier.'

'Detective Butterfield, yes, how can I help you?' Butterfield pictured Agent Adamson sitting in some large glass-walled private office with comfortable leather reclining office chairs and beautifully well-presented secretaries bustling about with buff coloured files. In contrast to his own office, he pictured Adamson's had plush carpets and floor to ceiling windows showing an expansive view over a golf course or perhaps a cityscape high up in a skyscraper complete with a helipad on the roof. The reality, however, was somewhat different.

'Probably a case of how I can help you,' retorted the detective. He was used to sparring with other law enforcement jurisdictions. It was an old game they always played. By instinct now they duelled the automatic game of one-upmanship based on who knew more than the other.

'Then how can you help me?' said Agent Adamson, with effort applying a friendlier tone which was far from natural for him.

Butterfield spoke, there was a long pause, then, 'Wow!' exclaimed Adamson when Butterfield had finished his summary. 'If this is even half accurate it's international and way outside both of our jurisdictions. I'll find out what I can about Wolf and his activities at a Federal level. You'll do what you need to do with regards to following up on this woman Lee Hyo-joo for your own investigation. We should both send this up the line to our superiors. It sounds to me like we're in the realms of the spooks at the CIA but I'll let my boss make that call,' concluded Agent Adamson. 'By the way, how did you crack this open so quickly?'

'Shrewd detective work, Mr Adamson, shrewd detective work!'

Agent Mick Adamson's impulsive scoff was audible. 'Very well, Detective Butterfield, have it your way.' The phone clicked dead.

#

Less than an hour later, across multiple time zones and 8,000 miles away, a secure phone rang in a white Range Rover parked in a quiet location close to Hong Kong's Peak. Plug, Guy, and Wendy had been discussing next steps and how to keep Wendy safe. Plug looked at the phone for a number, however, it was encoded with no caller identity. Following protocol he answered and offered nothing, not even a hello, awaiting the caller to speak first and identify themselves.

'Plug? Quinn here in London. Seems we have a situation in Hong

Kong and I need to give you a heads-up.'

Andrew Smith glanced at his wristwatch. 'Very early in the morning for you sir. Sorry to be the reason your night's sleep is disturbed,' Plug lied. His vintage Rolex sparkled in the sunlight and Plug noticed it was just passed 4:00 a.m. in London. He was delighted Quinn was disturbed. Quinn always called him Plug in public and contributed to the propagation of the nickname. Quinn was an overweight career civil servant who fancied himself as some sort of twenty-first century Mycroft Holmes character. True, he did report directly to the Director General of MI6 and was regularly expected to brief the Prime Minister. He also sported a formidable intellect and powerfully retentive memory for facts and data. Outside of work, Quinn's hobby was puzzles and he would join multiple pub quiz teams, usually helping them to win hands down even after copious amounts of wine, gin and tonics, and his particular passion, port.

Quinn continued, 'Seems the US have stumbled across a computer virus that can take command of North...'

'I know sir and I have Wendy Chen in my car with me as we speak.' Plug delighted in cutting him off mid-sentence. In the conventional protocol-laden spheres of diplomatic parlance in Her Majesty's Civil Service, interrupting a superior mid-sentence, certainly one as self-important as Quinn, was the metaphorical equivalent of a running kick to the testicles and Quinn was certainly not used to it. He was even more flabbergasted to learn Plug was well abreast of the situation, actively involved, and even in the company of one of the protagonists.

Quinn stuttered and spluttered, then spouted, 'Well who is she? What's she got to do with MI6? And why are you with her? Eh?'

Plug appreciated these were the small hours in London and his boss had been rudely awoken. He had an image of Quinn's rotund form propped up in bed by overstuffed pillows with a black satin eyeshade pushed up onto his bald forehead and brushed cotton paisley patterned pyjamas stretched over his portly belly.

'Wendy Chen is a Singaporean and, yes, she has a copy of the malware we believe can be used to initiate the launch of the Rodong-1 missiles. How she came by it is not important at the moment but it is accurate to say her life is in danger as a result. She's with an Englishman her…colleague.' Quinn picked up on the pause. 'Her colleague, who she's fallen in with is Guy Anderson. He's a British subject.' Plugs gaze flicked from one to the other. 'He's also in danger hence him reaching out to Her Majesty's Civil Service here in Hong Kong. With respect sir, can you tell me how MI6 in London is involved?' Knowing this was pushing his luck Plug hastily added, 'It may help us to determine our next steps sir.'

Quinn paused while thinking. Plug knew his angle would only be to avoid at all costs a diplomatic incident with the Chinese Government in Hong Kong. Britain's relationship with China was tenuous at best and he would pay scant regard for the lives of the two people sat in the Range Rover right now. Plug pushed the phone close to his ear so they wouldn't overhear Quinn.

'Ms Chen is a non-British citizen and presumably committed a crime of theft in South Korea. Neither is of concern to us. I recommend she turn herself over to the Hong Kong police and let them deal with that matter and her security. Mr Anderson might require protection and the best way to achieve that is to distance himself from Ms Chen pretty damn quick and get the next flight anywhere. With regards to our friends over the pond, I'll suggest to the CIA that they deal with Han Electronics through diplomatic channels and any shenanigans they're having with North Korea.'

'Thank you for your guidance sir. I'll be sure to pass your suggestions along to the parties involved.' With that he heard Quinn click off and presumably try to go back to sleep. Another near diplomatic crisis for Her Majesty's Government successfully averted in his tidy mind.

'What was all that about?' asked Guy. Wendy was looking anxious.

Plug looked at them both and saw the anxiety in Wendy pretty face. 'That was Her Majesty's Civil Service in London. Yes, MI6, and it seems the CIA are also involved. Don't ask me how. And I've been instructed to take the necessary steps to protect you both until this all blows over,' he lied.

Chapter 18. Payload

Seoul and Yongbyon. Monday morning.

The one aspect S.C. Lee truly loved about his job was the cutting-edge nature of the technology he got to play with. He had worked for Han Electronics since graduating from the Korea Advanced Institute of Science and Technology almost twenty years before. 'Heavens! It's more than twenty years ago now,' he realised. He rarely considered his career; he was quite content in his routine. But when he did consider it, he was simply proud to be part of a team that got to develop "really cool technology stuff." His staff would tell him this on the few occasions he took them for beers after work.

Amongst his other job title's these days was Chief Information Security Officer or CISO, a position which reported directly into the President and CEO, Mr Kim Sung-han. His boss trusted him implicitly. A trust which was reciprocated. For twenty years, their relationship had been built on this trust and mutual respect. S.C. Lee suspected he was the only person Mr Kim actually discussed ideas with as opposed to simply issuing instructions which was the usual modus operandi of Korean companies.

Their relationship had indeed been lucrative. Mr Lee was paid an agreeable salary and every year his CEO also saw fit to issue stock options to Mr Lee, which he never bothered to sell once they had vested. Once a year he would look at the growing balance for tax purposes and was pleased to see his personal value had grown to over US$10m. This was thanks largely to the measured and consistent growth of the company and therefore its value, and so his value. Occasionally S.C. Lee contemplated retirement and he had pipe dreams about what he would do with his time and money if he retired. Then, a really exciting project would come along, and it would confirm to him that his passion was technology. His fervour was problem solving and inventing 'really cool' things. Now, stood in the airy mountains outside Seoul in middle of a deserted field with a small, select group from his team at 5:00 a.m. on this cool, gin-clear, fresh August morning, was one such occasion.

Unmanned Aerial Vehicles, UAVs, or drones as they're more commonly called, are about as exciting as state-of-the-art technology can get if you're a nerd. At heart, S.C. Lee and the small skunkworks team he had assembled for this project probably redefined the noun nerd. For such seemingly innocent looking toys, drones or UAVs are a techie's dream, requiring a huge amount of technical innovation. The sheer complexity of building an aircraft, which is what they fundamentally are, is almost on par with building a passenger airliner. The airframe, power systems, avionics, navigation system, are all state-of-the-art, and all this must to be done on a miniature scale. For this particular beast, much of the technology had been developed from scratch or at best heavily adapted from Han Electronics existing intellectual property.

He looked around and appreciated the magnificence of the mountains, part of the ridge which ran the length of the Korean peninsula. He paused, tipped his head back and squinted into the clear-blue sky, the slightest breeze stoked his cheeks. 'Perfect!' S.C. Lee and his team could barely contain their excitement. Like kids on Christmas morning, few had slept much the previous night. When their collective alarms went off at 2:00 a.m. none struggled to jump out of bed. Some had even worked through the night, so totally committed they were to making sure their piece of this three-dimensional puzzle fitted together perfectly and, more importantly, didn't fail at 2,000 feet.

Conditions were perfect on the flat grassy field 25 miles east of Seoul in the foothills of the Taebaek Mountains, the mountain range that made up the backbone of Korea. The field had been earmarked for development into yet another golf course to compliment the more than 400 golf clubs South Korea could already boast. A very light, fresh breeze whispered from the west. The sky was cloudless, and the air was cool with low dew and humidity given they were now a few thousand feet in elevation. They were also only 10 miles south of the DMZ, the demarcation line splitting North Korea from South Korea. The field had been carefully selected because it was miles from the nearest town, there were no nearby power lines or cell phone towers, and no one to notice the ground being carefully flattened and mown over the recent weeks. All in all, the perfect conditions for the maiden flight of Han Electronics first prototype Unmanned Aerial Vehicle.

The small huddle of engineers worked out of the back of the scruffy, red, forty-foot container. The rusty container had been dropped off before sunrise and the driver dispatched back to Seoul to ensure the fewer people that witnessed this event the better. No one bar the essential team of ten core engineers knew what they were about. The thousands of emulations around stresses, manoeuvrability, longevity of flight, and the million other variables had been tested to exhaustion in computer simulations; however, nothing came close to the thrill of seeing the real bird take flight for the very first time. "Bird" was the operative word.

The team had named the drone Dogsuli, the Korean word for eagle. S.C. liked the name. It occurred to him the drone was very much like an eagle. Dogsuli was much bigger though, measuring ten feet long with a wingspan of thirteen feet. It was streamlined and had variable flared wingtips, driven by tiny servos for manoeuvrability, looking much like the Korean native bird. Privately he even hoped this might assist with detection avoidance with people seeing Dogsuli and thinking, 'It's only an eagle!' He also liked the name because the surveillance ability of the drone was exceptional, much like the eagle's exceptional eyesight. Finally, S.C. Lee mused, its true mission known only to himself, the real birds in their natural habitat lived all over Asia and every November many of the Dogsuli living in China would migrate in winter to the warmer climate of South Korea. It amused S.C. to think these birds would simply fly from China to South Korea, right over North Korea, oblivious to politics, the DMZ, and anti-aircraft weapons. How ironic.

At last the team was ready. Final software had been loaded, batteries charged, and tweaks made. The apprehension was electric as the ten-foot-long and thirteen-foot wide Dogsuli was reverently wheeled out of the container by all ten men. She was rested on the ground, facing into the breeze, with small chocks placed to brace each of the wheels. There she sat, majestic and powerful, poised for instruction. She was dormant now although oozing latent power. Dogsuli was beautiful. The ten men stood back and marvelled at their achievement.

For most, Dogsuli represented the pinnacle of their engineering careers to date. The upper fuselage was sandy matt yellow with grey camouflage to break the visible image if seen from above. The underside was light blue and grey so camouflaged against the sky if seen from below. There had been serious debate if they should go with the brown colour scheme of the native eagle or even their larger cousin the cinereous vulture. Both were common sights across Asia. The final conclusion was better to go for not being seen at all than being seen with the hope of mistaken identity.

In keeping with the eagle theme, the engineering team had adopted the name Houston for the flight control centre. This was the small isolated room which sat in the rear of the forty-foot container and consisted of an impeccably clean array of monitors, joysticks, and switches. All were linked to Dogsuli via both radio and line-of-sight laser where possible. The whole scruffy container was, on the inside purpose built for Dogsuli with the walls, floor, and ceiling all panelled with white Perspex. Spotless tool racks adorned every wall and the cradle housing the drone sat square in the middle. Two of the engineers would sit in Houston and monitor Dogsuli's every move. S.C. appreciated the humour and acknowledgement, giving due respect to the US Apollo Programme in the 1960s and 1970s; although hearing, 'Houston, we have a problem!' every time there was a minor glitch was becoming tiresome. Regardless, team's spirit was important, and they would always laugh and then get on with solving the problem.

Much of Dogsuli's activities were preprogramed. The flight plan, navigation, and surveillance goals were all pre-set, however, if manual intervention were needed then the human touch could be administered. Houston, by benefit of being in the container, was also mobile therefore, within reason, the control centre could be driven around if needed, making this drone ideal for military purposes. This was the official rumour allowed to circulate in Han Electronics: Han Electronics was moving into the defence industry sector.

When Kim Sung-han first approached S.C. Lee, his Chief Information Security Officer and confidant, summoning him into his spacious penthouse office to discuss the idea of building drones, S.C. had been very sceptical. This was a long way from Han Electronics Inc.'s staple of mobile phones and consumer electronics. It was also massively expensive for research and development costs. Intelligence, Surveillance, Target Acquisition and Reconnaissance capable Unmanned Aerial Vehicles, ISTAR UAVs, could cost tens of millions of dollars each to buy and billions to develop.

'Regardless,' argued Kim Sung-han to his Chief Security Officer, 'Korea is still technically at war, the Korean War never being formally declared as over, and we spend billions on defence technology from foreign vendors every year. Why shouldn't Korea develop their own technology?' He reasoned as his voice raised with the passion of his convictions, 'The US with Northrop Grumman and Europe with Thales are the major defence manufacturers, however, Israel, Germany, Norway and now obviously the Chinese with their China Aerospace Science and Technology Corporation are all getting in on the act! Yet Korea leads the world with smartphones, chip manufacturing, and software development so we should be capable of leading the high-tech defence industry? Eh!' With this, the President and CEO of Han Electronics banged his desk with his fist.

S.C. Lee had never seen his boss so animated and knew better than to question his thinking. After all, he did have a very good point. S.C. Lee offered to build a case study and asked if his boss would allow him thirty days to do so. 'You have ten days and assume an unlimited budget for the time being,' barked Mr. Kim, spittle flying from his mouth.

With this, S.C. Lee sensed he had been dismissed and, with excitement knotting in his stomach, S.C. Lee nearly ran from his boss's office and immediately assembled his ten brightest engineers in their regular whiteboard-walled "Ideas" meeting room.

That had been nearly six months ago and now, today, on this quiet and idyllic morning in a field full of wildflowers and fresh air smelling of recently mown grass in rural Korea, they were looking down upon their beautiful creation. It was the most intelligent and far-reaching project in the history of Han Electronics. This must not fail. S.C. Lee preformed the final action, removing eight, for luck, small USB's from his pocket. He placed them in a small compartment in the underbelly of Dogsuli and closed the hatch. The other ten engineers stole sideways looks at each other. None were aware of this part of the plan. S.C. Lee was known for his meticulous planning even to the point of obsession and all knew, or thought they knew, every part of the plan. Their expressions betrayed that none knew of this. S.C. Lee stood back and nodded towards two engineers who both nodded in reply and walked back into the container to seat themselves in Houston. As both tried to stifle their smiles, they started punching their keyboards and Dogsuli faintly hummed into life.

The remaining engineers stood back in a circle and gave Dogsuli due space. She was designed as a hybrid. She had a small traditional AVGAS powered engine driving a nose propeller for cruising long distance, 250 miles or ten hours on one tank of gas in this case.

She could also be flipped to an electric motor that powered the wing rotors for close-range work, where silence was necessary or no heat signature desired. It was a useful backup too when the fuel ran out and the batteries could self-charge from tiny photovoltaic solar panels on every upper wing surfaces. Lee's team knew this type of UAV is referred to as a Medium Altitude Long Endurance or MALE drone, although the engineers all referred to it as 'her', affectionately, in the feminine. For every one of the engineers, it was love at first sight.

The combination of internal combustion and electric power could give this UAV up to 375 miles or fifteen hours in one round trip depending on sunlight and winds. The final touch was a hara-kiri feature, adapted from the Japanese term for ritual suicide. In the event that the drone was caught or unavoidably crash-landed in enemy territory, small pipes of the highly flammable AVGAS fuel circulated around the airframe. This had the dual function of enabling weight distribution to be intelligently and dynamically adjusted in flight as well as providing an accelerant to seven tiny pea-sized parcels of pyrotechnic explosives dotted about the wings and fuselage of the drone. In the sad event of being lost in action, Dogsuli would simply self-destruct by detonating the small packets of high explosive and the accelerant of fuel would cause the whole drone to combust. Almost all components were made of light, combustible materials. The fuel would coat all meaningful parts of the aircraft in the flammable liquid so destroying it by fire before capture. S.C. Lee was particularly proud of this feature believing that all the Korean intellectual property could be safeguarded in the event of the drone falling into enemy hands. Afterall, he didn't want the Koreans to be caught out as the Americans had been in Belgrade in 1999.

The slightest puff of blue smoke spluttered from the little engine and flaps, rotors, rudder, and trims were all tested as she sat on the ground. The engineers sniffed the heady fragrance. The pleasant, sweet smell of the AVGAS mixed with that of the fresh mown grass. They mouthed silent prayers while the minutes passed. As the engine warmed to operating temperature, the avionics, software, and surveillance equipment were all tested in sequence. After what seemed an eternity, Houston signalled two fisted hands with thumbs pointing away from each other for the miniature chocks to be pulled away. The little craft revved to full power and shot away along the grass runway, gently getting airborne after 100 feet. The horizontal rotors would not be used for a runway take-off to save electric power.

Dogsuli cleared the ground, banked right, and gracefully climbed to the ecstatic applause of the engineers who were unable to contain themselves and were now hopping and dancing around like small boys while high-fiving each other.

After a pre-programmed sequence of aerial manoeuvres performed in the clear sky overhead, to the delight of the collective fathers, the two engineers in Houston confirmed to their boss, S.C. Lee, that Dogsuli was performing exactly as expected. They then asked for permission to go to the second phase of testing and conduct a longer cross-country flight. S.C. Lee smiled the affirmative and Dogsuli turned onto finals, lining up with the runway, flaps down, and prepared to land. She rocked her wings gently as she descended to kiss the grass field in a landing configuration. The approach looked perfect until the very last second when the flaps quickly retracted to 10 degrees and full power was applied. Dogsuli, as if sensing the playfulness of her creators, buzzed just feet over their heads causing all to dive for cover before she accelerated away on a heading north until the little dark spec in the blue morning sky vanished.

\#

In the centre of Seoul, Kim Sung-han sat back in the large leather chair in his presidential office and was reviewing his day's schedule ahead. It was early morning and he had come to the office at dawn. He was excited. Lee Hyo-joo was due back this morning and, even though it had only been two nights, his personal life had been empty without her. His private phone suddenly vibrated on the large highly polished desk and he grabbed it seeing the call was from his CISO, S.C. Lee. They had a policy of only discussing work over the phone if project codenames and implied speak could be used. Security was paramount between them, and phone communications were easily intercepted, he knew, as they had developed much of the technology Korean telco's used. Mr. Kim didn't need to interpret implied speak or project codenames this morning as S.C. Lee's giggly tone said it all. Dogsuli worked like a dream and had departed for her maiden mission.

He hung up on the short call, reclined in the large leather office chair, and reflected. The reality suddenly struck him. He was about to deliver the first strike in what might, if it all went very wrong, result in an all-out global nuclear war. As the assassination of the political minion Archduke Ferdinand in Sarajevo unwittingly catalysed the First World War, would Dogsuli catalyse the Third he wondered?

Around this time, now in stealth mode, the drone was flying at 20 knots at a height of 150 feet over the DMZ and into North Korean airspace. Too low for radar, too small for sonar, too quiet to be heard, and too high to be seen from the ground, and so no one noticed Dogsuli making her steady progress northwards.

#

Five hours later, Dogsuli killed her little AVGAS engine and gradually dropped from her cruising height. All the time she scrutinized activity above and below her. Now under the power of the electric motors she hovered 650 feet in the air near the North Korean defence facility in Yongbyon. Completely nondescript from the air, this location was believed to house one of the largest static missile siloes the Democratic People's Republic of Korea possessed. It was also understood some of these missiles were tipped with nuclear warheads.

Even though it was daylight, the heat sensors on the drone were highly sensitive and could detect a person's body heat on the ground below. The two pilots who sat at the back of a rusty old red container called Houston hundreds of miles away could only detect minimal movement on the surface. Probably small kids playing in the dirt or even large animals like dogs, pigs, or goats. The preconfigured software which determined the flight plan calculated it was time to deploy the payload.

The location for the drop wasn't directly into the Yongbyon missile base but 300 feet away above the commuter road used by the military staff working at the base. There were lots of small factories and worker accommodation in the area although intelligence photographs, many from satellites, suggested the factories were largely a cover for a very well protected military facility. Intelligence showed the facility had three shifts per day, seven days a week, all year round. Few of the staff had cars, some had bicycles, but most walked, or more accurately marched, to and from the base at shift change. These were the target.

Dogsuli quickly dropped to 30 feet above the ground, not enough for the rotors to kick up dust or barely be heard. The Koreans marched on the right-hand side of the road. It was along the right-hand side that Dogsuli hovered as she popped the hatch on the small underside compartment to allow the eight small USB drives to fall randomly into the dust on the side of the road. The job was done within a couple of seconds. Dogsuli rapidly gained height again. Without attracting any real interest, aside from some small children playing nearby who believed they had briefly seen a large bird. The drone recalculated her track home, turned south and leisurely climbed back to her cruising altitude. Only one of the eight USB's needed to be found and used. Now the trap had been baited, all that remained was to wait.

Chapter 19. A Plan

Hong Kong. Monday Morning.

It was a very tastefully appointed apartment. Guy stood, looked around and appreciated the good quality of the furniture and artefacts, mostly antique Chinese and colonial British. The morning sun filtered through the large windows accentuating the fine porcelain and exquisite glazes. Plug's apartment was in a gated compound in Mid-Levels, the posh part of Hong Kong. Since the British traders had 'leased' Hong Kong in 1842, the business of Hong Kong was purely that of a trading port. Berths in the harbour and storage sheds, which clung like the muscles and limpets to the narrow shoreline of Hong Kong Island, defined the island's economy.

To avoid the withering heat and humidity of mid-summer, the wealthier traders would build houses higher up on Victoria Peak, far above the berths, to benefit from cooler air. The slight breezes cooled, there were fewer mosquitoes, and it avoided the stench of the fragrant harbour itself. Today The Peak and Mid-Levels are still the most desirable areas to live, with most of the embassies and consulates housing their senior expat staff in these easy to secure condominiums.

Wendy was using the bathroom while Guy and Plug sat in the living room discussing Hong Kong politics and the job of diplomacy in Asia, all while sharing a large pot of English Breakfast tea. Guy broached the subject of the stylishly decorated apartment and tasteful collection of books, art, and sculptures. To his amusement, Plug actually blushed and confessed that as a confirmed bachelor he enjoyed surrounding himself with valuable antiquities both for their ascetic pleasure and investment value. He was an avid amateur collector and was even working on a book on the subject in his spare time. It was a small and beautiful apartment, looking down towards Central, meticulously tidy, with no feminine clutter or influence. Very much a wealthy bachelor's pad. Plug had invited Wendy and Guy to stay over for the night as he felt it was the safest option for them. Besides, he enjoyed Guys company and Wendy was very easy on the eyes.

Contrary to popular movies, Plug assured them the Secret Service didn't have a ready selection of safe houses on demand for the protection of defecting foreign master spy's, or organised crime lords who needed protection before spilling the beans on their compatriots.

He'd said, 'besides, no one will see you come or go from here and no one would expect you to stay with me so you're quite safe.' A discreet enquiry through diplomatic channels to the Four Seasons Hotel confirmed Wendy Chen's possessions which she had abandoned in her room had been packed and stored by the hotel, however, they were unable to release them as Ms Chen was a 'person of interest' to the police. The hotel had been told to contact them if Ms Chen arrived back at the hotel.

'I'm afraid you're going to need to wear the same knickers,' shouted Guy through the closed bathroom door.

'I'm not wearing any,' came the flippant response.

Guy caught Plugs smirk at the retort while he was head down pouring more tea. 'She's quite a girl,' said Plug who had clearly warmed to Wendy during the previous evening's dinner conversation. They had ordered in a Thai meal to avoid eating out. He liked Wendy, not least because she only called him Andrew.

'Oh, more surprises than a bag full of fortune cookies that one!' said

Guy rolling his eyes.

The intercom buzzed and Plug jumped up to answer it. He could see through the camera display the guest being stalled by the two security guards at the main gate. The guest held up his Hong Kong ID and Plug said, 'Let him up please.' A short while later there was another buzz from Security at Plug's specific block and the same protocol was followed. Eventually John's smiling face met them as Plug opened the door to his apartment.

'Strewth! No one's going to break in here in a hurry, are they?' John said with a smile. They had agreed the previous evening over the Thai green curry that they needed a plan. Guy explained to Plug he had involved his friend John, a software engineer who lived in Discovery Bay. He had run the malware in emulation and confirmed the code was real and in all likelihood was capable of taking command and control of the computers responsible for launching missiles.

They had called John and invited him to meet them at Plug's apartment the following morning. It made sense to get his input on the predicament considering he knew some of the details already and was technically the most well versed with the actual malware than anyone else other than the black hat who had coded it.

Guy made the introduction to Andrew as Wendy emerged from the bathroom still towelling her wet hair. She made towards the kitchen mentioning something about making coffee. Plug leapt up and cut her off, offering to do it, 'Please allow me. You should sit down with John and Guy.' Whether that was Plug being a polite host or the fact that he didn't want Wendy messing up his presumably pristine kitchen was unclear. Regardless, as Wendy bent to sit on the sofa, both men discreetly paused to watch her skin-tight jeans stretch over her peachy bum to see if they could determine if there was any sign of her wearing underwear. The momentary distraction was sadly lost on John.

While Plug was in the kitchen making coffee, Guy and Wendy bought John up to speed on the previous two days excitement since they had left his apartment in Discovery Bay. It seemed like an age ago and they were quite relaxed, almost detached, from the horror of being chased and shot at. John marvelled at the story with a look of awe and fear. The realization struck him that this was way more serious than he had predicted and cautioned them about as they had departed from his doorstep.

Plug emerged from the kitchen with four mugs of freshly brewed coffee on a tray. They were accompanying a packet of McVitie's Chocolate Digestives carefully arranged on a blue willow-patterned plate. 'Wonderfully English here in the Orient, to the point of cliché,' thought Guy. John just grabbed a biscuit and chomped into it.

After the four of them had collectively shared all they knew with each other and privately ingested the facts, Plug finally said, 'Where from here guys? We can't leave Guy and Wendy to the risk of being shot by a gang of unknown assassins. Also, if this malware is for real, are the South Koreans really looking to steal or worse attempt to launch the missiles? And if so at whom? They surely wouldn't prompt a missile attack at South Korea, that would be suicide, so then who? China? Russia? Would a South Korean industrial conglomerate be planning a false flag attack on the North's allies, and if so, why? There would be little or no gain and only huge downside. I find this all very strange,' confessed Plug. Guy locked his hands behind his head and looked heavenward and if searching for divine inspiration. John helped himself to another biscuit.

John sat on the sofa and looked thoughtful as he nibbled his chocolate biscuit; he was the only one who did. At last John said,

'I've been giving this a lot of thought. Your remarks are all correct Andrew. Why would a South Korean electronics company want to steal or launch North Korean rockets? We know the DPRK's missiles are technically inferior to the US missiles deployed in the South therefore there's no technical or intellectual property gain to be had. This can't be an attempt at vandalism. Sure, they might be able to take down one or two missile sites temporarily, however, I doubt the sites are interconnected so any damage is very localised and no more than an irritation. Most of the missiles are mobile anyway so again, pointless.'

He paused for a moment, looking one at a time at his audience. They were intrigued by his logic and the only audible sound was a distant clock ticking and the birdsong in the trees outside.

He continued, 'Even if they could damage the launch computers, they'll be easy to reformat and reinstall from a backup so there is no gain there either. The only conclusion I can come to is that this malware is designed to cause an unscheduled launch, assuming the weapons are fuelled. So, then the question is who are they aimed at? Surely not the South itself. But, and it's a big but, were the North to be seen to launch a preemptive attack on the South, Japan, or even their closest ally China, even if it's subsequently found to be accidental, it would immediately catalyse a response from the South and the US.

The DPRK have pushed their luck in the past, the sinking of the South Korean ship Cheonan in 2010 for example, although these have only been localised skirmishes. Were a nuclear missile fired, even if the warhead didn't detonate, I'd suspect the US would decide enough was enough and move to act on the DPRK. Sure the Chinese would probably grumble, but ultimately would not get involved fearing North Korea can't be trusted to control their weapons of mass destruction anyway. And if a rogue missile did hit a Chinese city, they would likely privately welcome, even discreetly support, the actions of the US.'

Plug, Wendy, and Guy were all sat looking at John. 'So,' Guy said, 'your logic makes sense but do you really think all this is about spoofing the US, possibly even with China's help, to forcibly act on Pyeongyang and ultimately rid them of their nuclear arsenal?'

'I can't possibly see another angle,' said John, reaching for another chocolate digestive. 'Fact is I've mulled through as many scenarios as I can and this is the only conclusion I can come to.'

'Then what are we to do?' asked Wendy, concerned about escalating tensions on the Korean peninsula and more specifically in context to her own safety.

'Ah,' offered John, 'you see that's where you come in. You have a copy of the malware. We could give this to the CIA, MI6, whoever, although they'll probably just do what I did and confirm that it works. The issue is what if this already has been deployed, or more likely is now in the process of being deployed in DPRK?'

'How would we know?' asked Plug, a bit unsure of practicalities of launching missiles.

John crunched into the biscuit; his spare hand cupped under his mouth careful not to spray crumbs over the expensive looking silk rug on the floor. 'Short of missiles whistling overhead or mushroom clouds on the horizon, you would see it on CNN,' replied John.

Guy spoke, 'so, the best-case scenario is Han Electronics does nothing with this code, fearing repercussions; although Wendy is still vulnerable given she has a copy which is still incriminating.'

Guy was careful how he described Wendy's predicament. 'And the worst-case scenario is all out nuclear war. Well that's a relief!' poked Guy with heavy sarcasm.

John agreed. 'Truth is I don't see much middle ground either. Even if Han Electronics does have a change of heart regarding this dangerous folly, Wendy is a loose end they would probably want tidied-up. You too probably by association now Guy. More likely, if your, err, - coming by this malware - causes them to accelerate their plans, this could all get very messy very quickly.'

Wendy was pale and tightly squeezing Guy's hand as they sat side by side on Plug's white leather sofa. 'I've done a little covert research myself,' said John who continued, 'There are three wild cards with North Korea's missiles. The first is that I have to believe Han Electronics have someone on the inside with detailed knowledge of the missiles and their launch protocols. It's probably either a very senior General with intimate knowledge of the systems or a worker at one of the storage locations. You see, firstly, you don't simply turn a key or press a big red button and missiles start flying, despite what Hollywood would have us believe. The missiles take time to prepare including fuelling them. They use a highly volatile rocket fuel, which is why they don't sit there with the tanks full; they need to be fuelled first to be ready for flight. Likewise, the warheads themselves are not permanently fitted; they're stored in a bombproof bunker nearby. For this malware to actually fire a weaponised missile would assume it knows when they are ready to be fired, such as a full rehearsal military drill.'

John went on, 'the second point is many of these missiles are mobile meaning they're never in one place for very long. Rather they're being shuffled around the countryside on portable launch platforms on trucks or trains. Again, this points to someone on the inside who either knows where the location of a mobile site will be, or the location of a static site to be able to target such as a purpose-built bunker. Okay, I presume Secret Service agencies, perhaps Andrew here, can figure out as much from satellite imagery as there will be dummy sites as well as real ones therefore to know the difference still needs inside knowledge.'

'Which brings me to my third point, which is this software needs to be installed. Because something as critical as missile launch systems can't be vulnerable to being hacked, they're not networked to anything else; they have to be completely stand alone. This means someone has to physically install the malware. I have to believe this is an inside job,' concluded John, with a smugness inbred only in computer engineers.

Plug had listened intently. 'So, this whole thing might be an inside job all along. A plot by a rogue element within the DPRK whose possible agenda is to overthrow the current leader Kim Jong-un?' It was rhetorical and he wasn't looking for an answer, more considering how he would feed this up his chain of command in MI6. Rich intelligence; indeed, it wasn't every day in the mundane life of a spook that they were fed such a well formatted story delivered on a plate.

'So,' John inserted forcefully before the conversation when off at a tangent. He wanted to interject to complete his train of thought as he had not quite finished. 'To conclude this, and protect Wendy while averting a nuclear war,' he added flippantly, 'we need to know who in North Korea is the inside man or more likely men, then we need to learn when and where the malware is due to be loaded.' John was not known in his mundane day job for theatrics, however, he was enjoying this and stood up and walked to the window. 'I doubt the diplomatic channels would work or be fast enough if they did. We need to solve this!' He spun around to confront the other three.

'How on earth are we able to do that?' Guy spluttered, the exasperation clear in his tone.

'We could approach Mr Kim Sung-han at Han Electronics. If he's involved he would know, or knows someone who would know, and we'll easily get his attention as we've got something he badly wants,' replied John drily. 'My recommendation is we blackmail CEO Kim to tell us who he's got on the inside in the DPRK. Now other governments are aware of the plan, Mr Kim will face treason if implicated, even a well-leaded rumour could destroy him and his company. He either needs to terminate the plot or execute it very quickly and hope it succeeds.'

Guy was holding John's gaze, not believing he was hearing a word of this from a sensible mate and colleague he had always admired for being completely rational. 'Go on. Exactly how would we do that? Call him up?'

Someone needs to go to South Korea, meet Mr Kim, and talk him out of it. And if that doesn't work, go to the Democratic People's Republic of Korea and stop this!' John was looking back pointedly at Guy.

Guy burst out laughing, 'You can't be serious! This is a job for government diplomatic and military channels. Besides what do I know about blackmail or nuclear missiles? I wouldn't know where to start! This is a job for his mob,' Guy said, pointing with his thumb to Plug. He slumped back into the sofa still holding Wendy's hand. 'Besides,' he mumbled 'we can't even get to Wendy's hotel room without being shot at. How would we or I possibly even get to the airport, catch a flight, and get to Seoul without causing trouble? I would have to believe they'll be watching the airport and the border crossings to China? We'd be arrested within thirty minutes of walking out of here.'

Wendy had been thoughtful and quiet for a while but then jumped in and said, 'If anyone has to go it's me. I got us into this mess in the first place. Where should I start?'

It was Andrew's turn to take sympathy and interject, 'Wendy, you're a brave woman, however, you are in too much danger already.' Plug was close to offering himself when he realised he would never be approved for such a mission and could hardly involve himself in espionage in Korea on a whim. He too stood and paced around the living room now, looking absently at his artefacts proudly displayed with impeccable care and spacial consideration.

'If anyone's going it's me,' insisted Guy.

'You're not going without me, death threats or not!' Insisted Wendy with even more force.

'But fair dinkum Guy,' John's Aussie accent emerging, 'You're right, how do we get you out of Hong Kong and into South Korea without the people who are out to get you knowing? And mind you, we still don't know who they are or who they're working for. My guess is they'll still try to finish the job they started.'

Plug looked up from admiring his Tang Dynasty pottery horse, 'Ahem, now I might be able to help with that one.'

Hong Kong. Seoul. Monday Evening.

Despite the seriousness of the situation and the fool's errand they may have talked themselves into undertaking, she couldn't help a little self-indulgent smile as she slid down into the excessively ostentatious cream leather seat. She pulled the complimentary cashmere pashmina around her shoulders and mentally checked another box on her bucket list. She was struck by the rich and complex smells of leather, cigars, and jet fuel. Wendy had never flown in a private jet before. She decided she wanted to make the most of everything the aircraft had to offer. The two pilots had made a fuss of her as she boarded, and the attractive middle-aged stewardess kept offering titbits of exquisite looking tapas and a selection of drinks. She suspected the stewardess, Mae, who formally introduced herself with a handshake, was probably just trying to alleviate her own boredom by keeping busy on the flight. This jet set lifestyle was routine for her, albeit her job.

Wendy was tempted to accept the offer of Champagne, however, on second thoughts and after catching a curious glance from Guy, she decided to avoid all alcohol and stick with the fruit tea. She didn't know what would happen once they landed so she thought it safer to stay fully sober. A nap in the fully reclining leather seat might be in order though. Mae seemed to be paying a bit more attention to the men. This didn't bother Wendy, they could flirt away, as she was happy and comfortable snuggling while appreciating the thrill of her first flight on a private jet.

Plug knew he would get into trouble. 'The British taxpayer had a right to expect their Civil Servants to be frugal with public funds…' he could hear Quinn say, going off on a rant about budgets again. That had never stopped him keeping a well-stocked cocktail cabinet in his own office and enjoying a sherry with every visitor thought Plug. Although, on reflection, he would have to concede a few bottles of Amontillado wasn't quite in the same league as chartering a private jet.

It was early evening and the warm Hong Kong air was stiflingly muggy, teasing relief with a late summer thunderstorm. The afternoon had been busy for Plug, dealing with the administration of arranging the private charter flight from Hong Kong to Seoul's Gimpo International Airport. Perret Executive Air Charters Ltd. had given the British Consulate-General an account secured by the British Government. He applied for diplomatic passes for Guy, Wendy, and John as he thought diplomatic passage would expedite their entry into Korea. He had driven them in the Range Rover to Chek Lap Kok, Hong Kong's International Airport's VIP terminal later that afternoon and escorted them through to security and immigration. To be on the safe side, his heavy Browning was secure in its holster under his jacket but none of them spotted anything suspicious.

Formalities over, he had passed an encrypted mobile phone to Guy with the explicit instruction to keep him fully posted on all their movements. They all agreed on pain of death they would. The men exchanged eye-to-eye looks and firm handshakes with a sense of marching into a medieval pitched battle. Wendy uncharacteristically went onto tiptoes and gave Andrew a kiss on the cheek with a whispered 'thank you' while Plug blushed bright crimson.

The VIP terminal had a separate and discrete entrance to Chek Lap Kok airport, well away from the hoi polloi in Terminals One and Two. It was quiet with only a few businessmen customers, some accompanied by an attractive assistant. There was also a gaggle of slightly drunken Chinese youths with funny clothes and even funnier haircuts. The VIP terminal oozed professional efficiency and service. Guy assumed these young lads were some teenage canto-pop band who were having fun squandering the novelty of fame and wealth. Wendy, John, and Guy steered clear of the boy band and lingered closer to the businesspeople waiting for the trolley buses to take them to their waiting Cessna Citations and Gulfstreams.

During the afternoon, John had assisted by taking Wendy and Guy to a small, quiet mall in Causeway Bay for a bit of shopping. At least they now had clothes and toiletries to accompany them to Seoul. Both were nervous in public, so the shopping was thankfully quick. Wendy had kept the form fitting jeans; however, she also went for a couple of practical businesswomen's white shirts with a business jacket. She also bought a sweatshirt and black woollen jumper to keep her warm. Guy had opted for polo shirts, a dark jacket, and chinos, believing they would pass in any environment.

Earlier that afternoon Guy, Wendy, John, and Plug had all reconvened back at Plug's apartment in Mid-Levels and replayed the plan. They sat, regrouped on the sofa in the same positions as the morning, the same benign magnolia coloured walls backdropped the richly coloured artefacts confirming their safety. Wendy had the USB drive, the original, and John had made a backup to a portable device he always carried. Upon arrival in Seoul Wendy would call Han Electronics and approach Mr Kim.

She would push him to agree to meet in a busy public place in Seoul. There were allowed to be no other parties present. Wendy would offer her original copy back so long as he confirmed that whatever plan this was going to be used for would be shelved. Of course, she had a copy for insurance and if she was harmed this copy would find its way to the intelligence agencies and, more importantly, the world's press, accompanied by a full disclosure of all that had gone on. If she were to come to any harm she would reciprocate and harm Mr Kim and Han Electronics as much as she possibly could. So long as he was good to his word, he would have to take in good faith that her copy of the software would never see the light of day. If Mr Kim disagreed, she would go public immediately and she had friends who would readily support and vindicate her doing just that. There was to be no requests for cash. It was a simple deal. Take it or leave it!

She would assume Mr Kim would have backup close by and hopefully he would assume she would have the same. It was a huge gamble, but they all agreed this was the easiest way out for everyone, if Mr Kim was agreeable to not follow through with whatever plan he had concocted. He also needed to commit to Wendy's safety assuming it was he behind hiring the contract killers in Hong Kong.

Wendy couldn't help feeling this was all depressingly naïve. Her attempt at foiling the plans of multi-billionaires and their corporations with their government connections was laughable. They had already tried to have her publically assassinated on foreign soil, therefore, to think she really had any leverage was beyond stupid. She felt like a very small black fly about to be effortlessly ground up in the machinations of some huge engine. The cogs not noticing her as they meshed together, and the little black fly crushed beyond recognition. Right here right now though, in the tight yet comfortable cabin of the Citation jet, she couldn't come up with a better plan.

In Plug's apartment earlier, they had jointly brainstormed and discussed as many options and variables as they could collectively think up. Plug offered the likely process via official government channels. John speculated on the Dark Web and hacker community. Guy offered some knowledge of military protocols, which he seemed strangely well versed in this given his job was as a consultant for a cybersecurity consultancy. The other three had looked at him with raised eyebrows. He shrugged and claimed the military of various countries were customers of Cyber Security Systems Ltd and he had some dealings with them before. This didn't convince any of the other three although no one pushed him any further.

Now, on the aircraft Guy had swivelled his seat around 180 degrees and faced John. They were still discussing the plan's finer details, however, there were no more alternatives and they couldn't offer any more outcomes. Would Mr Kim readily meet Wendy? Would he agree to her demands? Or would he simply dismiss everything offhand and continue to arrange to have her eliminated? Both were aware of the risk but none, including Plug earlier, could offer any more half-sensible ideas. To not act didn't appeal to any of them either. Wendy insisted without closure she felt she would never be able to sleep soundly or walk down a street without looking over her shoulder, anywhere, ever.

Soon Mae tired of trying to force-feed the two men morsels of tapas and retired to her seat. She bent her head over a mobile phone and, with earphones in, watched a downloaded movie. John dozed off, and Wendy too looked snuggly asleep, her legs curled beneath her. Guy found an action magazine and vaguely read the stories of scuba diving with whale sharks in Micronesia and hiking mountains in western China.

The 1,200 miles to Seoul took the Citation three hours and, with the one-hour time difference, it was late evening when they walked down the few narrow steps off the plane and onto the tarmac of the apron. They admired the polished white paint of the pretty plane, shining like a freshly raced stallion, the red port wing tip light still shining brightly as dusk fell.

Plug had arranged a car, and this met them as soon as Mae had escorted the party through the immigration hall offices of the VIP lounge and expedited clearing the entry procedures on their behalf. Guy and Wendy sat in the rear, while John rode shotgun as the black car sped them in silence from Gimpo International Airport to the discrete hotel Plug had arranged for them under assumed names in Gangnam. The drive took an hour. They checked in without their passports being required and there was no mention of payment. They were quickly shown to their large suite, no questions asked. Plugs diplomatic channels had arranged all this, it was impressive. Guy and Wendy couldn't help but grin at each other.

Plug had kindly arranged a suite in a block of serviced apartments. He had assumed the worst and that Mr Kim's sources in South Korea would learn of their arrival. He guessed they would first check the hotels, but a serviced apartment might slip under the radar. The large, comfortable suite had one lounge with two adjoining bedrooms both boasting ensuite bathrooms. Plug suspected they would all feel safer being close; he was right, and they were all privately grateful. The suite wasn't posh, simply clean and functional, and it looked comfortable enough. A serviced apartment for long staying businesspeople perhaps as there was even a small kitchenette. Their view was over the COEX Convention and Exhibition Centre in the middle of Seoul, on the south side of the River Han.

This was conveniently close to both the Han Electronics offices and where it was understood Mr Kim lived in the wealthy Gangnam district of Seoul. In the huge underground shopping mall attached to the COEX Centre and the adjoining office towers was the large and beautiful Starfield Library. The library was a glorious three-floor open-plan haven for readers and people-watchers alike. It was busy and public, spacious enough to house thousands of books while observing a reverence to reading and personal space. The huge cathedral-like gallery allowed people to be viewed from a distance. This was going to be the suggested meeting spot if Mr Kim could be coaxed into a meeting.

Once settled and refreshed, the three sat in the lounge area of the serviced apartment and Wendy pulled Mr Kim's business card from her bag and dialled the number from the secure phone. She kept her nervous doe-eyes on Guy as the receiving phone rang. Pyongyang was less than 150 miles from Seoul and the thought of short-range ballistic missiles that close made her task feel all the more unnerving now.

#

Kim Sung-han and girlfriend Lee Hyo-joo were relaxing in his apartment. The lights of night-time Seoul twinkled far below them, visible through the floor to ceiling windows. They sat at either end of an expansive black sofa. Dimmed, discrete lighting and fresh flowers in modern vases adorned the glass coffee table lending a pleasant fragrance to the plush ambience. Both enjoyed the tranquillity of the lounge in his apartment. The 180-degree view of up-town Seoul stretched out far below them through the large windows was very impressive, a cityscape panacea available only to the very rich. The sounds of the bustle of city life were inaudible at that height. The constant stop-start of traffic made for an impressive light show with red and white lights writhing in a grid-like pattern, looking like animations in a computer game. Only occasionally was there the very faint sound of a car horn or siren.

With light classical music playing somewhere in the background, Sung-han was working on his laptop. Hyo-joo was sat at the opposing end of the sofa, legs curled under herself to read. She had the occasional interruption, forcing her to grab the buzzing phone, read the message and type a swift reply, although he was never clear what she would be doing. Her few board positions wouldn't keep her so busy he would guess, and she seemed to have few close personal friends, but he never asked her what she was doing, and she never offered. They had an unspoken understanding to respect each other's privacy. She had only arrived back in Seoul a few hours earlier and had come directly to Sung-han's apartment where she showered, dressed in casual loose lounge clothes, and relaxed. She had kissed him formally and said the trip was good and that she had slept well on the long flight back.

They were comfortable together and sometimes one would ask a question of the other. Perhaps he would share an unbaked idea with her he wanted her help to form; or she would ask a politically pertinent question of him regarding some businessman or politician or more likely their wives. It was an intellectually comfortable and compatible relationship. Both had their space, both had their work and projects, both enjoyed each other physically, and neither felt stifled.

Kim found himself of late wondering if this woman was what he was looking for in a wife. He had inherited a legacy and now his thoughts were increasingly turning towards feeling he wanted to leave one also. He was of an age where he should be thinking of starting a family. Lee Hyo-joo was smart for sure although she was not from one of Korea's ruling families from which he would be expected to select a suitable wife. At his social level, marriages were as much a political and financial arrangement as a socially acceptable structure in which to procreate.

Breaking their peacefulness, his business phone rang. The CEO of Han Electronics frowned, his train of thought broken, and he was irritated to think someone would call him this late. It must be important plus few people had this number which he changed regularly anyway. There was no caller ID, which was odd. Regardless he pressed the green button and waited for the caller to speak.

'Hello, Mr Kim?' came the Singaporean accented voice.

'Who is this?' replied a nonplussed Mr Kim.

Wendy recognised his voice, 'Ah, Mr Kim, sorry to call you so late. This is Wendy Chen. We met in your office the other day. I'll be brief. You see I have something of yours I accidently removed from your office and I'd like to meet you to return it.'

Kim Sung-han threw an importunate look towards Hyo-joo who sensed his urgency. She felt the hair prickle on her neck and was alert assuming involvement and expecting he wanted her to participate. Kim Sung-han deftly put the smartphone on loudspeaker. Hyo-joo was poised, a hunting dog getting a whiff of the scent of its prey.

'I see,' said Mr Kim thinking quickly. He assumed the call was being recorded and didn't want to admit to knowledge of what it was she had removed or even the knowledge that she removed it. 'What are you proposing Miss Chen?'

'I'd like you to meet me tomorrow morning 8:45 a.m. at Starfield library by the magazine section. I'll come alone and I'd like you to do the same. I'll return what I have of yours and I have two simple conditions.'

'I see,' replied Mr Kim again, still looking at his partner. Hyo-joo retained a poker player's expression, although she did raise her manicured eyebrows at the mention of conditions. 'Can you tell me those conditions?' asked Mr Kim.

'I would prefer to do that face-to-face Mr Kim. I believe you to be a reasonable and honourable man and I believe if you give me your word on a requested condition that you'll stick to your word. You have my assurance I'll do the same.' Despite the knots in her tummy and slight quaver of her voice, Wendy felt emboldened now they were talking. After all, she was talking to the man she suspected was trying to have her killed.

Lee Hyo-joo remained enigmatic. Mr Kim said, 'have it your way Miss Chen. I'll come and find you at Starfield Library's magazine section tomorrow at 8:45 a.m.' He hit the red button. Wendy picked up on his omission that he was to come alone, however, the call was over so that was that. She didn't believe he really would come alone as much as she had no intention of being alone either. At least in a public place at rush hour she would feel a degree of safety.

'Well done!' smiled Guy. 'I'm sure that will have him thinking. Nothing more we can do until tomorrow morning now.' Wendy still had butterflies although her resolve was now feeding her bravery.

'I think he flipped his phone to loudspeaker, suggesting someone or some others were with him who he wanted to hear the call,' offered John.

'Probably,' suggested Guy, 'but it doesn't matter. If he's out looking for us now, I doubt he'll have any luck between now and tomorrow morning. No one knows we're here and I think the Library is a good venue tomorrow: public, open, many escape routes if needed, and difficult to cover them all. My guess is he'll want to meet Wendy and hear the conditions.'

Wendy and John looked at each other and nodded agreement. 'Nothing else to do now except try and get some rest,' suggested Guy. With no discussion on the subject, it was mutually assumed Guy and Wendy would share one bedroom with John alone in the other. They separated to their functional yet comfortable bedrooms. They heard John call his wife as he closed his bedroom door. Guy and Wendy took turns to shower and Wendy, wearing a fresh white tee shirt she had bought earlier, slid into bed next to Guy. She curled up close to him and tried to sleep. Guy held her tight within

236

the crook of his large arm. His smell and the hairy arm comforted Wendy.

Guy stared up at the ceiling listening for the slightest sounds in the corridor outside the apartment and wondering if sleep would ever come.

Yongbyon. Monday Evening.

Security procedures had been drilled like foundation piles into the staff at the Yongbyon complex. In fact, every day there was a security drill of some description. Some argued that at least the security drills helped break up the monotony of an otherwise tedious existence. There would be the national day parade soon, so drills were expected to be perfect. Party propaganda was constantly piped through the public address system and the missile installation as part of the Yongbyon Nuclear Scientific Research Centre was continually on a high status of alert.

They had to be ready at any time for an unprovoked attack from the imperialist South, the Democratic People's Republic of Korea's sworn enemy, who were under the political and economic control of the American aggressors. Byun Jae-hyung hated the Americans. Of course, he had never been to America but he knew he wouldn't like it. They had corrupted South Korea and therefore his blood relatives, and so by default, they were the sworn enemy of his family. He was proud of his nation and his Supreme Leader.

Byun Jae-hyung was a junior Support Engineer in the Yongbyon Nuclear Scientific Research Centre. He was also proud of his position and his intelligence. He was unlike his parents and siblings who were all farm labourers with rough hands and tanned skin. At 22-years-old, he was educated and people in the facility, indeed the people of the entire Democratic People's Republic of Korea, were safer because of what he knew and what he did for the country. He kept the weapon's computer systems operational and could fix problems when they occurred. He could programme patches and configure users' permissions. His bosses gave him recommendations and he hoped one day he could serve directly under his leader Kim

Jong-un. He would dream at night that Kim Jong-un knew who he was and appreciated what he did for the Workers' Party of Korea.

When he met girls, Jae-hyung would tell them this. Somehow, they never seemed as impressed as he expected they would be but no doubt they were deeply very impressed. He assumed they were even a little intimidated by him as few would ever agree to go on a second date. He had cut his hair in the style modelled by the Party Leader; this undoubtedly made him even better looking. 'Well,' he thought, 'if they didn't want a second date that was their loss.' He knew he was a very eligible man.

This evening, he and twenty of his comrades were walking in formation along the dusty verge next to the road leading to the Yongbyon facility when he noticed something white, plastic, and shiny on the ground. He stooped briefly to pick it up and recognised immediately what it was. He had used them at work for backing-up files and transferring software and updates. He put the USB drive safely into the breast pocket of his green one-piece army overalls. To lose such a tool was a massive breach of protocol. It must be returned to the complex. Ideally whoever was foolish enough to remove this from the facility could be traced and sufficiently reprimanded to never breach security policy again. This would then serve as a warning to others careless enough to remove memory drives from the facility, let alone lose them on the road where anyone could find and steal them. Byun Jae-hyung was appalled at this obvious security breach after so much training had been given to him and his colleagues.

This thought plagued him, and he deliberated how he should proceed as he continued to march in step along the dusty road, all the way from their Korean People's Army provided accommodation to the facility. His obvious action would be to immediately hand the USB drive into his superiors, although in doing that he might not get the deserved recognition for being the finder of this worrisome security breach. The other downside of that approach was not knowing himself what was on the USB drive. It was quite possible it contained information about the configuration of his network and as a Support Engineer he should be aware of this in case he needed to rectify any problems the security breach may have caused. Lastly, whoever removed the USB drive from the facility was undoubtedly a security risk and, even if they were reprimanded, they couldn't be trusted in future. It would then be prudent for him to keep an eye on them, if they kept their job, which he very much doubted.

Support Engineer Byun made up his mind. When he was sat at his terminal, having followed the handover procedure from his peer his shift was replacing, and, assuming he had no urgent matters to attend to, he would inspect the USB drive and see if it was clear who had removed it from the facility in the first place. He would also make a report to his superiors of what was on the USB drive and if he considered any of the files put their missile systems at risk. He fully expected his superiors would welcome this foresight and give him another recommendation. He daydreamed for a moment as he envisioned the reward and would stand proudly to attention as they recognised him. It might even assist his eligibility for a promotion, something he was currently preoccupied with.

Walking through the outer and then inner security gates, his credentials were presented to the security guards he saw several times every day. Today he smiled at their otherwise indifferent faces. Today he had an opportunity to shine. Today perhaps even his revered leader Kim Jong-un would come to hear of his loyalty he daydreamed. Today he would be busy. They had been tipped off to expect a launch rehearsal. This would be a full rehearsal of all procedures of a launch, barring the launch itself. The missiles would be cleaned, maneuverered, fuelled, and armed with warheads. The fuelling process is technically difficult so the launch systems needed to be flawless in their operation.

He arrived at the Administration Building behind the carpool sheds and followed the fluorescently lit grey walled corridors to the Information Technology Support Department on the ground floor and found his drab cubicle. It was a small room and Byun shared this with eight other staff members, all making themselves busy preforming routine inspections and support services. He replaced his colleague in the worn and threadbare office chair and prepared to settle into his shift, however, today would be different. He was passed the clipboard that captured the ongoing checks and open cases he would be expected to continue to work on during this evening's shift. The worksheets could all be done in software, however, not all his superiors had computers, so a paper-based system was still used. 'Good,' he thought out loud, 'Nothing urgent. Only routine checks and change requests.' Nothing as important as what he warmed in his breast pocket.

Once his colleague had cleared and packed his few personal items from the desk, saluted formally, and turned on his heel to leave, Byun Jae-hyung surreptitiously checked none of his eight colleagues were overseeing him. When he was satisfied he wasn't being observed he slid the USB drive from his breast pocket, hesitating briefly as his hand wavered over the small rectangular slot in the computer, before decisively inserting it into the USB slot on the front panel. He punched in a couple of commands to read the files on the drive and then sat forward on his chair to squint at the computer screen. This was strange he thought. He didn't recognize any of these files and, upon further opening a couple more, he didn't even recognize the code. Programming scripts scrolled up the screen before his eyes, mostly moving too fast to read.

Unbeknown to Support Engineer Byun Jae-hyung or for that matter any of his colleagues on his shift that evening, the files were automatically designed to download and execute without any further manual assistance. He was unable to determine what the files were or indeed complete his real mission of identifying the possible owner and therefore the culprit responsible for removing the drive from the Yongbyon facility in the first place. Byun Jae-hyung sat back with his hands locked behind his head and looked blankly at his screen unable to think what to do next. Surely someone had removed this USB drive from the plant and dropped it on their way home to their barracks. It looked like one of the standard USB drives they all used. The only other possibility was someone dropped it walking on their way to the facility but then who would do that. It just didn't make sense. He wracked his brain trying to think what could have happened.

He suddenly sat bolt upright. A knot tightened in his stomach. In a sudden panic he lurched forward and tore the USB drive from its slot. His mouth went dry and he broke into a cold sweat. With all colour draining from his face, he nervously looked around to see if anyone had seen him either insert or remove the USB drive. His hands started to involuntarily shake. He wasn't sure if they had seen him although his neighbour in the next cubical was startled by the sudden movement and looked over at Jae-hyung, such energy and speed of movement was rarely seen in the Engineering Department.

'Rat bit your arse Byun,' said the co-worker unsympathetically. Despite working closely together there was little friendship or comradery in the Engineering Department. He knew his colleagues didn't really like him and he wasn't invited to any social events with them. He knew they envied him and should recognise he was obviously destined for rapid promotions. Byun Jae-hyung stared open-mouthed at his neighbour, words unable to form on his randomly moving lips. His legs started shaking and he urgently needed to pee. He suddenly grabbed for the waste bin and buried his head in it. He was violently sick, the USB drive still gripped tightly in his right palm.

Meanwhile, moving even faster than Byun's retching, Stinger was travelling at 100 megabits per second through the fibre optic cables of the computer network and had found its target: the servers hosting the launch software for the missiles. In the Yongbyon datacentre facility, the network of computers hosting the elementary antivirus software and the Chinese made firewalls didn't even blink as the malware, spread like a cancer through the launch programme.

Stage 3 and Stage 4 in the kill chain of the hack were now realised. Stinger had been delivered, and its deployment had been successful thanks to the unwitting intervention of Byun Jae-hyung. Exploitation of the launch servers was now surreptitiously underway. In a matter of seconds the malware would be assuming command and control of the launch codes and sequence, from which there was no going back. Wolf would have been proud to see his elegant and precisely coded malware working so well.

In the hush of the remote forests of Yongbyon, hidden in the North Korean mountains, deep underground, beneath what had originally been the site of the nuclear research facility's huge cooling tower, slept six dormant missiles housed in concrete silos designed to keep them safe from any aerial bombing. Unbeknown to their masters, and much like a mythical dragon asleep for a thousand years in a folk story made up to scare children, the six medium-range Rodong-1 ballistic missiles were slowly stirring in their lair.

Seoul. Tuesday morning

John and Guy looked up in wonder at the library's glass atrium three floors above them. Guy had seen it briefly before, but this was Johns first time. The Starfield Library is an architectural delight built in the basement of the COEX Convention and Exhibition Centre, located in the heart of the commercial district in the southern part of the city of Seoul. Old Seoul is north of the Han River and houses the Grand Palace, the banking district, and the higgledy-piggledy lanes of Itaewon, the infamous shopping and bar area. New Seoul is south of the river and its high-rise shiny steel and chrome temples to capitalism are as new as any modern metropolis could possibly be. The tall buildings line very wide roads, meticulously laid out in a grid pattern, all serviced by a metro system and all the other amenities of a modern purpose-built city. At its heart lies the massive international convention and exhibition centre known as COEX; and at the heart of COEX lies the Starfield Library.

COEX is surrounded by prestigious office blocks and overpriced hotels, standing sentinel-like around the convention halls themselves. These are attached to the obligatory faceless shopping mall forming the artificially lit labyrinth beneath. In the centre of all this is one beautiful oasis of tranquillity: the Starfield Library. Its atrium reaches up nearly three stories from the basement of the mall to the huge glass ceiling above. Natural sunlight bathes the thousands upon thousands of books on the impossibly tall shelves. Some shelves are so tall the books are faux, as they can't possibly be reached. But the effect is still profound.

The light and airy space makes for a delightful retreat from the busy commerce conducted in the surrounding office blocks. There is a respectful hush in the huge library as people read, drink coffee, and take selfies whilst marvelling at the beautiful architecture and the literary tomes too numerous to count. At 8:00 a.m., as early workers using the library as a hub scurry through its many entrances to reach their respective office block's, bags in one hand and takeaway coffee in the other, John and Guy discretely conducted their reconnaissance.

Wendy had been in the ladies washroom in the mall for the last twenty minutes. First in a cubical, convinced she was going to be physically sick with fear. When the retching wouldn't come despite her unsettled tummy, she killed time in-front of the hand basins looking into the mirror and pretending to retouch her minimal make-up while at the same time having to hide her shaking hands if another woman came in. She had walked from their apartment to the mall in plenty of time, Guy and John flanking her on each side. August in Seoul was hot and sticky and, while the buildings are well supported with air conditioning, all three were perspiring from the early morning's humidity but more so from their underlying fear. They spotted no one who looked like they posed a threat, however, all three remained alert and anxious. Once in the COEX, Wendy peeled off to use the washroom while the lads went on to investigate the library.

The library is open plan, designed to allow people easy access around the mall and to the numerous entrances and exits to the surrounding office blocks. There are huge escalators taking patrons to the street level where yet more shops serve delicious coffee and cakes and where more access routes carry people to their offices and into the convention centre itself. The magazine racks and complimentary work desks are broadly situated in the middle of the floor in the flow of people transiting the library. At rush hour this is busy with the bustle of people getting to and from work but still with a dignified air of relaxed sophistication and learning as commanded by any library.

Guy and John, with takeaway coffee in hand, attempted to browse the library from all angles. They chose to stay together in the belief they probably stood out like sore thumbs anyway and individually they would be even more conspicuous. At least together they might pass for a pair of foreign delegates attending an event or working in one of the adjoining offices. Guy had concluded that if the Hong Kong assassins were in touch with Mr Kim or his associates, *if* he was indeed behind the contract to kill Wendy, then Mr Kim was probably aware she had a Caucasian counterpart. If Mr Kim's henchmen were also surveying the library, they would be looking out for such a man. Guy hoped the two together, with John looking every inch the tech-nerd that he was and Guy himself in his business casual dress, might provide them cover for their real agenda.

Neither man was sure of what they were looking for. They half expected to see scores of dark suited men filing in to cover every exit while talking into their shirt cuffs or long black barrels of sniper rifles slowly protruding from between the book shelves in an attempt to discreetly take aim at their unwitting target. As it was, Guy and John saw neither of these. All they saw were the usual humdrum Korean office worker bees, carrying their coffees, heading to their places of employment. The men sat at a reading desk together and browsed magazines, trying not to look around too conspicuously. Guy played with his phone, texting a running update to Wendy. As far as he could tell, conceding he was no professional at this, the people movement that morning looked much like he would expect any morning. He could see nothing he would consider unusual.

At 8:40 a.m., as agreed, John remained seated at the long reading desk. Guy stood and walked towards the huge escalators to ride to the upper level. By pre-agreement, John, the Asian looking of the pair would remain at the rendezvous point whereas Guy, probably the more likely to attract attention were he recognised, would observe from the higher ground and monitor the escape routes they had pre-planned in the event of needing to get Wendy out in a hurry. Their hearts were thumping with exhilaration. Guy was actually enjoying this whereas John was contemplating the stupidity of potentially endangering himself and whether he had really thought through the consequences to his wife and kids back in Hong Kong. John fretted that he'd not been entirely honest with his wife concerning the purpose of this trip. Regardless, they were now committed, and he was way passed the point of no return. Both Guy and John were wearing their discrete earphones. Wendy wore only one earpiece in her right ear, covered by her long hair and her phone tucked into her waistband hidden by her white blouse. She could hear the men and they could hear her conversation. At 8:42 a.m. Guy dialled the WhatsApp bridge number which conferenced himself, John, and Wendy together.

The washroom door suddenly burst opened and Wendy startled, her nerves stretched to breaking as the other woman briskly entered. Wendy was petite in contrast to the other woman who was tall and athletic looking. She was smartly dressed in a well-tailored professional black trouser suit, and black polo-neck beneath. An expensive looking single string of pearls completed the ensemble by adding the only colour. Wendy admired the beautiful suit and the way it flattered her femininity.

The woman popped into a cubical but emerged shortly after and stood beside Wendy in front of the hand basins as she retouched her flawless make-up. The two women flicked a brief smile at each other's reflection as they stood side by side checking their hair and pursing their lips. Wendy was struck by the other woman's beauty. Long raven hair cascaded down the full length of her back as she preened and retouched the dark red lipstick on her full lips. Korean women were renowned for their beauty; however, this woman was exceptional thought Wendy as she watched the woman's long immaculate fingers purposefully working the stick of red lip-gloss. The woman replaced the make-up in an oversized black handbag, which Wendy noticed was unusually large and also looked heavy.

Again, the two women gave tight smiles at each other's reflection and, after a quick check of her watch, the woman left.

At that moment Wendy's phone buzzed and she nestled the earpiece in her right ear and listened to John and Guy confirm all looked normal. It was 8:44 a.m. and Wendy should take her position near the magazines. Despite her looking at herself in the mirror for the last ten minutes, Wendy instinctively ran a quick final check of herself, squared her shoulders, steeled her nerve, and emerged from the washroom. Guy was coaxing her with encouraging words. John, who was listening, said nothing and continued to closely survey all patrons and passers by filing through the library.

From Guy's vantage point he watched Wendy emerge from around a corner and saunter over to the magazine section. Wendy did her best to control her breathing and not appear nervous. The wetness under her arms though betrayed her real state of anxiety. At 8:45 a.m. exactly, a tall well-dressed Korean man in a charcoal grey suit, white shirt, and red tie approached Wendy. She smiled her recognition. They didn't shake hands.

'Good morning Miss Chen,' came Kim Sung-han's commanding formal voice, quite startling her. Wendy had never been this nervous. She felt like she was a little girl at school brought up in front of the school principal for stealing cookies from the tuck shop. She was grateful she had just used the washroom, although it didn't stop her thinking she needed to pee again. Her profession demanded she reman cool in all situations, but this tested her mettle. Am I facing the person trying to murder me, she wondered?

'Good morning Mr Kim.' Wendy had feared how she would start this conversation. An apology seemed lame at this point. She didn't want to be confrontational either as, after all it was her crime that had started this whole process. She didn't need to worry as Kim

Sung-han led the conversation.

'Thank you for contacting me Miss Chen. You mentioned on the phone you had something of mine. Can you elaborate please?'

Wendy blushed. 'Yes. In your office last week, I took the liberty of reading your computer screens when you left the room and I noticed a piece of software code. It interested me and quite wrongly I downloaded a copy of that file to a USB drive. I have that drive with me now and should like to return it to you.'

'I see. Do you know what that software programme you claim to have stolen off my computer does?' Mr Kim was calm although his eyes betrayed his anger as he emphasised the use of the word 'stolen'.

'Yes, I do. I had a friend run the programme in emulation and I can see it's a malware designed to take command and control of,' she paused to select her words carefully, 'certain computer systems.' Given the public forum, Wendy didn't use any words that might attract attention if overheard. Both realised the conversation was likely being recorded by the other and neither wanted to say anything too incriminating.

'You have the USB drive with you now Miss Chen?'

'Yes.'

'I presume you have kept a copy?'

'For insurance, my insurance, yes Mr Kim, I have.'

'Then there seems little point in my asking for the USB drive back. On the phone last night, you mentioned certain "conditions".

What are these?'

Wendy steadied herself determined to regulate her wavering voice. 'I fear my life has been threatened. If you are behind this, it must stop. I also insist whatever plan you have for this malware must be abandoned. I can't imagine your endgame and I can see no scenario where this is in the best interests of humanity. Besides the USA, South Korea, and the North are all in diplomatic talks again so if your intentions are benign you should let diplomacy run its course.'

At this last comment Kim Sung-han's handsome face creased into a subtle yet sardonic smile. She might well be right he wondered, however, after decades of failed diplomacy he was privately sceptical. In the last fifty years every US President who had attempted to diplomatically engage with North Korea had failed.

From his elevated position Guy could clearly see Mr Kim and Wendy talking. He could also see the people movement around them. John was in clear view and all looked perfectly normal. Most of the people traffic looked like commuters heading to work. A few people were now using the library's workstation-style seating to read or more commonly work on their laptops and smartphones.

Guy casually became aware of someone standing close to him. He glanced sideways and noticed an astoundingly good-looking woman had sidled up next to him. She was smartly dressed in dark trousers and a short matching jacket with a tight black cashmere polo-neck complemented by an elegant string of pearls. She held onto the guard rail and stood so close a faint waft of perfumed hair aroused Guy's sense of smell. Guy instinctively absorbed the whole image in one discreet glance, while careful to not cause affront or stare as compelling as this beautiful apparition was.

The woman almost blended in with the other commuters but

something about the tasteful sense of dress, composure, and seeming lack of urgency to be going anywhere suggested this woman was unusual and out of place. She removed a phone from her large bag and proceeded to take random photographs of the library. This in itself was not unusual. The whole ambiance and scale of the modern library provoked picture taking. As Guy watched the woman in his peripheral vision, he noticed every second or third picture seemed to capture Mr Kim and Wendy. He was panicked.

All had gone well up until this moment. Wendy and Kim Sung-Han were meeting and talking. Wendy was relaxing now, stating her demands. But this lady in black changed the equilibrium. Guy wondered how to react. He didn't really expect Mr Kim to come alone; that would be naïve. Now being confronted with a picture taking security detail worried him. Black suited henchmen would have been easy to respond to. Guy wasn't overly tall although he fancied he could hold his own in a fist fight, however, a female photographer was different. Technically she was doing nothing wrong. Pictures of Wendy could make any subsequent follow-up easier though. It was this that caused him to fret. He quickly wandered away from the woman to ensure he could not be overheard and whispered to John, 'All okay your end?'

'Sweet,' was Johns reply. This was good. It suggested perhaps Mr Kim only had the one backup. He selected not to mention the woman to John through fear Wendy would hear and panic, so far, she was doing great.

Kim Sung-han held his steady gaze at Wendy and betrayed nothing of what he was thinking. As yet he had offered exactly nothing. He had not even conceded Wendy had stolen anything from him, merely used the term 'claimed to have stolen'. Wendy had stated her demands, said all she wanted to say, and now it was his turn. Mr Kim stood studying Wendy, his technical brain considering the variations on all she had said. That she had tested the Stinger software and was fully aware of its function didn't surprise him but that she claimed someone was trying to kill her did. Was this merely coincidence or a fanciful imagination? If someone was threatening her life as she claimed and she seemed genuine, this put a whole new dimension on the project. How could that have happened this quickly and who else knew about Stinger, he wondered.

Finally, after what seemed like an eternity, he said 'I presume you are recording our conversation. Please stop recording. You have my assurance on your safety.'

Wendy hesitated as Guy jumped in. 'Decline Wendy!'

Wendy continued to hold Mr Kim's stare as she took out her smartphone and pressed the red phone symbol, killing the call with Guy and John. She held the phone for him to see it was off. Kim Sung-han responded with a nod.

'Fuck!' Exclaimed Guy, louder than he'd intended.

'Thank you.' Mr Kim said. 'Regarding your first point, I assure you I'm not behind any threats to your safety!' He didn't disclose he had no idea who was. 'Regarding your second point, you're too late as the wheels are already in motion. Stinger was delivered to Yongbyon yesterday and I sincerely hope what Stinger will achieve will significantly accelerate the diplomatic process you referred to. However, even if these current talks fail, I believe Stinger will now change the balance of power on the Korean peninsula.'

'You plan to launch a nuclear armed short-range ballistic missile and think that will help diplomacy?' Wendy said with incredulity, staring wide-eyed at Mr Kim.

'Exactly,' replied Mr Kim with a benign smile he hoped would portray the worldly wisdom of a teacher explaining calculus to a 14-year-old. He paused, wondering if he should go on. Then making up his mind he said, 'For the last three generations of muddleheaded despots, the Democratic People's Republic of Korea has been humiliated and mismanaged, holding back and preventing one single, united Korea from being a true world power. Something must change this stalemate and Stinger could bring about this change. Keep your copy for "insurance" as you put it Miss Chen and, if it works, be proud you played a part.' With that he turned and walked away to join the melee of blissfully oblivious commuters still moving in ant-like discipline to their places of work.

As he walked away, he barely heard Wendy say behind him, 'but what if it doesn't....'

Chapter 23. Decision

Seoul. Tuesday Morning.

Guy had moved quickly towards the down escalator the moment Wendy ignored his instruction and turned off her phone. John had drifted closer and started browsing the section nearest to Wendy. Guy noticed the woman in black had quickly followed him to the down escalator and at the same time speech-dialled a number on her phone. There were three people between him and the woman on the excessively long escalator which provided a panoramic view of the whole library as it descended, therefore he felt fairly safe from an attack from the rear were an attack to come.

His focus remained fixed firmly on Wendy. As he walked briskly towards her, Mr Kim Sung-han seemed to conclude the conversation, turned, and walked away leaving Wendy to say something he may or may not have heard. From her pained expression it looked like she was pleading. Guy glanced over his shoulder and spotted the goddess who had also peeled off and was now walking in the direction Kim Sung-han had taken. As a passing glance for a split-second she looked directly at Guy, her expression unreadable. As beautiful as she was, Guy involuntarily shivered. There was something deep, shark-like, dark and threatening in those beautiful black almond eyes.

The trio met and decided to take a tenuous route out of the Starfield Library and back to their hotel. They walked out of the airy library and through the front of the building into bright sunshine and a fearsome heat. Seoul summers could be brutal with temperatures reaching over 30 degrees Celsius and humidity so high you could swim in it. They turned right and right again around the block, following the wide roads and taking care they weren't being followed. They were all shaken by the experience and particularly intimidated by the attractive woman who seemed to shadow Mr Kim. Even though their room was right behind COEX, they wanted to be clear no one was tracking their movements and could learn where they were staying should repercussions follow. After lots of looking over their shoulders and searching reflections in shop windows, they concluded there were no tails and they began to unwind a little.

The heat outside was blistering, typical for Seoul in August, and the three were relieved to reach the airconditioned apartment after the twenty-minute sweaty walk back from the COEX. They agreed the priority was to call Andrew in Hong Kong and share what they had learned. At this point they were unclear what, if any, their next steps should be. Their immediate safety threat seemed lifted but what could they do if Stinger was already in the process of deployment. Surely Seoul couldn't be the target were the missiles to launch as Mr Kim was still here in the city. It had to be some other location, perhaps Japan or China. Still the agenda wasn't clear. They reasoned, what possible gain was there to be had for Mr Kim should Stinger get as far as triggering a launch?

John seemed withdrawn. He'd spoken little since leaving the library, immersed deep within his own thoughts. *Had he missed something when he analysed the malware*, he wondered? Mr Kim's statement made no sense to him. "Stinger was delivered to Yongbyon" Wendy had reported he'd said. So there really was going to be a missile launch. John's analytical brain played through the scenarios. The more he considered the outcomes the more fearful he became.

They huddled around the coffee table in the lounge. The secure mobile phone Plug had given them was in the middle and they speed-dialled his number. Guy and John had cool damp towels pressed to their necks. Wendy had already splashed cold water on her face and changed out of her sweat-soaked shirt and into a white tee shirt.

'Hello. How's the kimchi?' Plug answered with his quick wit.

'No time for food yet,' replied Guy, suddenly realising he was hungry as the morning's excitement had overridden any thought of eating. A glance at Wendy and John confirmed the same thought had occurred to them too.

'Listen... Andrew, Wendy met Kim Sung-han,' again Guy had to catch himself before calling him Plug.

'Go on,' instructed Andrew, skipping all further formalities and his business tone kicking in.

Wendy spoke, 'Andrew, I spoke to Mr Kim on the phone last night and we agreed to meet this morning. He was very cagey although essentially admitted to Stinger. He told me Stinger has already been "delivered to Yongbyon yesterday", his words she stressed. 'He believes Stinger will do something to tip the stalemate in North-South negotiations and result in a unified Korea, which can then become a world power he believes.'

'He's patriotic. I'll grant him that,' said Plug, 'I wonder what he could mean by "Yongbyon's delivered"? We would know already if there had been missiles launched, even tests are picked up quickly by satellite and seismographs. Perhaps it's in play but hasn't yet triggered a launch,' Plug was thinking out loud.

John, who had been quiet all this time interjected, 'The launch programme takes command and control of the launch sequence. It's hard to disguise once it's in process, however, it won't activate without several other factors being aligned first. The rocket needs to be fuelled, warhead attached, and fuses primed, weights calibrated, and guidance system configured. Stinger could only then over-ride and reconfigure the flight path and activate the launch blocking a shutdown. It can only act once these preliminary steps have happened.'

'So, someone on the inside needs to do all this first?' interjected Guy.

'Yes,' confirmed John. 'It would take an entire team to prepare each missile for launch.'

'Then Stinger can only work if someone on the inside has already set the process in motion?' enforced Wendy.

'Yes,' agreed Plug. 'Every time there is a practice drill that's exactly what happens. What Stinger would do is override the drill shutdown procedure and actually force the launch as if someone really had pressed the button.' John nodded his agreement.

John went on, 'Unless a technician in the Yongbyon facility actually knew the malware had been installed, simply running up a launch drill would unwittingly result in a full launch sequence being completed by Stinger and the missiles fired.'

'Exactly,' said Wendy, Guy, and Plug in unison. Guy's lips cracked into a private smile as an amusing imaged flicked into his head when the engineers responsible for the shutdown suddenly panicked when they realised they couldn't. He said nothing, the moment not being appropriate to share his frivolous humour.

The quorum was silent for a while, each with their own thoughts as to the next steps. At last Guy chimed in, 'Andrew, you need to have your diplomatic channels get word to the DPRK military to warn them of the possibility of a security breach and the risk of a malware install at Yongbyon.'

'Easier said than done old chap. Diplomatic relations between Her Majesty's Government and the DPRK are pretty much non-existent now, given the current disarmament dialogue is with the United States. Sure, we can alert our cousins over the pond although I doubt that will be effective or that they'll act on it quickly. They were the ones to notify us and help fill in some of the blanks you'll recall!'

'Then the South Koreans?' asked John.

'We can try that,' conceded Andrew. 'Whether the North believe them is another matter. They might also be slow to act on what we tell them. If a drill is scheduled for the next couple of days, we could well be too late.'

'Thinking out loud, what are the chances of someone actually going to Yongbyon and warning them directly?' asked Guy.

Plug applied a little reverse psychology and picked up that question as his room-mates looked open-mouthed at Guy. 'It's very hard to get into the DPRK at the best of times. It's not open to general tourists and the tourist visa process takes months. Even if someone could get in, what would they do: knock on the gates of the Yongbyon military base and say in a plumy English accent, "I say chaps, you've some malware on your computers that will trigger a missile launch".' Andrew laughed at his own humour. His impersonation of a plumy accent, given he already had a plumy accent, did sound rather funny.

John re-joined, 'I can disable the malware if I can get to the computers. But I need to be physically there, there is no other way without a connection. The code's good and difficult to break once it's activated but I know I can do it.' He looked at Guy and Wendy. 'The person who originally coded the malware could do it, but then…' John trailed off.

'WTF! You guys aren't serious,' said Wendy, a look of horror and disbelief at the stupidity of the idea she was hearing being kicked about. 'Firstly, it's impossible for us to even enter North Korea. Then we need to get to Yongbyon and we can hardly hail a taxi. Then we would need to enter the missile facility and they'll not exactly welcome us in. And lastly we would need to find the control room, disable the malware, presumably with their permission, and walk out again. We would be caught and probably shot before we had been there two minutes, even if we could get over the border, which we can't!'

They all fell silent again, staring at the brown functional furniture and carpet in the room. Finally, Andrew broke the silence, 'Actually, we do have people in the North and while you were flying up there I did make some calls. You see, despite the image the press presents about the country and the inability for news to get in or out, the place leaks like a sieve and there are plenty of dissenters who would like to see the Kim regime fall. Sadly though, they're unable to coordinate themselves into any kind of movement, just a lot of impoverished, disgruntled people. We could get someone into the country and probably as far as Yongbyon. I agree getting into the base would be a problem and none of you even look or speak Korean.'

Wendy was quick to pick up on the implications of what Plug had said, 'You mean to say Andrew you actually anticipated we might need, and might even be prepared to venture into North Korea?'

Andrew sensed he was on thin ice. 'Well, I think it's best to consider all eventualities Wendy, after all, we would never have known about Stinger without your help.' Andrew was careful on his wording here spinning Wendy's theft of the malware as a positive rather than saying 'well this is all your fault after all.' They considered what Andrew had said and marvelled at the diplomacy. Even Wendy rolled her eyes.

'So, Andrew, what you're saying is you could actually get us into North Korea and as far as the nuclear facility?' prompted Guy.

'Look, this would be ridiculously dangerous. You would not have any government's official support, no infrastructure to help you, and if you were caught, which is highly probable, you would very likely be imprisoned for life, if not killed outright,' stressed Andrew.

John followed, 'And if not, several live nuclear medium-range missiles could well be fired into China, Russia, Japan, or possibly into us here in South Korea. The best case is many thousands if not millions of people would die and the worst case is we would be looking at a global nuclear war if it scaled quickly and other countries engaged.'

'Yes,' said Plug with a droll finality.

The trio all looked at each other. A resigned acceptance crossed them all. Guy said, 'Wendy, you can't be of help here. John can solve the problem if he can get in. I got him into this, and I would do my utmost to protect him. You can't help and, if we give this a try, you shouldn't come.'

'Fuck that!' shouted Wendy abruptly standing up, her eyes flaring wide with anger and with more ferocity than Guy had seen in a long time, 'I got us all into this mess and if anyone goes it's me!'

From the phone Andrew said, 'Team, you discuss this amongst yourselves. You can all play a part. Let me make some more calls and I'll call you back. Give me an hour.' He clicked off.

'Your mission should you choose to accept it…' mumbled Guy under his breath.

'It's stupid to even consider this,' stressed Wendy. 'Let's just get the next flight out.' She didn't mean or believe what she was saying. Wendy, of all of them, was keen to bring this to closure even if the consequences of getting it wrong were serious. She was physically small, a sheltered academically-oriented Singaporean, she had studied the violin as a kid, and her combat experience was nothing more threatening than girls' football at school, but she had never considered herself to be risk averse. The time had come to confront her real-world fears.

Guy looked at his mate, 'John, you've the most to offer and also the most to lose. You've a family, a beautiful wife and lovely kids all depending on you. Can't you simply write some software and give it to me to deliver?'

'Fair dinkum mate,' grinned John, 'but it's not that easy Guy, it's not "simple" and well you know it! I would need to be on-site. The malware code won't surrender without a fight, I'm sure of that, as Stinger was too well coded. Besides, it's my kids I'm thinking about. What world will they inherit and can their dad help improve their legacy.'

He thought for a moment chewing his bottom lip, anger suddenly flashed in his eyes, then he growled with a passion Guy had never seen before. 'Besides in a worst-case scenario and nuclear weapons do start flying around, there ain't gonna be much of a planet left for them to inherit, is there?'

The three of them sat back in their chairs, the discussion was over. Guy looked at his watch. It was mid-morning. 'So, if Plug can get us into North Korea, we're going?' Guy summarised looking at each of them. John and Wendy nodded in unison.

'Then we need a plan!'

Chapter 24. Dead End

California. Monday. Early Morning.

He had read the final forensics report attached to the email twice over. He had received it overnight and his open laptop now sat on the kitchen countertop next to a bowl of heathy breakfast cereal, juice, and a freshly brewed coffee. He allowed himself one good fresh coffee to start his day. It was 6:30 a.m. and Detective Brendon Butterfield had already been for a three-mile run. He was now cooling down while eating his breakfast, checking his emails, and planning his day ahead. Dawn sunlight streamed in through the windows of the small and tidy kitchen. It had been a fresh start to the morning although the sunlight promised another swelteringly hot day.

This weekend he had not officially worked, however, the Palo Alto case intrigued him. It had niggled him all the while he was doing chores and working out in the gym. He was delighted to finally get the full forensics report. Butterfield combed through it again for any helpful detail he may have missed. He was hoping this would add to what he already knew and might assist in closing the case. He was disappointed insofar as the report gave a lot of detail yet told him little beyond what he already knew.

The RDX and PETN chemicals used in the explosive at the apartment in Palo Alto confirmed Semtex, as McKenzie had told him. The balance of the two chemicals confirmed the mix was for commercial blasting. This could likely be traced to a batch stolen from a demolition site in San Jose a few months previously. A bit more research revealed the likely suspects in this theft were a couple of known criminals, known to the police as the Marx Brothers. While the Marx Brothers hadn't been charged with the crime due to lack of evidence, the theft pointed to them. Both were ex-military with explosives training, both with rap sheets a mile long, and both had served time for theft, assault, and various firearm and explosives related crimes. If Butterfield could interview them and prove the link to Palo Alto that might assist in at least clearing up the Semtex theft crime and tidy away one loose end in the death of Craig Sanchez. He made a note to himself to call the San Jose Police Department.

Otherwise the report contained little useful data to work with. Ballistics identified the gun used in the killing as a silenced Glock 19 9mm. The gun seemed to be untraceable and had not been used in any previous crimes. The four shots fired into the chest of Craig Sanchez were precise and fired at close range. They were positioned to rip the heart apart, which two of the bullets accurately did. The other bullets damaged the arteries and lungs around the heart. Such precision suggested to Butterfield a killer trained in assassination and not a random robbery or gang killing.

Interestingly, the device worn by Sanchez on his wrist was proven to be linked to the explosives and upon his pulse stopping triggered the explosion. This pointed to the fact that Sanchez was keen to ensure no trace of his work could be recovered even in the event of his death. Further checks with his FBI counterpart Senior Agent Mick Adamson had confirmed Sanchez as the likely identity behind the black hat known as Wolf. It seemed the FBI had a long file on Wolf although it lacked hard evidence to convict Sanchez.

The Korean lady, Lee Hyo-joo, was indeed in the area at the time of the killing. She had flown into San Francisco airport that morning and departed again later that evening. A woman fitting her description had booked a hotel, presumably to use as a base to freshen-up, but hadn't actually slept in the bed so recalled the chambermaid. Forensics had swept the room, at Detective Butterfield's request, and even though other guests had since used the room the search yielded nothing of interest relating to Miss Lee.

Either the chambermaid was meticulous in her cleaning or Miss Lee made a point of meticulously not leaving any trace of her stay. Butterfield knew which of the two scenarios he would bet on.

He had made a request to have an interview with Miss Lee via the South Korean diplomatic channels using Interpol, however, this involved time and a less than helpful diplomatic process. He doubted that unless Miss Lee willingly came forward to help the police it would go nowhere. There was a complete lack of evidence to pursue her formally with an Interpol Red Notice, the procedural way to request an international arrest warrant.

He was feeling impotent. Here was a sophisticated cyber-criminal living, formerly living, within his jurisdiction who had developed a malware that could theoretically launch nuclear weapons and start a nuclear war. The cyber-criminal had been murdered for his trouble and, despite believing he knew who the murderer was, he could do nothing to instigate an arrest. He also could not do anything about the malware the hacker had developed; this was all way above his pay grade. Lastly, a Singaporean woman who supposedly stole a copy of the malware is now being chased around Hong Kong and being shot at. This all made his adopted San Francisco look parochial.

All that was left for him to do was try and link the Marx Brothers with the death of Mr Sanchez. This might make him feel slightly better. He had nothing else to do except call SJPD and see if he could arrange a warrant to search the brothers' premises. Something might turn up. Still he owed Eitan a favour and then the case could be closed.

Detective Butterfield, washed then tidied away his breakfast crockery, threw on his linen jacket, and headed out to his M6. It was time to start another week.

Seoul. Tuesday Midday.

Wendy relished letting the hot water run over her body. She had been in the shower for ten minutes already. Her hair was washed, face and body scrubbed, and surplus hair shaved, more out of routine and to make herself feel feminine again. Now she stood and let the water run over her, hot and relaxing. What had she gotten herself into she worried. Bravado in front of the boys was one thing, however, here in a private moment in the steamy shower of the serviced apartment in Seoul, she was terrified. She was consciously incompetent and knew she was way out of her depth. She wanted to finish what she had started but was she seriously thinking of travelling to North Korea, being smuggled in, then attempt to break into a nuclear missile facility, then get out again, all without being caught? It was utter madness. They would kill her without hesitation - if she was lucky. The alternatives didn't bare thinking about.

There would be no record of her entry into the DPRK and she would simply be a missing person in Seoul she reasoned. Singapore might make some diplomatic gesture of a formal enquiry then the file would be discarded after a couple of weeks and her case resigned to the compost heap of missing persons lost abroad. Her parents would often wonder what became of their lovely daughter they were once so proud of. The loving daughter with such latent promise but whom never married, depriving her mother of a wedding banquet and her father of a grandson. The image of her grieving parents cut her to the core. Tears welled up in her eyes again and she upturned her face into the stream of water to wash them away.

John too had showered and changed shirts following the hot, sticky walk back from the Starfield Library. Guy had left the apartment to run to the faux French bakery on the ground floor next to the apartment block. They were all starving and Guy returned with arms full of bags containing pastries, sandwiches, and coffee. Guy called out to Wendy and she emerged from the bedroom in fresh clothes, her wet hair bundled up in a towel to dry. They had all had their moments of privacy and the commitment they had made to each other was now sinking in. None were prepared to show fear or apprehension, although they all felt it, and reality struck them with the folly of the quest they had agreed to embark upon.

John had called his wife explaining they were now in Seoul and he was working on a routine project where a customer had been hacked. He hated lying to his wife, however, there was no way he could be totally honest in this case. Besides, he justified to himself, he wasn't actually lying rather simply being a bit economical with the truth. The whole truth would scare his lovely wife and he would avoid that at all costs. She was the most precious thing in his world, she and their kids, and whatever happened they were his priority. He pledged to himself that whatever happened he would make it home.

Guy had offered to pick up the food. He had seen the patisserie the previous evening and hunger pangs had driven him to offer to get the food in once the call with Andrew had concluded. He too was wondering quite how he had gotten into this situation. He had texted his boss explaining he needed to take a few days urgent leave, without going into detail. He was wondering how this might end and how he might tell the story on the assumption he lived to tell it. He didn't fool himself what the worst-case scenario might be.

After many years consulting on the cyber-security industry's best practices and how companies and Governments could protect themselves from cyber-threats, he was privately excited to be really involved in something practical rather than hypothetical for once. Dodging technical shots from a smart-arsed Chief Security Officer in a plush company boardroom was one thing. Dodging lead shot on a Hong Kong street was quite another.

Guy loved excitement. Whether it be riding his Ducati motorbike on demanding roads in the Alps, skydiving in Australia, or snow skiing off-piste in Colorado, he loved to push boundaries and he liked to think he lived life to the full. A professional well-paying job gave him the cash to enjoy the creature comforts money can bring. A dynamic profession such as IT security was at the sharp end of the computer industry and gave the intellectual stimulation of a fast-paced career. Working with smart people like John also inspired him to keep his saw sharp. Real cyber-terrorism was a relatively new dimension he understood only from a theoretical perspective. Despite his reservations, this was exciting and the thrill was stronger than the pragmatic fear of probable death if it went horribly wrong.

Guy had not been formally military trained but he knew people desired leadership and John and Wendy seemed to have assumed a passive position to him. A responsibility he neither wanted nor needed although one he would take very seriously; John for his wife and children's sake and Wendy from some old-fashioned sense of chivalry. Where that sense of chivalry came from he had no idea and, of course, he would never admit that to a strong-minded woman like her anyway.

The three sat around the coffee table again ravenously chowing down on the sandwiches and drinks Guy had bought. Plug's secure encrypted mobile phone was still in the middle of the table and on cue it rang.

'Andrew,' sprayed Guy after hitting the green button, still chewing on a sandwich. 'We're all here.'

'Good. Any change of heart team? You've had time to consider the implications of what you're about to embark upon.'

Guy looked at the brave faces of his two colleagues who in turn looked him in the eyes. They all shook their heads and agreed they were still committed. Guy confirmed, 'No change of heart here Andrew.'

'Okay, let me fill you in,' commenced Plug. 'Needless to say, there is a roaring black-market trade between South Korea and the DPRK. Mostly this consists of western branded clothing, pornography, whisky, electronics, and oddly enough videos of South Korean boy and girl bands particularly BTS, 4TEN, 2Eyes, and the Wonder Girls being favourites.' Plug paused. The three shared blank looks with each other and shrugged.

'No,' continued Andrew, 'I've never heard of any of them either. Facts are, during the winter much of the contraband is smuggled over the northern border with China. The river freezes over and the trade can be plied on foot. Border patrols are easily bribed. In the summer this is harder, however, it seems many of these enterprising smugglers do runs from legitimate trawlers with dirigibles that are then met by North Korean trawlers and smuggled into the North that way. There is a sizable fishing port in Pakchon on the western side of North Korea on the Taeryong River that flows into the Yellow Sea as we call it. It's a way north of Pyongyang close to the Yongbyon Nuclear Scientific Research Centre. Seems the smugglers are terrified to take defectors out as that means execution on the spot whereas contraband smuggled in is relatively easy, even military sponsored some say.'

'So, we join a trawler here, get swapped to another trawler via dirigible in the Yellow Sea, and smuggled into the North in the fishing port of Pakchon?' quizzed Guy.

'Exactly,' confirmed Andrew, 'and there's more. Seems the smugglers are capable of getting you to Yongbyon too. Getting you physically into the facility is harder although not impossible they say. Apparently smuggling photographs out is common practice they claim, if my sources are to be believed.' Plug paused to let them consider what he'd said. 'No questions so far? Right. The North Koreans are supposedly decommissioning the Yongbyon nuclear processing facility. The cooling tower has gone, but the intelligence agencies suspect this maybe because they've now routed cold water underground from the nearby river to replace the cooling tower.

There is still a lot of activity on the site our satellite images show. It's suspected there is also a static missile silo there and given the proximity to the nuclear processing plant it's logical these would be nuclear warhead capable. They're likely to be the DPRK's Rodong-1's missiles, these are the reliable work-horse, mid-range missiles. There's no other reason I can imagen why Mr Kim would mention Yongbyon.'

'And you trust your sources?' asked John.

'I don't personally know them so, no, not as far as I could throw them,' confessed Andrew. 'These are our South Korean counterpart's people. But surrendering you is of little value to them, other than a patriotic pat on the back. The offer of hard money and even citizenship in South Korea for a mission completed for the second son of the leader, is, apparently enough to keep them focused.'

'Second son?' asked Wendy intrigued, her professional head automatically engaged.

'First son needs to stay in the North and inherit the family fishing business,' replied Andrew. 'The second son can integrate into the South and build the family empire there. It's even better that way should reunification ever happen, he can latterly bring his whole family to the South. The South Koreans will set him up financially and it's that long-term agenda that will keep the smugglers on plan.' John held his head in his hands, his shoulders shaking, it was unclear if he was laughing or crying.

'When do we leave?' asked Guy, trying to discern if the technical team member was indeed crying.

'There's a high tide at 6:00 p.m. tonight and there's a car on it's way to meet you at 3:00 p.m. this afternoon. You'll be taken to Ansan. It's a large modern industrial city on the west coast close to Seoul. It was formally a fishing port and now a major container terminus. It's just south of Incheon Airport actually, about three hours south-west of Seoul. It's a traditional old fishing town still with a handful of old fishing families. My man in Seoul will drive you three there.'

Andrew went on, 'I've not given him the full story. I've given him enough to stress the importance of your mission though. He'll take you through the introductions with the skipper and fit you out with supplies, clothing, and essentials for the journey. You'll be handed over to a North Korean trawler with a few cases of whisky in the Yellow Sea, and then be taken north to Pakchon. I've no idea how they'll get you off the trawler or to Yongbyon for that matter. Our man in Seoul vouches for him though, claims to have worked with these guys for years and says he's never been let-down.'

John raised his shaking head from his hands. He was smiling and hadn't been crying. Clearly the vagueness of the plan was counter to his logical and structured software engineer's mind. 'What could possibly go wrong!' he exclaimed with heavy sarcasm. 'Do the supplies include a Korean phrase book with useful phrases like: "Where do you keep the nuclear missiles?" I wonder? Oh, and get some seasickness tablets while we're at it please.'

Andrew was unclear if he was serious so remained silent for a moment. 'Look, I can't imagine how difficult this will be. Believe me, if I could see an easier way I would work on that. As we sit here now, the options are either you guys correct the problem, or we hope the problem just goes away. Frankly, the latter might happen, but if it doesn't the planet could be about to get an awful lot hotter.'

John nodded. 'Yeah mate, don't mind me. I get it!'

#

As the sun hit its zenith, Seoul reached a blistering 36 degrees Celsius on the street. For the occupants of the two white Hyundai Santa Fe's with tinted glass windows parked outside a hotel cum serviced apartment block, the air conditioning was a godsend, even a lifesaver in this heat. They had been sat there for three hours now, after driving in circles around COEX looking for the three faces on the pictures they had been sent.

The listening equipment had been picking up all it could. A discrete enquiry at the lobby of the serviced apartments, coupled with the passing over the counter of a thickly padded brown envelope told them which windows to aim their equipment at. The English being spoken confirmed when they had got the right room. While the conversations were in English, the occupants of the room were unaware the highly sensitive surveillance equipment could pick up voice resonance off the glass windows of the apartment so as to listen to the conversations inside the room.

One of the three, a Caucasian male, had been seen leaving the hotel briefly and buying food from the bakery below. The real intelligence though was the recorded conversations. The sophisticated software piecing together the conversations and even making educated guesses to the missing words if it were too quiet to capture them.

Less than five miles away as the crow flies, Talon was reading transcripts of the conversations. The transcripts weren't perfect and some of the software-estimated words made no sense. Thanks to her US education her English was impeccable though, and she could follow the gist of the conversation. She stood up and paced the room. They couldn't *really* be serious!

Chapter 26. Embarkation

Ansan. Tuesday Evening.

Peter Park enjoyed driving although this was an unusual assignment. It was a hot day and the three other people in his car meant the air conditioning needed to be on high for the whole journey. It was only a small car so with the three passengers and their backpacks full of provisions on-board, there wasn't a lot of room spare. He had been upbeat and chatty during the drive. He thought these people seemed a strange choice for such a journey to the North, however, he knew better than to question orders. Peter was young but smart enough to know the less he knew the better.

He had joined the staff of the British Embassy in Korea straight from university. He first joined the Honorary Consulate in Busan after graduating with a degree in international trade. He quickly worked through the ranks, demonstrating an aptitude for diplomacy and even more of an aptitude for playing the platitudes of politics, both within the British Civil Service and leveraging those within Korean political circles. Even though Peter was still a young man, the several Ambassadors he had served under recognised him as 'Mr Fixit': he spoke excellent English, he could think on his feet, and would quickly grasp the best outcomes, if not necessarily the right outcomes. He felt he could look forward to a good career with the British diplomatic service.

Of course, Peter hadn't been christened Peter. As a child he loved the Spiderman movies and at seven-years-old he announced to his parents one day that he wanted to be called Peter; the logical extension being Peter Parker, his alter ego. It stuck and, upon joining the British Civil Service, he found the English name was more useful than his native Korean one. It also had the added advantage of being memorable. Peter Park was a good man to delegate the awkward jobs to.

Coming off the highway from Seoul, he drove through the more underdeveloped areas, down drab side streets, and eventually parked his small Hyundai inside a large dingy boatshed near the docks in the old part of Ansan. He was acutely aware of satellite surveillance and naturally took every precaution to avoid being spotted by hidden cameras from far above. The boatshed would offer a degree of privacy.

Earlier in the day, he had called the hotel where Wendy, John, and Guy were staying and arranged for them to pack and leave their serviced apartment by a rear exit. He then gave instructions to walk a block and take a taxi to a public carpark where he'd meet them. Purely precautionary he had told them to allay their fears. He was being melodramatic. However, he had driven passed their hotel a couple of times at 2:00 p.m. and spotted two white Hyundai Santa Fe SUV's parked close by. The pair of inconspicuous SUVs' with tinted windows looked, to Peter's trained eye, like a dead giveaway. He kept this to himself; whatever these three were up to, the less he knew the better.

He also knew they were rank amateurs and so the less he spooked them the better too in his mind. His duties for the Embassy did involve some espionage, although he was rarely hands-on and more usually processing or compiling intelligence from the comfort of his airy office in the Embassy. His charges were under surveillance by someone and he would do his best to disrupt that, while avoiding being associated with whatever this madness was all about.

After meeting the three of them he couldn't shake off his feelings that this mission had failure written all over it. Being a career diplomat, he felt he could always smell failure and would always steer well clear. But he liked these people, they seemed friendly

278

and sincere – albeit completely out of their depth. The three-hour drive to Ansan was pleasant enough with Wendy making small talk in the front seat with him and the two men, both with their own thoughts, mostly silent in the backseats.

As soon as they were in the car, he had briefed them on the backpacks he had made-up for them. There were spare clothes, in sizes as best as he could estimate, bought from camping stores. Lightweight wet-weather gear was included as the skipper on the boat would provide heavy oilskins. There were food rations too, like energy bars and energy drinks. He had no idea the conditions they would be in so 'better to prepare for the worst' he thought.

He also provided cotton overalls, the type and colour known to be worn by the staff of the Yongbyon Nuclear Scientific Research Centre. They would not pass for native North Koreans for a moment although possibly as 'advisors from the DPRK's allies,' he'd told them. Wendy and John might pass as Chinese and Guy might just pass as Russian. He did have seasickness tablets also. John was relieved. A simple compass, paper maps, torches, and light sturdy boots were also in the backpacks.

He had no idea if these were needed or practical but how else could he be seen to have covered all eventualities of what they might need. Besides, his brief was vague at best. Guy had spent much of the drive studying the maps Peter Park had provided.

All Peter Park had been told was to make the connections to get three people, two men and one woman, to Yongbyon using their regular network of covert operators. On the drive he had paid close attention to seeing if they were being followed. As best as he could tell they were alone. The white SUV's he had seen outside the hotel hadn't found him. Perhaps the convoluted route the trio had taken had worked. Although if they were well-funded professionals, he would doubt losing them could be that easy.

Wendy squirmed out of the car, stretched, and wrinkled her nose at the smell of sea air, rotten fish, and oily machinery in the airy shed. The shed was mostly empty. Chains hung from the roof rafters, and wooden pallets were randomly stacked in the corners. The floor had aged puddled oil and rust stains streaked the walls. It looked like it was occasionally used for the storage of things needed for the boats and the docks. There were a few crates strewed around and a well-used battered forklift truck sat idly in one corner.

She had gotten out of the car and needed a loo. She looked around the large shed dubiously. Even if she found a toilet, she suspected the worst. John and Guy busied themselves rummaging through the backpacks confirming what Peter had already told them was in the packs and seeing if the boots fitted. Wendy confirmed her worst suspicions and found what was possibly the most disgusting workmen's toilet she had ever seen in her life, tucked behind the shed. Precariously taking care to touch none of the surfaces and using contortions known only to women she was grateful she'd carried a pack of her own tissues in her backpack.

Finally, they were physically ready and mentally prepared for the next stage of the journey. Peter walked them from the shed and along the road to the old quayside. Ansan was a large, modern, and thriving container and oil and gas shipping hub, however, this little part of Ansan had a smell of neglect and decay. The buildings were rundown, the roadsides had plants growing through the tarmac and were unkempt, and the small and medium-sized boats all looked tatty and rusty as they rested patiently against the quayside.

The only sound was the rhythmical squeaking of the old tires repurposed as fenders and the seagulls wheeling overhead. The fishy smell was really strong now and a few gangs of men, cigarettes hanging from their mouths, laboured around some of the boats, loading, fixing, shouting, and heaving. Some engines were running, adding their oily diesel smell to that of the rotting fish.

Wendy suspected she would normally hate this, but the kaleidoscope of colours on the quayside, all shades of fishing nets, cables, masts, rusty hulls and the lowering sun paling the blue sky behind made her yearn for her camera. Under different circumstances she would love to spend a day here pixelating the shades, shapes, faces, and the array of rich colours and tones Ansan's tired old fishing docks had to offer.

Peter walked along the quay and stopped at one trawler and shouted. An old man and a couple of younger lads quickly looked up like meerkats. The crew hastily beckoned them up the metal plank and aboard the boat, while craning their necks up the road to see if anyone was looking. The old man was clearly the owner-captain and the lads his boat hands. They looked grimy and sea hardened. No handshakes were offered, and the trio were pointed down latticed iron steep steps into the rusty hold of the boat while Peter spoke Korean to the captain. The boat hands stared open-mouthed after Wendy until the captain growled something in Korean and they begrudgingly tore their gaze away from her and got back to their jobs.

Shortly after, Peter came down the steps to the three loitering awkwardly awaiting instruction. He told them where to stow their bags and showed them a cramped cabin in the stern where they were to stay hidden until told they could go back up onto the deck. Peter explained none of the crew or captain spoke English and they would be there for at least six hours, probably eight. They would motor out to fishing grounds whereupon they would meet another North Korean trawler.

They would then transfer to the North Korean boat and be taken up the Taeryong River and on to the port of Pakchon, the town close to Yongbyon. The trawler looked dilapidated. Peter assured them the old captain was the best there was after a lifetime as a fisherman. He also still had family, a brother and two sisters, stuck in the DPRK. He didn't even know if they were still alive, but he still harboured the dream that one day Korea would be reunited and he would see his siblings again.

Peter shrugged. He had said enough. 'Good luck,' he said, as he shook hands with the three brave people he privately never expected to see again. 'I'll await further instructions and expect to see you back here once all this is over. Wendy, we'll enjoy the bulgogi in Itaewon in that restaurant I told you about.' He beamed and hoped his false confidence didn't betray his scepticism.

John and Guy thanked him and made vague confirmations to contact him, per his instructions, as soon as they were ready to get out of North Korea once the task had been completed. With that, Peter turned and scaled the cabin's steps again. They heard a further brief muffled dialogue between Peter and the captain on deck and then the three settled into the bunks in the small smelly cabin as the crew on deck readied the trawler for sea.

Peter Park walked back to the large old boatshed to collect his car and return to Seoul, his thoughts all about the three people he had just waved goodbye to. He pondered their mission, but the sense of doom still hung over him like a black cloud. There were no clouds, but 300 feet above him, hovering like an eagle on rotors in the quiet, still, early evening Ansan air was a barely visible Unmanned Aerial Vehicle. Dogsuli was watching and recording.

Chapter 27. General Park Dreams

Pyongyang. East China Sea. Tuesday Night.

Chairman Mao's Little Red Book rested on the small table beside his standard issue military bed. His status as General would afford him down-stuffed plump luxury, however, as he was used to a nori-thin mattress for his entire military career it was impossible to get a good night's sleep on any other bed. General Park was tired after the long day and he pondered the message from Talon, his daughter.

He had considered himself a good chess player but now the dimensions of this game had become exponential. The original plan was simple enough. A missile launch targeting a third-tier city in Japan would force a retaliatory response from the Americans. Even if North Korea were able to convince Japan and the US that it was accidental, the Americans would have no choice other than to fully attack the DPRK, albeit probably with conventional weapons. The world stage would expect it. The DPRK simply couldn't be trusted with weapons of mass destruction, even on the pretext of a deterrent. China would publicly protest, but then shrug and agree, sniggering behind closed doors at the technical ineptitude of their shit-kicking allies to the south.

Nestled near the southern coast of Japan is the city of Kure in the Hiroshima prefecture, close to the larger city of Hiroshima. It's a thriving city and has a long history as a naval base. It's best known for building Japan's largest warships, including in its heyday the Yamato. One reason the US targeted Hiroshima in 1945 with their own nuclear weapon was to cripple Japan's ability to float a navy.

From 1910 to 1945, before the US definitively removed Japan from the Second World War, the Korean peninsula was under Japanese occupation. The rule was brutal, with the Japanese army murdering any dissenters. Many of the ships and their Japanese crews came from Kure. In General Park's mind that made the city of Kure the obvious target. Tactically it was of little economic relevance to Japan, however, it had a bloody history and his Rodong-1 would inflict huge damage and loss of life. It would at last get the attention of Japan and the USA and, if it all went to plan, galvanise them into action against North Korea.

As he lay on his thin mattress in the dark his heavy eyelids closed. The twilight of consciousness rescinded into sleep and into his childhood dreams as it so often did. His aunty was the woman who reared him from a baby and the matriarchal figure in his life. She was the woman he owed his life to, and over the years she had told him many stories of the brutality of the Japanese soldiers and sailors from Kure. With tears in her own eyes she told him how, as a baby, he had been ripped from his mother's breast and thrown, crying, into the corner of the wooden hut where they had lived.

She told him of his mother's multiple rape and how his father was forced to watch until the entertainment became passé and how his mother's throat was then slit from ear to ear like a squealing pig. He would wake screaming as a child from his deeply repressed nightmares about Japanese soldiers. Sleeping in the same bed with his aunty, she would reassure him and cuddle him back to sleep.

Now he was an old man, his mother's sister, his aunty, long dead, yet sometimes the childhood nightmares would still wake him. He smiled now as he dreamed how the descendants of the murdering rapists, who so brutally killed his parents, and so many other of his ancestors would incinerate. They would never even know why.

General Park believed the United States would not retaliate with nuclear weapons. The response would be conventional with an initial cyber-attack disabling communications and critical infrastructure, such as it was in North Korea. Then there would be bombing of military installations around Pyongyang followed by land invasion forces from Japan and South Korea, backed-up with US troops. Much like Iran, the DPRK would economically collapse within a week and the invasion of key military bases and staff neutralised within a month. He didn't even believe his own KPA would put up much resistance once his defeatist, misguided, and conflictory orders were issued.

According to General Park and his old friend Chang Song-thaek, the Kim dynasty had misruled for long enough. It was time for the Korea's to reunite and become the global power they so latently deserved to be. His sleep was light and interrupted. He never slept well and he put this down to old age. He was always tired but could never sleep for long. This time his phone had disturbed him with an incoming message. He padded into the bathroom to wash his face then decode the message. What he read shook him out of his sleepy malaise.

Park understood little about computers or missile launch systems, but his staff had taken pains to explain it all to him and he got the gist. This malware would override the usual launch commands and trigger a launch with the target vectors set for Kure. All he needed to do was wait for the bang then rally some like-minded allies in the military hierarchy. Once done, they would arrest their President and the coup would be complete.

The US and her allies would attack, although arresting and handing over Supreme Commander Kim Jong-un for war crimes would prevent the wholesale occupation and international diplomacy would prevail. China would be invited to participate and would accept, still keen for an element of influence over the new Korea. A new government would be formed, and unification talks with South Korea would commence. Afterall, the Berliners tore down the Berlin wall and so Koreans will the DMZ.

But now he had two problems. The plan had been discovered and a small party of amateurs were intending to enter his country and scupper the plan. To even get this far implied other intelligence agencies around the world likely now knew of the Stinger plan or parts of it, they may even be discreetly helping.

He knew his own cyber-intelligence force was formidable so if other intelligence agencies such as the CIA, NSA, MOSSAD, and GCHQ knew, he feared the Chinese and his own intelligence staff would soon find out. He would be implicated whether involved or not. Enough of the other General's would get the scent of blood and covetously come after him and his position of influence.

His second problem was catching the three intruders who were now trying to enter his country. While he had no confidence they would complete their mission, until they had been apprehended he would feel uneasy. They needed to be caught and stopped. Talon's intelligence said they planned to infiltrate the nuclear base at Yongbyon. He knew that was impossible although it meant decisive action on his part. Besides, catching and watching their execution in front of his Supreme Commander might be the political keep out of jail card he needed right now.

He called his driver. He needed to drive through the night. He needed to catch the terrorists intent on destroying his plan and right now he certainly needed to put as much distance as he could between himself and Pyongyang until he had.

#

The weather had turned, and the open seas were getting rougher in the East China Sea. White horses tipped the waves in all directions except for the huge stern wake carved in the ocean's face following behind his magnificent blue-grey battleship. Admiral Young loved the bridge of the USS *Ronald Reagan*. She was one of the largest and most modern of all the United States Pacific Fleet. A Nimitz-class aircraft carrier with ninety aircraft and a company of over 3,500 crew, there wasn't a more formidable war machine on the planet. It was the 100,000-ton pinnacle of conflict evolution.

Admiral Young stood on the bridge and viewed the expanse of runway in front of him through the rainy glass. The support ships surrounded his floating airport providing a cloak of firepower. Even underwater a submarine was silently listening out, just as the aircraft launched from the carrier's deck would be watching out. As admiral, he was technically the ranking officer of the whole fleet, however, the captain of the USS *Ronald Reagan* ran this ship and Admiral Young was respectful enough to allow him to do exactly that.

The recent orders received were interesting though. New orders had instructed the fleet to increase speed to its full 30 knots and make course for the Sea of Japan, the sea between Japan and North Korea. The alert status had also been increased to DEFCON 2, only one step down from the highest threat alert being DEFCON 1, Nuclear War Imminent. Intelligence reports were suggesting unusual behaviour from North Korea again. 'What is the Rocket Man up to this time?' he wondered aloud.

As the two Westinghouse A4W nuclear reactors powered the massive momentum of the USS *Ronald Reagan* towards the seas between North Korea and Japan, Admiral Young gripped the rail on the bridge. After a successful naval career, he was only a few years off retirement. He was in a reflective mood and wondered if he would see a nuclear conflict in his lifetime. He hoped not, but with rogue states like North Korea there was no telling.

Chapter 28. Land

Pakchon, North Korea. Early Wednesday Morning.

On the western side of the Korean peninsular the weather was benign. A gentle easterly breeze only slightly rippled the Yellow Sea. The fishing trawler dipped and pitched on the grey water throwing a shallow white bow wave ahead of itself as dusk had fallen the previous evening. There was little roll to make the journey unpleasant and John hadn't been seasick despite his fears. All three lounged in the grubby bunks, keeping their thoughts to themselves, as the powerful diesel engine throbbed away beneath them. The captain checked in on them at one point, his stare for the most part scanning Wendy's feline form lounging in her bunk. Communication was impossible, however, a thumbs up seemed to convey all that was needed. As darkness fell, and the lights of the land were lost to the horizon the captain came below and beckoned them up and onto the deck. The light in the cabin was useless anyway and all three were bored.

The fresh air and clear night gave a most amazing view of the stars and the Milky Way; there being no light pollution to obscure the view. The three crew were relaxed, presumably the preparations were complete, but they had not reached the fishing grounds yet. Guy assumed they would at least make a token gesture to fish once they had been handed over to the other boat.

John was trying to figure out constellations in the mass of billions of tiny silver diamonds in the clear night sky. Wendy was impressed with the romance of the situation. Cool, fresh air, and a boat comfortably cruising over a calm ocean reflecting up at the stars. She was apprehensive about the forthcoming handover and what could happen in the DPRK yet right now she was relaxed as she stood next to Guy and slid her hand into his. Guy squeezed and held it. He too was anxious and, putting a brave face on it, smiled at Wendy and kissed her forehead. No words were needed.

After a couple more hours of motoring, Guy, John, and Wendy were passed cups of a hot flavoursome drink one of the crew had made. The taste was unidentifiable, salty and presumably some meat-based stock. While it wasn't cold now, Guy suspected this hearty hot drink would keep the crew going during winter expeditions when the wind was freezing and the sea was tempestuous. No one had eaten and none of the three wanted to tempt seasickness, so their provisions Peter Park had packed remained untouched. The three made themselves as comfortable as the boat would allow and they even slept a little.

A while later, lights could be seen in the distance. The captain shouted something and adjusted course slightly to head toward the lights. The silhouette of a second trawler slowly came into view and both boats turned off all lights. One member of the crew was working a flashlight, not trusting radio communications. Both trawlers slowed to a dead slow. At this point the crew started jumping about nervously while keeping a lookout on the horizon for any other boats. Backpacks were hurriedly brought on deck and the two trawlers came along side each other.

Lines were thrown between the boats and they kissed starboard to starboard. A metal gangplank was stretched between them although the small gap between the trawlers could have been easily stepped over. Old car tires encrusted with years of sea salt and green alga squeaked together and waves splashed up between the two coupling boats.

Guy was literally manhandled onto the gangplank and arms pushed him forwards while others reached to pull him across. Guy jumped down into the second boat then turned to see Wendy being mauled in the same manner. Lastly John was over, followed by a few cases which looked to Guy suspiciously like whisky, then the lines were untied and thrown back. Both trawlers engaged engines and put as much distance between themselves as quickly as they could. Shouts in Korean could just be heard over the engine noise as the boats separated and the exchange was complete.

In contrast to the trawler from Ansan that had not yet started fishing, this boat had already been fishing and had quite a catch of fish in the hold. Ice was packed over the fish and the dilapidated trawler laboured under the additional weight of the catch. The decks were slippery and the old boat stank of rotting fish and rusting iron. If the South Korean vessel was tatty, this North Korean boat redefined tatty. The few lights the boat had were turned back on although they were mostly useless.

In the darkness, with what little light the boat could offer, showed a trawler with more rust than paint. The nets and winches were all old and worn. Even the crew had a different persona: tired, resigned to exhaustion, and worn out looking. Again, it was clear none of the crew spoke English or Mandarin for Wendy's benefit. They were hustled below deck and this time actually boarded up into a hidden compartment of makeshift bunks forward of the fish hold. It was dark, wet, smelly, and claustrophobic. The North Korean captain was taking no chances of them being seen and in the darkness Guy and Wendy could hear John start retching.

The retching seemed to continue for an eternity. Guy and Wendy felt terrible for Johns predicament and the smell of his vomit turned their stomachs also. After a few hours, the craft ceased to rock as if the sea had become calm. They knew Pakchon was inland, up-river, so assumed they were now motoring up the Taeryong River and getting close to their destination; the sea voyage thankfully would soon be over. At last they heard the engine note change. The boat was slowing and the sounds of a noisy port, seagulls, and activity on deck permeated their temporary coffin.

It was still quite dark, and Wendy could just see by her Breitling watch it was close to 4:00 a.m. The trawler's motion finally stopped and the engine killed. It seemed they had all slept a little in the sensory deprived space. The boat bumped into the quay and they heard shouting in a guttural Korean tone. At last the boards and gear concealing the bunks was cleared. Wendy, John, and Guy tumbled from the bunks and tried to stand, their wobbly legs taking a moment to find purchase. Old well-worn oilskins and sou'wester hats were passed to the trio and they were beckoned forwards and on deck.

Once on deck, it was still dark, but they could see dawn was breaking. One at a time, they were passed a grey plastic crate of fish to hold on their shoulders and then guided off the boat and into the quayside. They were expected to carry the crate of fish, heads down, the crate and the large hats concealing their faces. They were then jostled towards an old lorry where they were pushed inside the back, and motioned to sit, hidden, behind yet more crates of smelly fish. Anyone giving a passing glance would only see fishermen unloading their catch off the boat and onto a lorry. The sun was cracking a line of light on the eastern horizon and several other trawlers seemed to be off-loading their catches at the same time. Little attention was paid to the three taller fishermen whose movements would have looked hardly fluid to an experienced seafarer's trained eye.

In the back of the lorry, Guy, Wendy, and John could see and whisper to each other for the first time in hours. John was ashen. A pale, wrecked man with huge dark shadows under his eyes, clearly exhausted after little sleep and hours upon end of seasickness. He tried to smile at them but guessed he looked as bad as he felt judging from their sympathetic gaze. More crates were loaded around them. The stench of the fish was overpowering, Wendy had never felt so totally dirty. Eventually, the lorry's engine was started and it bounced into life. Contrasting with the gentle, almost relaxing, ebb of the trawlers, this journey was painful.

The North Korean trawler had motored up the Taeryong River on the following tide to the large town of Pakchon. The Korean People's Army patrolled the Yellow Sea and the Taeryong River with fearsome looking Chinese made patrol boats, guns proudly mounted, prolific on their bows. For the most part they were looking for defectors which carried a high reward. The boats were sometimes used to smuggle people out of the DPRK. This meant it was usually the boats leaving port which would be boarded and searched. Those captured were often simply executed on the spot, along with the crew of the boats carrying them as a warning to others. The boats were then burnt and sunk so the families would lose that source of food and income. The refugees were unable to pay much and the penalties were high so there was little trade in human traffic out of the DPRK.

More common was the smuggling trade into the North. Every now and again an example would be made of smugglers, and more often than not, the soldiers and navy of the KPA would expect their commission on the smuggling activities, with payment usually in the form of some of the contraband itself.

Today the captain was lucky. His boat had not been stopped and searched. To be on the safe side he had two crates of Scottish whisky, always a favourite to bribe any navy boats taking an interest in him. The three people he had been paid to smuggle were tall and looked foreign therefore the biggest risk now was in getting them off his boat unnoticed. The tides helped insofar as they could make use of the darkness to offload their cargo. Other trawlers coming and going at that time meant the port would be busy with fishermen going about their business too. All he needed to do now was get them out of his truck and his job would be done.

He had been told to expect to have to get them back out again in a few days time. That was going to cost a lot more and frankly he had not been keen to agree to this. He hoped and fully suspected they would be arrested anyway and so not become his problem again. He even considered a tip-off to the police himself and save the risk of him and his crew being caught. But then the agreement with his South Korean contacts to extradite his second son was compelling and he concluded the risks, although great, were worth it. He was a gambling man and fancied the odds.

The sky was getting much lighter as the captain and his eldest son drove his lorry with the night's catch towards the town's fish market. Coming from the opposite direction, he was passed by a dozen KPA lorries full of soldiers, traveling at speed towards the docks.

'Looks like a big drill,' he commented to his son. 'The fishermen still on the quay will be harassed now.' They both laughed at their misfortune, relieved to not be caught up in this themselves. Unbeknown to him, these troops were an elite force sent from Pyongyang's AAA command and they were looking for something very specific.

The lorry ride was painful. Wendy grimaced as they bounced along the uneven potholed road. She was slim and carried little in the way of natural padding. Every jolt and bump the lorry drove over bashed her against the hard metal floor and she knew her legs and arms would be bruised black and blue. She tried sitting on her backpack but the road was so very bumpy, and it was hard to stay steady. Guy and John fared little better and had to stifle yelps of pain from every bump. Guy presumed the lorry's suspension broke years ago and so the flatbed simply rested on the axle transmitting every jolt from the uneven road.

John had quickly recovered from the seasickness now they were on land, although he still looked drawn and tired. Given the uncomfortable journey and stench of fish he feared this would bring the sickness back. He closed his eyes and pictured his wife and son's face's by way of a distraction. Could be worse he though, it could be raining.

They spoke little and then only whispered encouragements. Guy was doing his best to look out the back of the truck. In the half-light of dawn it was hard to make out much beyond monotone one-story grey buildings lining the road. However, he did see the convoy of KPA trucks heading at speed in the opposite direction, billowing dust behind them. He wondered to himself how much of a military presence they would see in this hermit country. The convoy seemed in an awful hurry.

The truck suddenly veered off the road and came to a squeaky halt a short way down a deserted side street. Another equally aged truck albeit a bit smaller, backed up to the fisherman's lorry and hushed Korean voices barked commands. The tailgate was opened and Wendy, John, and Guy were beckoned into the second truck. Nods of thanks were given to the fisherman and his son who visibly showed relief at being rid of their dangerous cargo. This second lorry was half full of timber with rolls of tarpaulin to sit upon and at least the suspension showed some promise of comfort. A young woman, no more than 20-years-old, jumped into the back with them and smiled at them with her brown teeth.

'Hi,' she said in a whisper.

'You speak English?' said Guy taken aback.

The bad teeth grinned nervously. 'Little English. My name is Ah-ga-sshi. Welcome to my country.' Her face broke into a grin at hearing herself speaking English to foreigners. 'I am sorry my bad English,' she rushed.

Wendy reached across and touched her hand, 'very nice to meet you

Ah-ga-sshi. Your English is very good.'

Guy hid his smile as Wendy was prone to prattle in Singlish in her home country and Guy though Ah-ga-sshi's broken English was better than Wendy's Singlish.

'My name is Wendy. This is Guy and this is John,' she gestured to the two men respectively. Ah-ga-sshi giggled and nodded a greeting repeating, 'Guy John.'

The girl said, 'we will help you get to Yongbyon. My father drives this lorry. He cuts wood. That is his job. My brother works in the research centre. He is a cleaner there.' She nodded to test they understood her. John guessed correctly she'd practiced these phrases.

The back of the wood truck was covered with an old and tatty tarpaulin cover stretched over a rusty frame. It presumably still kept some of the rain off the wood and now protected the four passengers from view. The lorry bumped along the road at a snail's pace, black smoke belching from the old engine. Motor vehicles were rare in North Korea but farmers were allowed them and, if they could afford to buy one, they would run it forever, improvising spares when needed. Guy studied the truck, it looked like an old Chinese copy of an old Japanese copy.

'Ah-ga-sshi,' started Wendy. 'How long will it take us to get to Yongbyon?'

Ah-ga-sshi looked confused and thought for a while, the words struggling to form. She eventually said, 'four,' counting on her fingers. Guy knew the nuclear research facility was in the mountains so he shared that he guessed the drive would take four hours and most of that would be at a slow steep climb. They should reach their goal by lunchtime. How would they actually get in was another question.

The sun was up now and the day was rapidly warming. Guy, Wendy and even John now nibbled on energy bars, sharing with Ah-ga-sshi. She giggled and relished the strange fruity taste. The old wood lorry trundled along, the wake of black smoke trailing behind them. Guy saw they were leaving the town of Pakchon behind. Peeping through a gap in the tarpaulin cover, the lorry was labouring uphill and the grey houses and low-rise buildings looked nondescript and depressing.

There was nothing quaint about Pakchon. It was a charmless struggling commercial town of featureless concrete. He could make out the silver river below and docks where they had disembarked. There was a flurry of activity around the docks where the army lorries were now parked. For a fleeting moment he wondered if the army were looking for his party. It couldn't be. They couldn't know they had arrived. How would they?

#

General Park stalked up and down the quayside watching his soldiers board the trawlers. There were a few grumbles of protest, only half-hearted though as the elite Special Purposes Force Command troops were brutal in their efficiency. The weapons they carried were intimidating and their attitudes were more so. Most of the fishermen simply stepped aside and allowed the strangely uniformed soldiers to go about their business. They were looking for something although it wasn't clear what. A manifest of all the boats that had come into port on that morning's tide had been compiled and each boat was being thoroughly searched. Every smelly, oil-stained inch was being probed. On several boats they found contraband, the fishermen fearing the worst. However, General Park merely stared indifferently and barked a command

297

to carry on the search. Whatever they were looking for, it wasn't pornography, counterfeit whisky, or DVD's of South Korean girl bands.

The wood lorry was well out of town by the time General Park conceded defeat and decided to move on to scour the town's fish market. Whatever he was looking for was either still at sea on a trawler, which they would search again on the next tide when the boats came in, or was already in his country. General Park was grumpy. He had not slept since the previous evening when he had received the message from Talon. He had hastily assembled the small unit from his base in Pyongyang and driven through the night to Pakchon. He needed to be personally involved in this operation. The General was unsure of what infuriated him more, that their plans had been discovered or the audacity that amateurs would attempt to enter his country to disrupt them. Either way he resolved this would end now.

Chapter 29. The Factory

Yongbyon, North Korea. Wednesday Midday.

The klaxons were deafening. Ah-ga-sshi covered her ears with her hands and slumped into a squatting position with her elbows on her knees. Her smile never diminished despite her fear. She almost seemed to be enjoying this. Guy feared she wasn't fully appreciative of the situation or, more importantly, the consequences of this all going very wrong. If she did, she would not be smiling. Regardless he had to admire the girl's balls, but right now he needed to move…

The four-hour drive from Pakchon to Yongbyon was without incident. The party of four were bounced around in the back of the lorry normally used to transport wood. At least they had rolled up tarpaulins to sit on which afforded some little comfort. John even seemed to doze for some of it. Wendy was convinced her butt was bruised black and blue following the earlier ride in the fish waggon with no suspension. Guy offered to check for her, but John ignored them and was not in the mood for banter, he was brooding to himself, so the humour faded fast. Guy and Wendy entertained themselves peeping through cracks in the tarpaulin cover at the mountainous countryside passing by. Both agreed, given the undeveloped, unspoilt nature of it, it was beautiful in a primitive way.

Ah-ga-sshi explained her father and eldest brother were sat in the front, driving. If they saw a roadblock, and were to be stopped, they would need to scramble out the back of the truck, run for cover, and hide before the lorry was searched. The truck was moving so slowly it was a plausible plan. Guy suspected the black exhaust trailing them would help make for a credible smokescreen. She explained if her father saw a roadblock he would signal to let her know. Whatever the signal was, it never came. The trio didn't fancy their chances although did appreciate the extreme risk her father was subjecting his family to. Guy speculated if they knew the mission's real purpose. It was probably irrelevant as they were caught, they'd be charged with espionage anyway which carried a mandatory death penalty in this trigger-happy country.

Guy studied Ah-ga-sshi as she sat on her hunches, she could hardly be described as attractive. Her squat stature, grubby moon face, bad teeth and shabby peasant clothes gave her the appearance of a National Geographic cover. But her ever-present smile and bright, black, intelligent eyes leant her a unique innocence and charm rarely seen. Wendy speculated her true motivation in helping them and learning English. Did she yearn for a better life outside the hermit dictatorship? Did she even know what life in the west looked like? Ah-ga-sshi's gaze rarely left either one of the three. I wonder what's going on behind that pretty smile Ah-ga-sshi, Wendy thought to herself.

The mountain road that ran from Pakchon to Yongbyon was modern, tarmacked, and as straight as the fields and rocky terrain would allow. The lower area was all agriculture with fields well-tended, but as the road climbed higher the land turned to more scrub, patches of trees, and old forest sprouted where the harsh brown landscape would allow. The nuclear research facility nestled comfortably on the banks of the Kuryong River which ultimately fed into the Taeryong River which, in turn, evacuated into the Yellow Sea where the trio had motored from hours before aboard the dilapidated trawler.

The weather was summery, warm and pleasant. As the wood lorry climbed ever higher into the mountains the temperature noticeably dropped a few degrees. The day was now comfortably warm, and fresh country smells greeted the tourists. Having to double-take where they were, and, were their mission not so dangerous they might even relax, take a stroll and enjoy the pleasant Alpinesque scenery.

Ah-ga-sshi explained in her broken English that her brother worked at the facility. With a sense of irony, she knew little else about the facility and what its true purpose was. Wendy, Guy and John had been well briefed and learnt the Yongbyon Nuclear Scientific Research Centre, as it was officially known, was an Experimental Light Water Reactor or ELWR designed ostensibly for 5 MWe power generation. However, it also provided the capability of processing uranium into plutonium or specifically tritium and lithium deuteride, the fissionable material used at the business end of thermonuclear weapons. This had been known for years to western intelligence services whose satellites closely monitored truck, cranes, and cooling tower emissions to estimate activity levels.

Lesser understood was the output in recent years since the cooling tower had been removed and the cooling changed to use water channelled from the Kuryong River. The cooling tower had been dismantled and, in its place, the underground bunker now housed the armoury of Rodong-1 missiles with the nuclear warheads stored close by. Despite the high-profile political dialogue between North Korea and the USA, the Yongbyon facility was still very much ready for action at short notice.

Spare land around the facility was farmed and the crops cunningly lay to dry over the missile silo covers. Ah-ga-sshi's brother both farmed the spare land and sometimes earnt money as a cleaner in the offices at the facility, or as she called it 'the factory'. She explained he appeared to be simple, gesturing with facial expressions, and so passed as a low security risk with easy access to most of the labs and offices as a cleaner. This was to be the trick to their gaining entry. Ah-ga-sshi would also sometimes help her brother in the plant for cleaning and farming duties when busy.

The arrangement was informal, but as her brother looked slow-witted, she would often go with him to help clean and therefore the security guards were used to seeing her arrive at the gate with her brother in the old lumber-carrying truck. They would frequently use the truck to deliver grain and move the harvested crops around to dry and then store them. They had security passes, but the guards were so used to seeing them they were rarely stopped, simply waved through, and the truck was almost never searched.

John and Guy never believed it could possibly be that easy. Three miles from the plant Ah-ga-sshi climbed from the back and sat in the front beside her brother and father. Before doing so, she had Guy, John, and Wendy lay flat and she arranged tarpaulins and wood over and around them. Even if the lorry were inspected the chopped wood would look benign and normal enough unless inspected closely. Nerves fraying, Wendy, John, and Guy lay rigid, even holding their breath as they felt the truck slow to a halt and Korean voices with hostile tones clatter loudly in their vernacular. The father was only dropping the lorry off and he wasn't going to wait.

The slow-witted brother slid into the driver's seat with Ah-ga-sshi sat next to him, still smiling at the security guards. Even speaking Korean, Wendy could determine the brother sounded like he had an intellectual disability, the slowness of speech was disenabled from the Korean being spoken. If he wasn't a retard, he's deserves a bloody Oscar she thought to herself. Wendy heard what she guessed was Ah-ga-sshi's father getting out of the cab, banging a couple of times on the cab door with the flat of his hand, and shouting his good-byes.

The sounds of boots tramping around the lorry permeated the tarpaulin thrown over them. Wendy gripped Guys hand, held her breath, and screwed her eyes up tight, expecting at any moment for the tarpaulin to be thrown aside and them to be discovered. Both their palms were sweaty, but the comfort was all that mattered. After an unbearable pause, the boots stomped on. The waggon's engine roared, gears graunched as the brother ground the gearbox into gear, and as he slipped the clutch the lorry lurched forwards again at last. Her lungs filled to bursting, Wendy exhaled and nearly yelped for joy at making it past this first step.

Guy heard John whisper 'fuuccckkkk,' under his breath. They were inside the Yongbyon Nuclear Scientific Research Centre facility.

#

Byun Jae-hyung had been in a state of panic since Monday evening. He had not slept, eaten, or thought about very much at all other than that cursed USB drive and what it might have contained. Following his panic attack Monday his supervisors had drilled him on his state of health, asking did he feel unwell and what was wrong with him. He professed it was something he had eaten and that he now felt fine. Indeed, he was pale, but he insisted he continue his shift. Once Byun Jae-hyung was confident he had been left alone he used all his IT skills to establish what files, if any, had been downloaded off the USB drive. He dare not plug it in again through fear it may still try to download unauthorised files. It was a case of exploring the network to look for code or files that should not be there. This was a difficult job. PC's, networks, and servers have many files and applications, not to mention their own protocols. In reality, it's thousands of files and millions of lines of code. Finding one string of code when you don't know what you're looking for, even if it exists, is close to impossible without the right tools and expertise.

Byun Jae-hyung was acutely aware he possessed neither and rather than confess what had happened to his superiors he decided silence was his best defence. To admit to finding a USB device outside the facility and then plugging it into his computer was gross stupidity at best and treasonable at worst. Either way it would end his career and bring disgrace to himself and his family.

The good news was that neither his computer nor the network of other computers had crashed. This suggested that, if there had been a malware on the USB device, it had either not worked or had not been fully installed. No ransomware messages had popped up like with the WannaCry virus nor were any obvious executable files trying to make contact with any others as best he could tell. As every hour passed and nothing out of the ordinary happened Byun Jae-hyung was able to relax a little.

The previous day the test drill for a missile launch had started so he was busy overseeing this and following procedure. This gave him little time to search for an unknown malware. Today the missiles were being fully fuelled and their ominous warheads added. They would be brought right up to the point of being fired. Byun Jae-hyung was aware in a matter of hours all the procedures would be followed and the drill complete. This would be over soon and, once over, the missiles would again be decommissioned, basically by reversing the procedure. The staff would then all stand down and his routine would once more prevail. Perhaps then he would have more time to explore if any viruses had made it into his network although by now he was expecting not.

#

Ah-ga-sshi's brother had nonchalantly driven the lorry into the research facility crashing the gearbox as he did so. He turned right into the carpark by the garages denoting the motor pool area. Rather than parking in his usual spot beside the motor pool area, he continued on and turned left around to the back of the sheds. This was sheltered from the security gate he had just passed through.

There was one administration block that could overlook where he had parked his truck, however, they would unlikely care should anyone see him. This was also the target location he needed to get his guests into.

The eastern side of the facility was the operational end of the Yongbyon Nuclear Scientific Research Centre. It consisted of the plutonium lab, reprocessing building, waste storage and decontamination building as well as the power plant itself, the ELWR. The western end of the site was the support and administration blocks. The motor pool was roughly between the two areas and also where the fire service kept their vehicles.

Ah-ga-sshi jumped from the truck cab and unhurriedly walked to the rear. She pulled the tarpaulin cover back while her bother stood guard pretending to struggle lighting a cigarette. She pulled the few logs off the passengers beneath. The same smile greeted them, and Guy quietly pledged to himself that if ever they got out of this, he would pay for her to visit a good dentist. The trio's eyes adjusted to the sunlight and they took their bearings of the shabby buildings surrounding them.

'Quick! Follow me,' she said, almost giggling with excitement. She ran behind the large shed that gave a rear entrance into the motor pool and, checking first, ducked into a door. The others followed, their eyes readjusting to the darkness. There were numerous old tractors and trucks as well as some new cars, a privilege only permitted to all but the most senior WPK leaders and military notoriety from the KPA. In addition, there were two large and well-equipped fire engines. The Red, shiny, and rarely used, Chinese manufactured Sinotruk fire tankers stood proud and ready for action. Off to the left of these was a large room full of firefighting gear and it was here Ah-ga-sshi ushered Wendy, John, and Guy.

'Please get in,' she pointed to the firemen's outfits hanging up. There was a jumble of heavy firefighting gear ranging from jackets and oilskins to full asbestos silver suits and helmets. The trio looked at each other then started to explore what would fit each of them. Ah-ga-sshi kept a look out by the door. 'Quick!' she stressed. 'We don't have much time.'

John adeptly fitted himself with a heavy black jacket, yellow oilskin trousers, boots, and a yellow fireman's helmet. Guy helped Wendy into a androgynous silver fire suit that would hide her female curves and then got himself into a yellow fireman's jacket and boots. Helmets covered their heads and much of their faces. Wendy had a silver hood, with glass visor, so the men each grabbed yellow facemasks with portable breathing apparatus too. They figured this would do a credible job of completely hiding their faces.

Guy looked around and saw a collection of firehose nozzle fittings. He grabbed two of the heavier ones and passed one to John. They clumsily followed Ah-ga-sshi back into the still deserted motor pool shed and stood by the door through which they entered. Wisely, Guy and John had picked up the heavy metal firehose nozzles as they both added to their overall look, and now made for a handy cosh if needed. Guy was anxious they were unarmed, and it looked like after eighteen hours of slow, uncomfortable travel it was all about to come to a head. He glanced at Wendy and again wished he had a camera. He stifled his laugh. Only she could look glamorous in a fully body asbestos silver suit, even if it did dwarf her.

Peering through the grimy door window, they saw Ah-ga-sshi's brother saunter across to the administration block, grey smoke from the now lit cigarette billowing behind him. He looked to the motor pool back door and gave the briefest of nods. He stepped aside and made way for two staff in one-piece military uniform leaving the administration block but neither paid him any attention. He gave them a clumsy salute then he disappeared inside.

'The computer room is in there,' said Ah-ga-sshi who gestured to the door through which her brother had just disappeared. 'We meet back here at the lorry, to get out again, be fast!' she said. Before any of them could ask or answer any questions, the deafening scream of the fire klaxon shattered the calm, Ah-ga-sshi covered her ears with her hands.

Nuclear Scientific Research Centre, Yongbyon. Wednesday Midday.

Dense black smoke started to billow from the windows in the top storey of the administration block as Guy, Wendy, and John walked across the road between the rear of the motor pool block and the administration block. A few people were already drifting out of the block, assuming this was another drill, and were startled to look up and see smoke wafting from the upper windows. To make it look realistic, Ah-ga-sshi's brother had found some plastic packaging in his caretakers' cupboard and this is what now blazed in a metal bin on the top floor creating all the smoke. No one was surprised to see three firefighters hurrying into the building although, had they stopped to consider the timing, they may have been struck by how promptly they had arrived; it was almost before the smoke showed.

They now pretended to fumble with their breathing masks to hide their features at close range. They looked inconspicuous so security guards and staff alike simply stepped around them in their desire to leave the building. The air prickled with excitement as staff realised this wasn't a drill and there was a real danger there was a fire somewhere in the building.

Ah-ga-sshi's brother had made his way back downstairs from the fourth floor where he had ignited the plastic packaging. He maintained his morose demeanour and no one spared him a second look as they were quite used to seeing him around sweeping, mopping, or emptying waste bins. He found the three firefighters and quickly loped passed them careful not to be seen interacting with them, however, Guy picked up on the cue and followed him as he led the trio around the drab corridors until they found the

Network Operations Centre.

The facility's computer servers themselves were housed in a separate adjoining room next to the Network Operations Centre. This server room was kept cooler and contained its own independent air conditioning and discrete firefighting equipment, including a Pyrogen system that would flood the room with the inert particles when triggered, displacing all oxygen, and thus extinguishing any fire. Most of the staff in the Network Operations Centre had left but a few staff remained looking anxiously at their computer monitors, the rehearsal for the missile launch was still in mid-simulation.

A second siren now sounded, even louder than the klaxon giving the fire alert. This new cacophony seemed to add yet more confusion to the few remaining people milling around the corridors and computer rooms. This siren was rarely heard yet all recognised it as warning of an impending missile launch. During previous launch practices it would be sounded for a short period to familiarise the staff yet, this time it remained on.

Undistracted by the fire warning Byun Jae-hyung remained at his station and monitored the launch procedure, it was largely complete. He stood-up and looked at his Manager, the head of the IT department. It was impossible to have a conversation over the two wailing sirens. He waited for the instruction to terminate the launch sequence and so begin the process to deactivate the missiles. This stage of the launch sequence was critical as the missiles were now fully fuelled with the highly volatile UDMH rocket fuel. Unsymmetrical dimethylhydrazine was the colourless liquid propellent used as fuel by the rockets and required careful handling. In the unprecedented event of a fire at the site the missile launch teams would not want to start the procedure of off-loading the fuel.

John guessed the missile launch siren sounded when the missiles were primed for launch or the concrete and steel doors of the missile silos opened, exposing the weapons to daylight and a clear flight path. At this point all pretence of disguise was shed and any satellite imagery from overhead would see six perfectly round missile launch tubes and six grey weaponised thermonuclear warheads poised for launch within them. Their intimidating red tips painted on the nose of the fifteen-metre-long missiles nestled just beneath the now opened silo doors. The missiles, proudly sporting the Democratic People's Republic of Korea red flag with a red star within a white circle and a thin white and thicker blue stripe top and bottom, they were, at last, about to be set free to wreak their havoc.

Now administration staff were running in all directions, to take their positions for the pending, assumed, launch. They knew it was a drill but, regardless, all took the siren seriously.

At first, to Byun Jae-hyung the fire drill looked routine. Now the administration block had a problem, but this was technically separate from the missile launch site and so one shouldn't disrupt the other. He just knew, he should stay at his station. For the power plant and the rest of the base it was business as usual. But now there was pandemonium. Never before had the base needed to deal with a missile launch drill and a real fire on the base at the same time. It had never been rehearsed.

Ah-ga-sshi's brother started exaggeratingly waving his arms and yelling in Korean. John presumed he was yelling the Korean for 'Fire', and Wendy, through her glass fronted helmet still marvelled if he really was slow or this was a very well calculated act. Certainly, his cries of alarm contributed to the rising panic in the few staff that had not yet left the building. Black smoke coming from the upper floor windows seemed to be much thicker now and the stairwells were beginning to seep heavy white smoke.

General Park sat in his usual ramrod straight posture in the front passenger seat of the first in the line of a dozen military lorries trundling up the well-cemented road to the Yongbyon Nuclear Scientific Research Centre. He wore his full military uniform so there could be no doubting his seniority, authority, and severity of the situation he wanted to be seen dealing with. His Special Purposes Force Command sat in the rear of the trucks, they were silent and professional. Their latent aggression ready to be unleashed on the target of their, so far, futile search.

The search of the docks and trawlers had proved fruitless as had the market town of Pakchon. The only thing left was to head straight to the Nuclear Scientific Research Centre and lock it down. The Nuclear Scientific Research Centre was sixty miles from Pyongyang, and he had been on the road since the previous evening with no sleep and an unaccustomed uncomfortable ride. His patience had worn thin and his mood thunderous. He looked through the windscreen of the truck at the white concrete road that wound upwards into the mountains ahead. There in the distance, perhaps three miles away, were plumes of black smoke. Realisation dawned and he pointed out of the windscreen and screamed at the startled driver. 'Step on it!'

Byun Jae-hyung was hammering away at his keyboard. His complexion ashen white. *This could not be right,* he thought. Launch protocols were governed by software his department had control over. The missile launch drill had gone well up to now with all procedures well rehearsed and running smoothly. The build-up to launch was perfect and now, just short of the launch command being given, they would reverse the procedure and slowly scale back the escalation and decommission the missiles again. But this wasn't happening. They were unable to arrest the process. None of the commands were working. Jae-hyung punched his keyboard with increasing aggression. His manager still sat a few cubicles away started hysterically screaming commands, all dignity and pretence of control lost. The missiles were actually going to launch and as computer operations chief it was all his fault. Finally, in a fit of panic, with the smell of smoke circulating in his nostrils, he too ran from the building.

Byun Jae-hyung knew differently. This was all down to the USB drive and the files he had allowed to corrupt their software. The malware had taken command and control over the launch computers and no actions he could take was stopping it. He knew the Korean People's Army had a sophisticated department focused on cyber-terrorism as he had met some of them while in China, being on technical training himself. However, he had never believed in a million years he would fall victim to this.

He wondered who the protagonist was. Was this developed by their enemies like the Americans, bent on provoking a war, or was it elements of his own government creating mischief for internal political gains? For the sake of his esteemed supreme leader, he wanted to solve this problem.

At this point, he was aware of being watched from over his shoulder. The cursor on the screen of his computer like a belligerent child was stubbornly refusing to move to his commands. The reflection in his darkened monitor showed two alien faces stood behind him. He jumped up and turned to see two firemen complete with breathing apparatus. He was about to protest. At first, he feared they had come to forcibly evacuate him; they would never grasp the criticality of what he was trying to do so he started to protest. Then one of them brought his right fist up straight and hard into his stomach winding him so hard he bent double with the pain. The fist came down a second time into the side of his face, knocking him hard to the ground. From behind them came a third figure dressed completely in silver. This one dragged him away from his desk, rolled him onto his front, and started to bind his hands behind his back with power cable.

Guy quickly pulled the chair out and swept his hand in a grandiose gesture for John to sit. John faked a curtsy and exaggeratedly cracked his knuckles over the keyboard. He had studied Stinger in depth and knew exactly what to do. It was going to be hard to crack but he would try and, if there was time, he would corrupt the malware and abort Stinger's execution codes.

To speed this process, he had coded his own software to override the locked screen, and pinpoint where Stinger interrupted the code to cancel the launch. This was simply a few lines of his own malware that looked for Stinger's signature and then corrupted the final executional elements of the code. It wouldn't remove Stinger, simply prevent the final launch commands from being carried out. John had coded this little malware back in Hong Kong and now he inserted his USB drive into the computer. Back on the PC's command line he ran the file he had christened Stingkill.

'Damn!' John exclaimed hitting the table with is fist, 'Stinger has locked the network! All these PC's are useless. They've been blocked from the servers. I need to get into the server room!'

For good measure, Wendy was still sat on Byun Jae-hyung's back and she had stuffed paper in his mouth to prevent him from making a noise. She was perspiring heavily in the fire suit. The punches delivered by Guy had floored the Korean although he was still conscious.

Guy turned and saw Byun Jae-hyung had a plastic card on a lanyard around his neck. He helped Wendy off Byun Jae-hyung, and, hauling Byun Jae-hyung bodily to his feet, Guy pushed him towards the server room where he swiped the card on the access lock. The server room door clicked open and Guy pushed him through into the cold room first, followed by John and Wendy. John quickly scanned the room and computer racks. He found a console connected to a server and punched the keyboard. 'This is what I need. I hope we're not too late,' he said as he inserted the USB drive into a slot on the server. Again, he typed the "run" command for Stingkill.

Outside they could hear a commotion. Fire engine sirens now added to the noise of the missile launch sirens and the fire bell klaxon. The real firemen were streaming into the building and running up the stairs, trailing hoses to extinguish the fire. In a couple of minutes they would be done, and the building would be crawling with security including the computer rooms.

'We're too late!' exclaimed John. 'It's too late to prevent the launch. The launch codes are set and directions installed into the missile guidance systems. These babies are going to fly in a few minutes. There's nothing I can do about it. I'd say we will have ignition in five minutes max. Stinger has delivered her payload and done her job beautifully.'

'We've got to do something John! We didn't get this far to fail,' gasped Guy. 'Can we block the launch manually? How about the silo doors, can they be closed?' John looked wide-eyed at Guy. Thinking.

Right at that moment, Byun Jae-hyung, who had been laying on the floor behind Wendy, recovered his breath and wriggled his hands free. He stood and charged headlong into his enemy in the silver suit. Fists flailing he had landed several punches into Wendy before she had a chance to react. Fortunately, the suit and silver helmet were strong and cushioned much of the blows. She instinctively raised her hands and launched a powerful kick into the groin of her assailant. Byun Jae-hyung reeled from the kick then, like a man possessed he recovered and launched another attack with clenched fists swinging wildly at Wendy. Wendy deflected the blows and pushed him backwards hard against Guy who had turned and saw the mauling Korean. Guy swung a right hook clipping Byun Jae-hyung's jaw and throwing him against the wall close to the entrance door. Blood burst from his mouth as his lip split and a few teeth were torn loose.

John was still seated at the console of the computer array. His fast fingers were flying over the keyboard searching for something he could do to arrest the launch.

Byun Jae-hyung was hysterically screaming abuse. Gobs of blood and saliva flew from his mouth as he spat and cursed his assailants. He believed these were the people responsible for his troubles leading from his finding the USB drive on the road outside the base. He neither understood this was Stinger's doing nor the goal of these three foreigners in his Network Operations Centre. Regardless, whatever their mission, he considered them the enemy. He paused to look for a weapon and saw the fire cabinet.

A red glass-fronted door covered the fire response equipment consisting of several powder fire extinguishers, an axe, a tap, a red water bucket, and the manual controls for the Pyrogen gas extinguishing system. This tool was automatically triggered, giving a five second warning if the fire sensors were triggered, but there was also a manual override. Pyrogen was a gas used to prevent a fuel bonding with oxygen and so extinguishing a fire. Large letters in red warned of the consequences of release and that no one must be in the server room at the time of release. He used his elbow to smash the glass-fronted cabinet and reached in.

He grabbed the axe and ran at Guy who was now on the offensive and had stepped between Wendy, John, and the frenzied North Korean. Byun Jae-hyung lurched forwards and swung the axe wildly at Guy. The large axe was heavy and had a momentum of its own. Guy leaned back and the red-headed axe swung in front of his face, clipping the breathing mask now hung around his neck. Wendy saw he had lost his balance and she sensed her moment to act. She ran headlong into Byun Jae-hyung and tackled him around the waist. He still held the axe although he couldn't swing it for Wendy had grabbed him around the midriff. All he could do was to use the butt of the axe raising it as high as he could before bringing it down heavily on her head. Wendy sank to her knees from the blow and Byun Jae-hyung again raised the heavy axe butt to drive another blow down onto Wendy's head.

'I've got it!' yelled John over the noise of the sirens, klaxons, and all the other din. Up to now he had ignored the fight behind him and was fully focused on the computer screen. He swung around in the swivel chair and jumped up, the breathing mask still swinging around his neck. 'I can't reverse the launch but I can close the silo doors. They're closing now! The launch will happen unless there's a failsafe I've yet to find. With the silo hatches closed the missiles will still launch but now explode in their silos.'

'You mean to tell me we're sitting within a few hundred metres of six nuclear bombs which are about to explode?' shouted Guy.

'Err, yeah! Now you put it like that!' John paused. 'The good news is they won't go thermal. Nuclear warheads need a very precise explosion around them to trigger the fission process that actually causes the nuclear reaction. That's not going to happen now. These are simply big-arse rocket fuel tanks that are about to explode. But it's still going to be big!' John added this as an afterthought. Guy frowned at him.

Byun Jae-hyung wavered before bringing down the heavy wooden axe butt on Wendy's neck. This would be the killing blow if well aimed. He was trying to grasp what the men were saying. He spoke a little English which he'd learnt for the purposes of using some of the computer equipment and software he needed. His bloody mouth worked silently as he tried to reform the words he had heard.

Guy saw the hesitation then the realisation in Byun Jae-hyung's eyes. Guy dived for Wendy, not to pull her away as it was too late for that, but to topple the embraced pair backwards and so destabilising the axe plunge. It worked. All three fell back against the wall and as the axe handle came down it managed a glancing blow off Guys arm.

The three bodies crumpled to a heap against the wall. Wendy squashed and sandwiched between the bulk of the two men. Her breath was beaten out of her, her ribs were burning, and her eyes watered with the pain. Byun Jae-hyung knew he was beaten. The second winding he had received moments before from being driven into the wall by Guy's tackle had sapped all strength. His arm went limp and he dropped the axe.

The moment stalled as all four people assessed the situation. Guy needed to get Wendy to safety and out from between him and the broken Korean. Wendy was convinced her ribs were cracked and knew she needed to disentangle herself. John's eyes flicked around the room to get a bearing for them to escape and Byun Jae-hyung momentarily saw his one final desperate option in his lost fight.

John's upright position allowed him to spot it before the other two. Surely not, he wouldn't, it would be suicide! Neither Guy nor Wendy from their mash of bodies could see Byun Jae-hyung's spare hand as he reached around. Shards of jagged glass still framed the red wooden door in the broken fire cabinet where the axe had come from.

His hand, wrist, and forearm were being lacerated by the razor thin summits of broken glass as he fumbled for his goal. Blood now streamed from his arm, but his movement was relentless. He grappled for the Pyrogen Extinguishing System and with his last remaining ounce of strength, lurched up, and with his full weight, grasped, and pulled down on the handle.

General Park's lorry screeched to a halt, kicking up plumes of dust by the security gates. The fire klaxon still screamed crisis through speakers posted around the base. His imposing stance and uniform screamed his authority long before his voice could. With no need, or time for formalities he demanded access for his twelve lorries and his Special Purposes Force Command troops, some of whom had already spilled out onto the road and had their automatic weapons pointing around the perimeter and at the gate guards.

The gate's security guards were already at a loss what to do since the sirens had broken the peace. Clearly there was a fire, they could see and smell the acrid black smoke streaming from the administration block's upper floor, flames were even licking the roof. However, now the missile launch sirens were wailing also suggesting an imminent missile launch. Were they at war? They hurriedly opened the gates as fast as possible then stood to attention and saluted General Park as his convoy rolled forwards again. The automatic weapons were still pointed at them by unblinking elite commandoes.

Nuclear Scientific Research Centre, Yongbyon. Wednesday Afternoon.

John needed to untangle his colleagues while he counted. Exactly five seconds passed, and the six Pyrogen fire extinguishing canisters arranged around the ceiling all suddenly spewed their high-pressure contents down into the small server room in unison. Gushing like an explosion of steam, the systems are fast and pervasive. They harmlessly and effectively rob any fire of its oxygen source and therefore snuff out fire with the minimum of damage to property such as computer stacks. Harmless, that is, to anything inanimate.

John was standing and realised the risk immediately. He'd pulled his oxygen mask back over his face and turned the valve for the air supply to start. Thankfully it worked. Guy had not been as quick, failing to see what Byun Jae-hyung had done. John took the few strides to cover the gap between himself and his colleagues and helped Guy pull on his mask also. He turned on the pressurised air supply from the buddy tank just as Guy started coughing, his lungs deprived of oxygen in the fast saturating Pyrogen atmosphere. Wendy, however, in her haste to get into the fire suit and concerned only about hiding her face, as the helmet did, never donned the breathing apparatus.

Still trapped under the heavy weight of Guy, her mouth opened wide and she started to convulse. Her already bruised lungs struggling for air, her gasps becoming fast, painful, and desperate. Byun Jae-hyung's arm had become pierced on one of the larger shards of glass. As the weight of the bodies on top of him acted to push him down so a large pinnacle of glass was forced still further, deeper, into his arm and this was restricting his movement. He was impaled and unable to move.

John grabbed Guy's shoulders and hauled him off Wendy. Guy scrambled to get himself upright, kneeling at first, then urgently started to help untangle Wendy from the limbs of Byun Jae-hyung whose silly hairstyle was now stuck to his head from blood and sweat. He was alive and also gasping for breath, his chest convulsing as his lungs instinctively heaved for more air. His bloodshot eyes opened and he captured the scenario.

He couldn't move his left arm. It was still impaled on the broken glass panel, the spike of glass wedged deep into his forearm. He couldn't stand or even sit upright, still slumped against the wall. With his free right arm and two legs he could and did grip Wendy in a deathlock. His hatred burned deep and his adrenaline overrode all other thoughts. If this last desperate act was going to kill him, he would take one of his protagonists with him too he reasoned.

Wendy was weak from lack of oxygen, her complexion through the fireproof helmet turning grey. Her mouth was wide open gulping for air, her eyes bulging with fear. Guy and John pulled harder to free her from the grip of her captor. He hung on tighter still. The weight of the wrestle pulled down harder on Byun Jae-hyung's glass-pinned arm and suddenly there was a pulsing shower of bright crimson as the radial and cubital arteries were severed by the spike of glass still holding him firm against the wall. The floor was becoming slippery with blood. John and Guy scrabbled in the gore to get a grip and pull Wendy free. Byun Jae-hyung smiled as he held Wendy fast with every remaining ounce of strength in his dying body.

At last, with a final shudder, the fight went out of the Korean and they could untangle Wendy. They dragged her to the door and opened it using the card swipe, pulling the now limp form of Wendy into the normal atmosphere of the office. Blue and red lights synchronistically swept the office, emitted from the fire engine outside the building. Klaxons and sirens still wailed their sense of impending doom, and still smoke filled the room from the fire above. They needed to get out and get away fast but Wendy was the priority. She lay limp on the floor with John and Guy kneeling either side of her. There was no movement in her body, no pulse.

The men quickly pulled down their breathing masks and Guy pulled the silver all-covering helmet off Wendy's head, her black hair spilling onto the floor as he did so. She wasn't breathing. John started clawing at the silver fireproof suit, undoing the studs and toggles around her neck and yanking hard at the ties. Guy tipped her head back with one hand and placed his other hand under her chin, wedging his thumb and forefinger in-between her teeth to force her mouth fully open. He placed his lips well over hers and gently breathed out. From the corner of his eye he saw her chest lift. John had managed to free the upper part of her suit. Guy repeated the action three times in quick succession. John placed his ear to her chest.

'There's no heartbeat!' he announced urgently.

Guy placed his mouth over hers again and repeated the exhaling then swivelled to compress her breastbone in five quick bursts. Anxiety such as he'd never known filled his thoughts. He repeated the steps knowing this was the best course of action. 'Come on Wendy!' he cried.

He applied his mouth to hers again. Finally she spluttered and gasped. Wendy gasped and gasped, her body gulping down as much of the beautiful oxygen as it could to replenish what had been lost. After a moment, Guy and John helped her first sit and then stand.

'It hurts to breathe,' she rasped, her hands on her knees as she grappled for air.

'We gotta move babe,' said Guy, pulling her arm over his shoulder.

John mimicked Guy on her other side. Wendy nodded limply. The fire hose nozzles they had picked up earlier still lay where they had dropped them upon entering the room. Guy and John stooped to collect them, Wendy hanging between them. They started running as fast as able out of the Network Operations Centre and into the corridor, back towards the building exit.

'Did what I think just happened, happen?' said Wendy, still coughing and the pain still tight in her chest. 'It hurts to breathe.'

'Later babe,' said Guy. He nodded towards the exit door at John. John saw it too. The way out.

As they rounded the corner in the grey strip-lit corridor, there stood two Special Forces soldiers in full combat gear. Both were armed with guns poised, but pointing to the floor, and both were confused about what was happening. The soldiers saw the three firefighters dressed in full equipment and raised their guns as trained. They thought surely these were two of their own men carrying an injured third between them. The third looked hurt with head lolled forwards hiding the face. The soldiers lowered their guns again.

As the three firefighters got closer, the soldiers realised the firefighters were not Korean and the security guards shouted to them to stop. Without missing a step and in unison, Guy and John continued right at them and swung the heavy metal nozzles to connect hard with the soldier's heads before any shots from the automatic weapons could be fired. The guards dropped like ninepins. John and Guy pushed passed the crumpled bodies as they reached the exit. Wendy regained her balance and shook off the men still supporting her.

'I'm okay now,' she whispered, holding her hands to her sore ribcage. 'I can walk.' Guy pulled his oxygen mask back on, and John, being Asian looking gave his to Wendy and pulled it over her head and face. In the confusion he might just pass for Korean.

'OK, now we need to put as much distance between us and this base as quickly as possible,' shouted John over the noise. They emerged from the administration block to be met with a melee of activity. Firefighters were working from the back of the fire engine: hoses running, ladders being erected, and orders being shouted. Commandos ran around securing their positions, unsure quite why, however, in the absence of other orders, that's what they were trained to do.

The three firefighters were noticed yet they didn't seem out of place and attracted little attention. Guy saw Ah-ga-sshi and her brother by their own truck. He signalled wildly to follow them. They looked odd now they were out of the building although not odd enough to warrant close inspection by the AAA Command troops given the other priorities.

Guy ran to the fire engine and climbed up into the empty front seats. John and Wendy followed behind and climbed into the rear seats. The engine had remained running to power its equipment. John looked through the windscreen and saw Ah-ga-sshi and her brother sat in the seats of their old rusty wood lorry. John waved his arm as a gesture to get away. They understood and started their own engine.

Guy had driven a lorry on several occasions before but never a fire engine and it took him a few moments to work out the controls. There were two gearsticks and an array of knobs and buttons he wasn't familiar with. He didn't want to get this wrong as, being surrounded by armed commandos, they would likely only get one chance of escape. Stalling the fire engine now would be catastrophic. He composed himself, tested some of the controls, and said a quiet prayer to anyone kind enough to listen.

John was exasperated. 'In your own time Guy. No hurry mate. Remember we're only sitting on half a dozen missiles that are about to get very hot… no pressure!'

'Thanks John. I thought you might like a minute to savour the moment' said Guy as he tested the engine's accelerator. 'You don't know when you'll have this opportunity again.'

'Very funny lads! Now can you get us the fuck out of here before we all incinerate,' rasped Wendy, her throat still horse. She bent forwards and wheezed for breath again, wincing as pain shot through her ribcage.

When he was sure he had not missed anything; breaks, gears, hydraulics, Guy depressed the clutch, eased the engine into what he hoped was first gear, and floored the accelerator pedal while releasing the clutch. The fire engine lurched forwards and Guy quickly selected a second gear in the close-ratio gearbox. She picked up a little speed and in the mirrors he saw startled firemen and soldiers scatter from flying hosepipes and ladders still attached to the bright red beast. He changed quickly into third gear and now the fire tender had momentum.

Guy heard gunshots and pings as bullets hit the back of the fire engine - hopefully they would do little harm as they would not penetrate all the metal walls and water tanks of the fire engine housed between them and the soldiers. Guy steered the truck left around the motor sheds where they had first hidden and found the firefighting gear. The backpacks Peter Park had given them still lay in there, but they were lost, no time to retrieve them now. Guy checked the gauges and as best he could tell the fuel tanks were full. It seemed there were two of them although the indicators were in Chinese characters. Wendy could confirm for him later if they made it off the base. A big if, he thought.

The fire engine gained speed as Guy continued up the gears and he swung the heavy vehicle hard onto the road approaching the security gates. The guards were still stood there, weapons poised should General Park issue further instructions. The fire engine showed no signs of stopping and, as Guy scanned the way ahead, he realised the road leading up to the Nuclear Scientific Research Centre from his left, the way they'd come, was blocked by two heavy green military trucks and a dozen soldiers.

A nanoseconds calculation told him he would not be able to crash though such a heavy blockade. Even if he could, that number of soldiers with automatic guns would have plenty of time to put more perforations into the fire engine's cab than a teabag. They would all be killed in seconds. He would need to turn right out of the gate and continue into the mountains, heading east, even deeper into the Democratic People's Republic of Korea and even further away from an improbable escape.

John put his arm around Wendy as they braced for impact. Guy drove the fire engine straight at the closed gates as the guards fired straight at the oncoming monster before leaping clear. Guy had ducked behind the wheel and heard the windscreen shatter as bullets thumped into the reinforced glass. The fire engine briefly lurched as it hit the locked gates, however, the momentum of the heavy wagon was enough to rip the gates apart on their hinges amid a shower of sparks flying glass, smashed wing mirrors and mangled metal. Guy sat up again and pulled the steering wheel hard right as fast as he could to avoid ploughing straight off the road and into the scrubland opposite.

The truck barely made the turn, screeching rubber and smoke coming off the protesting tyres as the red engine slewed sideways. Cognisant of John's warning, they needed to get as far away from the base as fast as possible. They had minutes at best, more likely seconds, before Stinger enacted her final instruction and attempted to fly the missiles. He really hoped John was right about the nuclear warheads not detonating!

Guy glanced into what remained of the now shattered wing mirrors and glimpsed a little wood carrying truck following close behind them. Ah-ga-sshi and her brother seemed to be gritting their teeth as they did their best to keep up. Guy changed up a gear and floored the accelerator again, heading east and into the mountains as fast as he could get the fire engine to go. They didn't have a moment to lose.

Chapter 32. Detonation

Tel Aviv, Wednesday Morning. Yongbyon, Wednesday Afternoon.

Tal sat in his usual blue walled cubicle in the Kirya building in Tel Aviv. He wore his standard tee-shirt and jeans and sported a five-day beard to compliment his techie image. His day had, so far, been routine and he was looking forward to seeing Dorit later in the afternoon. *'Only two more days to the Israeli weekend,'* he thought.

He had been on the early shift so with luck he would be finished by early afternoon giving him time to go to the beach and play football with his mates. Afterwards, rather than drink beer with them, he would dash off to the jeers and laughter of his friends to see his buxom Dorit. They may tease him but privately he knew they were envious. It had been a mundane shift up to now and his mind was wandering.

Over the last few days he had taken a particular and personal interest in North Korea. He had kept a close eye on news and surveillance. That his friend Eitan in the US had initially flagged the whole hacker angle then he himself had helpfully identified the probable hacker as Wolf had excited him, lending purpose to his job. Moreover, identifying Wolf's likely assassin Lee Hyo-joo had given him a personal angle in the case. He had studied her pictures in meticulous detail, examined every image of her he could find. He even felt a bond with this beautiful and enigmatic alleged killer. If Da Vinci had been fixated by Mona Lisa, so was he by Lee Hyo-joo. Now he was looking out for any further activity that might be related to the two and to, of course, North Korean missiles and the probable target of the malware. Suddenly he was struck by the amount of chatter he was getting from and regarding North Korea.

The first intercepts were offical and related to North Korea warning her two closest allies, China and Russia, of an imminent scheduled missile test. Then came South Korea, Japan, and China all claiming to have picked up seismic readings on the Korean peninsula, suggesting an earthquake or possible underground nuclear test, again, although this would seem to contradict the missile test warning. South Korea, Japan, and the US had not detected any missile launch activity on the Korean peninsula. The seismic readings suggested a sizable explosion but probably not nuclear, although it could be interpreted as a failed or suboptimal nuclear test. Afterall North Korea did have a history of failed tests.

What was odd about all this activity was that it seemed very real-time. Traditionally North Korea's protocol was to give several days notification of tests. This was mainly a negotiating stance on the part of North Korea's leadership leading up to requests for aid and was primarily designed to attract the attention of the world's media.

Compelling as they were, in politick speak they fell short of and were not to be confused with an act of aggression. However, all this chatter seemed to suggest the tests had happened before the warnings were issued. Tal quickly typed a summary to his bosses, knowing the interest they had in the activities of anything regarding North Korea and her missiles.

As far as he could tell, there had been some form of underground explosion and satellites were being focused to look for the thermal footprint and location. Was this in any way connected to the previous intelligence he had gathered, he wondered? It seemed too coincidental to Tal. The American and the European space agencies were busy lining up satellite imagery. He also saw the US navy had instructed the USS *Ronald Reagan*, with her flying armoury of ninety aircraft and her flotilla of ten warships, to not return to the Yokosuka naval base in Japan as planned and instead continue north into the Sea of Japan, close to North Korea.

Guy, who'd been paying close attention to the reflection of what remained of his wing mirrors saw it first. 'Hold on back there, the base has just exploded'. Suddenly the heat-blast was like standing behind a jet engine such was the roar and the raw heat wave that passed them seconds after a brilliant flash of light. Fortunately, they were facing away from the explosion. Looking into the light would have been blinding. The bright red engine had barely been on the road for a couple of miles after the sharp right turn out of the research facility following their crashing through the security gate. The little rusty wood lorry had been behind them before the blast as Ah-ga-sshi and her brother had been following close behind.

The road had visibly rippled underneath them, actually lifting and surfing the fire engine a little way, like a small boy's toy, before passing on ahead faster than the wagon was driving and settling the 10-ton fire engine back down again. The road surface was now crazed like a broken eggshell. They could see the ground wave still rippling in all directions across the rocky and parched landscape radially from the Nuclear Scientific Research Centre behind them. The energy released from the blast was staggering.

John was inclined to quote John Travolta as Vic Deakins in *Broken Arrow* and shout 'I say goddamn what a rush!' but the fear on Wendy's face told him this was no time to joke. The adrenalin-fuelled elation at having made it out of the base would need containing for the moment. They weren't safe yet.

Then the debris fell. Rocks, dust, wood, twisted and contorted steel began raining down around them, clattering on the roof of the fire engines cab. The steel's previous function was unrecognisable having been wrenched from its purpose by the force of the explosion and thrown with the brute force of Thor high into the air. It now showered down again like hail, hitting the ground hard all around them. Guy had the fire engine in top gear and was travelling at full speed while chicaning around wreckage from the blast as it bounced on the road around them.

What looked like a steel and concrete silo lid, 10-foot in diameter, slammed into the ground beside them with such force it half embedded itself into the hard ground and rocked the red engine so hard it nearly toppled over.

Guy swerved the huge engine around the obstacles as they fell. He glanced in the broken mirrors and was relieved to see the little wood lorry still glued to their tail, swerving in unison with the big red wagon in front. Lighter debris was still falling, and a doughnut of dust and smoke billowed behind them from the epicentre at the root of the missile silo that was now just a massive conical hole in the ground.

The fire engine and its wood truck tail had been battered by failing jetsam and had been fairly unscathed so far but then their luck ran out. A metal staircase plummeted from the sky and smashed at terminal velocity into the bed of the wood lorry flipping it like a tossed coin. The truck landed on its side and Guy glimpsed the image of the flying vehicle from the broken reflection in what was left of his wing mirror. He stamped on the brakes. The 10-ton fire engine slewed to a halt. John and Wendy were thrown forwards in their rear seats.

'Shit Guy. What is it?'

Guy leapt down from the driver's cabin and ran backwards to the crippled wood wagon, its skywards wheels still spinning in a lame attempt to gain a grip on the road again. The windscreen had smashed in and left a gaping jaw into the trucks cabin. Guy was nervous what he would find, and he fought the urge to turn and return to the relative safety of the fire engine. He braced himself for a gory shock. Ah-ga-sshi was bleeding from her head and moaning, lying across her unmoving brother. He looked in.

Luckily, they had worn their belts. He reached in to pull Ah-ga-sshi free. John and Wendy were behind him now and John barged in to assist. They could grip Ah-ga-sshi under her arms, and so pulled her clear through the gap that once housed the windscreen. Aside a nasty head cut that was bleeding profusely, she appeared to have no broken bones.

Wendy had the forethought to first bring a first aid kit from the fire engine. 'Lay her here and then get her brother, I'll tend to her,' she barked and beckoned to a flat bit of road. Smoke and dust still billowed around them.

Guy and John scrambled into the space that was once the rusty cab of the wood truck. Ah-ga-sshi's brother was in a bad way. John glanced at Guy, he had reached the same conclusion. Wendy was sat on the dusty asphalt road, working on Ah-ga-sshi, a swab held to her head where the cut was. She was laying prone and moaning, probably concussed, but she was alive with no obvious broken bones. Guy and John were trying to figure out the extent of the injuries to her brother. He was motionless, a few small cuts and scratches where the windscreen had exploded in, and he wasn't obviously bleeding externally.

It was eerie, the only sound was that of the fire wagon whose engine was still idling. Any wildlife was dead from the explosion or stunned and silenced by the blast. No birdsong, chirp of crickets, cries or squawks of any kind. The moonscape eeriness was unnerving. The only smell now that of the acrid smoke coming from the fires now raging in the scorched shell which was once the research facility.

Suddenly Wendy jumped up and shouted, 'Guys! Look!' She pointed towards the billowing black smoke where two of the green army lorries were moving ponderously towards them, navigating the debris that strewed the road. They were no more than half a mile away.

'Shit!' exclaimed Guy. 'These boys are like bloody cockroaches; nothing kills them! John, help me here. Injuries or not we need to get him free and to the fire engine.' John and Guy crawled into the cab and grabbed a hold of the limp body anywhere they could.

John said, 'On three,' and they heaved. At first the dead weight wouldn't move then, after a few more tugs, the limp form gave a little, the torso could be pulled forwards, and then it stuck fast again. Guy wriggled further in and could see the problem. One leg positioned at a very unnatural angle was pinned by the crushed footwell. He craned his neck around and saw a metal bar, part of the stairway that had hit the truck.

'Pass that,' he said, pointing and instructing John who saw the plan. John moved fast and grabbed the bar, bending it free from the wreckage. Guy rammed one end of the bar into the footwell as close as he could to the trapped leg. He planned to use the bar as a leaver to bend the footwell clear of the trapped leg. Another smell now greeted his nostrils, fuel, presumably leaking from the fuel tank.

'Seriously!' he muttered under his breath. 'I'll get leverage and you pull with all your weight,' instructed Guy. He stood and shouted 'Three!' then put all his strength into pulling the bar down. At first nothing happened and then the flimsy metal footwell grated and budged. John pulled the body clear through the hole that once held the windscreen.

John knelt beside the body and put his head to the body's chest.

'Breathing and heart's beating,' he declared with obvious relief. 'He's been knocked unconscious though.'

Guy surveyed the smashed leg. 'He's not going to be walking anytime soon. Let's get him to the fire engine. You help our girl,' Guy said to Wendy.

With a heave Guy hauled the limp brother up and, with the continuing momentum, deftly threw him in a fireman's lift over his right shoulder and hoofed the body towards the fire engine. John and Wendy had pulled Ah-ga-sshi up and gingerly walked her to the fire engine. Both brother and sister were manhandled into the rear seats and Guy pulled himself into the front seat. Guy looked behind them and saw the army lorries still stealthily picking their way through the chicane of debris, some still burning along the road. He scrabbled around on the dashboard looking for something.

'Now would be a good time to get going Guy. Whatcha doing?' called John to the front seat. He had clambered into the rear seats with Wendy to help tend to the patients.

'Hang on,' said Guy. He found what he was looking for. He ripped open the pack of cigarettes he had found and removed three. He put all three between his lips and with the companioning matches lit them.

'Not the best of times to develop a smoking habit,' called John, 'although, thinking about it, a better time doesn't come to mind.'

Guy sucked on the cigarettes and jumped out of the cab again. He ran to the wood lorry wreckage laying on its side and carefully placed the burning cigarettes on the ground, six inches from the spreading puddle of fuel. 'Come on you babies! One of you has to work.' He ran back to the fire engine and jumped in, pulling the door closed behind him and revving the engine as he slid the wagon into gear.

'Let's get the fire-truck outta here!' yelled John with a chortle. Even Guy and Wendy had to groan at that line.

'Very good, John, very good,' smiled Wendy, relieved to be underway again.

Wendy and John in the rear cab turned their attention to the injured siblings. The blood flow on Ah-ga-sshi's head had stemmed and she sat upright on the seat, eyes closed, breathing heavily. Her brother had been laid out straight on the rear-facing seats. He was still unconscious, and they let him lay there; best undisturbed, as the pain would be excruciating when he came around.

Wendy found scissors in the first aid kit and carefully cut away the trousers from the injured leg. She took care not to disturb the owner. The mess she found was horrible with a mangle of flesh, torn muscle, and white bone protruding from the compound fracture. It was bleeding although not badly.

'That's a relief,' said Wendy to John. 'The leg's smashed, however, the arteries are not hit. He's not bleeding badly but he's going to need medical help quickly.'

'Nothing much we can do for them now, other than get them to safety,' suggested John, who was feeling queasy. He avoided looking at the gore on the seat in front of him.

Guy was accelerating up the gears again as fast as able. His one goal was to put as much distance between him and the pursuing army trucks as possible. He was closely watching behind him in the shards of the rear-view mirror. He could see the two army lorries had made progress and were now close to the tangle of the wood lorry laying on its side in the middle of the road.

At that moment he saw what he was hoping for and a burst of flames shot from beneath the abandoned vehicle. The leaked fuel puddle had ignited. Seconds later the whole wood lorry burst into a ball of flames showering the roads width in an orange orb of fire and black smoke. For a moment the army lorries had stopped. They hadn't quite reached the wreckage and were not close enough to be touched by the fire although it had stalled them.

Guy saw them wait, paused like two large green alligators about to strike. Guy needed all the advantage he could get. He saw the two trucks stopped, wondering, then the front one reversed a few feet and then began to roll forwards again and smashed into the remains of the burning wood lorry, brutally pushing the still flaming and tangled wreck aside.

The might of the larger lorry powered through, heavy tyres crunching over the remains of the twisted metal ladder that had disabled the small wood truck in the first place. Now it was simply a case of whose lorry was faster, thought Guy, and he wasn't sure of his chances given he had the heavier vehicle.

#

'Was that explosion nuclear?' Wendy asked John.

'No. It was the missiles' rocket fuel, it's a highly combustible Liquid UDMH/AK27,' John couldn't help getting technical when the opportunity arose, 'exploding in the silos.'

John continued. 'The nuclear warheads wouldn't have detonated. They need a very precise and controlled explosion around them to trigger the thermal reaction. If they had, we would not be here. The explosion would have been hundreds of times bigger than that. We would have all been turned to a crisp of carbon within seconds.'

'Too fast to even know it had happened,' responded Guy.

John added 'I'd say Stinger took control of the launch, as designed, once the missiles had been primed and fuelled for launch under a test sequence. The Stinger malware took command and control of the launch and it couldn't be shutdown. I'd guess the Korean who attacked you Wendy in the control room back there realised the problem and was trying to abort the launch. That's why he had stayed back after the fire alarm. He knew they had a problem and was trying to rectify it. I wonder if he even knew it was a malware deliberately designed to do that?' John reflected speculatively. 'Guess we'll never know.'

Ah-ga-sshi was groaning and babbling in Korean. She was in shock. Wendy had no idea what she was saying but she wasn't lucid in any language. Wendy put her arm around her and made soothing noises. 'Don't worry. We'll get you to a hospital,' she said, having no idea if they even could or would before capture. Guy tensed his jaw muscles and wrestled the heavy rig as fast as he could along the twisting road. It followed the contours of the hills and there were no turn-offs, only a snaking asphalt surface heading higher into the mountains and generally east, deeper into North Korea and further from possible escape. Truth was he had no plan nor or even an inkling of a plan. His only priority was to try to outrun the two army lorries trundling determinedly behind them.

As far as Guy could tell they weren't gaining, if anything his red machine was pulling slightly ahead. He was running scenarios through his head. Had they radioed ahead to have the road blocked? He suspected not. Did he have fuller tanks of fuel so could he out distance them? He also suspected not. If he dumped all the water from water tanks would that give him more speed and better fuel economy. He thought possibly yes.

The scenery was rocky and barren. The Nuclear Scientific Research Centre was positioned in Yongbyon specifically because it was barren and in the middle of nowhere. The mountains could have been majestic in other circumstances, ideal for hiking and trail walking. Now they were bland, featureless, and offered no protection. Rocks protruded in every direction and the few brave plants and scrubby trees were brown and parched from the hot dry summer.

'John, you busy back there?'

'What did you have in mind?' replied John warily.

'Well, I was thinking we would probably go faster and further if we could figure out how to empty the water tanks of their water.'

'Good point, Guy. I'll come over.'

Careful not to disturb or step on the man's body lying prone on the seat in front of him, John deftly scrambled from the rear cabin into the front driver's cabin. The fire engine was still squealing around corners, Guy accelerating and breaking aggressively as the road demanded. The sweaty smell of the cabin now mixed with hot rubber and brake pads from the heavy vehicle. Truth was, John was happy to have a distraction from the mangled leg he sat facing in the rear. Wendy had strapped herself and Ah-ga-sshi into their seats with seatbelts and were rocking and lurching with the motion of the wagon being thrown around the bends. She had placed her feet against the unconscious brother to stop him shifting in the seat as he slept. Her ribs still hurt her from the previous fight and every bump caused a wince of pain, however, she felt her own issues paled against the agony of the siblings she felt responsible for, and she was hardly going to tell Guy to slow down.

There were no other vehicles on the road to avoid which was a blessing although Guy thought the distraction might be helpful as they headed eastwards. The sun had passed its zenith and the wagon's shadow had now crept in front of the engine. John had eventually scrambled next to him and started surveying the array of nobs and switches, trying to figure which, if any, worked the water pumps. He found the sirens and was greeted by a stern scowl from Guy. Next the fire engine was illuminated with arrays of flashing red and blue lights. A lesser scowl but a scowl never the less was the reply from Guy. None of the others had obvious functions and the Korean characters denoting function where useless.

'Only one thing for it!' announced John. 'Keep her steady would ya!' He opened the door of the cabin and, before Guy could talk him out of the folly, John had pulled himself outside onto the edge of the speeding fire engine.

The road was snaking higher now and Guy dropped down several gears, the wagon slowing as it climbed. John had shimmied down the side of the wagon and, gripping the rails with one hand, was testing the various red painted taps with the other. At last he found one that spewed water. He turned it off and, eyes streaming tears from the wind, climbed to the top of the fire engine to survey the road ahead.

'Good lad!' shouted Guy, realising what he was thinking. The road would crest shortly going through a natural pass between two peaks of rock. As the fire engine cleared the pass, John spun the tap wheel as fast as he could, water spewing over the dusty road saturating the surface. The road turned sharp left and Guy slowed, weaving the wagon from left to right giving the road surface a good coating of water. John left the tap on and scrabbled back along the side of the wagon to retake his position as shotgun beside Guy. They grinned at each other, both hoping for the same outcome.

#

General Park was livid with rage. Of his command of elite troops and twelve lorries, only these two remained. The others were dead and destroyed by the blast at the research facility. He had recognised the launch siren and knew the drill was real, however, he was unsure if it was to the point where Stinger could take control. If his guess was correct, Stinger had found its way into the base's computer system and had executed its job. To a point.

The missiles would launch but not to his timeframe. He had seen the fire engine race from its place in front of the administration block and assumed the protagonists sent to upset Stinger were on the base. He had immediately ordered what troops he could see into the two closest lorries and set off to pursue the fire engine. The explosion happened as his two lorries cleared the base, incinerating most staff and troops within the buildings and still milling around the base. Most poor souls were simply stood about outside the buildings having reacted to the sirens and unsure what to do next. He couldn't guess the total death toll but knew over forty of his men were lost.

The base was gone. His beautiful Rodong-1 missiles had not launched and had been destroyed in the process. Now his only option was to bring the terrorists back to Pyongyang for a public trial in the presence of his supreme leader. He might be able to sew a silk purse out of this pig's ear yet.

From the front seat of the front army lorry, General Park could see the fire engine was edging further away from them, however, it was a clear road with nowhere to hide. The small wood truck in the middle of the road had been a close call. His driver had only just stopped in time to avoid being engulfed in the fire as the lorry burst into flames. He recalled seeing this little rusty truck also leave the base and wondered at the part it played. Staff from the base, fearing the worst and spotting the opportunity to flee their posts, he pondered. In hindsight they had been wise. Had they then crashed their truck into falling debris and been burnt to death in the fire. Poetic justice if ever there was. They weren't his immediate concern. When this mess was over, he would investigate who they were and punish their families. Right now though, he had bigger fish to catch.

The army lorries lumbered up the rise as fast as able. The driver of the lead truck was concentrating hard and was doing an admirable job. That didn't stop General Park barking orders at him although the driver knew it was better to drive with a degree of care and stay in pursuit rather than recklessly crash off the road. The driver was going as fast as he dare for the conditions. The roads were dry, but gritty and dusty and the heavy army vehicles were hard to handle; their tyres treaded for rough terrain, not high-speed tarmac pursuits. As the first lorry peaked the crest the driver gunned the accelerator hard and changed up a gear, determined to gain on the fire engine now heading downhill.

As the road turned sharp left the driver's first indication of a problem was that the steering didn't respond to his input. The lorry continued straight, slamming headlong into the rock face on the tangent of the bend. The lead lorry bounced off the rock and spun on the wet road. The second lorry was too close to avoid impact and hit the first, side on, as it too slewed sidewards, grating into the rock face on the opposite side of the wet road. Both lorries stopped with an abrupt jolt. Their drivers and passengers dazed and confused. General Park regained his composure, opened the door, and, amid a barrage of curses, jumped down to inspect the damage.

'Clever people,' he muttered as his saw the wet road and realised what they had done. They had used water from the fire engine to soak the road on the blind bend, turning it into a virtual ice rink for the cumbersome big green goddesses. He surveyed the damage. It was hard to assess. The second driver was dead from the impact, neck broken. Stunned troops were now spilling from the rear of the lorries. Perhaps they could salvage one perhaps both vehicles. They would need time. Meanwhile the red fire engine in the distance continued to speed ahead, widening the gap between pursued and pursuer. General Park kicked the wall of a tire and cursed viciously.

Yongbyon. Wednesday Afternoon.

Wendy, John, and Guy breathed a collective sigh of relief. The fire engine sped down the mountain road and as they looked behind them, the army lorries were no longer following. John's idea seemed to have paid off and they were safe, at least for the moment. Sat behind the huge horizontal steering wheel, Guy could slow the driving down to a more sedate speed, adding a little comfort for the two injured passengers. The army trucks must have skidded on the wet road as hoped but the extent of their damage was unknown. Perhaps they had been delayed for just a minute or perhaps the lorries were irreparably damaged and out of the pursuit for good. The trio hoped this was the case.

Guy could afford a little breathing space now although they still desperately needed a plan. They also needed to tend to the injured brother and sister and decide how to best help them. Ah-ga-sshi was starting to make a little more sense. She was coming around from the concussion and even smiled at Wendy, until she saw her injured brother on the seat opposite. She let out a wail, dropped to her knees on the floor, and threw her arms across the injured man's chest, gushing Korean as she did so. The act must have hurt her own head as she grimaced with the sudden movement. Wendy put her arm around her shoulders and tried to subdue the heaving sobs.

'I don't know how but we'll get him patched-up' she whispered.

Wendy reached for the first-aid kit and slowly pulled Ah-ga-sshi away from her unconscious brother. They had been watching over him and his chest was still rising and falling, slowly and steadily, so at least he was alive. With the compound break in his leg they thought it best to let him sleep rather than wake to a lot of pain. He may have had other internal injuries too, it was impossible to tell. At least he was breathing and there was no sign of blood in his mouth, so his lungs were intact. Wendy pulled a pack of white tablets she assumed were painkillers from the first-aid kit and offered them to Ah-ga-sshi. She scrutinised them and took two, without water. She gestured the rest to keep for her brother and Wendy nodded.

John had remained in the front seat with Guy and broached the next pressing subject. 'We need a plan Guy. Where are we heading?'

'I've been wondering the same thing,' said Guy. 'I studied the area on Google Maps when we were still in Seoul although I didn't pay too much attention to the eastern side of the country. I recall after a few miles we hit another road running north to south and if we turn southwards we reach the next large town called Kaechon. I never assumed we would need to head east, deeper into the country. Per our plan I expected us to head back to Pakchon. At least it's remote. My guess would be the place is going to light up with military, helicopters, and emergency services very soon. They're going to need to assess the damage back at the plant and look for survivors. I'd give us one maybe two hours max.'

John added, 'If the lorries behind have radio's they'll likely be asking for air support to hunt for us too. In Red Bessy here we'd not be hard to spot from the air. I love her dearly but we need a new set of wheels!'

Wendy chimed in. 'We need to get these guys medical attention! Ah-ga-sshi is back with us, however, she's had a nasty bang on the head and probably needs a stitch or two. Her brother's in a worse way and he needs help before he gets septicaemia or something worse.'

Ah-ga-sshi had understood enough of the conversation and simply said, 'Kaechon' and waved her hand down the road in the direction they were traveling.

They fell silent, the adrenalin rush was abating and now the sober realisation of their predicament was taking president. There was thankfully still no sign of the army lorries behind them. They were all hit with tiredness, particularly John having slept little the night before. They were still wearing their heavy firefighting gear, and each struggled out of the kit, Wendy wincing as her sore ribs grated. Wendy felt dirty and sticky as the silver fire suit was impossibly hot and heavy and she guessed she had been sweating in it for a couple of hours.

After a while, they reached the road junction and again Ah-ga-sshi said 'Kaechon,' and gestured right. This road was also quiet with the occasional lorry trundling slowly along. Most seemed to be carrying lumber, stone, or aggregate of some type. Others seemed to be carrying the fruits of a harvest. Sweetcorn cobs, and root vegetables the most prevalent. Guy noticed how everything looked old, tired, and dusty, as if this were the graveyard for all the obsolete engineering the Chinese no longer used or wanted. He had travelled extensively in remote parts of China and 'developing' was certainly the adjective he would use, however, this looked even more retarded and underdeveloped. It reminded him of how China probably looked two generations ago.

John reached for the panel of switches again and this time turned the flashing lights on. Guy gave a curious look and John smiled, 'If we pass any emergency or army vehicles coming the other way, they may just think we're on official business.'

'Unless they're actually looking for us,' added Guy.

'In which case they'll see us anyway,' replied John, trying to avoid looking smug.

Six miles later, they passed a convoy of fast-moving army vehicles heading north, in the opposite direction, presumably heading to Yongbyon. Guy sped up again. It was mid-afternoon as they reached the outskirts of Kaechon. He was suddenly anxious, had the army vehicles realised who they'd just passed he worried?

#

General Park had supervised his troops traveling in the two damaged army trucks following the crash. One driver was dead, his neck broken with the impact, and a couple of his Special Purposes Force Command had minor injuries. The rest of his elite force from the 907th Unit he got to work trying to salvage one or both lorries. The sun was overhead now, and the sky was clear. It was sweltering work. It took them an hour. They swapped wheels and one axel and managed to get one of the damaged lorries serviceable. They continued carefully on their journey. They had nearly been thwarted by two traps, they didn't want a third.

After another hour they met a convoy racing towards Yongbyon. General Park stopped them to confirm what they knew. The Yongbyon Nuclear Scientific Research Facility had exploded and they were to inspect and contain. He asked if they had seen a fire truck heading toward Kaechon and they confirmed they had. He used their radio to order roadblocks around Kaechon and to stop and retain anyone in a fire engine. He then sent a message to his secretary at his home base in Pyongyang. He needed help from the one professional he fully trusted.

#

Ah-ga-sshi was feeling better, the painkillers had kicked in and she had assumed authority. Headache or not, she gave directions and navigated the fire engine around an industrial part of Kaechon. The town was nondescript and quiet with poorly maintained roads, grey concrete buildings, and a few drab looking plants and trees fighting for survival on the dusty patches of unused land. She directed them off the main road and after a few miles of unmade-up track they reached a moonscape of a quarry where either some construction was about to start or had started only to be abandoned. It was hard to tell which. Regardless, it was deserted.

Guy pulled up and spotted a large timber yard close by, adjacent to the quarry. Ah-ga-sshi gestured to drive the fire engine into the lumber shed and so conceal it from the air. The others were to stay in the wagon, but she grabbed Guy's hand and lead him to the rear of the timber yard. There she snuck around until she found what she wanted: another lorry, parked behind a huge pile of timber, the truck was old and dilapidated.

She slid into the driver's seat and reviewed the exposed wires dangling from under the dashboard. Twisting four strands together then brushing another two exposed ends together it started. Guy was even more in awe of Ah-ga-sshi. It seemed ignition keys weren't used in this country. He surmised she was familiar with this yard, and this particular truck. It was now late afternoon and the yard was still totally deserted. Closed for the day, the workers presumably home in their grey flats with their grey families.

Ah-ga-sshi then found several empty plastic fuel drums and a hose. Guy guessed the plan as she drove the lorry round to park next to the fire engine. She had Guy and John syphon as much precious diesel from the fire engine's tanks as they could hold, while she and Wendy carefully transferred her brother to the new vehicle. He still hadn't woken, and Wendy had done a passable job of cleaning the wound on his leg and loosely dressing it with a bandage she'd found in the first-aid kit to protect it from dirt and dust. But, she knew it would need to be professionally set and soon.

Fifteen minutes later they were travelling south again, this time with Ah-ga-sshi at the wheel of the new lorry. The honourable fire engine that had saved their skin was abandoned behind them. She travelled straight through Kaechon, continuing on towards Sunchon, the next major town. She told John, Wendy and Guy to keep their heads down. Wendy asked her at one point where they were going. She couldn't answer, she simply gestured forwards. As they were leaving Kaechon, they saw a lot of army lorries mobilised. They appeared to be about to set-up a roadblock, but the old quarry wagon rolled passed unmolested. In the nick of time they guessed.

#

The General assumed his targets would be making their way back to Pakchon, as per their point of entry into the DPRK according to Talon, his source in the South. How they ever managed to get this far amazed him. That they had actually fatally damaged the leading nuclear facility staggered him further and, unless he caught them, this would likely hold grave ramifications for him as the head of The Strategic Rocket Forces. He needed these three foreigners, badly. He had instructed roadblocks around Kaechon and all roads leading west. By the time he reached Kaechon the roadblocks were in place, stopping every vehicle. There was no sign of the fire engine and so far, no sign of the fugitives. But it wouldn't be long now he told himself. They must have reached Kaechon and would be trying to get back to Pakchon he concluded. If they were travelling they'd be stopped, and if they were hiding, they'd be found.

#

Ah-ga-sshi took control. She desperately loved her brother laying in the rear of the open backed lorry and it pained her to think he was badly hurt. Some of it was her doing; after all, he had cushioned her fall when their wood truck overturned. All she recalled was being suddenly thrown forwards, hitting her head on the windscreen, and then falling into him as the truck flipped on its side. It all happened so quickly. The rest was all blank. Now she had one priority, to get them all to safety. If she took her brother to a hospital now none of them would be safe. They needed to put as much distance between them and Kaechon as possible. Only then could she tend to her unconscious brother.

Guy, John, and Ah-ga-sshi's brother lay in the back of the lorry. The lorry was a 10-ton workhorse designed to lug rocks around the quarry. It was uncovered, however, the metal sides protected all from view. It was uncomfortable and gritty, being used for transporting tons of sand and rocks, although at least they were shielded from any onlookers.

Wendy and Ah-ga-sshi rode in the front cab. Ah-ga-sshi had found an old rugged workman's jacket and insisted Wendy wear it. She was fearful of lice but that was the least of her problems. An old rag was bound around her head to hide her mane of now dirty, matted hair. At a glance through the dirty windscreen she might pass for any other North Korean woman and Ah-ga-sshi with her short hair was androgynous if glanced at through the grimy windows sat in the driver's seat.

Wendy was left with her own thoughts and she contemplated Ah-ga-sshi. No one would call her pretty. Scruffy old clothes, untidily short cropped hair, a plain ruddy moon-shaped face worn from years of grafting outside in all weathers, bad teeth and work hardened hands with dirty broken fingernails. She was every bit as hard as her menfolk. But there was also a permanent engaging smile and a keen sparkle of intelligence in her brown eyes. And, Wendy noticed, she didn't miss a trick.

She drove on now with single-minded determination - get them all to safety and get her brother medical attention. She and her brother were well aware of the risks they took but the consequences went unspoken between them. As best Wendy could discern, she had no husband and loved her family.

Dusk turned slowly into night. Wendy slumped and slept, as did Guy and John in the rear. Their fitful sleep now came from exhaustion. Although uncomfortable with the rutted roads, weariness won over as Ah-ga-sshi drove slowly east through the night, passing Sunchon and Songchon without hinderance. As she drove, private and alone now in the darkness, with only one weak headlight struggling to light the pathetic road a few yards ahead, she let her tears flow freely down her dour cheeks. She was scared, scared for herself and even more scared for her brother.

Changjon. Thursday afternoon.

Talon was waiting. Having figured out how they got into the Democratic People's Republic of Korea she guessed they had planned to get out the same way, however, their route via Pakchon was impossible now. Every moving vehicle, whether engine powered or horse pulled, wheeled or floating, was subject to intense scrutiny. Five thousand troops had been drafted in and were posted on every dock, road, and railway around the area. The net was a close mesh and nothing larger than a mouse was beyond suspicion.

The way Talon figured it, to get out of the DPRK they had only two options now. The west coast was locked down as tight as a drum by the Korean People's Army. That left the fugitives heading north to try their luck over the border with China, or east, again via the sea, to find a boat that could loop around the coast to Goseong, the most northerly port on the east coast of South Korea. The Chinese border would be closely patrolled and guarded as usual.

At this time of year, in late summer, the Tumen River to the east and Yalu River to the west, which defined the natural border between North Korea and China, flowed fast and they were hard to cross without being spotted. In the winter the rivers would freeze over making crossings quite easy. The summers were different. The rivers were difficult to cross, well patrolled, with KPA patrolling the southern banks, and China's PLA, their ally patrolling the northern banks.

Her targets weren't stupid and if she were them, she would head for Changjon, the most southerly port on the eastern coast of the DPRK. If she were them, she reasoned, she would first get as far away from Yongbyon as she could, as quick as she could. Then she would chance her luck getting a small boat to Goseong from somewhere on the east coast and as far south as practicable, making the boat trip as short as possible. North and South Korea's navy's closely patrolled this stretch of sea although small boats could, and sometimes did slip the net, after all, it was how she had entered the DPRK from the South earlier the previous night.

She was there on the orders of her uncle, General Park. He knew they were resourceful and would evade capture from most of the fools that made up the 60,000 men and women of the Korean People's Army. He needed someone intelligent whom he trusted. He would prefer they were captured so he could personally deliver them to Pyongyang. This was the only scenario which would likely save his skin following the Yongbyon disaster. Were they killed in the process, so be it, although their capture was preferable. He would spin the story to his leader. He would explain how these terrorists had deliberately tried to provoke a nuclear war and shame the DPRK. Supreme Leader Kim would milk the trial and execution for the world to see.

They would be tried and executed as terrorists and while the west would decry the act and make loose gestures of further sanctions, it would all blow over within weeks; as it had with Otto Warmbier, the American student in 2017. Besides, they had plenty more missile bases and, following the recent rounds of peace talks with the US, the Yongbyon Nuclear Scientific Research facility was being slowly decommissioned as a public gesture of goodwill anyway.

Talon scanned the roads around Changjon through her binoculars. She had selected a spot on the hilltop overlooking the town. From her heightened position on the hill west of the port she could cover the railway and the main roads and follow most movement in and out of the town.

The sea lay to the east of the town, the high ground to the west. It wasn't quite dark enough for the night vision goggles yet although she assumed, if they were coming, they would wait until nightfall before trying to steal a boat. She would, if she were them. The west coast was closed to them. She'd ruled out the Chinese boarder, so that left the east coast as their only option. The only question then was could they make it as far south as Changjon. Frankly, she doubted it, but as they'd not been apprehended yet they had to be somewhere.

She was dressed for combat and prepared to camp rough for several more days if need be. Her KPA issued combat fatigues camouflaged her well against the scrubby undergrowth on the hillside and her backpack was well provisioned. She had no firm evidence they had even come to Changjon, yet it seemed to her logical mind that would be their target destination. They would be frightened, friendless, and desperate she reasoned.

Her uncle, the General, had spoken with her and suggested they may have help from one, possibly two North Korean nationals. That would make travelling across the country easier. Still, they needed to get out of the DPRK, and this is why Talon would lie and wait.

Despite being summer, the weather had turned unsettled. Like most of the month so far, the morning had started bright and sunny, then clouds had built during the day, the wind had picked up, and it looked like the rain could lash down at any time. This didn't faze Talon. She was well trained in all conditions. Like a spider, she would watch and wait, her prey unawares.

The truck had driven all through the day making its slow melodious progress with only a few stops when they needed to transfer diesel from the spare barrels to the lorry's tanks. Ah-ga-sshi hadn't slept and it was too dangerous to let anyone else drive. Should they be stopped, no one else would look or sound credible. She had avoided the larger towns of Sangsong and Wonsan, skilfully navigating the smaller roads around the towns rather than driving through them and risk meeting roadblocks.

The daylight brought a more cheerful perspective and Wendy woke with a craving for a latte and croissant with strawberry jam. Her ribs were still very bruised and sore, nevertheless, she kept this to herself. The daylight also stirred Ah-ga-sshi's brother. He wasn't fully awake yet, but he was mumbling and fidgeting. Guy and John in the back of the lorry had slept fitfully, however, at least they had got some rest and concluded their ward might wake anytime. It was a promising sign except the condition of his broken leg was a worry to them.

'Ah-ga-sshi,' shouted Guy, precariously standing to bang on the roof of the driver's cabin. She was following dust roads around the tatty town of Tongchon. She pulled over and parked under a tree to shade the lorry from view as much as possible. So far, while boring and uncomfortable, the journey had thankfully been uneventful. Ah-ga-sshi though was tired, dark bags had formed beneath her sore eyes.

'I think your brother is starting to wake. I have to believe we need to get water and maybe some food into him,' explained Guy, once Ah-ga-sshi had killed the engine. At one small town, Ah-ga-sshi had stopped near a roadside stall to buy very simple provisions of cooked rice and a watery soup with lumps of unidentifiable fatty meat floating in it. She'd also refilled a plastic container with drinking water. Her fatigue lifted the moment she saw her brother stirring.

She climbed into the back of the lorry and sat nursing and talking to him. She cradled his head and gently dripped water into his mouth. Reflex helped him swallow the water, but she stopped at trying to feed him. His lips were dry and chapped and he groaned nonsensically. Beyond the bandaging, they had left his leg unstrapped through fear the pain would be too much. Now they feared the pain would wake him fully. Ah-ga-sshi continued to drip small amounts of water into his mouth and she sobbed quietly to herself to see the distress her brother was in. They still needed to get him to a hospital to set the broken bone and prevent infection. Guy looked on with concern furrowing his forehead.

It was early evening and they believed they were getting close to their costal destination of the town of Changjon. The fuel had almost been used up and they were all tired and hungry.

Wendy was grouchy. 'I'm so hungry I'm hangry!' she declared.

'We all are my dear,' Guy retorted snappily, 'but that's going to need to wait. Priority one is to get this lad to a doctor and then get out of this country.'

John was bemoaning the loss of their backpacks, abandoned in the motor pool shed in Yongbyon when they purloined the firemen's clothes. 'I'd kill for an energy bar!' he announced.

Ignoring him, Guy continued, 'We'll get to the coast and try to find a way to steal a boat and head south. We're putting Ah-ga-sshi and her brother in terrible danger. If they catch us, well, we knew the risks whereas these guys have gone above and beyond...' Guy didn't finish his sentence. They all knew and were all humbled. Wendy hugged Ah-ga-sshi where she sat still nursing and cooing to her murmuring brother.

Ah-ga-sshi spoke in her broken English, 'We are close to the sea. Three more hours and we should be at Changjon. Then I can take my brother to a doctor.' She gestured to his leg. The trio nodded, embarrassed they'd dare to bemoan their hunger pangs. Ah-ga-sshi looked up at the lowering sun. 'We wait,' was all she said.

They decided to rest and wait until darkness to complete the trip. In darkness the trio could slide from the truck if there were roadblocks blocking the port town. Ah-ga-sshi was tired and slept curled close to her brother in the rear of the lorry. Wendy, Guy, and John found some scrubby bushes close to the lorry and out of sight of the road. They chatted and considered their predicament. Stinger had been thwarted. Whatever the malware's intentions, the launch had been averted and a nuclear explosion avoided.

Whichever country had been the target of the Rodong-1 launch, thousands, possibly millions, of people were now safe. It was unlikely they would ever learn exactly how close they came to annihilation. Of this accomplishment they should be proud Guy stressed. They now needed to get out of the country and they were hopefully only hours from that.

Talon saw the one headlighted lorry roll slowly down the road into the town of Changjon. She checked her watch; it was close to 1:00 a.m. and she had been fighting sleep. At first, she thought it was a motorcycle, given the one headlight, but the sound of the heavy engine reverberated off the hillside where she camped. It had to be them. What else would a 10-ton lorry be doing trundling slowly into this town this time of night. The night vision binoculars were of no value until the headlight was extinguished.

She quickly packed the groundsheet and camouflage netting she had hidden beneath into the backpack. She checked her sidearm and the knife she kept strapped to her leg then jogged down the hillside toward the town. Were she them, she thought to herself, she'd wait until the small hours and they try and steal a boat.

Talon smiled to herself. Her suspicion of their escape plan seems to have proven right. The hill had made for an excellent vantage point. A railway was tunnelled through the hill and she had a commanding view of the railway as well as the roads leading to and from the town. She could also see the port with a few ships and a flotilla of smaller boats, both military and commercial. This had to be them.

The lorry was slowly driving towards the port as if looking for a place to surreptitiously park. Talon ran down the hill and across the highway into the town, her army boots crunching the gravel of the dusty unswept streets. She hadn't seen her prey yet although she was confident this must be them. As she jogged passed buildings it was possible to follow the lorry from the sound of the engine. It was the only vehicle moving at that time of night. Ah-ga-sshi pulled up alongside a relatively new building with a blue tiled roof. They could see several jetties with a myriad of small watercrafts moored to them. It must be possible to steal one of them thought Guy.

The wind had picked up a lot near the coast and salt spray could be felt and smelt on the strong breeze. Furthermore, it was now starting to drizzle rain, an irritating wetness coupling with briny spray. It was notably colder too and they could see and hear in the blackness the ocean breaking her waves against the quayside.

'John, you come with me!' Guy whispered. 'We need a boat we can get working. Ah-ga-sshi, Wendy, stay here and look after the injured. Once we find a boat, we'll figure a way to get Ah-ga-sshi's brother somewhere comfortable until morning and then we'll say our good-byes and try to clear the port and head as far south as possible. The sea might be getting a bit rough clear of the harbour wall, although that may be in our favour,' tried Guy, convincing no one. John grimaced at the image.

Talon heard the engine die and from across the road dropped to a crouch and pulled the night vision goggles from her pack. The green hue filled her vision and her eyes adjusted to take in the human forms across the road from her. She saw two larger figures lope away in the direction of the quay, they were tall and didn't look Korean. Two smaller forms stayed in the back of the lorry with another laying prone in the back.

She had spotted the two men in the Starfield Library, failing to look inconspicuous. These were five people though. She watched and waited. This was them. She recognised the shape of the two men and Wendy Chen. The two men must have left to find a boat, and someone was injured, probably a Korean. Talon removed the night vision goggles and let her eyes adjust back to the darkness. The town had few lights, yet it wasn't quite pitch black and at close range the night visions would be a liability. Talon instinctively reached to the hip holster and checked her handgun. Stealthily she crept forwards.

The two women saw one another at the same moment. Talon and Wendy immediately recognised each other from the washrooms in the Starfield Library.

'Freeze!' was the shouted command for Wendy's benefit. Talon now stood not ten feet away from the back of the lorry. The gun was held professionally, with both arms outstretched and trained on them as they sat in the back of the lorry, still next to the injured brother. Her stance was solid, and she was ready to fire upon any sudden movement.

Talon looked at Ah-ga-sshi and said 'Ggomjjakma!' for her benefit then followed by 'hands behind your heads and, no, I won't hesitate to kill you.' Wendy slowly did as instructed and grimaced as her sore ribs pained her. Then Ah-ga-sshi slowly followed.

The fifth boat worked. The others were all well locked, however, the fifth was easy to start by simply jamming a screwdriver John had found into the ignition and forcing the worn lock hard clockwise to start the motor. The boat was small, no more than 12-feet long, open to the elements, and strewn with old fishing nets in the wooden hull. It looked old and neglected but the motor fired after a bit of coaxing. John scrabbled around to find the fuel cap and tried to see if there was much fuel. He found the cap although his efforts to see inside were futile, it was too dark to see much at all.

Guy nursed the engine to a gentle tick over and familiarised himself with the controls, not that there were many. A throttle lever, choke, and a wheel were all the little craft offered. The ammeter was broken and there was no fuel gage. John looked ominously out into the harbour. They could barely make out the green and red lights denoting the harbour mouth. The wind was picking up, even creating white tips to the small waves in the harbour. The rain was coming down more steadily now and they were both getting soaked.

'Let's go get Wendy and say our goodbyes,' suggested Guy.

'Do you think we should leave Ah-ga-sshi and her brother here?' posed John.

'I've been noodling on that question all afternoon. I think were her brother not injured we would give them the option to take their chances with us. With his leg as badly broken as it is though, he needs medical attention first. I think Ah-ga-sshi is a capable girl and will get her brother fixed up here then make their way back to their home. My guess would be than anyone who can associate them with us would have been killed in the explosion' concluded Guy.

'Guess you're right,' agreed John. He turned to walk back to the lorry, relishing the solid ground beneath him knowing it wouldn't be for much longer.

Talon approached the lorry not taking her eyes off the other two women. The man laying on the bed of the truck was motionless. With a graceful swing Talon stepped up into the back of the lorry not taking her aim off the two women. 'Turn around and kneel, keeping your hands behind your head.' The two women did as they were ordered.

Wendy didn't see the kick coming as Talon, in a sudden burst of anger, placed the gun back in her belt and, pirouetting 360 degrees, raised her right leg and delivered a brutal kick to the side of Wendy's head.

'That's for interfering with my plans!' she spat, the tone venomous. Not seeing the kick coming, Wendy hadn't braced herself and she flew across the bed of the truck, sprawling as she hit the steel sided wall of the lorry. Ah-ga-sshi saw the move and the momentary pause from Talon, her weapon in her belt. She saw her chance and in a split second decided to take it. She leapt forwards with the speed of a cat throwing her full weight into Talon's middle, tipping her off balance.

Ah-ga-sshi was much shorter than Talon, however, she was stock solid, her speed was formidable, and her anger frenzied. The two women collapsed in a tangle and Talon was too slow to reach her gun. Ah-ga-sshi pounced on her, punching her head, screaming in Korean. Wendy sat up and recovered her senses, her head ringing from the kick. Talon pulled her left arm free and brought a fist hard into Ah-ga-sshi's kidneys. The wind was pushed from her lungs and Ah-ga-sshi reeled, her eyes watering with pain.

Wendy, incensed, her focus narrowed to a single point of red, leapt at Talon with a fierce kick to her upper body that contacted with her hard in the shoulder. Talon yelped in pain as Wendy threw herself on Talon, fists flaying, thoughts of her sore ribs forgotten in her fury. The fresh rain had made the steel flatbed of the lorry slippery and the three women slipped and fell in a tangle of limbs from the back of the lorry, hitting the ground hard.

John and Guy heard the commotion before they saw it, and both sprinted towards the lorry. The women were writhing, sprawling and punching each other on the ground. The gun was still in Talon's belt and she wrestled to get it free. Guy and John rounded the back of the lorry in unison and absorbed the situation.

Guy saw the female soldier in combat fatigues struggling for her weapon and joined the fray, grabbing her right arm so to prevent her reaching the gun. Despite the army fatigues he suddenly recognised the woman from the library in Seoul. Wendy rolled clear and delivered two fierce kicks to Talons left leg but Talon, still on the ground had reached her handgun and pulled it clear of the belt and released one shot.

The gunshot at close range was deafening, and Guy reeled backward and screamed with pain. He grabbed his arm as Wendy delivered another resounding kick straight into Talon's face. She was rabid with anger, adrenalin fuelling an aggression she had never experienced before. Talon rolled backwards blood streaming from a nasty gash on her forehead.

John shouted, 'If the army are here, we need to go now!' He had only seen Talon, the one soldier so far, but assumed there were more of them close by. Surely the gunshot would attract attention. He leapt into the back of the lorry and lifted the dead weight of Ah-ga-sshi's brother onto his shoulders with a strength he didn't know he possessed. Ah-ga-sshi ran to help and assisted him to jump down from the back of the lorry. Together they ran from the fight and back towards the quay where the little boat puttered at her mooring, still tied to the jetty.

The gunshot thankfully wasn't well aimed, however, unluckily for Guy the bullet had skimmed his arm, an ominous shiny dark patch now spreading over his dark shirt. Talon was slumped on the ground blood pouring down her face from the cut mixing with dirty sweat and rain. Wendy grabbed Guy's uninjured arm and pulled him along at a run. She wanted to get as far from her dangerous nemesis as possible. The gunshot would attract attention and John was right, there was not a moment to lose. Guy dutifully followed Wendy realizing Talon still held her gun and, while she was momentarily down, she certainly wasn't out.

They ran as fast as they could and caught up with Ah-ga-sshi and John, who carried her brother in a fireman's lift as they were boarding the little boat. John saw Guy holding his arm, the soaking blood looking black in the darkness.

'You hurt?'

'The bullet skimmed me I think,' responded Guy, the adrenalin was overcoming any pain he might feel at this moment. Nevertheless, their priority was to get out to sea and away from the country where they would be executed for terrorism. Guy pointed with his good arm to Wendy towards the ropes securing the small craft to the quayside. She untied them as John and Ah-ga-sshi carefully lowered her brother into the hull of the boat and settled him as comfortably as possible on the old fishing nets. He was now moaning in pain.

The jetty was treacherous now the rain was making it slippery. Wendy fumbled to free the ropes. She slipped and fell backwards into the small boat just as the last line came free and Guy eased the throttle forwards and the propeller engaged to push the little craft into the harbour.

They heard a shout and turned to see Talon running onto the jetty. She was wet and her hair had become loose and bedraggled, rain and blood matting it around her face. She still carried the gun in her hand and seeing she couldn't catch the boat now she stopped, stood straight, legs spread her shoulders width apart, aimed and fired. Talon fired all her shots in rapid succession, the orange muzzle flash illuminating the pitch-black night, at the darkening boat until her gun clip was empty.

Chapter 35. The Sound Barrier

Sea of Japan. Friday Night.

The little boat crashed through the waves at the harbour mouth. The harbour itself was choppy, the open sea much worse. As she hit the open water the rough waves started lapping over the boat's gunwales. Guy's optimism regarding the sea's conditions were misplaced. The wind had picked up and cold seawater repeatedly hit the bows, spraying into the boat from all directions. They were already soaked to the skin and cold. Their optimism of escaping Talon was replaced by the misery of this journey and a fear the boat would simply sink.

Talon's bullets had come close, one ripping a chunk of wood from the side of the hull, but otherwise the little boat and its occupants were unharmed. They looked nervously at each other for mutual support. In the darkness the expressions were hard to read. None privately felt confident this would end well.

The sound of the shots had echoed all around the town like firecrackers. Guy worked the boat's small wheel and steered due east, nose into the swell, knowing they would be expected to follow the coast south and so be easier to track down for the KPA's navy. He suspected that if the navy launches weren't already looking for them, they soon would be.

He maintained the conditions were in their favour. For anyone trying to spot them in these conditions would be difficult, but the little unlit craft was a precarious escape option. Wendy was fussing over Guy's arm. The wound, while superficially messy, wouldn't kill him although every other aspect of their current predicament might, she thought with a grim shudder.

'Does this hurt?' Wendy asked, squinting in the darkness trying to assess the bullet wound.

'Like fuck yes! It's only a scrape though, the bleeding's not bad, and the saltwater will likely help. And it stings like crazy. Let's get well clear of the harbour tonight. Daylight will bring more options.' Guy was trying to sound confident. He wasn't convincing.

Ah-ga-sshi meanwhile tended to her brother who, lying uncomfortably in the bottom of the boat, was waking. His eyes had opened probably as a result of the cold water dousing him every other second. He wasn't fully awake yet and seemed to drift in and out of consciousness. Nevertheless, the leg would soon start to trouble him. There was no way sheltering him from the constant cold saltwater spraying over him.

Guy held the boat as best he could on a course taking them directly away from land, however, he knew it would be hopeless in these conditions to have any idea where they were. All he could hope to do was to travel east all night and then, as the sun lit the eastern sky in the morning use that as a bearing. In a few hours he would steer south-west and hope they would find South Korea. If, that was, they weren't sunk by the waves, apprehended by a North Korean patrol boat, or their fuel ran out and they were blown back onshore or out into the Sea of Japan to die of exposure.

John, Wendy, and Ah-ga-sshi huddled together for warmth, comfort, and security. Sitting on the old fishing nets in the middle of the little boat, their weight was helping as ballast. The rain and sea spray intermingled to ensure they were repeatedly soaked to the skin with no respite. They used their bodies as best they could to block the worst of the water washing over the lame brother. It was futile and shelter became indifferent.

John was anxious about the water in the boat and the plastic bucket in the hull beside the fishing nets found its purpose, as a scoop for bailing out as the water level rose around their feet. They took it in turns to bail water out, but it was a futile task. Still the engine plodded on, making some slow progress as the few lights visible on the land vanished from sight. Sleep would come to none of them this night. All they could do was huddle, bail, hope, and wait for the sunrise in their cold wet misery.

Talon stood on the wet quayside and scowled at the black ocean facing her. She had no idea if all or any of her shots had found its mark, she was simply shooting blind. The sound of the small engine was quickly lost to the sound of wind and waves. She was alone.

Talon contacted her uncle and shared the bad news. His night was going from bad to worse. His daughter as he knew her had failed him. He instructed her to stay on the dock and allow him to contact the navy base there. He would arrange for the navy search boats and she was to await further instruction. He was formal and it was an order. She would have one final chance to capture the terrorists.

#

DEFCOM 2 in practical terms for the USS *Ronald Reagan* meant stepped up patrols for the reconnaissance flights and a state of war readiness. While the alert status was authorised by the President of the United States and was national, the real danger was localised to Asia at this point. The USS *Ronald Reagan*'s patrol flights were with live ammunition and more rigorous drills for the crew who were now on full alert. The ship's crew were never entirely clear what was a drill and what wasn't, but Admiral Young knew, and this was the real deal.

Under this level of war readiness, arbitrary territorial waters meant nothing. His ships and planes would go wherever they pleased. Any resistance would be considered for diplomatic impact momentarily, however, the ships Warfare Officer wouldn't hesitate to use force. The USS *Ronald Reagan*'s motto was *'Peace Through Strength'* and that's exactly how Admiral Young would play it.

The threat this time was North Korea and Admiral Young was responsible for the safety and security of the whole Carrier Strike Group. As the closest American asset to the action, he would give them his full attention. Flights from the array of fighter jets were ordered to patrol the Korean peninsula and report any movement. Thermal drones with infrared aerial imaging capabilities were scrambled and they headed directly for the DPRK. It was still three hours to sunrise so the thermal drones were still the best long-range eyes the ship had.

On the bridge of the USS *Ronald Reagan* with the admiral, captain, and senior crew, stood the ships politically appointed general counsel. Unlike all other personnel on the ship, he reported directly to the General Counsel of the Department of the Navy in Washington and technically not to the captain of the ship. The job of the general counsel was to advise on legal protocol around maritime law and particularly warfare.

General Counsel Paul Abbott could not order, only advise the captain although they enjoyed a good personal relationship and, during officers' dinners, had many hypothetical and animated conversations over maritime law. Abbott believed it was appropriate to caution the captain on the protocol of violating DPRK airspace. The captain absorbed the advice and raised an eyebrow towards his more senior guest, Admiral Young.

'Fuck protocol,' was the admiral's gruff, and reasoned response to his captain in his husky southern drawl.

'As you were,' was the captains next order. Paul Abbott swallowed awkwardly and continued to stare through the rainy windows at the blackness in front of the ship. Privately he agreed, but he was happy in the knowledge he'd met his professional obligation.

#

Talon stood alone, soaked to the skin, and was met on the quayside by a KPA naval patrol boat. The orders had come from ahigh and the captain was not going to argue. However, he struggled to conceal his confusion when he saluted the passenger as she boarded. Even on the darkened docks, he could see she was facially beautiful with full lips and high cheekbones, although her face was bruised and bleeding with congealed blood matting her hair and smearing her face. Aside this, her combat fatigues and backpack simply created the image of a soldier's pin-up model.

She was well composed and comfortable with her equipment and she didn't accept his hand offered to steady her while boarding his boat. The distinctive smell of gunshot residue clung to her like a heady perfume. He guessed she was the cause of the gunfire which had awoken him earlier. She deftly skipped onto the boat and ordered them out to sea.

'Find them!' she barked.

The sea was relentless. The little fishing boat was bobbed around like cork jetsam. Ah-ga-sshi's brother was recovering and now aware of the pain in his shattered leg. He was in shock and moaned incomprehensibly as Ah-ga-sshi cradled his head and spoke soothingly in Korean. They shivered violently with the cold, teeth chattering. Guy realised they could all only take a few hours of this before succumbing to exposure. Weak, insipid sunlight breached the horizon and he could make out the baring east. Though the heavy grey clouds defused the sunlight, there was enough to figure if he kept the lighting sky at his eight o'clock, he would be moving south west, the direction of his goal, South Korea.

Aside the smell of the salt water constantly washing over him and the putrefying rotten fish smell of the fishing nets they sat upon, it was impossible to smell anything else. But suddenly he was struck by another stronger smell. It was just a whiff, but unmistakable. Petrol. A moment later the engine note changed then coughed and spluttered out.

Talon ignored the captain and crew on the patrol boat. She stood on the prow oblivious to the cold rain and spray from waves breaching the bow beneath her. She held the night vision goggles close to her face and robotically scanned the ocean. It was predawn and, while the sky was paling slightly in the east, she still needed the goggles to scan the black water surrounding them. The boat steered south following the coast, however, the swell was such that the small boat she was seeking could be 100 yards away and still hidden by white tipped waves.

They had at least an hour on her although her boat was both much bigger and much faster. If they had followed the coast it shouldn't take long to catch them. She trusted this fast vessel could reach the border with South Korea before the small fishing boat. She would catch them yet, and she relished the punishment she would deal out to the two women who thwarted her earlier. Not getting her own way was a very unfamiliar emotion to Talon.

'I'm at a loss guys. We've been travelling for three hours east and it's about 5:00 a.m. I'd guess we're about 10 miles offshore, adrift in the Sea of Japan. Now we're out of fuel and there's none spare in the boat. We're at the whim of the wind and tide. Frankly our only hope now is to be rescued. Realistically, if we are rescued it's gonna be by the North Koreans,' summarised Guy glumly to his four cold and bedraggled crew.

John felt wretched and heaved a heavy sigh, 'We were so close.'

Ah-ga-sshi's face looked drawn in the early grey light and she looked close to tears, while Guy looked bitter, all fight drained from him by the fatigue.

At the mention of the time, Wendy had glanced instinctively at her masculine wristwatch and verified in her own mind the time they had been at sea. In hindsight it would strike her as ironic that for a tool she wore on her wrist every day of her life, since treating herself to the luxury gift as a reward for winning the job with Cyber Security Systems Ltd, she had completely forgotten its secondary function.

She only looked at the heavy watch a hundred times a day and people would always comment on the size and weight of the watch verses the small frame that wore it. Wendy loved it. To her it symbolised her success: a petite woman punching above her weight in a male dominated industry. The weight of the watch didn't bother her; if anything, the heavy metal case reinforced confidence and security. She suddenly burst out laughing.

John and Guy exchanged sad glances with each other, both jumping to the same conclusion that the cold, wet, and fear had suddenly tipped poor Wendy's mental state. She's flipped, lost it…

With her strength ebbing, painful ribs and uncontrollable shivering making any movement awkward, she raised her left arm above her head in a clenched fist, the sign of power, the symbol of defiance!

She held the arm high above her head, still laughing like a drunkard. Guy and John now had their fears confirmed: Wendy had gone quite mad.

'My watch, you fools!' she burst. 'Look! My fucking watch! My beautiful Breitling Emergency!'

It took a second until the penny dropped for her two colleagues. John and Guy both gasped in disbelief. Blinking and confused, Ah-ga-sshi and her brother had no idea what was happening.

Guy broke into a grin and beckoned her. 'You beautiful creature!' He almost screamed it. She gave her shaking left arm to him. He held her hand and fiddled with the right side of the watch. The second large screw cap beneath the winder was tight and his cold wet fingers struggled to get a grip. He fumbled then stopped, putting his bloodless white fingers into his mouth to warm. He then shook his hand vigorously to get his blood circulating, attempted to dry his fingers under his armpit, and then tried again.

This time the screw cap moved, and he was able to unscrew it fully until it popped off and he could pull out the concealed wire antenna. At the antenna's full length, the cap came off altogether releasing a similar antenna on the left side of the watchcase. He pulled this tiny wire clear also. The act of releasing the two antennas activated the watch's built-in emergency beacon. That was the whole point of the Breitling Emergency wristwatch.

Transmitting a distress signal was the watch's secondary function after the primary yet comparatively mundane function of telling the time. The international emergency distress frequency is 121.5 Megahertz and any radio operator in the world on boats, ships, or aircrafts tend to have their radios set to receive on that channel as a pre-set, secondary frequency. Who knew when someone close by would send a distress signal and need assistance was the accepted logic. Wendy's watch housed a micro-transmitter that broadcast on 406 Megahertz intended for COSPAS-SARSAT low orbit satellites and the secondary frequency of 121.5 Megahertz. This was for radio receivers close by. Inaudibly, Wendy's wristwatch burst its cry for help to anyone listening.

Ah-ga-sshi and her brother had no idea what had just happened but in seconds the rest of the little fishing boat's crew had gone from utter despair to ecstatic jubilation.

'Crazy foreigners,' said Ah-ga-sshi to her brother. He nodded understanding.

'Is it doing anything?' asked Wendy. The watch was silent.

'Hopefully. We'll find out shortly,' said John, even his chronic seasickness forgotten momentarily. The five crew hugged. The Koreans were unsure why.

\#

On the bridge of the mighty USS *Ronald Reagan* the communications officer called out 'Sir, I'm picking up a distress signal about 30 miles north-west of our position. Confirming our escorts are receiving the same signal.'

'Any idea what it is?' asked the captain.

'Not yet sir. But it's small, only the distress call, no RT. COSPAS-SARSAT are relaying also sir. It's for real.'

'Probably a trawler but I suggest we assist then. CAG be good enough to send your boys to take a look please.' The captain of the aircraft carrier USS *Ronald Reagan* spoke to the Commander of the Air Group, the CAG, also technically a captain rank and responsible for the air arm on-board the carrier. Moments later two airborne F/A-18E Super Hornets flying at 5,000 ft, barely below the cloud base, banked hard left and flew the vector given.

At the speed of sound, they would be over the reference given in less than two minutes. Meanwhile a scrambled MH60 Seahawk Multimission Helicopter lifted off from the USS *Ronald Reagan's* rainswept deck heading for the same destination, their edgy four-man crew grateful for the activity.

Sunrise cast a grey diffused light over the ocean and Talon gave up with the night vision goggles now. She still ceaselessly swept the horizon and surrounding sea for any sign of the little craft. The bleak grey ocean pitched and yawed in all directions and she realised this was a needle-in-a-haystack search. Perhaps they had not followed the coast or perhaps she had sunk them with the whole magazine of shots she had fired after them.

'No, they're out here,' she thought to herself. The captain of the patrol boat ran towards her at the bow of the boat and saluted.

'We've picked up a distress signal. It's very close to us,' he waved his arm vaguely out to sea.

'Then full speed towards it. It must be them!'

The F/A-18E Super Hornet pilots slowed their planes as they approached the location. The F/A-18E's were fast although not optimised for slow flying so the pilots slowed as best they could without risking a stall. They dropped to 1,000 feet and surveyed the choppy sea beneath them.

'Visual!' shouted one over his radio; he knew his wingman and base would hear. The MH60 listening on the same frequency heard too.

Over the sound of the wind and waves constantly breaking over the bows of the little boat, Guy first heard and then saw the brace of fighter jets banking in formation in a lazy anticlockwise circle above them. They were fiercely loud and fast. He stood, as best he could, and waved his one good arm. At this height he couldn't quite make out the markings but prayed they didn't belong to China or North Korea. Regardless, in their current state, rescue was the priority now. He figured if they could see him, he looked the least Asian of the five of them.

Talon too spotted the jets performing their 360 degrees. She pointed the captain to the direction of the jets. They could only be a few miles away.

'Looks like they have company inbound too,' announced the lead pilot of the Super Hornets. 'I can see a North Korean patrol boat heading towards them. Five miles max.'

'Foxtrot One-Eight lead. This is Rotary Mike Hotel Six-Zero. Can you see how many people on board? Over,'

'Mike Hotel Six-Zero. Hard to see given poor vis. I'd guess four or five. One is waving and looks Caucasian. Over.'

The bridge of the USS *Ronald Reagan* was hushed as they listened to the radio transmissions between the fighters and helicopter. General Council Paul Abbott looked pensive.

'The boat is probably still in North Korean waters captain; however, a rescue would be defendable.' He smiled. 'Were our boys to slow the Korean patrol boat down I'd see no harm in that although better if we didn't fire first.'

The CAG relayed the message to the F/A 18's and the MH60.

Admiral Young knew navy jet pilots have a reputation for frivolous behaviour and the movie Top Gun did a lot to propagate that reputation. The truth is somewhat different. To avoid such antics that might risk both pilot's lives and US$50m taxpayers' assets, the pilot's behaviour is tightly monitored. Yet, there are occasionally combat situations where pilots are allowed a little situational discretion. Inside the F/A 18's pilot's helmets their smiles widened as the Super Hornet throttle grips were eased forwards.

Accuracy was something jet fighter pilots practiced religiously, height above the ground or sea and speed control. Both pilots accurately judged their height above the swell of the waves to be 30 feet and their speed to be 700 miles per hour, just below the sound barrier at sea level. This was about as close to sea level as they could get without actually floating on it. The accuracy of the distance between their wingtips was 20 feet and remained so as they approached either side of the North Korean navy patrol boat.

Talon remained on the deck as the patrol boat ploughed north-eastward through the heavy swell. It was slow going. The rain had momentarily stopped but the wind was still picking up spray as the boat crashed through the waves. Her first reaction was, 'What the hell!' A microsecond later she was thrown to the deck as the heat of the jet engines ripped across the patrol boat first followed by the most horrendous ear-splitting thunderclap. She had not time to assess the situation as seconds later the boat pitched violently forwards, close to pitchpoling as the boat was sucked into a trough of ocean then the opposing wave crashed over the boat lifting it up then nearly flipping it on its axis.

The wake of the jets created such a scar in the ocean it caused two 20-foot waves that broke over the boat in quick succession with such force the boat was temporarily wholly submerged. Talon instinctively gripped on for dear life, while white water engulfed the boat. The bridge was smashed in by the weight of water and many of the deck fittings were ripped loose. Water poured through hatches and the engine cut out. As the boat resurfaced and Talon gasped for breath, insult was added to injury as she heard the sonic boom of the jets as the Super Hornet pilots pulled vertical at 1,000 miles per hour.

Guy and John heard the commotion before they saw it; it was a couple of miles away. They heard the jet engine roar then saw the two jets flying very low and very fast followed by them abruptly climbing vertically. They then heard the sonic boom as the fighter planes passed through the sound barrier. Ah-ga-sshi screamed and flinched from fear, unsure what was making so much noise. She was further perplexed when she saw John and Guy belly-laughing like schoolboys and high-fiving each other. Ah-ga-sshi was fearful but smiled with them, guessing whatever it was, it was benign.

Wendy was shaking her head when heard the beat of the helicopter rotors and they all waved up as the winchman leaned over the side of the chopper to assess the situation. The huge helicopter proudly boasted the stars and stripes flag on the fuselage. Guy signalled five and got a thumbs-up by reply. The winchman prepared a cradle and a navy diver dropped down the line and into the small fishing boat and saw Ah-ga-sshi's brother was injured.

They helped him into the cradle, and he was winched clear of the little boat first. Second was Ah-ga-sshi, she was terrified but relieved to be clear of the boat and back with her brother. Already another crewman was competently tending to her brother with a thermal blanket and an injection, presumably pain killers. Wendy followed, then John. Guy went last and in the couple of minutes of peace, privately stroked the gunwale and thanked the little craft for its stoical effort of getting them out of the DPRK alive. He too was then winched aboard the MH60 and heard Rotary Mike Hotel Six-Zero confirm its bearing back towards the USS *Ronald Reagan*. John, and Wendy all looked at each other's sorry, bedraggled state, now wrapped in silver thermal blankets, and winked.

Talon surveyed the damage of the patrol boat. Thankfully no one was swept overboard or seriously hurt from flying debris although there was a few cuts and bruises. Some of the crew had inhaled water and were violently coughing and retching. One crewman had managed to restart the engine and they were back under their own power except valuable time had been lost and she could now see the US Navy helicopter winching her targets off their little boat.

It was too late to reach the boat's front mounted canon. They were only a few hundred yards away when she saw the fifth and final person being winched up. She squinted through her binoculars. He made a gesture with his free hand; he appeared to be blowing her a kiss.....

Sea of Japan. Friday lunchtime.

Admiral Young, General Counsel Abbott, the ship's Captain and two other men in naval uniform sat around the large hardwood table in the captain's private mess. The trio were amazed, on this warship the opulence was comparable to a presidential stateroom. Orderlies in whites served refreshments and the atmosphere was relaxed and cordial. John, Wendy, and Guy were sat, comfortably dressed in navy issue grey flannel jumpsuits and their wounds had been expertly attended to. Guy was at ease, his arm had been cleaned, stitched, and dressed. He expected he would be proud of the scar the bullet wound would leave in a few years; a story to tell his grandkids, he hoped. Wendy's ribs had been x-rayed and, while badly bruised, thankfully none were broken She appreciate the prescription of ibuprofen had kicked in.

Ah-ga-sshi and her brother were in the infirmary still. Her brother's leg had been operated upon and the badly broken bones pinned and set. He was on a drip to restore fluids but was fully conscious and even smiling, in awe of the facilities of the ship's hospital and the kind attention he was being given. The doctors were confident and reassured Ah-ga-sshi he would be back to normal in ten to twelve weeks. Ah-ga-sshi hugged everyone and this time the tears that flowed openly were for joy.

Guy, Wendy, and John sat at the dining table in the stateroom and relayed their whole story and were answering questions. As admiral of the entire Carrier Strike Group, Admiral Young was responsible for concluding the official report, a task he knew he would delegate to the capable General Counsel Paul Abbott. Abbott was asking multiple questions while taking meticulous notes. The two other men had introduced themselves by name only. They were clearly naval intelligence and had presumably been briefed by the NSA or CIA or whatever intelligence agencies were working with MI6's Plug and his boss Quinn in London. They asked if John would provide a copy of Stinger and he had assured them he would.

DEFCOM 2 had been downgraded to DEFCOM 3 and would be downgraded further once China and Russia had been briefed through diplomatic channels; and North Korea was trusted not to escalate, which was deemed highly unlikely. As embarrassing as this was for them, the explosion would be publicly spun as a missile test and North Korea's supreme leader would be photographed with images of large rockets and his Generals, congratulating them on a test successfully executed. The truth would only ever be known to a very limited few.

The whole story was astounding. Not least because of the sheer improbability of being able to break into and neutralize a nuclear weapons' base such as Yongbyon but also in three total amateurs being able to get into and out of The Democratic People's Republic of Korea and wreak such havoc. John as an Australianised Hong Kong national, Wendy as a Singaporean, and Guy as a Brit were aware they probably had no legal obligation to tell the American's everything, however, they were grateful for their rescue and saw no cause to be anything other than fully cooperative. Afterall, the original black hat who'd developed the malware was American. They knew they had even assisted in diverting an international incident which may well have catalysed a nuclear war.

They were quietly proud of what they had done and assumed their own governments might also want to debrief them. The Americans and the British, following the kind assistance of Andrew Smith, deserved the full story although they couldn't see how they had broken any laws, other than in North Korea; laws they were unlikely to ever be charged for breaking. John would need to keep a low profile in Hong Kong and perhaps he could contain his story to a business trip to Seoul. He fretted quite how much to tell his wife. If he thought Talon was formidable, she'd obviously never met his wife. Wendy, likewise, would avoid any diplomatic escalation in Singapore. Wendy thought aloud about her excuse for being away from work for a few days.

'A big game fishing trip in Korea that got lost Wendy, really, really, can't you do better than that?' John fell about laughing.

'Probably more believable than the truth,' she smiled back. Under the table she had found Guy's hand and held it tight.

When the interviews were concluded and no further questions could be asked, Guy said, 'So what now?'

'Our doctor suggests you stay with us for a couple of days for observation. Then we'll get you to an airport in Japan and you'll be free to go wherever you please, presumably your hometowns,' offered the admiral.

The three agreed they would all like to get back to Hong Kong and back to their more mundane jobs of working for a cybersecurity consulting company and preventing cyber-attacks through the more traditional hands-off method using software. There was a pause, the obvious question still pending.

'What of Ah-ga-sshi and her brother?' asked Wendy. 'They're the real heroes in all this you know.'

The admiral smiled, 'I think we'll let them decide that, don't you? If they want to go back to North Korea, we can probably assist with that' he said with a twinkle in his eye. 'But my guess would be South Korea would welcome them with open arms and will

383

look after them, if, that's their wish. We can brief the appropriate channels in Seoul.'

General Counsel Paul Abbott endorsed the admiral, 'We have the diplomatic channels that can facilitate that. I'm sure even American immigration would be an option after the President has been briefed. And he will be briefed, I'll see to that, and ensure their part is fully appreciated.'

The admiral had a sudden notion and added as an afterthought. 'Perhaps you would like to broach the subject with them Wendy? Given your profession, I guess you're well trained for such conversations and it would make our jobs easier.'

Wendy lit-up, happy with the idea, 'I'd be pleased too sir!'

The admiral dismissed them with warm handshakes, and they retired back to the ship's infirmary. They each had their own beds in a private room in the sickbay. The hospital facilities on-board the ship were amazing and designed for combat casualties. As it was, aside a few routine accidents, the ship's hospital was totally underutilised. Following an inspection by satisfied doctors they were left alone to rest.

Guy was flipping through the channels on the in-room TV. He had stayed in hotels less well equipped than this, he thought as he plumped his pillows behind his head to settle into a good movie. A small impish face appeared at the door window of his room and the door opened. Someone slipped in and closed the door quietly behind them. Guy laughed as the little body slipped into bed beside him and snuggled up to him, curling her body into his.

'Be gentle, my ribs are killing me,' she whispered.

'Girls on top then, and mind my dressing, I'd hate to bleed all over these nice white sheets,' he whispered back.

They slept, a long deep comfortable sleep, the gentle motion of the USS *Ronald Reagan* barely noticeable.

Pyongyang. Sea of Japan. Saturday.

It came as no surprise. He sat in the luxury of the leather seats in the back of the staff car as he was driven back to his army base in Pyongyang. He carried nothing personal in his uniform but for the small copy of Chairman Mao's Little Red Book in his breast pocket, his only emotional attachment to his daughter. He pondered the events and how destiny conspired against him and his like-minded comrades to remove the flawed dynasty that had misruled his beautiful country for three generations. Such dreams they had as young men. He heard the army radio crackle in the front seat, his driver responding.

His orders to his driver were to take him home, however, he knew his driver was now receiving alternative orders. Arguing was futile. Someone would have to take the wrap for Yongbyon, and he saw no other real alternative except himself. He was old and tired and the last few days of the Yongbyon ordeal had exhausted him. He was passed his prime and knew retirement was long overdue. He had only kept his position because his leader had valued him, up until now; and to a lesser extent, he wanted to oversee the career of Lee Hyo-joo, Talon, his daughter.

He reflected on what he could have done differently. He knew the plan was a bold one albeit with risks. The unforeseen. Stinger falling into the hands of some very capable amateurs, he had not seen that one coming. He now expected to be taken to a military prison, possibly even the Gang Gun Military Academy in the suburbs of Pyongyang, where he would be held, questioned, and possibly tried for a crime such as treason.

If his leader was deeply displeased, he might even face the same fate as his old friend Chang Song-thaek. If he did, he would face it with dignity. Afterall he knew what to expect. His regret was only that the daughter he cherished would probably never learn that the man she thought of as an uncle and mentor was really her father. But then he considered if he died disgraced it was probably better that way.

Talon should be back in Seoul by now. Her failure to capture the terrorists who had foiled their plan was relayed to him personally by radio earlier that morning. He failed to communicate his disappointment to her and perhaps that was for the best. He could at least try to protect her from being associated with the failure. He hoped that whatever fate befell him, his beautiful and talented Talon would continue his fight. He thought of his dear long dead Aunty who had raised him and loved him from a baby and told him stories about his parents. She'd told him about the wars, the Japanese, and the hardships. He wondered if one day their granddaughter would avenge their murder. He hoped so. That thought gave him peace.

#

Guy looked at his reflection in the mirror. He had not shaved his head or his chin in days and the disposable plastic razor rasped as it cut through his fuse-wire bristles. The infirmary of the ship was hardy a five-star hotel although he had never felt more comfortable in his life, enveloped in the warm dressing gown and slippers they had given him. He splashed his face with water to remove the residue shaving cream and emerged from the bathroom. Wendy, similarly dressed, was sat on his bed. She stood and rubbed his smooth chin in her cupped hands. 'Shame, I like a bit of rough,' she whispered as male nurses would be close by. She stretched onto tiptoe and kissed his freshly shaven cheeks then slid her lips around to meet his.

He pulled her close to him and recalled their first kiss at the door of his apartment. It seemed like a lifetime ago. It had only been a week and during that time they had probably saved the world from oblivion. His thoughts drifted to his legacy, or moreover, what his legacy might be. A marriage, children, grandchildren? He'd never seriously confronted these thoughts, but he wondered if perhaps now he should. Saving the world was a story his hypothetical grandkids would never believe. *Was this woman his destiny,* he thought as Wendy parted his lips with her tongue; Jesus, it's only been a week, what will next week be like, he wondered?

Awkwardly a large male nurse came in and coughed discreetly. 'Phone call sir. It's a secure line from Hong Kong and patched in with London.'

Guy took the phone from the nurse while smiling lamely at Wendy; wow, that woman aroused him. 'Guy Anderson,' he announced, gently pushing Wendy's mischievous hand away that had somehow wriggled its way inside his dressing gown and was caressing his buttocks.

'Guy!' announced Plug, his public school accent betraying his identity before he needed to say anymore. 'We've Mr Quinn from London on the line with us too.'

'Mr Anderson, pleased to make your acquaintance. I'm Quinn from Her Majesty's Civil Service in London. We'd like you to meet us as soon as you're back in Hong Kong if we may. I'm on a flight over later today.'

Quinn was polite yet the invitation was more like an instruction.

'I'm in trouble am I, Mr Quinn?' asked Guy, eyeing Wendy who was sitting on the corner of his bed coyly twiddling with her bathrobe belt. Her long smooth legs were crossed before her, her uppermost foot waving, conducting a tune playing in her head.

'Far from it, old chap. We'd like to express our sincere thanks to you, Miss Chen, and John Choo too if possible. We've been working with the Americans, South Korea and even China, and all are very grateful for the job you've done. That situation could have all got very messy if you three hadn't stepped up.'

'Thank you, Mr Quinn. We should be back in a couple of days,' replied Guy.

'One more thing, Mr Anderson, and no need to answer right away, but Her Majesty's Civil Service, particularly MI6, is always on the lookout for capable people. Give it some thought, would you? Talk more when we meet. Pip Pip,' Quinn dropped off the call before giving Guy a chance to respond.

'Call me when you know when you'll land Guy. I'll come pick you up from the airport,' said Plug and he too dropped the call.

Guy was left holding the dead phone, ingesting what he had just heard. Wendy looked up at him, still sitting on the corner of his bed. She gave him her coy look under heavy eyelids. She saw the male nurse had left them, and reached out, pulled the hem of his bathrobe towards her. She whispered, 'right here, right now.'

Available now, book 2 - **Deadly Protocol**. Join Wendy, Guy, and Talon in the next instalment:

Prologue. The National Security Agency

Moscow. Friday 13th May. 2016.

'Geeez!' He said out loud. Ivan Komarov lifted his tired arms and pulled the headset off his head. The twang of Metallica's *"Black"* album still audibly blared from them as he threw them down on to his desk next to his well-worn keyboard. Ivan stretched extravagantly and shook his arms and wrists to stimulate the blood circulation back into his thin, pale fingers. They were sore from typing. His black tee-shirt was sticky from sweat even though his small room was cool. Moscow weather in May could still be cold, as it was on this grey and windy spring day. Flurries of heavy raindrops sporadically splattered the apartment's one grimy windowpane concealed behind the drab blackout curtain. As a precaution, the thick black curtain was in two layers, with a sheet of tinfoil clumsily glued in-between the two layers.

Ivan slumped back in his chair and rolled his head to ease his tired neck. He looked away from the huge monitor on his desk and rubbed his temples. It had been a marathon session and he was mentally exhausted. His fingers were stiff and tired, and his eyes were so raw he found it hard to focus.

The low-level computer code still played in front of his eyes as he looked up at the bland, whitewashed wall in front of him. He needed to tear his eyes away from the computer screen. He screwed up his eyes and rubbed them carefully with the heels of his hands. The flashing cursor and programming commands he'd been wrestling with for the last thirty hours still danced and flickered in the mottled darkness behind his closed eyelids. Backslashes, parentheses and strings of commands were temporarily burned into his retinas. They would fade soon, but right now, the inside of his closed eyelids danced with shapeless colours like an unfocused Bolshoi ballet.

Despite his exhaustion, his smug grin widened, his tired brain buzzed with exhilaration. This high was far better than any drug; and heavens knew, he'd tried them all. Ivan was delighted, he was still struggling to come to terms with the brilliance of what he'd achieved. *Am I tripping?* he wondered. He looked across the small room towards his bed as if searching for an anchor, a point of reference. The person laying in it was gently purring, the thin blanket half covering her rising and falling ribs as she slowly breathed, sound asleep. No, he wasn't tripping. The skinny woman in his bed was real enough. Tatyana.

He wanted to wake her and shout from the roof tops about what he had achieved in the few moments before. Few people would understand the relevance, the sheer cleverness of his hack but Tatyana would understand. The American National Security Agency was the ultimate test for any hacker. And Ivan Komarov had beaten them. This was the gold medal, the Grand Prix, the Michelin Three Stars of his profession. Mortals wouldn't understand what he had, moments before, succeeded in doing. Even his fellow hackers would struggle to grasp the genius and subtlety of the summit he'd just peaked. Ivan rolled his shoulders to ease their stiffness. He slouched and looked around at his drab room. It looked like a rubbish tip and it smelt bad he realised. There were discarded soda cans and congealed fast food boxes on the floor. Dusty spider webs hung in the corners of the ceiling. Right at this moment though, he needed to look at anything simply to avoid looking at his monitor again which had been pixilating his retinas for the last thirty hours.

His room was like any other apartment room in a typical flat in Moscow. It was very messy, but functional, and he called it home. At 23, he was smart, good looking, and he'd completed the hack of the century. He felt invincible, he was a god, albeit a very, very, tired god.

The apartment was cool, and now he shivered. Ivan focused on the upturned crate he used as a coffee table. The ashtrays were spilling over, and metal foil strips, lighters, smeared lines of white powder, and candles lay strewed across his coffee table top, bearing witness to the chemical inducements he'd used to help his thinking and his stamina during the last thirty hours.

Tatyana's naked body, with its shock of long, peroxide white hair, partially covered by the thin blanket, still lay on his bed in the foetal position with her back facing towards him. Her heavily tattooed arms and back displayed a psychedelic pattern of symbols and runes, interwoven with skulls, roses, and barbed wire. No doubt she was making a statement of some description, but he had no idea what, nor did he care. Her breathing was slow and steady, so at least she was alive, she'd accompanied him using the chemicals during the marathon hack. Given his adrenaline-fuelled elation he needed to do something to unwind. He considered sex for a moment, but she was sleeping, and he really was too exhausted. He killed the music playing from the computer and the faint beat of Metallica's "The Unforgiven", abruptly faded.

The NSA, America's National Security Agency, supposedly hosted the world's most elite hacking group, the Goliaths of cybersecurity. Based at Fort Meade in Maryland, this group of world class hackers are employed to defend America from cybercrime while paying scant regard to the privacy of any one person, company, or even nation state. The internet is their playground, and they come and go wherever, and whenever they please. Within the agency, is the department called the Tailored Access Operations, or TAO. This group of white hats (in theory the good guys in the world of cyberweapons and espionage) are considered the pinnacle of everything 'cyber'. That was until Ivan managed to infiltrate their network with his own remote access trojan and prove he was better.

Within the NSA, cybercrime, cyberterrorism, cyberwarfare, and cybersurveillance all fall under the auspices of the TAO. The TAO only recruited the best, the smartest coders America has to offer. Whether Harvard graduates or high-school code-kiddies, the name given to talented young people with an aptitude for hacking, the cream of these would be approached by the NSA to test for their dream-job of working for the TAO. The TAO only selected the very best recruits. Following exhaustive penetration testing exams, background checks and psychometric profiling, the elite are given the privilege of defending their country from the world's cybercriminals. So what if the territorial boundaries drawn on maps didn't apply to the world-wide-web, or the world of cyberspooks. Afterall, everything in the internet is connected to everything else. Surveillance geeks can apply their trade worldwide, from anywhere.

But Ivan knew that was the catch, and that was his mission. As with any 'profession', hackers needed specialist tools. In order for the TAO to be good at their job, they needed to build those tools, the specialist tools of their cybertrade. Just like a good builder needs plumb-lines, spirit-levels, trowels, and tape-measures, so a good hacker needs specialised computer codes - the programmes used to hack other computers. The tools, in this case, are malwares, spyware, trojans, viruses, and a comprehensive database of known hardware and software vulnerabilities. No IT vendors were safe from the tools which hackers can use to exploit their victim's computers, networks, and even their mobile phones. All software has vulnerabilities - ways to mess with it, ways to change its behaviour, and ways to steal what it knows. Ivan believed the TAO owned the world's best and most comprehensive toolbox.

So, how ironic it would be then, if someone were to hack the NSA and steal those very tools. Ivan was good, dangerous, and he knew it. He had a fierce intelligence, coupled with a gargantuan ego, and he had always set his personal goals very high. "I'll hack the NSA", he'd bragged to his friends one night after numerous vodkas. They'd all laughed at him. He even recalled Tatyana asking him how he'd do it; then goading him, betting him that he couldn't do it...

I'll show them! As Ivan slowed his breathing, scratched his ribs through his tee-shirt, and ruminated on his achievement, he knew he wanted to gloat and brag to his friends and colleagues. However, Ivan also knew he couldn't. Not yet anyway. The downloads needed to happen, and this was going to take a few hours, days, even weeks perhaps. Hacking or breaking into an organization was one thing. Stealing what they possessed without them knowing was another. He wasn't even sure himself yet what a rich seam of gold he had hit upon until the downloads had started to happen. The TAO called them their Ops Disks – the term they used for their toolkits of malwares. He needed to scrutinise them with the detail an entomologist would scrutinise his insects under a microscope. If his belief was correct, he'd already exfiltrated the Ops Disks, and would next download what the TAO labelled ECI, for "exceptionally controlled information." This would be the spring that never ran dry. The gift that kept giving - well, until the TAO discovered the breach.

Now that his malware was installed within the NSA's network, the files he wanted to steal from them would be discreetly seeping over to his servers and this would continue until his exfiltration malware was discovered. The TAO might spot the identity theft, the file transfers, but he felt he had disguised this well enough for his virus signatures to avoid detection. Over the coming minutes, hours, weeks and months, the entire database of the TAO's known computer vulnerabilities, and the toolkits they used to exploit them would be downloaded to him. The holy grail of everything of relevance in the world of cybersecurity. After all, Ivan figured, why would an apprentice bricklayer need to buy or build his own tools when he can simply steal the tools from the master mason?

Not since the leaks of Edward Snowden in 2013 would the American Intelligence Agencies be thrown into such turmoil. Of course, Ivan Komarov would need to cover his tracks. He couldn't be an individual; he couldn't even be Russian. He needed to be an amorphous group, a collective, with no face, no address, no country, purely a vapour that floated unanchored, like a will-o'-the-wisp, in the virtual world of the internet. He was untraceable and untouchable. No one Nation State or religious faction could either claim him or disown him. He could touch everyone, he could be everyone, but no one could see or touch him. He was as omnipotent as a god, he reflected.

The girl stirred and groggily sat up. 'What are you doing?' she groaned in a croaky voice.

'I'm finished and I need to rest, my head is killing me' Ivan replied. He reached for a bottled water.

She stood unsteadily and pulled the blanket over her shoulders, more to keep warm than preserve her modesty. Tatyana wasn't modest. Piercings and tattoos adorned her body and her nudity was irrelevant to her. Tatyana's world was binary. She was either hot or cold, awake or asleep, hungry or not-hungry, high or sober, money or no money. Her thin legs looked ungainly like a foal learning to stand for the first time. She walked over to Ivan and massaged his shoulders, wrestling with the blanket to stay draped over her. Ivan leaned back and gave a sigh of relief letting her rub his tense neck muscles. She looked at the monitor. The light-green computer code, vivid against its black back pane was scrolling up in one window, dashboards in other window's alluded to activities on remote networks in foreign datacentres.

'Want a line?' she said, looking at the chemical debris on the coffee table. Her slight accent betraying her as not native to Moscow.

'No, I'm tired and could sleep for a week' Ivan replied. He was too tired to consider a stimulant, he had used plenty of cocaine in the last thirty hours and now he only wanted to sleep, and to dream of his achievement. A happy dream he wanted to wallow in and enjoy.

'Suit yourself' Tatyana moved to the coffee table, swishing her long peroxide white hair over one shoulder in anticipation of bending over the table and closing one nostril with her forefinger, but then she paused. She turned and looked up at Ivan.

'You did it?' she enquired; eyebrows raised.

Ivan gave a sleepy, smug smile. 'Yes! I've hacked America's National Security Agency.'

#

He slowly stood, his body creaking as he eased himself upright and scratched his flat tummy under the crusty, shapeless tee-shirt. Ivan squeezed around the coffee table and slumped down onto the vacated bed. He pulled a crumpled rug over himself, closed his weary eyes, exhaled loudly, and was asleep in seconds. Tatyana stood over him and looked down at his still, exhausted form. He was fast asleep, his lips twitching as he slid ever deeper into a contented dream, the dream of a winner.

'You clever boy!' she whispered under her breath as she pulled the rug higher up, to cover over his shoulders like a mother would to her small child.

She knelt beside him and gently stroked his fair hair. She watched him for a full five minutes to satisfy herself he was deeply asleep. Then she found her clothes. Old Jeans, boots, bra, distressed black Pussy Riot tee-shirt, and her signature black leather jacket. She sniffed the tee-shirt and frowned but pulled it on regardless. With a last glance towards the bed to confirm Ivan was still sound asleep, she sat herself down at his computer monitor, fingers poised over the keyboard. Her bosses will be pleased she thought to herself.

Tatyana's fingers flew over the keyboard, but she took care to be quiet. First, she brought up a pornography channel and ran that in one window, so should Ivan wake and catch her using his computer she'd have an excuse. 'You were sleeping, and I was bored!' she'd pout. Ivan would grumble, but he'd buy her argument. They used each other for sex, and pornography was a common enough recreation for them both. In the two months they'd been spending time together the sex had been wild, open, and frequent. Ivan hadn't been hard to seduce, and Tatyana had enjoyed this part of the contract. She hadn't even needed to fake; with Ivan the sex was fulfilling and natural.

Regardless, he was dead to the world now. She cast an eye over him, his breathing had slowed, and Ivan was snoring lightly. Next, she scrutinised the downloads which he had started. The downloaded files were being sent to a remote server so that should the police or the FSB (the Federal Security Service of the Russian Federation, the successor to the infamous KGB) explored what Ivan had been doing, no criminal evidence would be on his computer. She typed her own string of instructions onto the keyboard, adding her own commands onto the remote server taking yet another back-up of these downloading files, this time to a secondary remote server. One which only she controlled. Lastly, she unzipped a small pocket on her leather jacket and removed a tiny black plastic thumb drive.

She slid this thumb drive into a USB port on the computer and a new window popped opened, presenting her with the command line and inviting her to run the programme. Tatyana hit "Enter" to execute the programme. This was the forensics software which would recreate everything Ivan had been doing for the last thirty hours. RAT's, commands, malware programmes, keystrokes, etc. Everything Ivan had done in his hack would be captured and recorded on her small USB drive. This would take a little time. Despite the computer being extremely well-spec'd and fast, there was a lot to process and download. She amused herself by surfing the porn channel until the download was complete. Finally, once done, she replaced the thumb drive back into the pocket of her leather jacket, zipped it securely, and deleted all the logs of her activity off Ivan's computer.

Lastly, Tatyana closed the porn channel and checked on Ivan, he was still deeply sleeping. She knew he would sleep for hours. Normally she'd wipe down the keyboard with nail-polish remover to remove fingerprints, however this time she'd leave them. If he had a hidden camera, she'd use the porn-surfing to defend her actions. Better leave the evidence there Tatyana thought to herself. One less lie. Wiping down would raise even more suspicion. The downloads he was intermittently stealing from the NSA's servers would fully happen over a few weeks, but the rich seam of gold he'd hit had already yielded a huge cache of files. These files needed to be analysed, but there was no mistaking the magnitude of the hack.

This find, in the world of twenty-first century cybercrime, was equivalent to Howard Carter, the Archaeologist, discovering Tutankhamun's tomb a hundred years previously.

"Can you see anything?" Carter was asked in 1922, as he had first peered into the pharaoh's tomb.

"Yes, wonderful things!" Carter had replied.

Tatyana had no idea quite what Ivan had discovered yet, but like Howard Carter, she knew they were wonderful things, and the world of cybercrime and cyberespionage would be irrevocably changed forever.

Tatyana stole Ivan's neck scarf from off the back of the door, and slipped out of his apartment, quietly clicking the door closed behind herself. She skipped down the four flights of stairs to the street. The day was overcast, blustery, grey and cold, and she smelt rain on the air, but the excitement she felt insulated her thin body. She found her regular nearby cafe and ordered hot food and coffee. She dialled a number on her mobile phone and gave an update to the anonymous male voice that answered. While Ivan slept and dreamt, Tatyana finished her food and coffee then wrapped Ivan's scarf around her neck, paid her bill, and took a taxi back to her own apartment. She preferred her motorbike, but the weather was still too cold for that.

Three months after Tatyana had made that phone call, and Ivan's malware had been watching and carefully downloading the TAO's crown-jewels of cybersecurity, an organisation called the Shadow Brokers announced themselves on the world stage. Shadow Brokers were the anonymous hackers who claimed to have hacked the NSA. The Shadow Brokers needed to fulfil three objectives. First and foremost, they wanted the world to see how clever they were. While careful to retain autonomy, they wanted other hackers the world over to be in awe of the brilliance of their work. To show they had hacked the NSA, the world's greatest cybersecurity agency, and stolen their deepest, darkest secrets.

However smart the TAO's white-hat hackers thought they were, Ivan, under the guise of Shadow Brokers was smarter. To prove his point, he even exposed real people who were members of the National Security Agency's hackers in the Tailored Access Operations department. Martin Williams had been a former employee of the TAO and was publicly outed and humiliated on Twitter. It proved career limiting for Mr Williams. Ivan Komarov had never met the man, but he felt he knew him like he knew his own brother.

The Shadow Brokers' second goal was to humiliate America as a nation. That the world's ultimate hacking organisation could themselves be hacked was too good not to publicly gloat over. This needed the world stage, and what more laughable way to cause the Americans to squirm than via social media and Wikileaks. Even the world's printed media and television networks couldn't ignore the enormity of the story with news networks including CNN and the BBC all running editorials and debating the extent of the hack and speculating who was behind it. "We hack Equation Group," the Shadow Brokers bragged, "We find many many Equation Group cyber weapons." Equation Group had been the name given to the TAO by the Russian cybersecurity company Kaspersky.

Pundits speculated this was 'proof' the Russians were behind the hack.

'A false flag attack aimed at demonising Russia', decried others.

Third and lastly, Ivan liked money, although this was only a minor concern. As a dedicated black-hat coder and hacker, he could easily make good money. But to have people pay Shadow Brokers for the tools he'd stolen was a nice touch. In a flurry of flamboyance designed to embarrass the Americans yet further, the stolen hacking toolsets were offered for sale on the Dark Web. Any state sponsored hacker, or militant religious group wanting to evolve beyond their AK47's could buy these publicly, well almost publicly, available tools. It was a smokescreen. Anyone trying to buy the tools even paying with cryptocurrencies would be open to scrutiny, as would anyone attempting to receive payment. Sure, Ivan knew cryptocurrencies could be anonymous but that wouldn't stop the NSA, FBI, and the CIA trying to follow the money.

An uneducated global news media lapped-up the story as did Ivan and his friends, who laughed and celebrated all weekend by buying vodka-champagnes in their preferred nightclub in Moscow. What better way to share the glory of the greatest hack ever than to publish it on social media? If Goliath hadn't exactly been felled, at least his loincloth had been ripped off, and his wilting inadequacies exposed for the world to point towards and laugh at.

Ivan realised that, for the last few months, he'd been seeing less of Tatyana. They still moved in the same social circles, but her sleepovers were becoming less frequent. He didn't care, he was a god, and he could have whatever his heart desired. Afterall, he was the hacker who hacked the NSA.